The Kirkwood Scott Chronicles

1

Stephen Black

The Kirkwood Scott Chronicles – A New Jerusalem © 2020 by Stephen Black. All Rights Reserved.

All rights reserved. No part of this book may be reproduced in any form or by any electronic or mechanical means including information storage and retrieval systems, without permission in writing from the author. The only exception is by a reviewer, who may quote short excerpts in a review.

Cover designed by Don Noble of Rooster Republic Press

This book is a work of fiction. Names, characters, places, and incidents either are products of the author's imagination or are used fictitiously. Any resemblance to actual persons, living or dead, events, or locales is entirely coincidental.

First Printing: October 2020
Potter's Grove Press, LLC
http://pottersgrovepress.com

ISBN - 978-1-951840-19-8

Dedicated to my wife, Fionnuala, and our children, Adam, Hannah, and Rebecca. Without them, I am nothing, and I am so grateful for the love and support they show me every day.

Contents

CHAPTER 1 - THE DEATH OF MAURA MILLER...............................1
CHAPTER 2 - FOR EVERYONE WE'VE EVER LOST 7
CHAPTER 3 - A MOST PECULIAR VISITOR.................................14
CHAPTER 4 - LOVE IS A FOUR-LETTER WORD...........................18
CHAPTER 5 - NO GRAVE FOR THE DEAD 22
CHAPTER 6 - KISS FROM A GHOST..27
CHAPTER 7 - TOY SOLDIERS...33
CHAPTER 8 - SO MUCH TROUBLE..40
CHAPTER 9 - BURN, BELFAST, BURN 45
CHAPTER 10 - THE TOWER..50
CHAPTER 11 - MY LAST DOUBLOON 57
CHAPTER 12 - TOMMY 61
CHAPTER 13 - PERMANENT 4TH OF JULY...............................66
CHAPTER 14 - PLANEING 101..72
CHAPTER 15 - THE CAR CRASH THAT USED TO BE YOUR COUNTRY 81
CHAPTER 16 - STEP INTO MY PARLOUR.....................................88
CHAPTER 17 - A BRIEF HISTORY OF HELLFAST..........................92
CHAPTER 18 - A STARC INQUISITION..99
CHAPTER 19 - A STROLL THROUGH THE CITY 104
CHAPTER 20 - THREE BECOME TWO.......................................108
CHAPTER 21 - GIRO 113
CHAPTER 22 - THE PRIESTESS 120
CHAPTER 23 - I THINK I NEED A DRINK...................................125
CHAPTER 24 - A PINT OR SEVEN 131
CHAPTER 25 - CIRCLING THE WAGONS 136
CHAPTER 26 - INCURSION...141
CHAPTER 27 - SHIFTING SANDS..146
CHAPTER 28 - THE PORTUGUESE PROPHET............................154
CHAPTER 29 - JACK AND THE MAGIC SEED.............................160
CHAPTER 30 - COLD TURKEY 165
CHAPTER 31 - BAD NEWS DAY...170
CHAPTER 32 - DRINKING TO FORGET 175
CHAPTER 33 - DESERT ISLAND FRY UP....................................178

CHAPTER 34 - OUTFLANKED	183
CHAPTER 35 - TROJAN HORSE	187
CHAPTER 36 - THE GRAVEDIGGER	191
CHAPTER 37 - COMMUNION OF BLOOD	194
CHAPTER 38 - ROUTINE 33	203
CHAPTER 39 - WINE TIME	212
CHAPTER 40 - STUDY STRATEGISTS	218
CHAPTER 41 - CHANGE OF PLAN	223
CHAPTER 42 - AN UNEASY ALLIANCE	227
CHAPTER 43 - MEREDITH THE MAIDEN	232
CHAPTER 44 - 17/4	239
CHAPTER 45 - FIRST NIGHT NERVES	246
CHAPTER 46 - WHO CUTS THE GRASS AROUND HERE?	252
CHAPTER 47 - BOMB GIRL	258
CHAPTER 48 - A SPOT OF TROUBLE	266
CHAPTER 49 - BUYING TIME	274
CHAPTER 50 - BURY YOUR DEAD	278
CHAPTER 51 - MEN ARE LIKE DOGS	285
CHAPTER 52 - CRICKET IS A FIVE-DAY GAME	288
CHAPTER 53 - A QUIET NIGHT IN	292
CHAPTER 54 - THIS TROUBLED LAND OF OURS	297
CHAPTER 55 - WE ARE WHO WE ARE	303
CHAPTER 56 - RETURN TO HELLFAST	310
CHAPTER 57 - WE ARE GODS	316
CHAPTER 58 - THE DEAD HEAL QUICKLY	322
CHAPTER 59 - TRADING WITH THE DIRTIES	327
CHAPTER 60 - FOR MEREDITH	332
CHAPTER 61 - DAMN THE COMPANY	335
CHAPTER 62 - IT MEANS NOTHING TO ME	342
CHAPTER 63 - MY LITTLE ARIANA	347
CHAPTER 64 - HELL TO PAY	352
CHAPTER 65 - ONE NIL TO THE GOOD GUYS	356
CHAPTER 66 - HOME TO ROOST	360
CHAPTER 67 - INJUSTICE FOR ALL	367
CHAPTER 68 - SMELLY PANTS	378
CHAPTER 69 - A VERY CHARMING IDIOT	383
CHAPTER 70 - AN UNPALATABLE OFFER	388
CHAPTER 71 - THE MAN WHO HATED MANKIND	393
CHAPTER 72 - TIME IS RUNNING OUT	398
CHAPTER 73 - GETTING AHEAD IN THE AFTERLIFE	403

CHAPTER 74 - BRIDGE OVER TROUBLED WATERS	407
CHAPTER 75 - A TERRIBLE BEAUTY	412
CHAPTER 76 - SAVING SKELLY	425
CHAPTER 77 - THE STREETS RUN RED	431
CHAPTER 78 - EVEN THE DEAD NEED REST	436
CHAPTER 79 - I DESTROYED THE WORLD TODAY	443
CHAPTER 80 - AND SO IT BEGINS	448
CHAPTER 81 - AMBUSH AT THE BLACK HOUSE	454
CHAPTER 82 - THE REGIMENT THAT NEVER WAS	462
CHAPTER 83 - HELL HATH NO FURY	468
CHAPTER 84 - BACK TO THE BATTLE	474
CHAPTER 85 - BROKENHEARTED	478
CHAPTER 86 - THE ROAD TO BRUSSELS	483
CHAPTER 87 - A COMMON FOE	491
CHAPTER 88 - SARCASM HASN'T REACHED PARIS YET	497
CHAPTER 89 - MESS OF A GIRL	500
CHAPTER 90 - PIG UGLY SOLDIERS	505
CHAPTER 91 - TEARS FOR A STOLEN CHILDHOOD	512
CHAPTER 92 - SLEEPING THROUGH THE APOCALYPSE	517
CHAPTER 93 - FIGHTING TALK	522
CHAPTER 94 - WAR STORIES	527
CHAPTER 95 - GOING IN HEAVY-HANDED	532
CHAPTER 96 - THE NUMBERS MAN	537
CHAPTER 97 - DINNER IS SERVED	542
CHAPTER 98 - GAME CHANGER	545
CHAPTER 99 - I'M KIRKWOOD SCOTT	557
CHAPTER 100 - THE END OF EVERYTHING	561
ACKNOWLEDGEMENTS	567

CHAPTER 1 - THE DEATH OF MAURA MILLER

She ran through the smoke and the horror on all sides towards her death, towards all their deaths. It mattered not, for living was no longer an option, not if he wasn't there to share it with her. If she could not live with him, then she would die by his side.

The young woman slithered down the muddy slope, oblivious to the chaos all around her. Ahead, a navy-blue forest of musket and metal trudged inexorably down the slope on the opposite end of the valley. Smoke pricked her eyes, drawing tears, and her nostrils flared at the acrid stench of gunpowder. Rotten eggs, rotten luck, rotten everything.

She hurdled a stricken horse, lying helplessly on its side, intestines exposed by God only knows what instrument of death. So many to choose from on this day. The terrified beast kicked out feebly as, leaping it, she caught a glimpse of its once-proud rider, his limp body trapped beneath his former mount. Eyes glazed, staring up at her, a look of utter bemusement on his blood-caked face. It wasn't meant to end like this. Skewered on a French lance, watching with mildly detached curiosity as your life force soaked effortlessly into your tunic. Medals, glory, promotions. Wasn't that what he had been promised, what they had all been promised? Lies. The lies of pompous, deluded, old men. Butchers lying to the butchered.

Ahead lay her goal, not more than a hundred yards. Amidst the clamour, they stood firm, a square of red facing the sea of blue descending upon them. She flinched as another volley sounded from the front line, slamming into the French ranks. Horses slid to their knees, throwing their riders into the ground with a sickening impact. Those not killed by musket balls were pitched within bayonet range of the British line, where they were gleefully dispatched by raw teenage recruits and hardened Peninsular veterans alike. Cries for mercy were ignored. There would be no parley given, it was too late in the day for that. Too much had been witnessed on either side. Sights and sounds that the survivors would take to their graves and beyond.

As she wove across the muddy, ravaged terrain, she watched the French artillery on the far side pour hot, metallic death down into the valley. Detached puffs of smoke and dull thuds were followed almost instantaneously by the scream of the incoming cannonball. She slowed a fraction and watched its relentless trajectory, slack-jawed, as it bounced once before careering into the front of the Allied square. Burly soldiers were tossed aside like skittles, legs and arms removed from torsos as the wrecking ball bounced a second time near the colours. An imposing officer frantically tugged on his horse's reins as the ball narrowly missed removing his head from his shoulders. The ball continued along its indiscriminate journey, bouncing again before cutting a gory swathe through the rear ranks. She watched mesmerised as it rolled beyond the square and past her before coming to rest—steam and smoke fizzing from the still sizzling projectile. One lump of metal, one of thousands pitched into the valley from both sides. They called it a battle, but that only painted half the picture. It was a massacre, a bloodbath, an abomination against all that was good and just in the world.

The square regrouped. The discipline drilled into the troops during months of monotonous training back home, now coming to fruition and saving lives. One gap, one chink, one man not knowing his role and position, and the French cavalry would flood through, slicing and hacking at any unfortunate soul within reach of their cruel blades. Blinded by the stinging smoke, traumatised at the brutal deaths of their friends and comrades, the regiment somehow held firm, shuffling together until a more compact, but still intact, formation emerged. Another thunderous volley sounded from the front ranks, and the French charge was repelled again.

"James, James," she screamed, her voice straining to be heard above the tumult of the battlefield. "James Miller. Show yourself." She hitched her skirts, her ankle boots sucking her into the mud with every step, the square seemingly further away than ever. Less than a hundred yards ahead, three dozen muskets were trained upon her. The men were tired beyond words, dazed and inclined to fire at any man, woman, or beast who came within range. All it took was one twitchy finger, the tiniest squeeze of a trigger, and the entire line would let loose a wave of lethal lead.

"Who's there?" An authoritative voice rose from behind the line, holding steady. A voice of steely control amidst the bedlam.

"It's a woman, Sergeant. A bloody woman."

An eerie pause followed as dozens of pale faces peered through the smoke towards the young woman staggering towards them, struggling to remain upright over the uneven terrain, trampled beyond recognition by the passage of tens of thousands of men, horses, and wagons. Vivid red hair fanned out wildly from porcelain features, a drizzle of freckles decorating the bridge of her narrow nose. Thin, bloodless lips and piercing green eyes belied a doggedness and determination which fuelled this maddest of dashes.

"God in heaven, I thought I'd seen it all this day," the initial voice boomed out, fringed with a hint of incredulity. "Open ranks boys. Let her through, let her through."

The front rank of kneeling men edged aside, opening a gap that widened as those behind did likewise. Seeing her opportunity, the woman accelerated and, in doing so, lost her balance and stumbled. She reacted immediately, regaining her momentum and scuttling on hands and knees into the interior of the square. She raised her head and exhaled, taking in the devastating sights around her. The dead and dying were stacked against ammunition boxes, surrounding the tattered regimental colours which hung limply at the centre of the formation. All about her, the groans of the grievously wounded filled the air, left to their own pitiful devices, as a handful of officers roared orders to the lines of red-coated infantry forming the walls of the square.

The young woman blinked and swallowed hard, the enormity of where she was beginning to settle on her frayed spirit. When she opened her eyes again, she found herself looking at the forelegs of a horse. Squinting upwards, she settled on a formidable figure astride a black stallion. It's wide, staring eyes and flared nostrils giving it the impression of some creature dragged from hell itself. For isn't that where she was now?

"And what have we here?" The figure leaned forward to study her in greater detail, his dark eyes and gunmetal grey moustache and sideburns dominating craggy features. She realised from his demeanour and uniform he was an officer, a man of rank and importance. But what was he doing atop his horse? It was the very essence of madness, for he undoubtedly presented a sitting duck for eagle-eyed French sharpshooters stalking the British formations.

"I'm Maura...Maura Miller. I'm...I'm pleased to meet your acquaintance, sir. I must find my husband. James Miller...Private James Miller. Can you direct me to his position, please?"

The officer's eyes drilled into her as if examining her very soul, and for a second, they were the only two people on the battlefield. Finally, he smiled at her, but not a kindly smile, more a cruel smirk, before nodding towards a pile of bodies by the colours.

"I'm afraid you've had a wasted journey, my dear. He's somewhere at the bottom of that heap. Went down early but fear not. He wouldn't have felt a thing. Cannonball clean took his head from his shoulders."

Maura gagged and struggled vainly to keep down the contents of that morning's pitiful breakfast of porridge. She failed and blushed with embarrassment as she retched on all fours in front of the stallion. A dull reverberance in the distance vaguely registered with her before the officer spoke again, his clipped, controlled tone barely masking a shard of malice.

"Now, now, my dear. No point getting theatrical. There's plenty more healthy young bucks in the line willing to make an honest woman of you."

The surrounding clamour began to once more overcome Maura's senses. The bellow of commands, and shrieks of agony. Above it all, however, was the sickening scream of cannon. The French batteries had now found their range, and huge clods of black earth rained down upon the square from near misses all around.

"But, he was my life. He was…"

Colonel Augustus Skelly wheeled away and gazed into the distance as if admiring a sunrise over a tranquil meadow. He watched as the cannonball tracked a perfect pattern from the far ridge before starting its descent towards where he and his men helplessly awaited it.

"He's dead. We will all be dead before too long. Now grab a musket and make yourself useful." His snarl brought Maura to her senses. Just long enough to witness the cannonball bounce once before smashing into the front of the square.

That's when she saw hell for what it truly was.

CHAPTER 2 - FOR EVERYONE WE'VE EVER LOST

"So, that's what a square is." Meredith looked up from her phone, eyes alight with understanding. "I thought it was a place, like a courtyard, but it's actually a military formation. Who knew?"

"Obviously, Wikipedia did," replied a distinctly unimpressed Kirkwood, seated beside her in the back seat of the battered Nissan Micra as it rattled along the narrow country road, sounding as if it could disintegrate at any moment. "And there was me thinking the only square you knew was the caramel variety."

"You're going to get a dig in the face if you keep insulting my intelligence, Kirky. Ashgrove College, remember. Ashgrove. I've more GCSE's than you have clean pairs of socks." The dark-haired teenager returned to her phone screen, brow furrowed in concentration beneath the black beanie hat, which rarely left her head. Kirkwood could not help but smile. Meredith Starc, how far you have come.

"Only squares I see are sitting behind us in the back seat, isn't that right, Samuel?" quipped the permanently upbeat Harley from the passenger seat. She reclined back, boots off, her feet resting on the dashboard while the man-mountain Samuel hunched over the steering wheel to her right, eyes fixed on the road ahead. The Northern Irish countryside revealing itself to them as the little red car spluttered round another sweeping bend.

"I would be much more comfortable if you would put your feet down and position yourself properly," deadpanned the mulleted giant. "My superiors would not take kindly to us overcoming the armies of darkness, only to end up dead in a ditch because some disobedient teenager couldn't sit properly in a car." He shot her a stern stare, before returning his attention to the road ahead.

"Shush, grumpy. I'm wiggling my toes," replied Harley, bright eyes sparkling beneath her multicoloured mane. "Do you know how long it's been since I've been able to do this?" She rotated her ankles, admiring them like a modern-day Cinderella setting eyes upon her glass slippers for the first time.

Samuel smiled sheepishly, suddenly aware of his faux pas. "My apologies, young lady. That was thoughtless of me."

Harley fixed him a mournful expression before it proved too much, and she dissolved into a fit of giggling. "Oh, relax, Samuel. Honestly, you're so easy to wind up. Over ten months in a wheelchair taught me to grow a thick skin if nothing else. Just you keep your eyes on the road in case we hit any stray cows. Honestly, I thought Ardgallon was in the back end of nowhere, but this place really takes the biscuit."

"Yes, madam," replied her normally dour chauffeur, the hint of a smile ghosting across his granite features.

"Hark at her ladyship," chirped Kirkwood from the back. "Ardgallon is the original one-horse town. I've seen more life at a wake."

"Yeah, until we turned up and did that whole saving the world thing." Meredith looked up from the screen of her phone and smiled humourlessly.

"Yeah," repeated Kirkwood. Suddenly he was back on the bridge watching helplessly as Dobson fell to the ground in front of them, dead at the hands of William. Even Harley, who had chattered incessantly since they left her home village, fell quiet.

It was Samuel who broke the silence, sensing the downturn in the atmosphere amongst his young companions. "Dobson would insist we continue, we cannot afford much time to mourn. The Scourge will not wait long before renewing its offensive. Skelly and his Company are many." He looked in the rear-view mirror and caught Kirkwood's eye before continuing. "You three are all that stand in their path. Dobson knew that which is why he protected each of you for so many years. We must honour his memory by carrying on, no matter how much it might gall us."

Kirkwood nodded sombrely. He looked across at Meredith, but she remained engrossed by the contents of her phone screen. Harley had returned to admiring her toes. They all had their own ways of dealing with the trauma of that morning, it didn't mean they missed the old tramp any less.

"So, we go back to where it all started then? I'm still not convinced. I'm not even sure if it's there anymore. It's been years, and it's not as if I've gone looking for him during that time. He always came for me." An image of his last visit to the Study seared across Kirkwood's mind, the odious Skelly leaning forward in his armchair to mock and taunt him.

"I'm afraid there is no other choice," replied Samuel, flicking the car's indicator before turning left onto a road Kirkwood knew only too well. They were nearing his family home, the place where he grew up, nestled in the rolling countryside on the outskirts of the busy market town of Omagh. The house from where they buried what was left of his father all those years ago.

It was as if Samuel could read the young man's thoughts. "The Portal has been closed, but that was a defensive measure on our part. We need to go on the front foot now, catch them while they're still licking their wounds."

"It says here a fully formed military square in Napoleonic times could consist of as many as 700 men," interrupted Meredith. "So, if they all died with that lunatic Skelly at Waterloo, are you telling me there are that many psychopathic ghost soldiers queuing up to tear us apart limb from limb?"

Samuel sighed. "Possibly. Skelly and the Scourge have considerable resources at their disposal. So far, we have only encountered an expeditionary force. Rodriguez, William, Gunther, they are merely the tip of the iceberg." He returned his attention to the road, aware they were drawing nearer their destination.

"Well, good job Dobson introduced little old me to this merry band." Harley turned around to face her newfound friends in the back seat. "You saw what we did on the bridge back there. We kicked serious ass. I'm not afraid of anyone or anything now we've got this Present thingy on our side."

"Presence," corrected Samuel. "And it's not a thingy to be carelessly tossed about. It's a devastating force that needs to be nurtured and used wisely. Which is where I come in."

"Charming," replied Meredith, tossing her phone aside. "I'm bored with all this war stuff. Just point me in the direction of the next bad guy, and let's get this show on the road. The sooner we wipe this lot out, the sooner I can see Emily again. I know she's trying to get to me. She wouldn't come back without contacting me again."

For once, Harley had no answer. She stared out the passenger window at the passing fields, where plump sheep grazed lazily. Despite the two young women having bonded so seamlessly following their meeting on the bridge, it was obviously a bone of contention that Emily had revealed herself to the rainbow-haired teenager instead of her former best friend. Kirkwood shifted uneasily in his seat. He had yet to tell Meredith the ghost girl had also appeared to him the previous night at the bed and breakfast, or the reason Emily was keeping her distance from her best friend.

Samuel once more was the one to fill the silence in the car. "Patience, Meredith. If Cornelius taught me anything, then it was that. We will need more than brute force if we are to win this battle. We can dispatch as many of the Company as we want, but they will only keep coming. They are a many-headed beast, yet they have one heart. A rancid, blackened lump of flesh that drives them forward. Skelly."

"Which is why we're going to Kirkwood's house?" queried Harley.

"Exactly," the big man replied. "Skelly knows he is vulnerable if he exposes himself on this plane to the three of you. The Presence is the only force that can defeat him, which is why he has fought so desperately to keep you apart. He will be in that accursed Study preparing his next move. Which is why we must strike now, without hesitation."

"I don't even know if my toy soldiers are still here," grumbled Kirkwood. "For all I know, Mum took them to New Zealand with her for my nephew."

"It's a long shot I agree, but if we can locate and destroy the Skelly figure your father bought you all those years ago, we can use it to summon him here. And then finish him once and for all."

"I still vote we rip this Company apart one by one with our newfound super-duper powers, rather than chasing our tails in deepest, darkest Tyrone."

"Shut it, Meredith," snarled Kirkwood. "I trust Samuel. What he says goes, ok? He hasn't let us down yet." The dark-haired girl pouted, folded her arms, and stared defiantly ahead.

"She might have a point," offered Harley. "I mean, how can snagging some rusty toy soldier protect us. We can do magic stuff now. Did you see that Gunther guy's head go up in flames back there? That was us!" She jabbed a thumb in her chest to emphasise the point.

Samuel crunched down the gears as the little Micra howled in protest at negotiating a tight corner. "Because," he muttered through gritted teeth, "Cornelius told me so. Last night, after we met William and the others, we talked for many hours. He confided in me what must be done if he didn't survive the battle on the bridge." His voice returned to its usual emotionless monotone.

"It was as if he knew," he added plainly. "And his word is good enough for me."

"As it is for all us," Kirkwood added sharply. "Isn't that right, ladies?"

"Hell yeah," yelled Harley, thumping the dashboard with the palms of her hands like a demented drummer.

"Meredith?" Kirkwood arched an eyebrow towards his back-seat companion.

Meredith simply nodded, her eyes glistening. "Yes, of course." She turned towards Kirkwood, smiled sadly, and took his hand. Her touch was ice cold.

"Okay then, let's do this. Keep going straight, Samuel. We're about ten minutes from the house."

He squeezed Meredith's hand back and returned her smile. "For Dobson. For Emily. For everyone we've ever lost," he whispered.

CHAPTER 3 - A MOST PECULIAR VISITOR

Bernard Thompson, or Mr. Thompson, as he preferred to be known, considered himself a good neighbour. A very good neighbour, truth be told. So good that he assured Mrs. Scott, when she departed for New Zealand to visit young Katie, he would pay extra special attention to her property. Not for nothing had he been elected Neighbourhood Watch Co-Ordinator for this part of the town. It had been a unanimous decision. Granted, he and his wife had been the only voters, but he liked to think he had the silent support of all the residents of Greenvale Drive.

Which was why this morning, he was paying particular attention to the young woman striding up the driveway towards the Scott residence. He had a perfect view from his front window and didn't like what he saw, not one little bit. Bernard prided himself on being able to deduce a lot about a person's character through first impressions. Thirty years in banking had fine-tuned this skill, and he now sought to put it to good use in this new chapter of his life. Yes, retirement was proving just as busy given the various community and charity projects he had thrown himself into with gusto.

There was something about her swagger, which displayed an arrogance not becoming of a young lady with such delicate features. Her alabaster pale skin was accentuated by a mass of flame-red curls tied back in a ponytail. By her attire, it looked as if she had come straight from an equestrian event, dressed in tight cream jodhpurs, fitted tweed jacket, and black riding boots. Bernard strained to see further down the driveway, but there was no sign of a car or horse for that matter. What a peculiar young lady, he thought to himself.

"Bernard, your coffee is ready," his wife called from the kitchen. "Do you want me to bring it through, or are you having it in the conservatory?"

"I'll take it in the conservatory, dear. I'll be there in two ticks, there's just something I need to check out first."

"Right-oh. But don't be long. It will get cold, and you're such a grump when that happens."

Bernard didn't hear his long-suffering spouse as he was already out the front door and making his way towards the perfectly pruned privet hedge that separated chez Thompson from the Scott address. Bernard was particularly fond of Mrs. Scott and always looked out for her. The loss of her husband was such a tragedy, yet she had raised such a delightful young lady in Katie. He had a soft spot for the Scott ladies. There was a son as well, Kirkwood, but he had seen little of him since the boy left for university some years ago. A strange child from memory; bit of a loner, kept to himself.

"Excuse me, can I help you?" The young woman was almost at the front door now. Was she lost? She didn't look lost, such was the assured manner with which she carried herself.

She turned, took two steps towards him, and cocked her head to one side, considering a response before a sly smile slipped across her features. Bernard swallowed involuntarily, his mouth suddenly very dry. There was something about the young woman he didn't like. Something he didn't like at all.

"No need to excuse yourself, sir," she beamed. "Is the lady of the house at home?" She flicked a loose strand of hair from her face, revealing startling emerald eyes and a smattering of freckles across the bridge of her nose.

Bernard stalled, struggling to formulate a suitable response. He abhorred liars, given his strong Christian faith, but was reluctant to tell this peculiar visitor too much about Mrs. Scott's present circumstances.

"Er...no. She's not in. Can I help at all?"

The young woman emitted a peal of laughter as if enjoying some private joke at his expense. Bernard felt the hairs on the back of his neck rise in unison. This wasn't going at all as he had expected. Elizabeth would be wondering where he was, and she was right—he despised lukewarm coffee.

"If you want to leave your name and number, I'd be happy to pass them on when she returns. I'll...I'll just go back inside and get a pen and paper, alright?" He half-turned, keen to make his excuses, and be rid of this awkward encounter as quickly as possible.

"Not to worry," the woman replied, dismissing his offer with a flick of her hand. "She has something which belongs to us, but I'll call again. I'm often in the area." Was that a hint of a Dublin accent he detected? She turned sharply and started to stride down the driveway again.

"Are you sure? I mean, it's really no..."

The young woman stopped and looked over her shoulder, fixing Bernard Thompson with a stare he would take to his grave. Was it his imagination, or were her eyes now a deep brown, almost black? He could have sworn they were green.

"That's enough questions for one day, Bernard. Now be on your way before your coffee gets cold. We all know how much you hate that." She smiled again, watching as the blood drained from the irksome little man's face. She doubted he would be bothering her next time she called.

They rarely did.

CHAPTER 4 - LOVE IS A FOUR-LETTER WORD

Love...

Hate...

Why did all the worst words have four letters? His old nursemaid, Clarissa, had beaten him senseless once as a child when he dared to direct a certain four-letter insult in her direction. Barbaric treatment of a child, but it taught him a lesson. He never used it again.

Fire...

Pain...

So much pain.

Skelly dug his gnarled nails into the deep pile carpet of his beloved Study and hauled himself, one agonising inch at a time, into the armchair. To look at him, you would have wondered why. His skin was unmarked, and he gave no visible sign of the horrific ordeal he had just endured. He had anticipated his superiors would have been displeased by the debacle at the bridge and was prepared for unpleasant repercussions. But their response had taken his fear of them to a new, unparalleled level. They had drawn a line in the sand, leaving him under no illusions that this was his one and only warning. Were there to be a repetition, there would be no reprieve next time.

Was that such a bad thing, he thought to himself through gritted, yellowed teeth, as he struggled into an upright position. He reached with a trembling hand for the glass decanter on the table next to him and poured a considerable measure of the dark, red liquid within. Never had he needed it so badly as the pain threatened to consume him, to burn him alive from the inside outwards. His skin was aflame, every inch of it screaming for relief, blessed release. Throwing decorum aside, he gulped down the contents of the tumbler before refilling it with equal haste. A second lengthy swig allowed him to sit back and wince as the agony subsided slightly.

The momentary reprieve allowed him to gather his swirling thoughts into some sort of order. Skelly snarled. Dobson had completely outmanoeuvred him at the portal. The fourth child had been wholly masked from him; he had no inkling as to her existence. Dobson must have drained himself dry to conceal her from Skelly's tendrils, for they had been everywhere. He had been so close. The boy Scott had been in the palm of his hand exactly where he wanted him. And as for the street urchin, she had been of no use to anyone slumped in a doorway, numb to everything except where the next drink was coming from. He had been on the cusp of a momentous victory, even the remaining presence of the one known to her kind as Emily was but a minor inconvenience.

The fourth child. A cripple, no less. Appearing from nowhere at the eleventh hour, like those damned Prussians had on the eastern flank, crashing into Boney's Imperial Guard, the finest fighting force known to man, reducing them to a bedraggled rabble running for their lives through La Belle Alliance all the way to the little bridge at Gnappe. They said it was like shooting fish in a barrel, those who led the pursuit. How he would have loved to have been amongst them, sabre whirling, cutting the frog scum down from behind. If he hadn't been lying dead eight miles back on the slope of that accursed ridge with his lads. It was a French blade in the end that finished him off, but the blame lay entirely with the coward who had sat atop the ridge watching his regiment being torn apart.

Betrayed by a so-called friend. And for what? Nothing.

Skelly finished off the second measure and rolled his shoulders, the pain subsiding with each passing second. A few more glasses and he would be back to full strength, able to give his undivided attention to the farce at the bridge. Gunther, a loyal and dependent lieutenant, was gone, and that spineless wretch William was currently having his eyeballs fried on those oh, so delicate cheekbones of his. Only Rodriguez had left the field of play with any kind of honour intact. In any other circumstances, the destruction of Dobson would have been a cause for great celebration. But his acolyte, Samuel, had equipped himself well and now guided a united Presence.

Together they were a force to contend with, the only power capable of hampering his grand strategy. He had underestimated the old fool but wouldn't fall into the same trap again. The only way he could get matters back on track was to separate the three brats. Yes, divide and conquer, get them on their own and watch them whimper for mercy. On their own, he could play with them as he saw fit, defenceless puppets on strings, just as before. He would have Scott jumping through imaginary hoops, the urchin slumped in a comatose stupor, and the cripple crawling at his feet. There would be no mercy. She and the others would be ground into the dirt like the worthless worms they were. And as for the other one, Samuel, he had a very special place for him.

Skelly relaxed a little and sank back into the plump confines of the armchair. He raised a finger, and flames shot upwards from the expansive fireplace to his right. They provided no heat, for he needed none. Instead, they were for aesthetic effect and helped him focus. He stared into the flickering furnace, steepling long, bony fingers under his voluminous chins.

"They'll expect me to come at them. Well, let them think that. A tactical withdrawal is sometimes necessary. Draw them into a false sense of security, and then..."

The flames roared a foot higher in the air as if doused with petrol. Skelly smirked and took in his luxurious surroundings. How he loved this room. It was one of many in the Tower. He had visited many of them and, as for the remainder, prayed to all that was unholy that he would never have to experience the terrors within them.

"But as for you, my dear Kirkwood. I think it's high time you and your new chums got the guided tour. There's so much fun to be had."

Fun. A three-letter word. Much more like it. Skelly chuckled hoarsely as he poured himself another drink.

CHAPTER 5 - NO GRAVE FOR THE DEAD

"That's it there on the right."

Kirkwood shifted uncomfortably as Samuel slowed the car before swinging right onto the gravel driveway, which led up to his childhood home. It felt like a herd of elephants had stampeded over his grave. In so many ways, the house looked just the same, but in others, it was like setting eyes on it for the very first time. He clenched both fists until his knuckles blanched to contain the rush of memories and emotions threatening to submerge him. He was home. The home his father was buried from. He was that small, bewildered orphan boy again.

"You okay?"

Meredith's soft words returned him to the present and the reason they were there. Although only acquainted a handful of days, the two of them had acquired an almost telepathic bond, normally only forged through years of friendship. Another Presence based side effect, he mused. It was a totally new experience for him, being this exposed and vulnerable before another human being. Not even his ex-girlfriend, Natasha, had managed to prise open the shutters where he stored his darkest thoughts. The OCD, the grief, the trauma all stored away under careful lock and key. Yet, Meredith had breached his defences effortlessly or rather he had allowed her to. Weird, yet he embraced and welcomed it nevertheless. He had craved such connection all his life, and now, at last, it was before him in the form of this grungy, grumpy mouthpiece.

"Yeah. Just getting my bearings," he lied. "I've got the key here somewhere. Digging a hand into the front pocket of his jeans, Kirkwood fumbled and fidgeted before producing a ball of metal. He wrestled with an assortment of fobs and key rings before triumphantly holding a small, silver key aloft.

"It's pretty sad you have more key rings than actual keys," sighed Meredith, raising an eyebrow as she climbed out of the car onto the driveway where Samuel and Harley already awaited them.

"My sister always brought me one back from her travels," offered Kirkwood, joining them to form a loose circle in front of the detached bungalow. "So, big man, what's the plan of attack?"

Samuel furrowed his brow before speaking, it always seemed such a burden for him. He was a man of few words, preferably none, but now realised the baton of responsibility had been passed on, and the others looked to him for leadership.

"Skelly is many things, but he's no fool. He will never show himself personally on this plane as that places him at risk. Even he would be no match for the Presence now it has been released by you three coming together."

"Coooool," beamed Harley, barely able to contain her glee at this information.

"But he still has ties. He was born, lived, and died here prior to transforming into his current guise. Ideally, we would be seeking to locate his grave, find his actual remains, and destroy them once and for all."

"Well then, what are we doing here?" groaned Meredith. "Can't you wave a magic wand or whatever it is you guys do and transport us to his grave? Give me a shovel, and I'll dig the old goat up in no time. What?" She looked at the other three who were staring at her with a mixture of disbelief and revulsion.

"Alright, calm down, Buffy. Why don't we wait until the expert on these matters has finished talking?" Kirkwood nodded for Samuel to continue.

"Thank you, Kirkwood," replied the gentle giant, oblivious that Meredith was pulling a face akin to a bulldog chewing a wasp. He turned to face her without warning, and she guiltily averted her eyes downwards towards her Doctor Marten boots, her face as red as them.

"You will find there is no grave for Skelly, we do not know his final resting place. Probably in some unmarked grave on the battlefield with his colleagues. Bodies are recovered from the Waterloo site every year. But to date, neither Skelly's remains or any of the 49th Somerset Regiment have ever been found. It's as if they never fought in Wellington's army that day."

"Yet, we know they did." Kirkwood chewed his lip. "How does an entire regiment disappear in a puff of smoke, written out of the history books? It makes no sense."

Samuel nodded. "For now, all I can say is that Sir Arthur Wellesley and Colonel Augustus Skelly had a rather complicated relationship. What's the phrase...History is written by the winners? Well, Wellington was ultimately the victor that day."

"So, it's bad blood? All because two crumbly old soldiers had a bit of a fallout?" Harley looked up at Samuel incredulously, who towered a good foot above her.

"Basically...Yes."

"Well, I'm glad that's all cleared up then. Now, let's get on with killing him and his loser friends." She crossed her arms, a stern expression on her youthful features. Samuel swallowed hard. He wasn't used to this level of scrutiny. How on earth had Dobson put up with it?

"While we have no body, the essence of Skelly continues to linger on this plane. Which is where you come in, Kirkwood. The key, please." Samuel held out a bucket-like hand and nodded towards the younger man. Kirkwood complied obediently, still none the wiser as to why they were standing outside his old house.

Samuel sensed the growing frustration within the party. "We are going back to where it all began, my young friends. The medium through which Skelly first got his rancid claws into Kirkwood and this plane of existence." He turned his back on them and strode towards the front door.

Harley looked hopefully towards Meredith for an answer to their cryptic guide only for the taller girl to shrug her shoulders. "Don't look at me. I haven't a Scooby-Doo what he's talking about." She looked at Kirkwood, who sported a dogged expression.

"Kirkwood? You still with us?"

"Come on,' he replied. "Let's finish this."

CHAPTER 6 - KISS FROM A GHOST

Kirkwood teetered unsteadily as he peered over the rim of the opening into the murky roof space. He flicked on a pen torch retrieved from his mother's 'odds and ends' drawer in the kitchen and scanned the cavernous expanse, guided by its weak beam. He was greeted by a chaotic scene. Boxes piled high, their sides marked with black felt tip pen. It was an Aladdin's cave of bric-a-brac, a lifetime's possessions accrued but then tossed aside when his mother decided to up sticks and jet to the other side of the world to be with her beloved daughter and grandson. And though she would never admit it to him, further away from her oddball loser of a son.

"Can you see anything?" Harley's voice filtered up from below. Kirkwood glanced down to where she and Meredith stood on the landing below, staring hopefully up at him.

"It's a mess up here. I'm going to have to climb in and have a look around."

He set the torch on the ledge and used both hands to lever himself up and into the roof space. From below, there was a muffled grunt.

"Hey, careful," shouted Harley. "You're mashing the mullet."

"Sorry, Samuel," said Kirkwood, now able to swing around onto his hands and knees and look down at his companions. Why his mother hadn't installed a drop-down ladder, he would never know. Forcing him to clamber atop the big man's formidable shoulders to initially prise open the attic door.

"That's quite alright, Kirkwood," replied Samuel, tenderly rubbing his jaw. "I was feeling a bit hungry, so the opportunity to chew on your boot was most welcome."

Meredith sniggered. "It's beyond me how we now house the most powerful force in the universe, but between us can't lay our hands on a box of rusty toy soldiers."

Kirkwood spent the next twenty minutes rummaging through every corner of the roof space until finally admitting defeat and calling down to the others. "It's not up here." He crouched on his haunches and winced in frustration. It had to be here somewhere. Surely, she didn't take them to New Zealand with her.

"So, what do we do now?" asked Harley in dismay.

"Kirkwood, can you think of anywhere else they might be?"

"Okay, okay. I'm thinking."

"Wondered what the noise was."

"Shut it," hissed Harley, elbowing Meredith in the ribs in a decidedly unfriendly manner. Even the normally placid Samuel shot the dark-haired girl a disapproving look.

Above them, Kirkwood rubbed a hand furiously through his unruly mop of brown hair in an attempt to spark flagging memory banks. Think Kirkwood, think, where could it be?

"You really are an idiot; you do realise that?"

"Shut up, Meredith!"

"What? I never said a word." Meredith's aggrieved voice drifted up from below.

"Oh, for goodness sake, you numpty. It's me."

Kirkwood looked up from where he was crouching and squinted into the gloom. As his eyes gradually adjusted to the murky light, he could just make out the outline of a figure in the far corner of the roof space. A figure which he recognised with astonishment as it stepped forward towards him.

"Emily!"

"At your service, kind sir." Emily curtsied extravagantly, daintily hitching the hems of her flimsy chiffon dress between thumb and forefinger. Her striking pale features and platinum blonde hair accentuated the ghostly image she presented to Kirkwood. "For the saviour of the planet, you're not the sharpest tool in the box, are you?"

"Is everything alright up there?" Samuel's voice had a concerned edge. Kirkwood looked wide-eyed at the waif in front of him, uncertain as to how to respond.

"Oh, relax, Kirky, they can't hear us."

Kirkwood nodded before shouting down. "Yeah, I'm fine, just found another box. I'll be two minutes."

"There, that wasn't so difficult, was it?" Emily smiled mischievously and perched herself on a cardboard box opposite Kirkwood. "Two minutes is all I need. Soooooo, how have you been? Pleased to see me?" She smirked and flicked her hair back coyishly.

"I'd be more pleased to see you if you didn't keep making these unannounced appearances and scaring the living daylights out of me." Kirkwood stood and arched his back, the top of his head brushing the attic eaves.

"Occupational hazard, I'm afraid." Emily smiled sweetly at him, and Kirkwood blushed despite his best efforts not to. As dead girls went, she could be very persuasive. "Now, let's talk, we haven't much time. Are you seriously telling me you don't know where the box is?"

"I've looked everywhere," hissed Kirkwood. "If it was going to be anywhere, this is where it would be. All Katie's junk is up here." He indicated the box Emily was sitting on. "That one contains more cuddly toys than a teddy bears picnic."

"Which is exactly why I chose it to sit on," beamed Emily, stretching her legs before crossing them at the ankles to emphasise the point. She grinned as Kirkwood steadfastly maintained eye contact with her, despite the rising flush in his cheeks.

"Hurry up," bellowed Meredith from below. "I'm starving."

"Coming," replied Kirkwood before turning to Emily again. "This isn't the time for games. Help me. Please."

"Oh, very well, sad sack. Honestly, you living have no sense of humour." She sat more upright and placed both hands on her lap in as demure a fashion as one could, given the location and circumstances.

"Look around, Kirkwood, and what do you see?"

"Er, boxes?" replied Kirkwood dully, struggling to grasp the thrust of the question.

"Yes, you ninny. But cardboard boxes. And your collection of toy soldiers were kept..."

"In a metal box. Of course. I kept them in one of my Dad's old toolboxes. So, when Mum saw it, she's..."

"Put it in the garage." Emily finished the sentence, her words dripping with sarcasm. "Nice one, Brain of Britain. What would you lot do without me?"

"Then why did you leave her?" Kirkwood regretted the question even as the words were leaving his mouth. "Sorry," he added. "I shouldn't have said that. None of my business."

Emily shifted position slightly and sighed, her eyes containing a great sadness. "It's alright, you don't need to apologise. It's just best Meredith and I don't meet at the moment. Not like this anyway." She stood and flattened out her dress, before stepping forward and standing on her tiptoes, planting the gentlest of kisses on Kirkwood's cheek. He closed his eyes, instantly flooded with a soothing calm he had never known before. Suddenly it didn't matter, nothing mattered, he just knew everything would be alright. Somehow.

"Promise you won't tell? I'll reveal myself to Meredith when the time is right. Now is not that time. She's not ready emotionally, and me appearing is only going to distract her from what's important right now."

Kirkwood sighed. "Okay. You really have me wrapped around your little finger, don't you?"

"There's nowhere else you'd rather be. Now hurry along. And Kirkwood?"

"Yeah?"

"Be careful. They're close. Very close."

CHAPTER 7 - TOY SOLDIERS

The garage shutters squealed in protest as Kirkwood raised them. Situated to the right of the bungalow, it housed several wooden rows of shelving along either side of its length. His mother had sold her immaculately maintained Mini years ago once her free bus pass arrived when she reached pension age. Even before then, though, she rarely drove it other than her weekly excursions to the supermarket and church. Kirkwood was on the insurance but could count on the fingers of one hand how many times he had sat behind the steering wheel. In Belfast, he had no need for a car given most locations were within walking distance or via public transport. There was also the small matter of him being over the legal limit most weekends, typically ensconced in a city centre bar with Gerry and Grogan.

"If it's going to be anywhere, it's in here," he announced, starting to root through the first shelf to his left. "It was a red tin, I'm certain of that. Bright red. Spread out and get looking."

Samuel and Harley complied, starting on the shelving to their right. Kirkwood's eyes frantically scanned the garage, Emily's final words still reverberating round his skull.

"Is there a Burger King in Omagh?" asked Meredith, still loitering by the garage door. "I could eat a scabby horse. I'm that hungry."

"You poor wee thing," replied Harley, rolling her eyes. "It's been a good two hours since you've eaten anything. I don't know how you're still standing."

"There's a McDonald's in the town," replied Kirkwood. "Now would you two stop bickering and get looking? The sooner we find this box, the sooner you can get your face fed, Meredith."

Meredith groaned and reluctantly started to check the shelf beneath the one Kirkwood was ploughing through. There followed several minutes of silence, interrupted only by the rattle of boxes being opened and their contents examined. A cold sweat began to form on Kirkwood's forehead as tendrils of panic coiled around his throat. *It isn't here, it isn't here. What if she did take it to New Zealand?*

His mood darkened as the minutes passed until a whoop of delight from Harley had them all spinning in her direction. Kirkwood turned to see the teenager running manically around the garage with a red metal box raised triumphantly above her head.

"I've found it, I've found it," she hollered before chucking the box to Kirkwood as she passed him. He juggled it before clutching it gratefully to his chest. The others crouched around as he tipped its contents onto the concrete garage floor.

"Come out, come out wherever you are, Skelly. For you, the war is over."

All manner of plastic and metal figures bounced off the concrete before coming to rest before their eager eyes. There were stern

German paratroopers, pristine Crimean cavalry officers sitting resplendently upon their mounts, and dour World War One Tommies, plucked shellshocked from the trenches. Yet, despite rifling through the contents of the box several times, the jewel in the crown could not be found.

"I don't suppose you could have a word with your bosses and teleport us to the other side of the world?" Kirkwood scratched the back of his head in dismay. "For it looks like we're screwed. If it's not in this box, then my mother must have..."

"Looking for something?"

They rose and turned in unison to be greeted by a sight that sent a collective shudder through their ranks. Standing at the bottom of the driveway was a red-haired woman dressed as if she had hot-footed it from a show jumping event. She held out her left hand to reveal a small metal figure in an outstretched palm. The object of their desires—the Colonel, Skelly.

"Who the hell are you?" snarled Meredith, her fists clenched in balls by her side.

The woman laughed a high-pitched peal that belied an underlying hardness.

"Oh, Meredith, how very rude of me. Allow me to introduce myself. I'm Maura Miller from Dublin's fair city, where the girls are so pretty." Her laughter turned into a leering smirk. "Well, much prettier than the riff-raff they find on the streets of Belfast these days."

"You want to say that again?" Meredith growled, taking a step forward until Samuel placed a restraining hand on her forearm.

Their eyes met, and he gave an almost imperceptible shake of the head.

"Very wise, Samuel, very wise. I see Dobson chose well when selecting his successor."

"You are of them," replied Samuel, showing no emotion. "I had heard there was a woman in their ranks, but until now, thought it only a myth."

"Well, welcome to the 21st century, my friend. Or rather the 19th in your case. I believe you were already six hundred years in the ground when I breathed my last at Waterloo."

"Wait a minute," said Kirkwood, looking from Samuel to Maura in disbelief and back again. "There were female soldiers at Waterloo?"

"Not soldiers, camp followers. And this miserable wretch obviously found her way into the square at the end. No doubt looting the pockets of the dead."

The smirk slipped away from Maura's face. "I died looking for my James. And I found him in the end, my brave husband. He died a hero's death, which is more than I can say for your leader. I hear he cried like a baby when William winkled his brains out from between his ears."

"That's enough." Samuel's roar made Kirkwood and Harley jump in unison, even Meredith was startled.

"Sorry," purred Maura. "Looks like I struck a nerve there. Anyway, it's been great getting to know you all, but I really must be on my way. The Colonel's a very impatient man and will be wanting this little trinket delivered forthwith." She began to place the tiny figure in the inside pocket of her jacket when Kirkwood, Meredith, and Harley strode forward in unison, joining hands as they did so.

"We are three, but we are one, we are three, but we are..."

Maura clicked the fingers of her free hand, and Harley was lifted off the ground before being flung forward, where she sprawled on the driveway at the feet of her assailant. Before the others could react, she had secreted the tiny soldier and replaced it with a flick knife which she held to Harley's throat, dragging the rainbow-haired girl to her feet with alarming dexterity.

"Way, way too slow children. Your little tricks might have worked on the bridge, but I can assure you I am a cut above my colleagues when it comes to combat. One move and this little bitch gets her throat cut. Don't try me."

Kirkwood and Meredith, still holding hands, looked on helplessly. It was Samuel who acted next, taking a step forward while raising his two palms in a placating gesture.

"Do not harm the girl. She is an innocent. If blood must be shed, then let it be you and I who do so, in fair combat." Harley could do nothing but blink in return, the sharp edge of the blade preventing her from speaking.

"Sorry, I don't do fair. The French didn't do fair when they took my man from me, so why should I start now? The girl stays with me as a little extra gift for the Colonel. I'm keen to progress within the organisation, and this will do my career prospects no harm at all."

"So be it," replied Samuel, betraying no sign of panic. "But a message for your Colonel. Should he harm one hair on the girl's head, I will flay him to the bone."

"Ha!" Maura flew her head back and laughed. "Given I now possess his last connection to this dung heap of a planet, I've no idea how you're going to accomplish that, but I wish you well. You might have closed the Portal, but we are far from done with this planet. It will be ours."

With that, Maura and Harley vanished. Meredith rushed forward to where they had been, before turning towards the others, her hands on her head. "Samuel, do something. We have to get her back." Tears began to roll down her cheeks, the cocky, streetwise persona evaporating to unveil the real Meredith Starc beneath.

Samuel looked several shades paler than before Maura's sudden appearance. This had not been part of the plan. Kirkwood looked frantically around, hoping for Harley to pop out from behind the adjacent hedge and declare it had all been one massive, if deeply unfunny, practical joke. There was nobody else there—no Dobson, no Emily, all his guardian angels were otherwise engaged. Even old 'Nosy Pants' Thompson next door was nowhere to be seen, which was particularly odd as his front curtains were forever twitching.

"Would somebody please say something?" cried Meredith. "I've lost Emily, I've lost Dobson, and I think I'm losing my mind. I am not prepared to lose Harley into the bargain, given I only met her earlier today."

Kirkwood looked at his scuffed shoes before speaking again. "Guys, I think I might have an idea, but you're going to have to pull a few strings at your end, big man." He looked towards Samuel, who nodded for him to continue.

"You're not going to like this Meredith, and I promised her I wouldn't say anything but..."

CHAPTER 8 - SO MUCH TROUBLE

"You've talked to her? And never told me?"

As explosions went, it was a spectacular one, even by Meredith's volcanic standards. Kirkwood narrowly avoided the first right hook, anticipating it and swaying back on his heels, but had no answer for the ensuing rugby tackle which landed him on his back. Meredith straddled him; raining blows down upon her supposed friend in a fashion Mike Tyson would have been proud of.

"You lying, cheating piece of dirt." She punctuated each word by bringing a clenched fist down upon Kirkwood, who struggled to adopt a foetal position to curtail the assault. The punches weren't particularly painful, and he battened down the hatches, hoping Storm Meredith would blow herself out and become amenable to a civilised conversation.

In the end, Samuel had to intervene, effortlessly lifting a still flailing Meredith off her victim. With one hand, he brought her to her feet and wrapped his massive arms around the distraught young woman. Kirkwood staggered to his feet, before leaping back as Meredith again lunged for him. Thankfully Samuel regained his grip despite her best efforts to wriggle free.

"I trusted you. Trusted you. And you repay me by stabbing me in the back and sneaking around with my best friend." She opened her mouth to continue but was overcome by emotions and turned her head aside, sobbing into Samuel's barrel of a chest.

"Meredith, I..." As so often in his life, when he most needed them, the words eluded him. He turned away and kicked a pebble as hard as he could in frustration across the driveway. Samuel waited a moment before speaking.

"Meredith and I are going to take a little journey to this McDonnells place your kind speak of. When we return, the three of us are going to discuss what has just taken place and our next step forward. I'll expect you to be here when I return, Kirkwood."

"Yeah. Ok," mumbled Kirkwood. "And it's McDonald's, by the way. And another thing, you don't even know where you're going."

"I'm a supernatural entity with unbelievable power. I'm sure I can find the local fast food joint, as you people refer to such establishments." He led Meredith to the Micra, opening the car door and ushering her into the passenger seat. She complied without uttering a word, the fight seemingly gone from her. Not once did she look in Kirkwood's direction.

When they returned, it was obvious Samuel had used the journey to apply his considerable diplomatic skills. Meredith said little as she consumed her Big Mac and fries at an alarming rate. It was only as she scooped the last of a Dairy Milk McFlurry into her mouth and drained the dregs of a strawberry milkshake that she spoke softly, her voice still laden with hurt.

"I've discussed this with Samuel, and for Harley's sake, I'm prepared to hear you out on this one. But I'm not happy. I'm confused and feel betrayed."

She lowered her head and shattered the heavy silence with a lengthy slurp from the milkshake. Kirkwood looked to Samuel for guidance, who simply nodded for him to talk.

"Emily has appeared to me twice now. Once last night at the B&B and today in the roof space. On both occasions, she has warned me about what lay ahead and offered me advice. Like she did when she appeared in Harley's dreams. And on both occasions, she made it very clear I was not to tell you she had contacted me."

"But...but....why?" Meredith looked up from her milkshake, pale blue eyes filling with tears.

"I'm not certain," replied Kirkwood. "But I think it's as if she feels that she's already hurt you enough. You talk about betrayal, but she thinks she betrayed you. By taking her life, deserting you when you needed her most. She showed weakness when strength was required."

Meredith flinched and stared at Kirkwood in disbelief. "Weak? I've never thought that of her. It's not for me to judge why she killed herself. I have no idea what sort of place she was in when she made that choice. Skelly was no doubt playing all sorts of mind games with her. God knows I've thought about doing it enough times myself since her funeral."

"I've read your letters to her, Meredith. Some of it was pretty harsh. I know you were hurting when you wrote them..."

"And blocked or horribly hungover most of the time," added Meredith grimly.

"Yeah. But while she hasn't come out and said it to me, I think that's what lies behind her reticence. Plus, you've had other commitments competing for your time. Defeating Skelly, preventing the Scourge from reducing the planet to a pile of smoking rubble."

Samuel spoke softly, but his sincerity was unmistakable. "Emily has crossed over, a deeply traumatic and confusing process, believe me, I know. Since then, she has been by your side every step. The graffiti, in Harley's dreams, and the appearances before Kirkwood. She might not have been visible to you, but the effort required for her to manifest herself on this plane must have been immense. It's all been for you, Meredith, it's all evidence of her deep love for you."

He gently took her hand and looked into the young woman's eyes. "You're hurting, but so is Emily. I need both of you if we are ever to see Harley again. Forgive her and forgive Kirkwood as well. He meant no harm and was placed in a terrible position."

Kirkwood dared to meet her eyes, and once more, the telepathic connection between them flickered into life. They stood as one and met in an awkward but heartfelt embrace.

"I'm sorry, I should have said," whispered Kirkwood as he buried his head in the nape of her neck.

"And I've got to stop flying off the handle at the slightest wee thing," replied Meredith. "I just miss her so much, and it's frustrating I can't see her, talk to her. She was...is....my best friend."

"I know you'll see her soon. It's just going to take a little time for her to...AAAAARGHHHH!"

The two of them separated and fell to their knees, clutching their ears in agony. The female voice screaming in their heads was unmistakable despite the excruciating pain she seemed to be in. Only Samuel was unaffected as he sprang from where he was sitting to their aid.

"What is it? What's wrong?" His normally calm veneer vanished as he watched his young companions squirming on the ground. But as suddenly as the anguished voice started, it cut off with a strangulated gasp.

"Did you hear her? It was her, wasn't it?" Meredith whimpered, reeling from the vicious aural assault.

"Yes," replied Kirkwood, clambering onto all fours. "It was Emily." He looked up, his face twisted with distress. "She's in trouble, Samuel, so much trouble."

Samuel frowned. "I was hoping it wouldn't come to this, but events are moving fast." He placed a comforting hand on first Kirkwood's shoulder, then Meredith's, causing the pain to instantly subside. "We need to leave. Now."

CHAPTER 9 - BURN, BELFAST, BURN

Fire appliances from the surrounding areas screamed along the main arterial routes towards Belfast as news of the blaze spread. The first alarm sounded half an hour before the store was due to close, and staff and customers alike initially thought it was a fire drill or a false alarm at best. Wardens in fluorescent vests began to herd reluctant shoppers towards the lifts and escalators. Many scowled and aired their thoughts, annoyed that their shopping expedition had been cut short. Beleaguered management, with rapidly fraying patience, explained the need to vacate the premises in a prompt and orderly fashion.

All that changed when the first nostrils flared at the smoky aroma filtering through the upper floors of the historic Carruthers Building, which housed the modern Prestige store. Sitting in the heart of the city centre, office workers and school children filtered past unaware of the events unfolding inside. Irritated murmurs became shouts of concern as mothers started to pick up the pace, ushering their wayward children towards the exits. There was a roar of complaint as two women, laden down with bags, collided while negotiating a corner. A lone cough rapidly multiplied as a thin blanket of smoke began to lazily drift across the building's upper floors.

It was nine minutes after the initial alarm sounded that the first flame could be seen from ground level, popping its head over the ledge of the flatbed roof like a nervous archer peering over a castle parapet. As the seconds passed, the fire, encouraged by a stiff breeze, swept across the top of the building until it burnt bright like a fiery crown atop the iconic Redstone structure. For over a century it had taken pride of place in the city centre skyline, imperiously unmoved as the decades crept by and the city morphed into its current guise. It had witnessed countless bombings and multiple shootings within its vast shadow. It had survived everything the world could throw at it. Until now, but the furnace engulfing it was not of this world.

Panicked shoppers were now spewing out onto Royal Avenue, as the first police officers to arrive fought to curtail curious onlookers from prying too near. The roof was an inferno, and a funnel of smoke began to spiral high across the city, where it could be seen for miles. The wall of dense, choking fumes spread word of the blaze quicker than even social media could, despite the best efforts of Twitter and Facebook. The wail of approaching sirens announced the arrival of the fire crews, soon to be joined by a fleet of ambulances to treat those suffering from shock and smoke inhalation. Prestige management was later to appear before the cameras, proudly announcing that the quick actions of their shop floor workers undoubtedly saved lives. They were less forthcoming about the origin of the fire, heeding legal advice not to comment until the findings of a formal investigation were known.

That investigation would take months as forensic experts painstakingly raked over the charred ruins for evidence, which was then subject to extensive laboratory testing. It was rumoured that a welder working on the roof had left a blowtorch unattended. Others spoke of a lit cigarette not fully stubbed out by an employee after an unauthorised smoke break. The more extreme religious elements claimed it was the wrath of God after Prestige decked out a display window with rainbow flags in support of the city's recent Pride parade. Holy flames from above striking down the unclean and impure, a modern-day Sodom and Gomorrah.

Skelly had a good chuckle at that one, for there was nothing holy about the fire, which reduced the Carruthers Building to a smouldering husk. No, for all their efforts, the true source of the blaze would never be known. What they did know was that it spread rapidly as if spurred on by some unidentified accelerant. Ripping through the listed building, the modern sprinkler system, and heroics of the firefighters unable to contain its malevolent progress. The skies darkened, but while many prayed for saving rains, they never arrived. Instead, the winds picked up, driving the flames almost horizontally across to adjoining buildings. One structure alight soon became two, became three, and before long, the entire block was a hellish scene. It was a miracle no one was killed, but for one unrecorded casualty. Behind the Prestige building, industrial waste bins were soon smothered by flames, their crackling tongues licking along the walls on either side. Wood, plastic, paint it all succumbed to the searing heat.

It was a sight to behold, Mother Nature, at her most merciless. Nothing could stand in its path, bar one figure. Had the beleaguered firefighters been able to battle down the alley to the rear of the building, they would have been greeted by an incredulous sight. For there, standing in the eye of the firestorm was a lone figure, defying the temperature and cruel flames. It was impossible, but there he stood, dressed from head to toe in black designer clothing. His full black beard glistened as equally dark eyes gleefully watched the face on the wall blistering and melting before him.

The face of a young, finely boned woman, her sombre features succumbing to the fearsome furnace now consuming all. The bearded giant took a step towards the wall, impervious to the flames which licked at the flaps of his three-quarter-length coat. He cupped a hand to his ear.

"What's that?" he enquired, sarcasm dripping from his voice like poisonous honey, sweet yet deadly. The Mediterranean lilt to his accent would have been seductive, were it not for the deadly intent evident in his eyes. Eyes which wouldn't have looked out of place on a great white shark, stalking its prey from the icy depths.

"Oh, Emily, why so quiet all of a sudden? You normally have so much to say for yourself. You and your little friends."

A huge slab of masonry from the main building crashed onto the wall to his right, shaking the alley and causing an alarming crack to zig-zag the length of Emily's face. Sergeant Martim Rodriguez took another step forward until he was within touching distance of the wall. All around him, the city burned.

"Looks like this hot spell is doing nothing for your looks, witch. But you may get used to it where you're about to go."

Rodriguez lifted a foot and planted it squarely against the wall at the crack's epicentre. The impact caused it to lengthen and widen before that entire section of the wall collapsed into a formless mass of bricks and dust. It and the street art adorning it were no more.

If a bystander were to listen keenly, they might have caught the snatch of booming laughter above the cacophonous noise of the stricken building. A deep, Portuguese baritone. Nobody would have heard the tortured screams of Emily O'Hara, though. The screams of a girl who was already dead.

CHAPTER 10 - THE TOWER

Harley awoke with a loud sneeze, rising and shaking her head to dispel the feather duster someone had mischievously dangled under her nose. Recovering from the exertion, she opened her eyes to be confronted by a plush, burgundy carpet an inch from her face. As she struggled to work out where she was and what she was doing there, a deep, sonorous voice interrupted her jumbled thoughts.

"Ah, there we are, Maura. Our guest has decided to join us at long last."

Harley pushed herself up with both palms to be confronted by a pair of beige tweed trousers directly in front of her. They sat atop a pair of expensive-looking brown brogues polished to a gleaming sheen. The bottom half of the mystery voice's ensemble was completed by a pair of garish yellow socks that wouldn't have looked out of place at a rave party. Harley sensed she was no longer in Omagh.

"No need to get up on our accord, my dear. Although I doubt you'd be able to even if you wanted."

A ruddy face loomed into Harley's field of vision. A swollen bulbous nose and unruly charcoal eyebrows sat atop a pair of twinkling eyes within a wrinkled face. Whoever this old man was,

Harley immediately realised he was no friend. She struggled to get onto her hands and knees, but a sharp pain to the small of her back sent her sprawling face-first into the depths of the carpet again.

"You'll stay where you are, you wee bitch," a female voice snarled from above. Harley looked over her shoulder, recognising it immediately. Towering above her was the woman from Kirkwood's house, still decked from head to toe in riding gear. The only difference was that her mane of flame-red hair now flowed freely over both shoulders and halfway down her back. She was beautiful, her stunning looks only marred by the sneer which seemed a permanent feature on her face.

"Shush, Maura. Now, where are your manners, that's no way to treat such a distinguished guest." The old man spoke like he was the lord of the manor, and it suddenly dawned on Harley as to where she was and who was addressing her.

"Skelly," she said between gritted teeth. "You're that sad old perv who's been knocking about Kirkwood's head all these years. Is this the best you can do, sending a woman to fight your battles?" She flinched, expecting another painful intervention from Maura, but her assailant simply glowered down at her.

Skelly chuckled before sinking back into his armchair and rested swollen fingers beneath his numerous chins. Harley took the brief respite to scan her surroundings. The floor to ceiling bookcases to her right, the imposing oak table in front of her, and the roaring fireplace to her left which should have been scalding yet emitted no heat. A chill ran down the length of her spine. She was in the Study, the place Kirkwood had described to them when recounting his horrific history with one Colonel Augustus Skelly.

"Rodriguez said you were a little firecracker, and he wasn't wrong. Full of vim and vigour, aren't you? Reminds me a little of the day I first met you, Maura?"

Maura snorted in disgust. "Hardly. This little runt wouldn't have lasted five minutes in our world, sir. The likes of her were dispatched to the asylum where their sort belonged."

Harley considered a reply but bit down on her bottom lip. She was impulsive, but the enormity of the trouble she was in was dawning on her. No point in poking the bear any further. She had to buy some time, gather her bearings, and try to figure out what the hell she was going to do. Surely Kirkwood and the others would work out where she was and race to her aid. What was the point housing the most powerful force in the universe if it couldn't be utilised to help a friend in need? And boy, was she in need right now.

"You really are the most disagreeable young lady." Skelly lowered his hands and frowned at Maura before returning his gaze to Harley, lying prostrate in front of him. "Although I must say I'm a tad disappointed, Miss Davison. Here I am, honoured by the presence of Dobson's secret weapon, and you don't seem to have an ounce of fight left in you."

"I'll show you fight, you fat slug." Harley snapped and lunged towards Skelly before a searing pain exploded across the left side of her rib cage as Maura's riding boot connected with it. She slumped to the floor again, gasping for breath as the pain ricocheted around her slight frame.

Skelly clapped his hands together like an excited schoolboy. "Oh, excellent, this kitten does have claws after all. A bit of the old fighting spirit. Perhaps I could have made use of you after all in the square. What say you, Maura?"

Maura sighed and made no response, never taking her eyes off Harley, who was now curled in a ball trying to ride out the wall of pain threatening to consume her. She swallowed hard to hold back the bile rising from her stomach, although part of her would have taken great satisfaction in decorating Skelly's spotless shoes with the contents of her stomach. Finally, it was too much to bear, and she let loose a low, miserable moan which she barely recognised as her own voice.

Skelly leaned forward again. "Bit winded, are we girl, eh? I feel your pain. I got one in the ribs once from a damnable beast I was grooming for parading in front of His Majesty. Cracked God only knows how many ribs. Still paraded though, nothing half a bottle of brandy couldn't sort out." He chuckled and gazed fondly into the raging fire, recalling some former glory.

"What do you want?" panted Harley, struggling to suck oxygen into her throbbing lungs. "They'll come for me. We're not scared of you. Didn't you pick up on that earlier at the bridge?"

Skelly frowned momentarily, cocking his head to one side as he considered her words. "Yes, that was an unexpected setback, I'll give you that. Dobson is a wily old foe. Or should I say was..." He almost purred with delight as he watched his words hit home. A single tear traced a lonely path down Harley's cheek.

"Oh, I do apologise," mocked Skelly, feigning concern. "Have I offended you? How very remiss of me. Here..." He learned forward, producing a yellow handkerchief from the breast pocket of his jacket and holding it out towards her. "Never let it be said that Augustus St. John Skelly wasn't a gentleman."

Harley swatted the garish offering aside. "Go to hell," she grunted.

"Ha," retorted Skelly, rocking back on his heels and slapping a thigh in delight. "Who's to say we're not there already, Miss Davison? But let me help you out if I may." He raised a hand and clicked his fingers. Harley let out a protracted wheeze as the pain in her side departed as quickly as Maura's riding boot had delivered it.

"There, isn't that better?" continued Skelly. "Now, I know what you're thinking. Your wonderful new companions are going to ride to your rescue and put nasty old Skelly and his evil cronies well and truly in their place. Well, I'm afraid I can't allow that to happen. You see, while you may think I'm running this show, I am but a mere cog in a much bigger machine. The lovely Maura and I must follow the orders of our elders and betters. Isn't that right, Maura?"

"Yes, Colonel." Maura lifted her gaze from the prone Harley and nodded curtly. "Although if this is the best the enemy can come up with, then we have little to fear. Capturing this one was like snatching sweets from a baby." She allowed herself a humourless smile before reverting her attention to Harley again.

"Ah, yes, captured," smirked Skelly. "For that is what you are, my little friend. Although I prefer to regard you as my guest. An insurance policy if you may. For while my employer's plans may have been temporarily derailed on that blasted bridge, they regard it as a minor blip. They very much still have eyes for your little lump of dirt. I've given them my word that I'll deliver the goods, and once I get the bit between my teeth, I'm not the type of man who backs down and walks off into the sunset."

"Neither are we," muttered Harley. Let them talk, she thought. The more information she could squeeze out of Skelly, the better. Knowledge is power, wasn't that what they said? Skelly was full of hot air and loved the sound of his own voice, but it was buying some time for the others. They would come for her—she was certain of that much.

Skelly either ignored her or was oblivious to the response. He reached into a trouser pocket and produced the miniature figure which Maura had beaten them to at the bungalow. "You see now that I've got this, and now that I've got you, I can sit tight and claim the higher ground, wait for your chums to rush to your aid. And when they do, I've got a few delightful surprises in store for them."

Harley fought back the tears threatening to overwhelm her. She was tough, had been through so much in recent times, but this was a whole new ball game. In the face of this blizzard of bewildering events, she opted for a bland, practical response.

"So, I'm stuck in this manky old Study until then?"

Skelly grinned, revealing two rows of rancid, decaying stumps. "Oh, you think this is it? Well, allow me to give you the guided tour." He threw out both arms in a theatrical flourish. "Welcome to my humble abode, Miss Davison. It has many rooms, and I've an extra special one reserved just for you. Somewhere you can rot away the rest of your pathetic existence if need be. Welcome to the Tower."

Something snapped inside Harley, and she propelled herself upwards, wanting nothing more than to pummel Skelly's obscene face to a shapeless pulp. She collapsed again in a heap, inches from the feet of her intended target. Instinctively she knew, for this time, Maura had made no effort to stop her. Frantically she urged her legs to respond to her commands, but they lay crumpled beneath her. She pinched her thigh. Nothing. No sensation or response. She couldn't move a muscle.

"Sorry, I forgot to mention," smiled Skelly. "How rude of me. Now that you're not in the company of your new friends, I'm afraid it's back to square one. And there are no fancy wheelchairs here for you to swan about in. You'll just have to make do. Crawl around like the disgusting little worm we both know you are. You're playing with the big boys now. And you're losing big time."

He threw back his head and laughed, a coarse sound that reverberated around the Study. Maura joined in on cue, and Harley finally succumbed to the tears. She buried her face in the sumptuous embrace of the carpet and whispered a silent plea.

"Help me, guys. Please help me."

CHAPTER 11 - MY LAST DOUBLOON

The journey back to Belfast was draped mostly in silence. The Micra's tinny radio told them all they needed to know. A major fire had broken out in Belfast, consuming the Carruthers Building and spreading to several smaller premises in the vicinity. Firefighters from all over the country had responded to the blaze and were now battling to bring the flames under control. There were no reported fatalities, although several people had required hospital treatment for smoke inhalation and shock. The damage to property was believed to be in the millions. Soon, the centre of the city would be no more than a blackened ruin.

It was Kirkwood who spoke first. "Maybe she's okay. I mean, I know the alleyway is behind the Carruthers Building, but that doesn't necessarily mean it spread there." He shrugged, unconvinced by his words, spoken more to fill the gloomy silence than to instil any sense of hope.

"Oh, wise up," snapped Meredith, before correcting and composing herself. "Sorry, Kirky, but you felt what I did. Emily was in agony like she was burning alive. Then this..." She pointed at the radio in helpless disgust. "She's gone, isn't she?"

"I can't sense her, no," mumbled Kirkwood in response. "She's only appeared to me twice, but after the first time, I always sensed she was close, looking over us. But now...nothing."

Samuel spoke from the front, glancing periodically in the rear-view mirror. Kirkwood and Meredith had remained in the back, neither of them wanting to take Harley's seat beside their mysterious driver.

"She's no longer on this plane, I agree, and I'll bet my back teeth Skelly and his goons are behind the fire." As they neared the outskirts of Belfast, they were greeted by an ominous cloud of thick, black smoke drifting across the city landscape. "He has Harley now in addition to Kirkwood's toy soldier, so the odds have shifted in his favour." He returned his gaze to the unfolding motorway in front, deep in thought.

"There must be something we can do," pleaded Meredith. "Aren't we meant to be the all-powerful, all-conquering Presence? We are three, but we are one. All that malarkey." She looked to Kirkwood for support, urging him to pick up the hopeful thread she was unravelling.

Kirkwood was in no mood for pandering. "We house the Presence, Meredith, and with Harley gone, that power is pretty much wiped out. Yes, Skelly can't get at you or me through OCD or alcoholism..."

"I wasn't an alcoholic," interrupted Meredith. "I just drank a lot, that's all."

"Yeah, right. An awful lot." Kirkwood continued, unimpressed by his friend's protestations. "But I haven't an earthly what we do now."

"I wish Dobson was here," replied Meredith. "He'd know what to do."

Samuel nodded sadly. "He would have, but he's gone, so we will have to make do with what we have." The car suddenly swerved violently to the left as Samuel steered it without warning onto the hard shoulder, slamming on the brakes. Kirkwood and Meredith were thrown forward, only their seatbelts saving them from exiting the vehicle via the front windscreen.

Samuel turned around in his seat to address them, a rare glint in his eye, replacing his normally dour demeanour. "But if Cornelius taught me anything, it was always to have a Plan B tucked away for a rainy day."

"Well, as rainy days go, we're in Noah's Ark territory here," winced Meredith, rubbing her neck tenderly after their abrupt stop. "Go on, then, let's hear your masterplan."

"The portal at the bridge was closed to prevent the Scourge from decimating this plane, but..." He paused, savouring the delivery of his revelation.

"Oh, hurry up, Samuel," moaned Meredith. "I can only bate my breath for so long." She was distinctly unimpressed by the theatrics of their normally monosyllabic guide.

"It doesn't stop us from moving in the other direction. I think I can figure out another path to get us to Emily, and in due course, Harley. A back door, so to speak, that Skelly won't be expecting."

"Go on. I'm listening now." Kirkwood looked at Meredith, who nodded eagerly, her sarcastic side no longer on display.

"We have access to sixteen planes via this portal, and each of them allows us access to sixteen others. And so on, an infinite number of parallel realities. Parallel versions of other worlds, but more importantly, also parallel versions of this one."

"Okay," said Meredith slowly. "So, you're saying there are other versions of Earth?"

"In which case, there must be other versions of Belfast," continued Kirkwood, expanding her train of thought. A huge smile began to break across his face. "Versions where the Emily graffiti hasn't been burnt to a crisp."

"Exactly," Samuel concluded. "And if we can reconnect with Emily, I'll bet my last doubloon she can lead us to Harley."

"Doubloon!" Meredith snorted with laughter. "You really must fill us in on your backstory one of these days."

"I will," nodded Samuel. "But first, we have work to do. It's time I called in a favour from an old friend of Cornelius." He turned back round, cranked the Micra into first gear and pulled out onto the motorway again.

Kirkwood and Meredith exchanged bemused looks. "Best stay buckled up, Kirky," the dark-haired girl beamed from under her black beanie hat. "I've a feeling this ride is only going to get bumpier before it's over."

CHAPTER 12 - TOMMY

He was waiting at the roadside a good ten minutes before they arrived. Several motorists passed in either direction, paying scant attention to the slight figure huddled inside an oversized parka and equally baggy khaki green combat trousers. Beneath the hood of the parka was a grey face traversed with decades of wrinkles. A week's stubble did nothing to allay the scruffy exterior, nor did the mop of dark curls in serious need of a visit to the barbers. He looked as if a hot bath and three-course dinner might kill him, but that was all part of the act. Let the enemy underestimate you, lull them into a false sense of security.

Beneath the clothing was a lean, muscular figure, not carrying an ounce of fat. He could run a seven-minute mile, give you a hundred press-ups and then do it all over again. He prided himself on his stamina and strength. For a dead man, he was in the best shape of his afterlife. Trained for moments like this, moments when his particular set of skills were required. He narrowed his cold, cobalt blue eyes against the low evening sun as the little red Micra approached, indicated, and pulled in beside him. Picking up a rucksack at his feet, the man swung open the front passenger door and deposited himself in the car beside Samuel.

"Thank you for agreeing to this, Tommy. I apologise for the short notice, but our situation has taken an unexpected turn for the worse."

"Not a bother, Samuel. Least I could do. I heard about the business at the bridge. I'm sorry for your loss. Old Dobson stank to high heaven, but he was a good egg. They broke the mould when they made him." He extended a hand that Samuel shook warmly. Kirkwood detected a strong Northern English accent when the man spoke. Yorkshire perhaps?

The man threw back the hood of his parka and turned around to face Kirkwood and Meredith. "So," he laughed. "What have we here? The famous Kirkwood Scott, hero of Ardgallon, and his trusty sidekick, Meredith Starc. Pleased to make your acquaintance."

"Less of the sidekick, mate," mumbled Meredith, cautiously returning his offered handshake.

"Kirkwood. Meredith. Allow me to introduce Tommy Mainwright. He's one of our own."

"Ha," roared Tommy, his laughter reverberating around the interior of the small car. "Not that I had much of a say in it. One minute I was patrolling your fair land with my troop, the next, they were scooping up bits of me from the adjacent fields. The same boyos who got your good father." Tommy's cheerful disposition vanished. "My condolences, young man. Ignore my roguish charms. I'm here to help you and will do all I can to reunite you with your friends. No offence taken, I hope."

Kirkwood eyed the quirky character before responding. "None taken. And thank you. For your condolences, I mean. And er...the same to you?" He let the question hang in the air, uncertain as to what the etiquette was when addressing the undead.

Tommy broke the potential awkwardness with another booming guffaw. "Oh, don't worry, best thing that ever happened to me. One minute I'm in a crap job, getting paid peanuts to get shot at and bricked, the next I'm living the dream with Mr. Dobson and his fine body of men...er and women...I mean people."

He nodded at a glaring Meredith. "Sorry, love. I'm still trying to get my head around this political correctness lark. I'll always be a child of the '70s."

"Hmmm, alright, Sid James. I'm prepared to put up with all the misogyny you can hurl in my direction if it means you get Harley and Emily back."

"Tommy is an expert in the area of portal transportation. It's a tricky business at the best of times. Get it wrong, and there can be rather disturbing consequences." Samuel wrinkled his nose as if recalling some unpleasant event from his past.

"Yes," Tommy breezily chirped. "There's nothing worse than nipping back to 18th Century Venice and discovering you've left your lungs and liver in 20th Century Rio. Damn messy."

"I can imagine," replied Kirkwood, shifting uneasily in his seat. "Please, tell me we're not going back to 18th century Venice. My conversational Italian isn't what it used to be."

"No," replied Tommy, before pausing and eyeing them innocently. "That's Italian for no, by the way." He winked mischievously at Meredith, who, despite her best efforts, rewarded him with the tiniest of smiles, a corner of her mouth, nothing more, but it was a start. Barriers were being breached, and icy exteriors broken.

"So, what now, Sir Samuel?" asked Meredith, rocking nervously back and forth. "We go now, right? The longer we sit here twiddling our thumbs, the more danger we are putting my Em...I mean... Emily and Harley in." She blushed and took a sudden interest in her fingernails.

"She's all our concern now, Meredith." Samuel's soft voice encouraged her to look up and meet his kind, brown eyes. It was like engaging with a six-foot-six puppy, utterly irresistible. She shrugged her shoulders and nodded.

"I know, it's just not many people had what we did. And, if anything, it hurts even more knowing she's out there somewhere, yet I can't talk to her. At least before, when she...did it, there was a sense of finality to it. This way, it's like I'm on a rollercoaster. One minute my hopes soar, the next I'm crushed and right back where I started again."

She bit her lip and gazed pensively out the window. When she felt Kirkwood taking her hand and squeezing it gently, she reciprocated the gesture. "I'm sorry, Kirky, for having a go at you earlier. I know Emily has her reasons for keeping her distance, and you were both trying to protect me. Friends?"

Kirkwood considered her sternly before breaking into a conciliatory smile. "Friends. Just stop calling me Kirky, or I'll be forced to put your head through that window."

"If you've both quite finished," interrupted Samuel. "We've matters to attend to." He nodded at Tommy, who took the prompt.

"Okay, kiddies. Not only am I a master of *planeing*, as us industry insiders refer to it, but I also know a thing or two about getting ourselves about dear old Mother Earth in a far more effective manner. I'm sure you two are sick of the sight of this rust bucket?"

"Too right," groaned Meredith. "I think my butt went numb about thirty miles back. And our driver leaves a lot to be desired." Samuel's brow furrowed slightly, but he chose to ignore the jibe.

"Well, I have good news for you then, young lady. I'm about to upgrade you all to first class. It might be a little unsettling at first, but you'll soon get used to it. It's the only way to see the world." He grinned, revealing an unusually bright set of teeth, given his otherwise battered appearance.

"Hold on tight. You're about to embark on the ride of your lives."

CHAPTER 13 - PERMANENT 4TH OF JULY

For such a slight woman, Maura lifted Harley from the floor of the Study as if she was a bag of feathers, effortlessly hauling her over one shoulder. Harley didn't remember losing consciousness but had no recollection of leaving the room. Her next memory was being carried up a narrow, twisting flight of stone steps. As she hung over Maura's shoulder, she considered struggling and tensed her muscles in anticipation of launching an assault.

"Don't even think about it," warned her captor. "If I let go, it's a long way down. Especially for a worthless cripple like you."

Harley relaxed and concentrated on her lower body. She thought of the interminable physio sessions she had endured and strained to flex her leg, even an inch, but nothing. She couldn't wiggle a toe, let alone kick out and effect an escape. She felt nothing, not even the comforting tingle which had previously reassured her there was light at the end of the tunnel. She was right back to square one, back to that night on the bridge when...

Maura stopped and swung around, with Harley finding herself facing a narrow slit in the wall. It was the kind of window that archers fired from in those stupid Robin Hood movies her little brother, Aidan, used to watch. She couldn't make out a thing and assumed it was night, the only light coming from a burning torch set into the wall on an iron bracket. *Were they in a castle?*

She heard the tired creak of a reluctant door opening before being unceremoniously dumped onto a damp stone floor. Maura glared down at her from the open doorway, making no effort to disguise her pleasure at Harley's plight.

"Enjoy your stay. I hope everything is to your satisfaction. If it was me, your throat would be slit, and I'd be feeding you to the pigs by now, but the Colonel knows best. I'll be back to check on you later." She sneered and spat on the ground next to where Harley lay, a considerable globule of saliva which disintegrated upon contact, spraying back onto the young girl's cheek.

"Bitch," retorted Harley, but her words were unheard as Maura pulled the heavy wooden door closed behind her. Once shut, Harley heard various bolts being secured into place. She sighed and closed her eyes. Now was not the time to panic, but she could feel a ball of anxiety building in the pit of her stomach, growing and gathering momentum like a runaway snowball mowing down helpless skiers on an alpine slope.

"Calm, Harley, calm," she intoned over and over in an effort to dispel thoughts of her plight. Suddenly the excitement and drama of the day's events subsided. The adrenaline tap within dripped to a halt, and she wanted nothing more than to be back in Ardgallon with her parents and annoying little brother. She missed her little room, the familiar sights, and sounds. Even that bloody wheelchair which had imprisoned her this past year.

She was in a different sort of prison now, one made of impenetrable stone and wood. Harley blinked away tears and hauled herself into a seated position, arranging her once more useless legs so she could take in her surroundings. On all four sides, she was greeted with foreboding granite walls. The door in front of her had no window or hatch, the only light coming from a small grilled window set high in the opposite wall. Harley doubted she could have reached it, even if she had the use of her legs and a trampoline. The window must have been a dozen feet above her.

A bright flash, vivid reds, and yellow streaks lit up the tiny window and cast an unnatural glow across the cell. Harley shielded her eyes with a hand, waiting for her sight to adjust to the unexpected illumination. The light dimmed a fraction but remained, revealing a familiar figure sitting in the far corner of the room.

"Emily!" Harley's voice rose in delight at the sight of the ghost girl who had previously only appeared in her dreams.

"Hey, roomie. So, what do you make of our new pad?" She rolled her eyes theatrically. "It's hardly the stuff of fairy tales, but I guess we'll just have to make ends meet until something better comes along."

"What the hell just happened? Oh, my God." Harley cupped both hands to her mouth before dissolving into tears.

"Oh, relax, Harley," sighed Emily. "And I thought I was the drama queen. We're in enough trouble without you flipping out on me." Realising her tough approach had little effect on the distraught teenager in front of her, she crawled over and awkwardly patted Harley on the shoulder.

"I'm sorry," bawled Harley between shuddering snorts and gasps. "It's just my legs...and Skelly and...and...I MISS MY MUUUUMMM." She thrust her face into Emily's collar bone while simultaneously throwing both arms around the older girl's neck. Emily looked aghast before woodenly returning the embrace.

"There, there. It'll be alright. Auntie Emily is here now. Oh, wow. Please stop crying, Harley. I haven't a clue what to say in these situations."

Harley released her vice-like grip a smidgeon and faced Emily, their noses separated by less than an inch.

"Where are we?"

Emily smiled. "I can answer that one anyway. Welcome to chez Skelly. This is where the lecherous old rat hangs out. I haven't had the guided tour yet, but I hear it's quite the pad. Unfortunately, all his en suites are booked up this week, so we've been forced to slum it."

"But...you don't get me, Emily. *Where* actually are we?" Harley's eyes widened like saucers in the unnatural light, which bounced off her already multicoloured hair, creating a kaleidoscope of shades and hues.

"Now, that's a slightly trickier one." Emily wrinkled her nose, weighing up the options, before continuing. How do you break such news to an already hysterical, hyperventilating teenager?

"Well..." She drew a deep breath. "We're not on Earth, that's for sure. Did Samuel explain all that plane business to you?"

Harley nodded and sniffed simultaneously.

"Well, my best guess, and it's only a guess, is that we're currently residing on another plane. I haven't been allowed out on day release, but from the cacophony outside, I think we're better off where we are for now."

As if on cue, a thunderous crack reverberated through the walls, and the light outside shifted to a spectacular cobalt blue. "It's permanently the 4th of July out there. Must cost them a fortune."

"Are we in hell?" Emily thought Harley's eyes couldn't widen any further.

"I don't know," she replied simply. "I've seen a lot since I passed over, but I'm not sure such a place exists. Or maybe it does, and this is it. Either way, I don't plan on hanging around here to find out." She placed a hand on each of Harley's shoulders and pulled her most serious expression. "You and I, girl, are going to put our heads together and form an escape committee."

"But how?" Harley poked her thigh in frustration. "I can't even move these stupid things. I'm no use to anyone unless I'm with Kirkwood and Meredith. Skelly has seen to that."

"If you're expecting tea and sympathy from me, young lady, then you're talking to the wrong girl. You've lost the power of your legs, temporarily I might add. I've lost my life permanently. All because of one stupid, drunken, spur of the moment decision. You'll see your family again one day. I won't." She smiled sadly at Harley, who placed a palm on Emily's cheek. For a ghost, she was surprisingly warm.

"Sorry, Em. It's just..."

"It's just nothing. I'm not interested in your legs. I can't feel mine either. I'm interested in this..." She rapped Harley's forehead with a knuckle.

"Oww. What did you do that for?"

"And this." Emily placed her palm flat against Harley's chest. "For I know you've got enough heart to move mountains and part oceans. Never mind getting us out of some poxy prison in a parallel universe. I need you, Harley. We need each other. It's the only way we will ever see the others again."

Harley blew her cheeks out just as another thunderous clamour rocked the room. This time she didn't flinch a muscle such was her renewed conviction and focus, inspired by Emily's words.

"Okay, then. What do you need me to do?"

"Pin your ears back, my little friend," beamed Emily. "You're going to love this."

CHAPTER 14 - PLANEING 101

Kirkwood retched again, and what was left of his stomach contents finally consented to exit his body. His shoulders shuddered as he tottered back onto his haunches in front of the toilet bowl, his skin covered in a clammy, cold sweat. As *'planeing'* went, it had not been the best of introductions.

"Are you bringing up a lung in there?" enquired Meredith from the other side of the bathroom door. "Hurry up. Mrs. Morgan said dinner will be ready in five."

"I can't believe you can think of food at a time like this." Kirkwood rose shakily to his feet before turning on the cold tap and splashing water liberally about his face. He leaned against the sink in the tiny bathroom and studied his pale pallor in the mirror above the sink. "I look like death warmed up," he remarked to nobody in particular.

"Don't be coming out with comments like that in front of Samuel and Tommy. We don't want to be accused of deathism." When it came to sympathetic travelling companions, Meredith was not scoring highly.

Despite himself, Kirkwood gave his ghastly reflection a grim smile. "You're such a little ray of sunshine, Ms. Starc." He dabbed his face with a towel before unlocking the door to find an impatient Meredith standing, arms folded, on the landing.

"Flip, Kirky, you look rough. You been on the hard stuff?"

"Feels like it," answered Kirkwood. "Come back, crappy little red car, all is forgiven. That was utterly dreadful. How you can stand there and even contemplate food is beyond me." The smells wafting up from downstairs were doing nothing to calm his churning innards.

"Oh, stop being such a big wimp. It wasn't that bad." Meredith turned and bounded down the narrow staircase towards the dining room, two steps at a time, her thick boots making her sound like a herd of baby elephants had invaded the Ardgallon guesthouse.

Kirkwood shook his head and followed at a more sedate pace, steadying himself against the banister. When Tommy had gathered them on the roadside and asked them to hold hands and close their eyes, he had been utterly unprepared for what was to follow. It was as if his brain had departed his body via an ear lobe and been used as a football by a passing gang of marauding Vikings, before being haphazardly shoved back in place. Several seconds of dizzy weightlessness was followed by a bone-jarring impact, then nothing.

He could have been out for ten seconds or ten hours, he didn't know, but he woke up face down in the little bed he had slept fitfully in at Mrs. Morgan's guesthouse in Ardgallon. Meredith was sitting across from him on the opposite bed, yawning and attempting to untangle a knot in her hair. That was when the first wave of nausea struck, and all else was forgotten in a desperate dash for the bathroom down the hallway.

They entered the dining room to find the forever fussing Mrs. Morgan setting knives and forks at a table occupied by Samuel and Tommy. She smiled broadly as they took their seats at the table. "Ah, our young friends have finally joined us. Well, I hope your journey helped you work up an appetite. I've enough here to feed an army."

Meredith gave their amiable host an enthusiastic thumbs up while Kirkwood smiled in as grateful a fashion as he could muster. Tommy and Samuel eyed him up from the opposite side before the former burst into laughter.

"You're looking a bit green around the gills there, young fellow. Did you not enjoy our wee jaunt?"

Kirkwood stared back as if Tommy had two heads. "I'd rather stick needles in both eyes while running over hot coals." He winced as Mrs. Morgan appeared beside him and, with a flourish, placed a plate of heaped steak and chips in front of him. Perched on top was a duo of greasy fried eggs. Kirkwood swallowed hard before meekly thanking their host.

"Aye, it can be a shock to the system. But once you've planed a dozen times or so, you should be grand. Thanks, Mrs. M." Tommy flashed the rotund landlady a rakish grin before launching into his meal with relish.

"A dozen?" whined Kirkwood. "This will be the death of me. Owww! What was that for?" he hissed at Meredith as she rammed an elbow into his ribcage.

"What did I say to you about inappropriate death-related comments?" she whispered under her breath. Samuel looked at them, a baffled expression adorning his features, while Tommy only giggled as he munched on a chip.

"Never worry. Samuel and I are too long in the tooth to get upset over the occasional faux pas from the land of the living, aren't we big man?"

"We have more to concern us," replied Samuel, attempting to restore a degree of gravitas to the conversation.

The four of them ate in silence for a while, Kirkwood managing to keep down several chips between sips of tea. The hot drink settled his stomach, and he was considering a mouthful of steak when Tommy spoke.

"Now that you've had your first taste of planeing, all be it a short hop within this realm, I'll explain what's going to happen." He adopted a grave expression, causing Kirkwood to abandon all plans of negotiating the steak. Even Meredith set down her knife and fork. However, she continued to chew noisily on a mouthful of bread and butter, which had accompanied their meal.

"We're going to be planeing from here to another version of here if that makes sense. You'll still be in Northern Ireland, but it will be a very different version of the place."

"As in, 87 years in the future version," added Samuel.

"Yes, the year of our Lord 2099."

"Wow," was all Meredith could muster.

"Indeed," continued Samuel. "As you might expect, it will look a little different from what you are accustomed to, but I'll allow Tommy to explain the mechanics, given he knows the terrain far better than I do."

"You mean, you've been there already?" asked Meredith, mouth now open in astonishment.

"I'm a planer," explained Tommy simply. "It's my job to put myself about and recon what's happening on other planes. In the old days, we were called scouts. Been doing this for roughly thirty-five of your years now, so I'd like to think I know what I'm doing."

"So how many planes have you visited?" asked Kirkwood, his interest growing by the second.

"Well, let me see now," mused Tommy, sitting back in his chair and scratching the stubble on his chin. "This is my home plane as I breathed my last on this fair island. From here, I can access sixteen others, as you know. They are what we call the Inner Circle. I've chalked up all of them, piece of cake, that lot. Then it starts to get a little more complicated."

"What do you mean?" Meredith leaned forward in her chair, by now totally engrossed.

"Well, of the Inner Circle, the Scourge now control three of them. It was from one of these that they attempted to gain access to this world on the bridge. Thanks to you good folk, though, that never transpired. I worked on all three of those planes before we had to withdraw. We lost a lot of good men on those worlds. And women." He stopped and stared wistfully out the dining room window for several seconds before gathering himself and continuing.

"Sorry, I digress. It gets trickier as each of those sixteen planes within the Inner Circle leads to sixteen more. I'll let you do the maths around that."

After what seemed an eternity, Meredith raised a finger in triumph "Two hundred and fifty-six! That's a lot of planes."

"I don't have your mental skills Miss Meredith, so I'll show you instead." He bent down and pulled up his right trouser leg to the knee, revealing a muscular, toned calf. From the ankle to the knee, it was covered in uniformed rows of black circular tattoos, each no more than an inch in circumference. "Call this my roll of honour. Each time I visit a plane, another one is added."

"Awesome," cooed Meredith, stretching closer to inspect Tommy's artwork in more detail. "Look. There's little numbers set in each one. 75, 109, 207. You've been to two hundred and seven alternative universes." She rose and looked at Tommy in newfound awe.

"If you say so," said Tommy, looking sheepish as he rolled his trouser leg down again.

"So, you've been to over two hundred versions of this planet?" Kirkwood looked as impressed as Meredith with the figures.

"Oh, no," replied Tommy. "Not all of these are versions of your home. There are countless other worlds, galaxies, and dimensions that your kind are blissfully unaware of. This lot..." he added, pointing to his leg, "...are only the tip of the iceberg. Try multiplying sixteen by sixteen for the next sixty years, and you'll get a taste of the numbers we are talking about. It's beyond both your and my own understanding."

"Utter head melt," nodded Meredith sagely.

"So, where are we going?" asked Kirkwood. "The Inner Circle?"

"No," replied Samuel, taking over the briefing. "You'll be what's known as double planeing. Skipping the Inner Circle and travelling to a plane within the next orbit."

"Northern Ireland in 2099? I wonder if the politicians are still arguing?" joked Meredith, earning an appreciative chuckle from Kirkwood.

"There are no politicians where we're going. Actually, there's not much of anything left." Tommy speared a chip with his fork and chewed on it, apparently unwilling to say another word on the subject.

"Well, don't just leave me hanging off the edge of a cliff," urged Meredith. "We'll need some background info about the place."

It was Samuel who bridged the silence. "This is a Northern Ireland untouched by Skelly or the Scourge to the best of our knowledge. It does not appear to be anywhere near the top of their list of priorities for reasons that will become obvious when you get there. So, because Skelly never was there..."

"Emily never died," finished Meredith.

"Correct," nodded Samuel. "Emily O'Hara lived a full life on this plane. Her legacy and essence are incredibly strong. So much so that it is our best way of connecting with her, and finding out where Skelly is holding them."

"Sorry to be the eternal pessimist." Kirkwood looked reluctant to elaborate, but Samuel gestured for him to do so. "But how do we know they're even capable of being rescued? Skelly has no heart. What if he's..."

"While Tommy is a planer, my skill relates to seeking. I can sense souls, even if they are light-years from me. It's an internal radar Dobson helped me to develop when I passed over. Their essences are weak, indicating they are far from us, but I can guarantee you that the souls of your friends are still with us."

"Yes!" Meredith clenched a fist, which she then used to punch Kirkwood on the forearm.

"Bugger off, Starc."

"Serves you right for being such a harbinger of doom."

Samuel chose to ignore their antics. "If you journey to the plane where Emily's essence is strongest, it's our best bet of pinpointing where she is. And when you find Emily, you find Harley."

"And three will become one again. The Presence will be activated, and we can go on the front foot against Skelly. Finish him once and for all." Tommy's face was etched with determination.

"Woah, back up a bit there." Kirkwood looked Samuel in the eye. "When we journey to the plane. Don't you mean yourself as well? As in the four of us. We've lost Dobson. I don't think I can do this without you, Samuel."

"Yeah, big man." Meredith looked horrified at the thought of continuing without the gentle giant. "You're my guardian angel. You saved me back in the graveyard from those psychotic brothers and risked everything for us on the bridge. I want you with me every step of the way."

"And I will be, young Meredith." Samuel reached across and placed a huge hand on her wrist in a surprisingly tender fashion. "But with Dobson gone, the responsibility to protect this plane lies with me now. I cannot neglect my duty. Tommy will take good care of you both. My place is here."

"But you're a seeker. How are we meant to find Emily and Harley without you?"

"Worry not. I am sending one of my kind to aid you. The Company may be many, but so are we. Trust me, this is how it must be."

Meredith placed her free hand on his and smiled. "I do trust you, all of you. Let's do this, then." The four of them shared a moment of silent solidarity, each taking a private moment for thoughts of those who were not with them around the table. Dobson, Harley, Emily. They owed it to them, whatever the sacrifice, whatever the cost.

CHAPTER 15 - THE CAR CRASH THAT USED TO BE YOUR COUNTRY

"Are you sure I can't make you up something for the journey?" Mrs. Morgan fussed over them as they bid their farewells on the front step of the guesthouse.

"Honestly, Mrs. M, I'm good, thanks," replied Meredith. "I'm fit to burst."

"Meredith Starc turning down food?" sniped Kirkwood. "This truly is a day of firsts."

"Button it Kirky," she snapped, raising a hand as if to slap him. Kirkwood ducked for cover behind Tommy, not wishing to feel the wrath of her backhand.

"Thank you as ever, madam, for your hospitality. It is always appreciated." Samuel performed an awkward bow, causing the jovial landlady to blush furiously.

"You otherworldly types are such charmers," she gushed. "Gentlemen, every one of you."

"Wait...you know about?" Meredith pointed from Samuel to her and then back to their mulleted guide again.

The pensioner threw back her head and laughed heartily. "Och, do you think I came down in the last shower. Of course, I know. Cornelius Dobson visited me many years ago and explained the importance of our little village. When I realised what was at stake, it was the least I could do to help out whenever he and his kind passed through." Her eyes misted over as she spoke of their departed friend. "Yes, Cornelius and I go way back, the old rogue. Such a loss."

Samuel bowed his head in silence, and even Meredith was at a loss for words. They eventually bid farewell and made their way down the driveway. Parked at the bottom was Samuel's old Micra, last seen before they planed outside Belfast.

"I'm not even going to ask how that got here," sighed Kirkwood.

"Ha," laughed Tommy. "Sometimes it's best to just go with the flow. This more traditional mode of transport will take us down to the bridge. I wasn't going to put you through the joy of planeing for the sake of a five-minute car journey."

"Much appreciated," replied Kirkwood, barely recovered from the exertions of his first supernatural trip.

The journey passed in silence as they drove through the mostly deserted village. It was now late evening, and the last light of the day was sinking over the horizon as the shadows lengthened and claimed the sleepy hamlet for themselves once more. At the bottom of the main street, the road swung to the left, revealing the nondescript little humpback bridge. The bridge where earlier that day they had thwarted the most evil power in the universe from laying waste to the planet.

Samuel pulled over onto a verge at the foot of the bridge and turned off the ignition. He turned round in his seat to face Kirkwood and Meredith in the back. "Ready?"

"Not really, but it's not as if we've much say in the matter. Come on, Meredith." Kirkwood unfastened his seatbelt and climbed out of the car, Meredith following suit. The four of them gathered at the base of the bridge. Samuel looked at all three individually before speaking.

"This is where I must leave you. Find Emily's essence. From there, she will guide you to where she is being held. I will remain here until your return. Before long, we will all be united again, of that I am certain."

"Sure you don't want to tag along?" enquired Meredith hopefully, but the big man was already walking back towards the Micra. He performed an excruciatingly slow three-point turn before the car lurched back towards the village and out of sight.

"Warrior. Leader. Useless driver." Kirkwood shook his head in resignation before turning to face Tommy. "I take it this is the bit where I get violently ill again?"

"It shouldn't be as rough as your first time," answered Tommy. "But we're double planeing this time, so listen up. We will plane into an intermediary Circle, realign, then plane again immediately to our destination. The realignment shouldn't take more than five seconds. Whatever you do, don't let go of my hand when we do, no matter what you see or hear. Are we clear?"

"Yeah," replied Kirkwood reluctantly.

"Crystal, comrade." Meredith saluted their unlikely guide and held her hands out to either side. She shot Kirkwood an exasperated expression.

"Come on, cowardly cat, the girls need us. Do you think wee Harley would be standing here shaking in her boots if it was one of us needed rescuing?"

"You're right," conceded Kirkwood, gathering his resolve and taking her hand. "As my old mate, Gerry would say, let's make like a banana and split. I'm ready, Tommy."

The three of them stood, eyes closed, in a tight circle. At first, there was nothing bar the chirping of starlings in the trees overhead. In the distance, Kirkwood heard the steady drone of traffic from the nearby main road. He was tempted to take a quick peek at Meredith as the seconds ticked interminably by, but resisted as there was too much at stake. Just as he was about to ask Tommy if there was a problem, he felt himself being flung skywards by an unseen, overwhelming force. His head lurched to one side, then the other like a Formula one driver negotiating a chicane at speed. Meredith's grip on his hand tightened to the point where he feared his crushed knuckles were going to pop out of their joints.

Then a second of nothing. The pressure released, and he hung suspended, adrift and serene before the descent began. The wind whistled past his ears as the noise intensified, a rattling, screaming runaway train of air and some tremendous energy. Kirkwood tensed for impact, his stomach performing cartwheels. At any second, he expected his feet to hit the ground, shattering every bone in his body, hurtling him into indescribable pain, his body a mangled mess of...

"Okay, I want you to open your eyes on my count of three. Do not, I repeat, *do not*, let go of my hand." Tommy's voice spoke into the darkness, a calming authority.

"One..."

Kirkwood realised, almost as an afterthought, that his feet were on solid ground again.

"Two..."

He blew out his cheeks as a solitary rivulet of sweat traced a lazy path down the side of his jaw.

"Three!"

His eyes shot open to be greeted by a vast green expanse. They were surrounded by sweeping, lush lawns, which stretched as far as the eye could see. Beyond him and over Meredith's right shoulder, a young woman sat on a wooden bench. She looked at him and smiled, friendly blue eyes set beneath a peroxide pixie hairstyle.

"Hi," said the girl.

"Hi," replied Kirkwood, not knowing what else to say.

Meredith glanced over her shoulder before fixing Kirkwood with a bewildered look. "Who are you talking to?"

"That girl," he replied, suddenly realising the young woman was dressed in a billowing pink taffeta ball gown and box-fresh gleaming white trainers.

"What girl?" hissed Meredith, craning her neck in all directions. "There's no one here." To her left, Tommy sported an amused smile.

"Just passing through?" asked the girl, maintaining eye contact with Kirkwood and blanking Meredith.

"Yeah, something like that," said Kirkwood.

"Okay then," smiled the girl, crossing her ankles and flattening out the folds in her dress. "Well, I guess I'll be seeing you around then, Kirkwood Scott."

Kirkwood blinked. "Wait, how do you know my—"

His world turned upside down again as he hurtled upwards into the brightest of blue skies. Kirkwood screamed, convinced he was going to collide with the sun, as it loomed ever larger in front of him. He squeezed his eyes shut as a myriad of multi-coloured bubbles danced across the back of his retinas. He was vaguely aware of Meredith laughing, a piercing, near-hysterical cackle. He chose to ignore it, solely intent on surviving this current phase of the plane without soiling his clothes or losing his mind. Whichever came first.

Then there was nothing. Blissful silence and a welcoming darkness that Kirkwood succumbed to like a toddler snuggling into a comfort blanket. He tensed, conducting a mental inventory to ensure all his limbs and vital organs were functioning as they should. He chanced opening an eye, revealing he was lying on his side in a small, bare room. Its sole window covered by a metal grill. Standing next to it was a short, stocky man dressed from head to toe in mud crusted camouflage clothing. He surveyed whatever lay outside with beady black eyes, his five o'clock shadow reminding Kirkwood of one of the bad guys from a spaghetti western movie.

"Took your time, Tommy," he grunted, raising the biggest gun Kirkwood, an aficionado of countless war movies, had ever seen. "I'll be with you in a minute. Just need to let the locals know who's boss. They can get a little excitable at this time of the day." He pointed the monstrous weapon through the grille, took aim at an unknown target, and squeezed the trigger. Unleashing a deafening racket, which had Kirkwood and Meredith squirming on the cold concrete floor, hands pressed to their ears to lessen the din.

Drawing the firearm back into the room, he peered through the grill, before grimacing and averting his attention to the room's most recent arrivals. Kirkwood and Meredith rose warily to their feet as the gunman set his weapon against a wall before enveloping Tommy in a suffocating hug.

"Good to see you, Tommy boy. What brings you to our beautiful city this time?"

Tommy extricated himself from the shorter man's embrace before replying.

"I've a little favour to call in, old friend." Turning to his travelling companions, he nodded towards the shorter man. "Kirkwood and Meredith, allow me to introduce Major Nathaniel Deacon, Officer Commanding, Sector 8 Security Solutions."

The soldier grinned at his new acquaintances. A grin that was welcoming yet vaguely unsettling at the same time. "Anyone who's a friend of Tommy Mainwright is a friend of mine. Welcome friends to the car crash that used to be your country."

CHAPTER 16 - STEP INTO MY PARLOUR

Harley awoke with a gasp as if she had been underwater before bursting above the surface, lungs aflame. She realised her nails were digging into the dirty stone floor, drawing blood. She scrambled into a seating position, back to the wall, and frantically scanned the cell. Outside, it was thankfully silent, the pyrotechnics of earlier having finally relented. She had succumbed to a deep sleep, watched over by Emily until the muddled dream dragged her back to consciousness.

"They're coming, Harley. I sensed it too."

Emily's pale face peered out of the gloom from the other side of the room. She broke into an infectious smile, which Harley could not fail but return.

"My dream. I saw you. On a wall. Except it wasn't you, it was a painting. What do you call it? Graffiti, that's the word."

"That would be right," smirked Emily.

"Except it was dark. I could hear gunfire. And explosions, like something out of a war movie."

Emily's smile tightened. "Yeah, I guessed that was what woke you. They're coming, Harley, but it's a very dangerous path." She crawled across the floor to where Harley was seated, taking her hands. "Which is why we need to help them as much as we can."

Harley laughed in exasperation. "Help? How can we do that, holed up in this dungeon? I can't even move my legs."

Emily squeezed the younger girl's hands tighter. "Harley, listen to me. You might not be able to move your legs at this present minute, but you are far from useless. You're one of the Three. The Presence courses through your veins connecting you to Kirkwood and Meredith. Let me help you channel that, cast it out from here, like a beacon."

"You mean, like in the Batman movies?"

"Exactly. The more we can do to guide them to us, the quicker we can get out of this dump. And when the three of you are back together, then God help that rat, Skelly."

Harley creased her brow and nodded, new hope ignited within her. "Okay then, let's get started."

∞ ∞ ∞

Several hundred floors below them, Colonel Augustus Skelly, flinched from his own slumber. He wasn't getting any younger, so could be excused a power nap in the midst of another hectic day at the coal face. He wasn't averse to delegating responsibility, but who could he trust at such a critical stage of proceedings? Gunther was no more, while Rodriguez and the Drummer Boy had both let him down badly in recent times. Maura had potential but, no, she wasn't quite ready, and he was loath to call up other reinforcements yet. The Company were fighting on many fronts, so it was up to him, and him alone, to juggle resources and oversee proceedings.

It was the power surge that had stirred him. A surge that immediately engaged his mental cogs. The enemy was on the move. Skelly closed his rheumy eyes and inhaled deeply through his nostrils, before breathing out again, a watery, diseased rattle. He dug yellow, curled fingernails into the arms of his chair, before opening his eyes again. They were now a milky hue as if cataracts had instantaneously formed and blinded him. Yet, Skelly was anything but blind. Instead, he was now looking far beyond the confines of the Study.

"Now, where are you, Samuel, you irksome little fly? Buzzing around inside my head, depriving me of what is rightfully mine." His voice rose to a roar, and his left hand shot out in front of him with surprising dexterity, forming a fist. Skelly smiled and opened it to reveal the remains of a fat housefly squashed on the palm of his hand.

"Got you, you bugger."

He leaned forward to inspect it, his bulbous, misshapen nose almost touching the dead insect. "Tell me where you are, Forsaken One?" he hissed as the icy fireplace to his right erupted, covering the entire Study in an eerie, hellish glow. A tongue more befitting of a venomous viper shot out his mouth, long and sinewy, before claiming the fly. Skelly sat back and chewed on the disgusting morsel before swallowing and licking his lips.

"Exquisite," he sighed, opening his eyes again to reveal they had returned to their original watery form.

Rodriguez stood before him, although no door had opened in the room to admit him. The bearded Portuguese giant stood nervously in front of his malignant master, awaiting orders. The silence between them stretched for several minutes before Skelly acknowledged his presence.

"That was good work in the alley, Sergeant. Verging on impressive. So, I'm prepared to give you another chance. More than you probably deserve, but at present, my resources are stretched, and you're the best of a bad bunch."

"Thank you, sir." Rodriguez relaxed an inch, but nothing more. "Tell me what needs done, I won't let you down again."

"You had better not," snarled Skelly. "Or next time I won't be quite so forgiving. You don't want to end up like the Drummer Boy, do you?"

"No, Colonel. That won't be necessary."

"Well, then, listen up. Your little friends are in need of a personal visit."

"Belfast, sir?"

"Indeed. But you'll need your hard hat for this one. Belfast has changed an awful lot since your last trip there."

CHAPTER 17 - A BRIEF HISTORY OF HELLFAST

Kirkwood and Meredith jumped in unison as another explosion reverberated through the basement of the building. A fine shower of dust from the ceiling above coated them, causing Meredith to sneeze violently into the cracked mug she was cradling in her hands. She muttered an apology before hurriedly taking a sip of coffee, determined not to offend their gruff host. It was almost undrinkable, but she swallowed hard, somehow keeping it down.

"Get that down you, girl. It's kept me going for the best part of two years. Might not taste great, but it keeps the old engine ticking over."

"Er, yeah," replied Meredith dubiously. "Who needs Starbucks?"

Tommy smiled wryly. "If it's good enough for 'The Deacon' then it's good enough for us. He knows this part of Belfast like the back of his hand and has kindly agreed to escort us to where we need to go."

"And where would that be exactly?" asked Kirkwood. "Because it sounds like World War Three out there, and I'm not much use to anyone with my head detached from my shoulders."

"World War Three," guffawed Deacon. "You've a bit to get caught up on, lad."

Tommy shot Deacon a warning look. "I think it's perhaps time I provided a potted history of where we are and what's out there before we move on, don't you all agree? I'm sure Kirkwood and Meredith have a lot of questions, but time isn't on our side here."

Kirkwood and Meredith nodded, the latter playing anxiously with the ends of her black, grimy hair and bitterly regretting not having availed of the shower facilities at the guesthouse.

"Be my guest." Deacon sat back and extended a hand. "The floor is all yours, Corporal Mainwright."

"Lance Corporal," corrected Tommy, looking a shade embarrassed.

"This…" he announced, indicating the bare basement around them, "…is what's left of Queen Street Police Station, Belfast city centre. Currently, the headquarters of Security Solutions in what the locals charmingly refer to as Hellfast. The year is 2099, and the city you two used to call home is utterly unrecognisable."

"Security Solutions, that's catchy," scoffed Meredith. "What are you, a souped-up version of the PSNI?" Deacon looked up angrily from his coffee but said nothing, causing Tommy to hastily continue.

"You have to realise, Meredith, this is an alternative version of your country and its history. In this world, the Troubles never finished. There was no peace, the warring factions never got around the negotiating table. It all just kept going until it…"

"Fell apart," muttered Deacon darkly.

"But what about the police?" said Kirkwood, barely able to believe what he was hearing. "The army, the forces of law and order. Where are they?"

"We're the only law and order that matters now," replied Deacon, setting his rifle on the cheap laminated table around which they sat.

"Really?" replied Meredith, raising an eyebrow and folding her arms simultaneously. "Security Solutions? You sound more like a burglar alarm company than the only hope for civilisation."

Deacon opened his mouth to respond until Tommy placed a restraining hand on his shoulder.

"It's all gone, Kirkwood. The British pulled out; the Irish pulled out. Utter chaos reigned. The United Nations had a go at it and failed. Even the Americans considered getting involved but thought better of it in the end."

"Damn Yanks are always sticking their noses into other people's business. For once, they got it right. Would have been another Vietnam for them."

"So, who's running the place? The paramilitaries?" Kirkwood was struggling to process the flurry of information being fired in his direction.

Deacon snorted but said nothing. A small, circular orb attached to his battered flak jacket glowed, and a crackle of static erupted from his earpiece. He listened intently before speaking into the orb.

"Roger that. Proceed as planned. Updates every 300. Out."

"The IRA? The loyalists? None of them exist as you knew them. Politics and ideologies went out the window once the priorities became clean drinking water and filling your belly. It's everyone for themselves out there now. There are loose alliances, ghetto gangs who control a handful of streets here and there. Catholic, Protestant, Buddhist, nobody cares anymore. All that matters is staying alive."

"My father died for this," whispered Kirkwood. Meredith heard him but said nothing. Sometimes, even words were worthless. Instead, she spoke to Tommy.

"There must be something. What about these burglar alarm guys? Who's paying them? It's not as if they're doing it for the craic?"

"Once the governments realised the situation could not be salvaged in '27, they organised a mass evacuation. Those who could be saved were brought out by the UN and housed in huge camps on the border. The biggest one was in Donegal, up Innishowen direction. It's still there today. They call it Gracetown."

"Must be near half a million living there. Good people by and large," said Deacon, a hint of fondness softening his harsh tones. "It's where I go for my R&R. Clean air, fresh fish. I want to settle there if I ever make it out of here."

"So, what are we left with?" Kirkwood asked the question, although he wasn't sure he wanted to hear the answer.

"This mess," laughed Deacon.

"Northern Ireland is technically an independent state. The UK and Irish governments struck a deal whereby they washed their hands of it and ended any political or economic claims they had over it. As I said, even the Americans didn't want anything to do with it. The UN policed the border and turned a mile either side of it into a no-go zone. You got caught in there, and you normally ended up with a bullet in the back of the head. There's no way in or out unless you know the right people and pay enough to make it worth their while. Not that anyone particularly wanted to come here. It was hardly a top tourist destination after that. Nobody cared."

"Until they struck gold," sniffed Deacon, a disgusted look on his face.

"Gold?" Meredith looked at Tommy as if he had taken leave of his senses. "In this dump? You're kidding me, right?"

"No, hang on, he's right," blurted out Kirkwood. "In the Sperrin Mountains between Omagh and Monksbridge. There were always rumours about it, then some big American company started to survey the area and confirmed there was a seam there. Last I heard they were exploring the commercial viability of mining the area. There was always stuff in the local paper about environmental damage and protests."

"Spot on, Kirkwood," agreed Tommy. "Just after the UN pulled out the company involved hit paydirt. The biggest seam in living memory. I'm talking worldwide. Billions upon billions potentially. That's when the big investors came sniffing. If the world's governments weren't prepared to lump the cost of policing this dump as you called it, then the multinationals were more than willing to sign off the cheque."

"Which is where we came in," said Deacon, with a grim smile. "Security Solutions is the biggest private security firm in the world. You name it, we've been there, done it and got the t-shirt. The Middle East, Russia, Canada, we've had boots on the ground in them all."

"Canada?" exclaimed Meredith incredulously.

"That one's for another time," replied Tommy. "Now moving swiftly on. Once the pigs got their snouts in the Sperrin feeding trough, they hired Deacon and his employers to provide security for their burgeoning operation. Keep the locals in their place and ensure the mines kept producing. The area was rather unimaginatively named Sector 1."

"Damn good job, we did too," added Deacon sourly. "Too good, unfortunately. Next thing, they want the adjoining areas secured to bolster supply routes. Some suit has the bright idea of expanding, and Sector 2 was born. Next, there's talk of gold in the Mourne Mountains as well, so we get Sector 3. Turns out, the whole sodding country is sitting on the biggest gold reserve in the known universe."

"Are you telling us Belfast is the richest place on the planet?"

"Hard to believe, I know," replied Deacon. "The whole country is viable when it comes to mining opportunities. Sector 1 remained the hub of the machine, but satellite mines were established in each of the six counties which make up Northern Ireland. Then another in Hellfast itself, meaning we ended up with eight sectors. And for my sins, me and my people got stuck here, in the crappiest of them all. Sector 8."

Meredith let out a low whistle. "Thanks, Samuel. Seems like you've pitched us out of the frying pan and into the fire. No wonder you weren't that keen on accompanying us."

"Oh, shut up, Meredith," snapped Kirkwood, rounding on her. "You know fine well Samuel would be here with us if he didn't have responsibilities elsewhere. I don't care where we have to go if it means getting Harley and Emily back."

"Sorry," replied Meredith sullenly. "Sometimes, I don't engage my brain before opening my mouth."

Deacon rose to his feet and yawned, stretching his arms extravagantly in the air. "Well, I don't know about you time travellers, but I've just finished a fourteen-hour shift and need some serious shuteye. Your quarters are on the floor above. Tommy, you know your way around. I'll leave it to you to give our esteemed guests the tour. Food is at six bells in the morning. We move out at seven." He picked his trusty rifle from the table. "As you were."

The three of them watched as the sturdy soldier sauntered out of the bare room into an equally bare corridor lit by stark fluorescent lighting.

"Who died and made him boss?" asked Meredith, a look of deep displeasure on her face.

"He's alright," replied Tommy, rising to his feet. "If I have to go outside his compound, and unfortunately we do, there's nobody else I'd rather have with me when *the you know what* hits the fan."

"And where exactly is that?" asked Kirkwood, already dreading the answer.

"Let's get bedded down for the night," replied Tommy. "If you think today was crazy, then you're in for a real treat tomorrow."

CHAPTER 18 - A STARC INQUISITION

They ascended the flight of stairs, their weary footfall echoing upwards through the murky stairwell. Kirkwood squinted into the gloom and estimated at least three floors still rose above them as Tommy pushed open an emergency exit revealing another artificially lit corridor. A row of identical red doors ran alongside one side of the corridor. There were no windows, and Meredith groaned as Tommy opened one of the doors to reveal their sleeping quarters for the night.

"You're seriously not expecting us to sleep on those? Come back, Mrs. Morgan, all is forgiven."

Kirkwood peered over her shoulder to be greeted by three grubby mattresses, bedecked with equally grimy sleeping bags and pillows. A filthy sink with rusted taps was the only concession to en suite status.

"Er...where am I expected to wee, out the window? Oh, that's right, show my face at the window, and I'm likely to get it blown away by some shotgun-wielding maniac outside."

"There are toilets and a shower block on the floor above. Now stop complaining and sit down. I'm away to scrounge some food."

Tommy dumped his rucksack on the tiled floor and sloped out of the room.

Kirkwood rolled his eyes and collapsed onto one of the mattresses. "You know what, M, I'm so tired I don't think I care anymore. I could sleep on a clothesline." He sprawled onto his back and let out a long yawn. "For a flea-infested doss house in the middle of a war zone, this is actually quite comfortable."

Meredith joined him on the adjoining mattress and swivelled to face him cross-legged, a troubled expression causing her brow to crease beneath her beanie hat.

"Are you going to tell me, or do I have to drag it out of you?" Her eyes narrowed as she prepared to scrutinise his reaction to her question.

"Drag what out of me?" Kirkwood struggled to keep the irritation from his voice. "Meredith, I'm hungry, I'm tired. We are facing God only knows what tomorrow, and you decide to start the Spanish Inquisition again. Can't this wait till the morning?"

"No, it cannot," was the waspish reply. "When we planed, I heard you talking to someone. Who was it? And don't tell me I imagined it for I know what I heard."

"It was nothing," mumbled Kirkwood, desperate to avoid eye contact with his pale-faced interrogator. Meredith missed nothing, and when she got a sniff of something, it was like a dog with a bone. Incessant, relentless, impossible to deflect. He prepared his defences for the coming verbal assault but already anticipated he was on exceedingly shaky ground.

"Don't treat me like I've just floated up the Lagan on a bubble, you numpty. Spill." Her piercing eyes bored into his skull, turning any pretence at resisting her advances to mush. Kirkwood was already wavering, conscious Tommy would be returning soon when the coup de grace was administered.

"Was it, Emily?" The accusatory tone in her voice snapped the final band of resistance within him. The floodgates opened.

"No, it wasn't Emily." He dropped his shoulders and finally met her stare. "Didn't you see her? When we planed into the park?"

"Park? What are you talking about? We were in a quarry. I didn't see a single blade of grass."

"Really?" Kirkwood scratched his messy mop of brown hair. "You didn't see the girl? In the ridiculous dress, like some deranged contestant from Strictly Come Dancing."

"I saw what I saw, Kirkwood. Who was she? What did she say to you?"

"She said *hi*. And...er...I said *hi* back to her."

"Oh, my days." Meredith slapped her forehead and rolled back onto the mattress in disbelief. You really are the king of small talk. Didn't you think this might be important? She might have known something which could help us."

"Don't have a go at me," sniffed Kirkwood indignantly. "I'm in the middle of the most surreal, terrifying experience of my life, and you expect me to turn into Hercules Poirot. We planed, I'm staring at some bonkers elf girl dressed in a pink, fluffy ballgown, and next thing we're holed up with Rambo and his mates." He scratched his nose before flinging his arms in the air and staring at the ceiling in frustration.

"Okay, Okay. Calm down, you big wuss." Meredith breathed deeply before continuing. "Just think. She must have said something else. There has to be a reason she was there." She looked at him, more in hope than expectation.

"She said she'd see me around. And she knew my name. That's it." He clicked his fingers in triumph as the last memory of the plane slotted into place. "She said, *I'll see you around, Kirkwood Scott.*"

Meredith sat bolt upright, hands raised to her temple in disbelief. "She knew your name? Don't you see the significance of this? She might know something. To help get us to Emily and Harley. Instead of whatever kamikaze mission old Tommy Boy has lined us up for in the morning."

"Or, she could be one of the Company trying to lull me into a false sense of security," Kirkwood countered gloomily.

"Ever the optimist, aren't you, Kirky?"

"Pots and kettles, Sansa. Pots and kettles."

"Sod off. I'm much more beautiful than her. Common Stark girl with a K." She flicked a lock of her shoulder-length hair back in false vanity.

"Yeah, Yeah. You wish." He smiled for what seemed the first time in forever. She could be the most infuriating creature alive, but the grungy girl in front of him had a heart the size of Texas. He was glad she was by his side to face whatever lay ahead in the morning.

"I promise I won't keep anything from you again. Total transparency from now on."

"You better. Or this boot of mine is going so far up your backside, you'll be chewing the laces for the next month." She lifted one of her red Doctor Martens and waved it in his direction.

Kirkwood laughed, long and hard. It was the best possible medicine at a time like this.

"Sorry to interrupt the little party." Tommy entered the room, carrying two paper bags. He sat down on the spare mattress and began to unpack them. Kirkwood and Meredith looked on hopefully as a familiar, mouth-watering aroma wafted within range of their nostrils.

"This might not be the Hilton, but the mess cook does the best bacon sarnie this side of Huddersfield." He lobbed a couple of grease-stained parcels into their eager hands, before producing three steaming polystyrene cups from the other bag.

"Get stuck in," he proclaimed with a satisfied smile. "Now, how do you take your tea?"

CHAPTER 19 - A STROLL THROUGH THE CITY

He was a big man but went to ground easily, his head striking the tarmac with a sickening crack. Rodriguez leaned back and inspected the carnage around him with a contented smile. This was where he was in his element, on the front line, going toe to toe with the opposition and getting the job done. He stepped over the lumbering brute he had just downed with a clubbing right hook. Beyond him, a second man kneeled, dazed and bloodied. He glanced up, and seeing his grinning assailant approaching him, held up a hand. Enough was enough. He had no more fight left in him.

"Aww, you don't want to play anymore," beamed Rodriguez. "But I was just getting started. You guys are no fun." As he reached the second man, he delivered a devastating kick to his ribcage. The man gave a pitiful grunt and curled into a ball. Rodriguez knelt and leaned into his ear.

"I'm going to spare your life, but only if you promise to help me out with some directions. Would you care to assist?" He took the little finger of the man's left hand and bent it back. "What's that? I can't quite hear you." He applied additional pressure, and a hideous crack rang out, the injured man emitting a high-pitched scream.

"Yes. Yes. Whatever you want," the man sobbed. Rodriguez nodded and released his hand, allowing him to nurse the mangled digit.

"That's more like it. I have always found the Irish to be such genial hosts whenever I visit your land. Now, let me explain. I'm looking for a girl...or rather a painting of a girl."

∞ ∞ ∞

Within minutes he had located it. In a part of the city that was new to him, across the city and over the river. Rubble pitted the streets, making them virtually impassable for traffic. Not that there seemed to be many vehicles that hadn't been gutted by fire. They sat dotted about, silent sentinels harking back to a time when they served a purpose. People didn't need cars now. Nobody was going anywhere, anytime soon.

Rodriguez strode purposefully towards his target, finally setting eyes on a familiar landmark. He was aware of eyes following his progress from the shadows, there being no street lighting to guide his path. The only light came from a fire blazing somewhere off to his left. It cast the wall before him in a sinister orange glow. The distant crackle of flames the only sound to be heard.

"Ah, there you are, my lovely. You've relocated." Rodriguez stopped and admired the artwork before him on the wall, stretching as far as he could see on either side. In its midst, the face of a young woman staring defiantly out at the chaos before her. What sights she must have beheld down the years, yet here she was, unscathed by human hand. Dobson had taken extra special care of her, but Dobson was no more. A distant explosion drew Rodriguez away from his thoughts. These humans had an uncanny knack of destroying everything they touched. All you had to do was give them a little free rope, then sit back and enjoy the horror show, which inevitably unfolded.

Belfast 2012. Belfast 2099. It mattered not to him. All he had to do was follow orders, stay alert, and he would soon be back in Skelly's good books. With Gunther gone, he preferred to work alone now. Bitter experience had taught him that, and he was sick of taking the can for the failings of incompetent colleagues. No, from now on, Martim Rodriguez was a lone wolf on a very specific mission. He approached the wall and planted an extravagant kiss on Emily's cheek as she silently eyed him in profile.

"Ah, Miss O'Hara. I'm afraid you are allowing your dumb friends to walk straight into my trap. But do not worry. When I've dispensed of them, I fully intend to pay you a personal visit in the Tower. It's high time you and I became better acquainted with one another." The huge man raised a hand, clicked his fingers, and was gone. Another explosion rocked the area formerly known as Belfast's Titanic Quarter, now just another ruined area of a once vibrant city. This time it was nearer and was accompanied by a strangled scream which abruptly cut off as it rose in volume. This was no place for a young woman to be out on her own, yet Emily O'Hara remained unbowed. Had anyone passed her at that moment, they might have taken a second look, as the cracked, chipped paintwork seemed to come alive and glow with a new urgency. The colours making up her features dimmed then glowed again as if a beacon had been activated, triggered by the departure of the Portuguese man of war.

∞ ∞ ∞

Indeed, a beacon had been activated. As many worlds away, two young women sat in a dank cell facing each other, their eyes ablaze with intensity and purpose. They spoke as one, the whispered mantra barely audible above their ragged breathing.

"We are three, but we are one."

"We are three, but we are one."

CHAPTER 20 - THREE BECOME TWO

Kirkwood slept fitfully, slipping beneath a veil of jumbled dreams, where Harley and Emily featured prominently. When he awoke, he could remember little, bar a vague sensation of foreboding. Time was not on their side. Outside there was welcome silence, allowing him an opportunity to process where they now were and what was expected of them. He didn't know what lay outside the confines of the old police station, but whatever it was, he felt utterly unprepared without the calming influence of Samuel by their side.

"You can't sleep either, then?"

He turned his head to one side to reveal Meredith's outline in the gloom. She was raised on an elbow facing him, her pale features in juxtaposition to the surrounding pitch black.

"Nope."

Meredith sighed. "I think it was that bacon sandwich. My mother always said you should never eat anything after nine at night."

Kirkwood chuckled. He was learning quickly that you could always rely on Meredith to raise a smile in even the direst of situations.

"What? You never scoffed a pizza and then spent half the night dreaming you were being chased by a sixty-foot meat feast?"

"Oh, yes, but I don't think you could dream up our present predicament even if you tried."

"Well, that's true. What delights lie ahead for us today, do you reckon?"

"No idea." He turned onto his side to face her. "But I'm sure Skelly will soon work out we are here and send a welcoming committee the second we step outside. He's good like that."

"I'm starting to realise that. I guess we'll just have to take on the chin whatever he dishes up. At least we've got Sleeping Beauty over there on our side."

She pointed towards the far corner of the room where Tommy's snores could be faintly heard. Prior to bedding down for the night, he had filled in some more of the blank spaces as to why they were in this futuristic version of Belfast, risking life and limb to rescue their missing friends.

"Emily is out there. All we have to do is hone in on her, and the rest will take care of itself." He made it sound so simple when they both knew it was anything but.

"Do you think the Company is here?" Meredith's voice rose out of the darkness again, causing Kirkwood to finally give up on whatever faint hopes he had of returning to sleep.

"Oh, undoubtedly," he replied. "There's no show without punch. But they will be less cocky now. We showed them on the bridge what we're capable of."

"Yeah, but we had Harley then. We were three." The darkness could not conceal the pessimism in Meredith's voice.

"Stop it, gloomy drawers." Kirkwood's tone was more gentle than chiding. "We did alright when it was just the two of us. Harley was...*is* the icing on the cake."

"I guess." Meredith sounded far from convinced, causing Kirkwood to try a different tact.

"Okay, then, look at it this way. Do you want a drink?"

"Do I what?"

"This minute, this very second. Do you want a drink?"

"No."

"Well, that's the Presence. If you were on your own now, you'd probably be climbing up the walls, willing to give a kidney for half a bottle of Buckfast. Agreed?"

"I suppose."

"I suppose nothing, Meredith." Kirkwood's tone was less conciliatory as he sought to drive home his point. "It's the same with me. If I was on my own right now, Skelly would be crawling all over me, filling my head with all sorts of intrusive, disgusting thoughts. I was a slave to him and his damned dice for years. You set me free from that."

"The Presence set us free. Both of us."

"Whatever. But my point is just because Harley isn't with us at the minute doesn't mean we are useless; doesn't mean we're beaten. There's still stuff we can do. And as long as we stay positive and keep fighting, Skelly doesn't get a look in."

The rattle of automatic gunfire sounded in the distance, followed by shouting. Kirkwood strained to hear but could not make out what was being said. He clutched at a hazy memory before sitting upright and unzipping his sleeping blanket. Within seconds, he was fumbling for his boots in the murky half-light. Dawn was struggling to break outside, but the sun appeared less than enthusiastic to share its life-affirming rays with a city where death and darkness were not for budging.

"What are you doing?"

"It's just hit me. We're in Queen Street Police Station. Doesn't that ring any bells with you?"

Meredith thought long before answering. "Not really. That time I got arrested for stealing a toothbrush they took me to Musgrave Street."

"Noooo, you numpty. Even back in our day, Queen Street was derelict. It was round the back of Boots Chemists..."

"Yeah, that's where I nicked the toothbrush..."

"No, think you airhead. Where does Queen Street lead you onto?"

"Castle Street?"

"Yes. And if you cut across it?"

"Mulberry Square." There was a short pause before the penny dropped. "That's it! We're just around the corner from where Emily's graffiti was."

"Exactly. And I'll bet my last pound coin if we head over now, we'll find it's still there. Why else would Samuel insist on sending us here? That's how we communicated with her. That's how we find out where Harley and Emily are."

"Well, then, what are we waiting for?" replied Meredith, leaping to her feet. "We could be there in five minutes. We could..."

A torch swept across the room, freezing them in their moment of revelation. A familiar voice spoke from behind it.

"Five minutes? Try five hours if we're lucky. And around 5000 rounds of high-velocity ammunition. Belfast has changed a bit since you two last staggered around it." Tommy's voice was tense, as he laid out what lay ahead of them.

"I don't care," hissed Meredith, raising an arm to shield her eyes from the torchlight. "I'm getting to her today if it's the last thing I do."

"There's every chance it will be, with that attitude," replied Tommy.

"Well, then, show us what we need to do." Kirkwood was on his feet now, boots laced.

"That's why I'm here," said Tommy. "Now get your gear together and follow me. It's time you met the rest of the team."

CHAPTER 21 - GIRO

Tommy led them along a series of identical, dimly lit corridors, and up a further flight of stairs. The dilapidated station was a concrete maze, and before long, Kirkwood and Meredith had utterly lost their bearings and were incapable of finding their way back to their sleeping quarters.

"This place is like the Tardis," moaned Meredith, trying to keep pace with Tommy. "We must have walked for miles."

"Not much farther now." Tommy turned a corner, and they found themselves facing a metal door with an emergency exit sign above it. Kicking it open with his foot, he led them out onto a steel stairwell, which took them onto the roof of the building. A fresh wind whipped around them, and Meredith shivered as the icy air assailed her. The roof itself was flat and featureless, except for a triangular canvas tent pitched at the far end. Standing beside it with his back turned to them was a chunky figure surveying the city landscape as dawn broke over it.

"Morning, Deacon." Tommy's greeting was met by a grunt in return. "How's Sector 8 looking today?"

Deacon lowered a pair of binoculars and turned to face them. His five o'clock shadow now looked as if it was well past six-thirty. If he slept, it had done nothing for his shattered demeanour. Bloodshot eyes were complemented by puffy bags beneath them. The man needed a holiday about six years ago.

"It's hard to say," he muttered, before producing a roll-up cigarette from one of the many padded pockets which festooned his filthy flak jacket. Juggling his rifle under an armpit, he pulled a match from another pocket and struck it against his chin. It flared into life, and he was soon sucking greedily on the cigarette, encasing them in a cloud of nicotine smoke. He stared at the cigarette like it was the great love of his life before addressing them again.

"There was a bit of action over at the Castle. You might have heard that about an hour ago. None of our patrols were involved. From the chatter, seems like it was a squabble between two Dirties over who owned a particular corner of the upper floor."

"Dirties?" Kirkwood looked towards Tommy for guidance.

"It's what they call the inhabitants of Sector 8," explained Tommy. "When Belfast descended into anarchy, any decent, law-abiding folk fled for the border. What we were left with were the absolute dregs. Car thieves, burglars, you name it. It was like Christmas come early for them when law and order moved out. Deacon and his people do the best they can, but it's carnage out there. No schools, no hospitals, nothing recognisable is left. Just the dirt on the sole of your shoe."

"Not strictly true." Deacon took a final long drag from his cigarette, sucking out every gram of toxicity before tossing it aside. "There's the Priestess across the river."

"Sorry, this girl is lost again," interjected Meredith.

"See over there?" Deacon pointed out into the gloom. "Down by what used to be the harbour. Some mad-ass religious freak who says that these are the end times, and she has been chosen to guide the people into the Promised Land. Or some mumbo jumbo like that." He turned, opened the flap of the tent, and disappeared inside.

"Excuse him," apologised Tommy. "Social etiquette and manners aren't exactly essential criteria for his job description. The Priestess tends not to bother us as long as we don't bother her. But her influence is growing, and that's a concern. Dirties keep flocking to her, more out of desperation than any great desire to be indoctrinated into her ways. She guarantees three warm meals a day, shelter, and clean drinking water. Those are persuasive arguments when you're cold and starving to death."

"You can hardly blame them," murmured Kirkwood.

"Yeah," agreed Tommy. "But the big chiefs at Security Solutions are keeping a close tab on them. If she stays where she is, well and good, but our drones have detected increased infractions by her people over the river onto this side of the city. She's a nuisance at the moment, but it will come to a head one of these days, and Deacon is counting down the minutes. He loves a good scrap."

The flap of the tent opened, and Deacon's head popped out, indicating for them to join him inside. They filed in to be greeted by a wooden workbench running the length of its interior. It was bedecked with all manner of wires, tools, and random bits of metal. At the far end, a figure wielding a red-hot soldering iron sat hunched over a sizeable circuit board. Deacon coughed unsubtly, and the figure looked up, before switching off the solder and setting it carefully on the bench. He stood and walked towards them, hand outstretched.

"Hrrrrrr. Aghjjj Gyttyyioooh."

Deacon shuffled uneasily. "It might help if you removed the mask before you introduced yourself."

The figure paused as if considering the advice, before flicking up the welding mask to reveal a plump, jovial face. "Hi, I'm Giro. Well, that's not my real name, but nobody can ever remember or pronounce it, so Giro has kind of stuck." He bowed to each of them in turn before enthusiastically shaking their hands until Meredith worried her arm was going to drop off.

"Giro, these are our visitors I told you about. Kirkwood and Meredith. And you know Tommy, of course."

"Ah, yes, me and my little round friend go way back, don't we buddy?" The two of them laughed before a protracted bout of play fighting and hair ruffling ensued. Kirkwood and Meredith smiled awkwardly, not sure what to make of the exchange.

"Maybe these two need to get a room?" whispered Meredith.

"Yeah, bromance is alive and kicking in 2099," replied Kirkwood, maintaining his forced grin.

Giro extricated himself from the scuffle and turned his attention back to them. He had greasy black hair fashioned into a terrifying bowl cut, which sat inches above a pair of jam jar glasses. His chubby cheeks and sparkling brown eyes gave him the appearance of an incredibly cute, if slightly unhinged, hamster.

"Hi, guys. Welcome to 2099. Where do you hail from?"

"Well, I'm originally from Omagh."

"Sector 1," corrected Deacon.

"And I'm from Bangor. Sector none of your business, Deacon." Meredith shot the cranky commander a warning look, and the grizzled soldier glared back but remained silent. "Where are you from originally, Giro?"

"Oh no, I'm from Bangor too," grinned Giro, dropping into a broad Northern Irish brogue. "Or what's left of it." He noticed Meredith's embarrassment and laughed to spare her blushes.

"I'm really sorry. I shouldn't have…"

"Wise up, wee girl." He removed his glasses and began to clean them with the bottom of a suspiciously unclean t-shirt. "You're right, in a way. I'm sixth-generation Hong Kong. My great-great-grandparents used to own a restaurant on the Dublin Road. I'm born and bred Norn Iron, but I put on the Chinese accent as part of the act."

"Act?" Kirkwood was at an utter loss.

"Yeah, since I joined this lot." He jabbed a thumb in Tommy's direction. "Thought I'd rebrand myself when I passed over. You know, play the whole crazy Asian genius thang." He inspected the glasses and, satisfied with his efforts, balanced them again atop his pudgy nose.

"You mean, you're dead?"

"Yup. Five years next month. Or is it the month after?" Giro shook his head, dismissing the thought like a bothersome bluebottle. "Anyway, here I am, living the dream as Sector 8 electronics and communications expert amongst my many other skills." He bowed extravagantly, eliciting a giggle from Meredith. She was warming rapidly to the little man.

"Yes, Giro is one of ours," explained Tommy, gazing fondly at him like a doting father. "He's a seeker, like Samuel, but can also plane and has been embedded here since he passed over. Dobson sensed the strategic value of this plane some time ago and insisted we had someone in situ. Don't ask me how he knew, the man was exceptional. Always one step ahead of the Scourge and ten steps ahead of the rest of us."

"Deacon tolerates me as long as I keep his chronically bad comms system up and running. Without me, the patrols wouldn't have a cat in hell's chance out there. That right, grumpy?" His jibe was rewarded with a scowl from Deacon.

"Tolerate is the word. Now, are we going to get out there and do this or what? The longer we wait, the more likely the locals will be up and about. I'm tired, hungry, and could do without a firefight today. Too much paperwork to fill out for those clueless idiots over at One."

Tommy nodded. "Okay, you have a point. Let's get out there and find what we're looking for. It's time you earned your corn, Giro."

"Don't worry," replied Giro with an enigmatic smile. "I'm all over this one. Seems I'm getting a little help as well. Follow me." He bustled out of the tent and began to cross the roof towards the stairwell, which led back to the floors below.

"Help?" queried Kirkwood.

"Do you want the bad news or the good news?" asked Tommy as they began to follow Giro down the stairwell.

"Always the good." Meredith flashed him an unconvincing smile.

"Well, I'll explain down in the briefing room, but it looks as if your buddies are doing their bit to guide us to them."

"And the bad?" asked Kirkwood.

"We're going to have to travel to hell and back to get there," grumbled Deacon.

CHAPTER 22 - THE PRIESTESS

Flanagan clutched his ribs as he reluctantly limped towards the complex entrance. Back in the day, it was the place to be at the weekend, alive with bars, restaurants, and nightclubs. The adjoining arena hosted the city's ice hockey team, and all the big singers performed there. Swift, Perry, Bieber. As a young boy, he sat perched on his granny's knee, and she would play their songs to him on her ancient CD player. Yes, the complex had been the place to be seen. But at this very minute, it was the last place to be, for it meant he had messed up big time.

The two guards at the entrance doors stood aside, eyeing him with a mixture of pity and contempt. Flanagan trudged inside onto the central walkway. On either side, units had been converted into mass dormitories. Mattresses and sleeping bags covered the floors while bunk beds lined the walls. Hundreds of pairs of eyes followed him as he made his way to the broken escalator, which led onto the mezzanine floor above. Flanagan steadied himself at the bottom as every step sent shards of pain racing through his body. The brute must have broken at least half a dozen ribs, and he was afraid to look at his mangled fingers. Flanagan considered himself a hard man, but he had been no match for the bearded giant they encountered on what should have been a routine perimeter patrol. At least he had walked away from it, unlike Ramsey, but right now, he thought his patrol partner may have been the luckier of them.

He sucked in air between his teeth, trying to funnel the pain away to a remote part of his mind, allowing him to focus on the matters at hand. She would be displeased at the incursion but even more displeased at their inability to deal with it. An eye for an eye and a tooth for a tooth, that was how she managed affairs. To those who rose to her high standards, great favour awaited. Well worth tolerating all the religious mumbo jumbo she and her inner sanctum spouted. Yet for those who disappointed her, less favourable fortunes lay ahead.

As he reached the top of the escalator, the sanctum was revealed to him. On either side, her congregation stood. Young and old alike, decked head to toe in red clothing. Red, the colour their Saviour had bled on the Cross for them, covering them in his protective bliss as they now formed the vanguard for his glorious return to Earth to establish a new kingdom. He didn't believe a word of it but played along. To earn the coveted 'red' meant extra rations, more comfortable dwellings, and the pick of the women. Flanagan could choose his bride from amongst the prettiest girls the Priestess surrounded herself with—her Maidens of Purity. He had been besotted with Cassandra since joining their ranks, and she now reclined before him at the foot of the throne, avoiding eye contact as Flanagan approached. "Halt," a voice purred, dripping with poisonous intent.

Flanagan dropped to one knee, head bowed, biting his lower lip and resisting the urge to scream. It felt like a knitting needle was being repeatedly stabbed into his ribs while his left hand emitted a steady, sickening throb.

"My Priestess, I bring you news of an intruder."

"An intruder? And where is this intruder, Flanagan? For I see only your sorry self, quaking before me."

"He overpowered us on the northern perimeter. Ramsey's dead, he snapped his neck, I've never seen such strength in a man. I barely escaped with my own life." He chanced an upward glance to gauge her reaction to his words. He knew his very life was now hanging by a thread.

The Priestess sat on an angular throne, welded together from a mishmash of electrical appliances and bits of metal scavenged from the surrounding area, atop a dais constructed from wooden pallets. At her feet sat several Maidens of Purity, all attired in flowing white dresses to befit their status. The Priestess, in contrast, was dressed in tight black jeans and a matching t-shirt. She looked down wearily at Flanagan, her jade coloured eyes languid like a well-fed cat dozing in front of a roaring fire.

"Where is he now?" she spat, entirely unimpressed at the inadequacy of the explanation. She was slim and petite, no more than five-foot-tall, although the clunky biker boots she wore added several inches whenever she stood. A mass of loose raven curls cascaded down to the small of her back. The first time Flanagan set eyes on her, he thought she was the most beautiful woman he had ever seen.

He would have done anything for her, he still would, but now his motivation was fear as opposed to infatuation.

He snuck a look to where Cassandra sat at the foot of the throne. She nodded for him to continue, an almost imperceptible gesture. All around, the eyes of the Red bored into him. Flanagan's throat was dry, his skin clammy, but he knew he needed to continue, to somehow talk his way out of this horror show.

"He tortured me, my Priestess," he stammered, raising his swollen, twisted fingers by way of explanation. "Made me tell him where the wall was, the Wall of the Prophets." The words petered out as he struggled to regulate his breathing.

The Priestess raised an eyebrow, the closest to surprised she would ever come. She picked a long, curved fingernail against a jagged shard of metal jutting from the throne's arm. Painted ruby red, they were in vivid contrast to her black clothing and pale skin. Although barely middle-aged, her demeanour and mannerisms emitted an aura of venerable wisdom.

"The Wall. Deacon and his devils would have no interest in our holy place, nor would the heathens at the Castle. Yet I sense evil is close by. In these end times, the minions of the Deceiver will constantly seek to torment us." She lifted a finger and gestured for a hulking Red to approach her. After receiving whispered instructions from her, he made off at pace towards the escalator leading to the ground floor, flanked by several other heavies.

"I will retire to pray over this disturbing turn of events. Cassandra, Melissa, join me." She rose, and the congregation fell to one knee in reverence. The Priestess picked her way through the throng, stopping to stoop and whisper in Flanagan's ear as she passed.

"You have failed me, Flanagan. Consider yourself fortunate I'm in an affable frame of mind today. Next time may not be the case. And, as for your beloved Cassandra, if I ever catch you so much as looking at her again, I will have both your hands as a sacrifice to our Saviour." Her sparkling eyes blazed as she rose and disappeared through the remainder of the crowd towards her private quarters, followed by the two Maidens.

Flanagan remained kneeled as the Red dispersed around him. After several moments he was alone but alive, and for that, he was grateful. His body ached but not as much as his heart did for the loss of Cassandra. The Priestess had spoken. His dream of social advancement within her ranks was dead in the water. He sobbed silently, part relief, part regret.

CHAPTER 23 - I THINK I NEED A DRINK

"We are here." Deacon jabbed a grubby finger at a tattered, faded map that vaguely resembled Belfast city centre. Kirkwood and Meredith, seated on either side of him around an unsteady circular table, nodded in unison. He could have been showing them a map of Rome, such was its grimy condition. Indecipherable words and symbols adorned it. Belfast had changed an awful lot since they last walked its streets.

"And we need to get here." He moved his finger across the map to where the dense mass of grey and brown gave way to a blue section of the map.

"That's the docks area, right?" asked Kirkwood. "The Titanic Quarter. I used to run around it on my lunch breaks. Or rather, Skelly made me run around it. Good old Routine 11."

Deacon looked at him quizzically before reverting his attention to the map and continuing. "This Titanic Quarter you refer to is now known as New Jerusalem. It's the one part of the city we have no control over. The Priestess runs the show over there."

"How?" challenged Meredith. "Aren't you lot meant to be the law in this city, sector, whatever you call it?"

Deacon growled and appeared to have an internal dialogue with himself before responding. "Sure, we could go in there heavy-handed, clear it out, but at what cost? Our job is to maintain the peace, even if it's an uneasy one. If we tried to take over New Jerusalem, it would be a bloodbath."

"So, you stay in your corner, and she stays in hers?" Kirkwood picked up Deacon's logical thread.

"Basically," explained Giro from across the table. "We have our channels of communication with the Priestess. Messages can be exchanged if required. But sometimes it's best letting sleeping dogs lie. Or in her case, one seriously rabid bitch."

"Doesn't that give her the upper hand, though?" pressed Meredith. "I'm no strategic mastermind, but giving up the docks to her, doesn't that give her control of Belfast Lough?"

"Maybe back on your plane, Meredith," replied Giro with a tight smile. "But, it's a whole new world out there. When the Army withdrew from Belfast, and it all fell apart, they mined the lough. Going in and out of there is playing Russian roulette with God knows how many tonnes of high explosives. The Priestess knows that too, so keeps her feet well and truly on dry land."

"Why are we going there if it's a virtual no-go zone? Plus, the mural of Emily is in Mulberry Square, less than five minutes' walk from here." Kirkwood looked over at Tommy, who was studying the map with feverish intensity. He looked up, as if unaware the others were in the room, such was his focus.

"Because that's where Giro says her essence is strongest. And we go where the seeker tells us to go, even if it's the other side of the planet. He's the best one this side of the Inner Sanctum." Giro's chest visibly swelled, looking like it might burst with pride. His smile lit up the room, and Meredith melted a little more at his infectious personality. Kirkwood smiled, pleased to see his normally surly companion so at ease. A happy Meredith was one of the few things he asked for any more.

"When I was told you two were paying us a visit and the reason, I cast out the net and got a weak signal from New Jerusalem. It was a sniff at first, a strand, nothing more, but I've developed it ever since. I've gone out with patrols as close as they go down there and zeroed in on the source. It was hardly anything, but since your arrival, it has increased in strength. Your friends, Emily and Harley, they're clearly together and working hard to tell us how to get to them."

"And Mulberry Square?" asked Kirkwood.

Giro pushed his glasses further along the bridge of his nose. "I'm sorry, Kirkwood, I've checked it out myself. Her graffiti is no longer there."

"But they're alive? And together?" Meredith's voice was tinged with a fragile, faltering hope.

"Oh, most definitely," nodded Giro. "They're combining to strengthen their essence. It's like a radar, and I'm picking it up loud and clear. In New Jerusalem." He looked nervously towards Deacon. "At the Wall of the Prophets."

"Wall of the Prophets?" asked Kirkwood and Meredith as one.

"Wonderful," sighed the grizzled soldier. "Their most sacred and therefore heavily protected site. We would need a small army to get in and out of there."

"Which is why we're not sending one." Tommy looked at each of them in turn. "We need to get in, get what we need, and then leg it pronto. Giro, how accurately can you tell us where the essence is?"

"Given its present strength, within ten metres, easy."

"How long is this wall?" asked Kirkwood.

"Long enough that planeing in even slightly out of alignment could be the death of us. That's good, Giro. Get me the grid reference, and I'll plane in with one other person. Any more than that and I'd struggle."

"How come?" asked Kirkwood perplexed. "You were able to double plane the two of us almost a century into the future. Surely, a hop across the city is a piece of cake for you."

"Normally, yes." Tommy straightened from the map. "But there's something about New Jerusalem. I don't know what that crazy woman and her followers are up to, but there are forces at work that restrict my ability to plane, like a protective barrier. The best I can manage is myself and one of you two." He glanced awkwardly from Kirkwood to Meredith and back again.

"You want to separate us?" Meredith felt her jaw drop open.

"Yes," replied Tommy starkly. "I know the consequences, Meredith, but I'm afraid there's no other way. This is the only way we can connect with your friends and find out where they are."

Without realising he was doing it, Kirkwood began to chew anxiously on a fingernail. He looked up and said what the others in the room were all thinking. "If we physically separate, then we are leaving ourselves wide open to Skelly. He can play on our weakness, attack us where he knows we are vulnerable and exposed."

Meredith took his hand and squeezed it. "If it's the only way to find the girls, then we have to do it. Think of Harley, Kirkwood. Think of what she must be going through this very minute."

The penny dropped, and as it did, so did Kirkwood's head into his hands. "Harley. Oh my God, I didn't think. Her legs..."

"You see?" Meredith's words were gentle, carrying no recrimination. "But if there's a tougher cookie on this or any other plane, I'm yet to find them. She would do it for us. She *is* doing it for us. She and Emily are doing everything they can to unite us all. If that means me having to go cold turkey in a padded cell for a day or so, then I'm prepared to do it."

Kirkwood nodded, wanting to believe, but icy tendrils of fear were already rising from the pit of his stomach and threatening to choke the words as they formed in his mouth.

"But the thoughts. The second I'm separated from you, I'm back in the Study. I'm rolling the dice. The 49..." His words trailed off, and all Meredith could do was take his other hand and look imploringly into his frantic eyes.

"You can do this, Kirkwood. As can I. There's no other way."

Kirkwood snorted, not sure if he was going to laugh or cry. "Things must be serious if you're calling me by my proper name."

"Don't worry. Normal service will be resumed shortly. Let's get the girls back first." She smiled, her pale face lighting up with a softness she had fought so hard to conceal during her time on the streets.

Suddenly aware they had an attentive audience, Kirkwood coughed self-consciously before turning to address the others.

"Okay, let's do this. Tommy, when do we go? I'll get my sick bag ready."

"There's no need for that lad," replied the usually jovial Northerner. He knew the message he was about to deliver would be a difficult one for the young man to hear. "You're going nowhere. It's the young lady I need for this job."

All eyes turned on Meredith, who smiled shyly and adjusted her beanie hat before replying. "Do they still make Buckfast in 2099? I think I need a drink."

CHAPTER 24 - A PINT OR SEVEN

Meredith's dark humour punctured the heavy atmosphere in the briefing room, and a welcome wave of shared laughter washed over them. Even Deacon managed a grin, although it made his sullen features craggier than ever. Outside in the corridor, heavy boots and low conversation could be heard as the men and women of Security Solutions faced another day on the front line. There was no respite, no R&R in their immediate futures, only long hours of dull routine punctuated by terrifying, violent excursions into the city. Hellfast worked hard to earn its nickname and had no intention of relinquishing it any time soon.

"If we're all agreed, then this is the plan," said Tommy.

He spoke slowly and deliberately, maintaining eye contact throughout as he carefully explained what lay ahead for them. A patrol was to take Deacon, Meredith, and himself as close as was safe to the perimeter of New Jerusalem.

"Once there, I will plane Meredith and myself in. Deacon will provide cover, allowing Miss Starc to make contact and figure out where the girls are. Then it's back out again, hopefully before we are noticed."

"Hopefully?" Meredith was far from convinced.

"It's not an exact science," conceded Tommy. "While we have a fair idea of what we are heading into, we can't be certain."

"And what exactly am I supposed to do when we get there?"

Deacon grunted, indicating words were imminent. "From what we know, the Wall of the Prophets was a peace line erected during the Troubles to keep the warring communities apart. After the peace, it became something of a tourist attraction. You know the thing. People signing their names, taking selfies, adding bits of graffiti. It ended up a piece of living art. Load of hippy nonsense if you ask me, but it helped keep the dollars and euros rolling into the city."

"I think President Will.I.Am visited it. All the big names. It became iconic." Giro nodded sagely.

"Will.I.Am? Black Eyed Peas? Became the President of the United States?" Kirkwood could not hide his incredulity.

"No more far-fetched than Ronald Reagan," answered Giro. "Two terms. Massively popular."

"Do you think Emily is trying to communicate with us through this wall?" asked Meredith. "Like she did back in Mulberry Square?"

"Exactly, Meredith," replied Tommy. "The Priestess claims God speaks to her at the Wall via his Prophets. There have been reports of all sorts of weird stuff going on down there, ceremonies, and wild parties. A load of nonsense, but it's all part of New Jerusalem's appeal to the Dirties. Food, shelter, and dance yourself silly until the Rapture arrives. Somehow, that's where Emily and Harley's essence is strongest."

"Sounds just my cup of tea," quipped Meredith. "Welcome to the end of the world. Bring your own drink."

"I don't intend to hang around long enough to find out," replied Tommy, starting to fold away the map. "Samuel has me well briefed as to your particular...er...vulnerabilities. The sooner you have all reunited again, the better. Meredith, I'm confident we can be back here safe and sound long before withdrawal symptoms kick in with you."

"Withdrawal?" replied Meredith indignantly. "You make me sound like a right wino." She folded her arms and pouted, causing Kirkwood to smirk.

"Meredith, you were necking enough tonic wine and vodka to stock a medium-sized off-license. By right, you should be crawling up the walls as we speak."

"Possibly," she reluctantly conceded, rolling her eyes. "But I never touched the drugs. Left all that crap to Danny and his saucer-eyed mates. I did have some standards."

"I'm actually more concerned about you, Kirkwood" Giro frowned. "Meredith can cope with a few shivers and a headache. You, however, leave yourself vulnerable to Skelly and a routine. I can't afford to have you zoning out to the Study if you planed into New Jerusalem. Which is why you're staying here."

Kirkwood opened his mouth to argue but realised the futility of it and said nothing. Meredith stared smugly at him, as Giro continued. "You won't be hung out to dry, though. I'll be staying with you. Hopefully, my particular skill set will be able to deflect any incoming advances from Skelly."

"Are we ready now?" asked Deacon impatiently. "I'm tiring of this talking shop. High time we got out on the ground and kicked some backside. I've a Sector to run once this little escapade is over." He glowered at Tommy, keen for the briefing to end.

"This escapade as you refer to it," said Tommy icily, "is all part of a much bigger battle that you have little awareness of, Major Deacon. You think keeping tabs on The Priestess and a few Dirties is hard work, then be thankful Skelly, and the Scourge isn't unleashed on this dump. They'd have a field day, and you wouldn't have a clue how to repel them. It's because we've a vested interest in this plane and embed guys like Giro that you've still got a city to police. You'd do well to remember that."

"Noted," grumbled Deacon, before pushing back his chair and rising from the table. He didn't look particularly happy with the state of affairs but was unwilling to take the discussion further. We'll rendezvous in the yard in 90. Get your people sorted, and don't be late. Giro, with me." He stalked out of the briefing room, followed by the diminutive seeker who gave a cheeky wink as he followed the grumpy soldier.

Tommy turned to his young companions. "You guys ready for this? It's a big ask, I know, but unfortunately, it's all we have to go on at present."

"I was born ready," joked Meredith before adopting a more serious expression. "But first, I need some breakfast before I can even think about saving the planet again."

Tommy laughed, a deep gulder from the pit of his stomach. "Well, they do say an army marches on its stomach. Let's hit the mess and see what the cook can rustle up. Kirkwood?"

"Born ready?" he scoffed. "You really are a prat, Sansa." Try as he might, he could not prevent a grin from sweeping across his face.

"Yeah, well, if I'm reverting back to my former raving alco state, then I might as well line my stomach first. Although your hypocrisy is noted. If I recall correctly, you aren't averse to a pint or seven yourself."

"At least I drew the line at paint stripper."

Tommy held back slightly as the bantering duo walked into the corridor. Dobson had chosen wisely. To face what they had and emerge unscathed on the other side required courage, intelligence, and perhaps most importantly, a sense of humour. Kirkwood Scott and Meredith Starc had it by the bucketful. He only hoped they could maintain it in the face of what lay ahead.

Tommy Mainwright gritted his teeth, took a deep breath, and followed them out of the room.

CHAPTER 25 - CIRCLING THE WAGONS

"Laters, Kirky." Those were her last words to him before she hopped into the back of the armoured landrover, and it rumbled out of the compound yard. As it veered left and out of sight, Kirkwood caught a brief glimpse of a nondescript street before two heavily armed guards closed the rusting steel gates. Harley, and now Meredith, were gone, they all were. Gerry, Grogan, Natasha, Katie, his mother, his father, they all left him in the end. All except Skelly, old faithful himself. Kirkwood Scott suddenly felt very alone. He looked up at the dreary grey sky, expecting to see Skelly and his demonic denizens descending, ready to pluck him skywards before dropping him to certain death.

"Care to accompany me to your quarters, sir?" Giro's words brought him back to the reality of the yard. All around him, the station was humming into gear. Kirkwood marvelled that, despite it being 2099, the favoured mode of transport for Security Solutions patrols were battered armoured landrovers, not unlike those used by the police and army a century ago. Half a dozen of them sat parked in a row opposite him, all bearing the scars of numerous street battles. Their original gunmetal grey paintwork was chipped and, in many places, decorated with fire and paint damage. Petroleum and paint bombs also seemed to have remained the missiles of choice amongst those opposed to the current occupying forces.

"If we must," replied Kirkwood. He followed Giro across the yard, weaving a path through the dozen or so soldiers preparing for the day ahead. There were as many women as men, but they all shared the same tired, resigned faces. Hellfast had sucked the life out of them; they were merely surviving now, counting the days to their next precious period of R&R when they could escape the mundane horrors of Sector 8 for a few days. Suddenly, Kirkwood had a sense of how his father must have felt, waving goodbye to his family and heading off into the night to fight a mostly unseen enemy.

"We can set up in my room," shouted Giro over the noise of the metal beasts across the yard, roaring into life. The morning patrols were heading out, and a sense of chaotic purpose had enveloped the yard. "It's a bit more private there should things get a bit hairy." He took the stairs two at a time to the first floor, displaying surprising energy and agility despite his pudgy frame. Somehow sensing Kirkwood's unspoken surprise, he shouted down to his new charge who was struggling to keep apace.

"Black belt in Taekwondo, believe it or not. Second Dan. Not that I get much opportunity to train these days."

"The only black belt I ever had held up my school trousers."

"Ha," roared Giro, stopping at a nondescript door and fumbling in the pocket of his cargo trousers, before producing a key and opening it. "Samuel said you were a dry wit. He loves a good giggle, our Samuel does." He entered the basic but spacious room. Bar the regulation bed, desk, and chair, most of it was taken up by an assortment of metal contraptions spouting wires on a series of shelves running along the far wall.

"Some of my works in progress," he offered by way of explanation. "Excuse the mess. I don't entertain very often."

"You should see my place. Never worry."

Giro swept a bundle of clothing off the chair onto the floor, where it joined a collection of odd socks and stained t-shirts. He beckoned for Kirkwood to sit down before planting himself on the lumpy, single bed.

"Join the armed forces and see the world. Yeah, right." He grinned, a heart-warming trademark smile which few could resist, Kirkwood included.

"Pardon my nosiness," asked Kirkwood, curiosity getting the better of him, "But how come you ended up...here?" He blushed furiously at his inability to tactfully form the question.

"You mean how I died and ended up in this palace?" For a second, Kirkwood was caught off guard by the stern expression of his host until the latter could retain the facade no longer and fell back onto the mattress cackling manically.

"Oh, your face," spluttered Giro after taking several minutes to gather his breath and composure. Kirkwood waited patiently, content to play the straight man. When Giro finally ceased chuckling, he attempted to engage in serious conversation again.

"It's just..." Oh Lord, how could he word this. "You don't seem the soldierly type." Kirkwood inwardly groaned and scanned Giro's features for the tiniest clue as to his true reaction to the question.

"I'm not a soldier," was the plain reply. "Not all of us were. Dobson cast his net far and wide when he recruited. Tommy, Samuel, guys like that, they all hail from military backgrounds. I'm just an electronics geek who, one day, wasn't looking where he was going and stepped out in front of an articulated lorry on its way to Belfast. Splat." He shrugged, dismissing his violent, sudden death in an instance.

"And you ended up here?"

"Yeah, after several years of intense training. Dobson put us all through our paces before he trusted us operationally. He took one look at me when I passed over and said I was primarily a seeker. It's all I've known since. I went all over the planes, then he sent me to this luxurious residence." He spread his arms out to take in their less than sumptuous surroundings.

"It's hardly the Ritz, I agree."

"It's what I do now," replied Giro. "Dobson knew something the rest of us didn't. The significance of this plane, and the need to have me in situ for when the time came. Plus, Deacon isn't that bad, once you get to know him. There's a heart beating inside that grumpy old chest somewhere. He would give his left arm for every man and woman on this base."

"Hmmm, I look forward to seeing that caring, sharing side of him. So, what now, Giro? Do we just sit here and wait for Skelly to come a-knocking?" Kirkwood glanced around the room, his nerves on edge, expecting to be summoned to the Study at any second.

"Relax, Kirkwood. I'll be able to sense any approach in advance. If one even comes. If it does, then Skelly will have met his match. I'm more than ready for him. Before you know it, Meredith and your other friends will be reunited, and all will be well again. I've heard all about your victory at the portal. Talk is, the Presence has never manifested itself so powerfully in a trio. Dobson chose wisely; he always does."

"Really?" Kirkwood raised his eyebrows in genuine surprise. "We're that good?"

"You closed a portal. Took on three of the Company on your first outing and blew them away. That's not to be sniffed at. Skelly's running scared, he's not used to being given the run-around. That's why he's throwing the kitchen sink at us now. We've got him on the back foot, I'm certain of that. Just you wait and see."

"If you say so," replied Kirkwood, not entirely convinced. "I guess we wait then." He settled back into the chair, every fibre of him on red alert for the tell-tale signs that forewarned of a summons to the Study. Giro lay back on the bed, folded his arms behind his head, and within minutes was snoring gently, glasses still perched atop flaring nostrils. It was a far from comforting sight but, if Dobson believed in him, then who was he to doubt his new protector's capabilities.

"Come back safe, Meredith. Safe and soon."

CHAPTER 26 - INCURSION

"These wagons aren't exactly built for comfort, are they?" yelled Meredith above the roar of the landrover engine. She lurched across the bench she was perched on as the diesel-guzzling beast rounded a corner, almost landing on Deacon, who sat facing her in the rear of the vehicle.

"So awfully sorry," he bellowed back. "Next time, I'll make sure the Roller is valeted and back from the garage." He placed a coarse hand on each of Meredith's shoulders and planted her next to him on the bench. Wedged between the gruff Colonel on one side and a smiling Tommy on the other, Meredith decided to say nothing more and instead focus on maintaining her upright position.

"Don't worry," Tommy shouted in her ear. "Not much longer. I'd say another mile to the drop off point."

"Wonderful," muttered Meredith. Tiny reinforced glass portholes on either side of the landrover offered a minimal view of the passing city. What she did glimpse did nothing to raise her spirits. Rubble-strewn streets and dilapidated buildings with no discernible landmarks gave her no indication as to what part of the city they were travelling through. By Meredith's rough calculations, they should be in the city centre, navigating streets she once knew well. Nothing was familiar. They could have been trundling through downtown Chernobyl for all she knew.

Her thinking was shattered by a series of heavy thuds on the roof of the landrover, causing her to leap in the air before falling back down onto the bench between her two escorts.

"What the hell was that?"

"Just the Dirties messing around," replied Deacon. "Lobbing breeze blocks off the top of buildings." He held his rifle tightly between his knees and leaned forward, opening the hatch between them and the driver in the front. "What's going on up there?"

The driver stared intently ahead through the metal grill affixed to the front windscreen, while his colleague in the passenger seat held a finger to her ear, listening to a garbled radio transmission on a radio earpiece before turning to update her Commanding Officer.

"Activity on the western side of the Castle, sir. Could be an ambush. Hawkeye recommends we give it a wide berth and cross the river at Bravo Bridge."

"Do it," barked Deacon. "And keep me updated." He pushed the hatch shut and settled back onto the bench. "Nothing of concern, just the locals, trying to goad us. Any excuse to have a scrap. I think they get bored sometimes fighting amongst themselves, so decide to have a pop at us."

"That was more than a pop." Meredith pointed in amazement towards the roof of the landrover.

"It will take more than a couple of rocks to get through that. The best armour plating money can buy. We lost too many good people that way in the early days, so I made it my mission to ensure the last batch of vehicles were upgraded."

They travelled on without further incident for several minutes before the vehicle slowed and rolled to a halt. Meredith heard the driver talking to someone before the vehicle jolted forward again over what felt like a series of ramps.

"Is that us on Bravo?" inquired Tommy. Meredith noticed for the first time he was clutching a handgun with a stout barrel. Realising she was staring at it, he patted it almost tenderly. "Just a bit of reassurance. Hopefully won't have to resort to it." She nodded uneasily at him, wishing it was all over, and she was back at Queen Street with Kirkwood. Kirkwood. It was hard to believe that less than a week ago, they had never met, but now he was her rock, the one she turned to every time this crazy new life threatened to overwhelm her.

"Out of the frying pan, into the fire," she mouthed silently under her breath.

The landrover swung sharply left before lurching to a halt. Deacon pushed back the hatch again and held a hurried conversation with the driver before turning to Meredith and Tommy. "Okay, this is our stop. We're about five hundred metres from the outer perimeter of New Jerusalem. This is as close as we go without ruffling the Priestess' feathers. When we leave the truck, we head left, fast as possible, until I tell you when to stop. Pearse in the front will cover us until we get there, but then they'll have to back up onto Bravo, and we're on our own. Clear?"

"As mud," replied Meredith solemnly.

"Good. Then let's go."

He leaned forward and unbolted the rear doors of the vehicle before hopping out to take up a kneeling stance, sweeping the immediate area with his ever-present rifle. Meredith heard a door opening and assumed Pearse was adopting a similar position at the front of the truck. Tommy gripped her forearm, and taking a deep breath, she propelled herself from the bench and out through the doors towards whatever awaited them outside. Her boots crunched on gravel underfoot as they ran at a crouch, Deacon leading the way, surprisingly swift and agile for a man of his years. Meredith found herself wedged between the sour veteran and Tommy behind, urging her to keep moving.

"Lower, Meredith. Stay low."

Out of her peripheral vision, she glimpsed the landrover turning in a tight arc before rattling off, presumably back to Bravo Bridge. Without warning, Deacon veered right, down a series of steps that brought them into a hollow containing the remnants of a children's play park. Rusted swings hung redundantly opposite a steel slide, which housed an array of rotting leaves and other detritus.

"In here." Deacon led them under the sloped wooden roof of what used to be a den where kids would shelter from the elements when the unpredictable Irish weather intervened and stopped play. Deacon crouched to a knee again and waited for Meredith to regain her breath as she stood wheezing beside him, bent over double, hands on her thighs.

"The youth of today. No stamina."

"Youth of today? By my calculations, I'm 105 years old. Give me a break, Deacon."

"Whatever. This location okay for you, Tommy?"

"Yeah, it will do. All I need is a couple of minutes."

"Okay. I'll provide cover and wait here. The truck will be back in ten minutes. It's a tight window, time-wise, but if we stay this side of the river any longer, we'll attract attention. Good luck to you both." With that, he was off, scampering across the play area and up a slight incline, where he flattened onto his stomach, sweeping the area ahead through the rifle's sights.

Tommy took Meredith's hands in his own. "You ready for this?"

"Do I have any choice?"

"Not really. We are going to plane no more than half a mile, it's blink of the eye stuff. They call it the Wall of the Prophets. It's their holy place and always guarded, but we have the element of surprise. I'll cover you. Their essence is at its strongest there."

"So, that's where I can connect with Emily and Harley?"

"We think so. Our intelligence tells us the Priestess believes God speaks to her, instructs her through the Wall. Everything adds up. If Emily and Harley are trying to communicate with us, then you're the person best placed to pick it up. We plane in, you find the message, and we plane out again. Simple."

"What could possibly go wrong?"

"That's what I like about you," grinned Tommy. "Your boundless optimism. Now let's do this."

Meredith nodded, took Tommy's hand, and closed her eyes. When she opened them again, they were there.

CHAPTER 27 - SHIFTING SANDS

She ran.

The crack of pistol fire indicated their arrival had not gone unnoticed. Ahead of her, the Wall loomed, a twenty-foot-high kaleidoscope of colour and creativity. Tourists from all over the world travelled here to add their own tribute to the fledgling peace that was supposed to take root in their country a century ago. If only they knew how naive and futile their hopes had been. 2099 was the reality. Everything was broken, irreparably lost.

Meredith screamed as a lump of rock exploded at her feet, shattered by a high-velocity bullet. All around her was a deafening noise, she had no idea where Tommy was or what he was doing. They had planed into the middle of an ambush. The trap had been sprung, and there was nowhere to hide. Meredith tripped and fell forward, throwing out both hands to break the fall. Her palms exploded in pain as the top layer of skin was removed by sharp shards of rubble. A millisecond later, her knees followed suit, leaving her breathless and sobbing on the ground. Blinking away the tears, she looked around frantically for Tommy.

She found him less than a dozen feet away, lying facing her, pistol still gripped in hand. He stared vacantly at her, a trickle of blood flowing from a single bullet hole to his forehead. "Tommy!" The tears accelerated along with her heartbeat, a quickening drumbeat of terror battering her ribcage.

"They knew."

"Of course we did, my child. The Prophets reveal all to the righteous."

Meredith looked up to be greeted by a grubby biker boot that proceeded to grind down upon her outstretched hand, exacerbating the pain she was already experiencing in her flayed palms. She cried out, earning a peal of laughter from her tormentor. Blazing green eyes, framed by a mass of soft, black curls tumbling down either side of an angular face. Dressed top to toe in black, Meredith doubted if she had ever seen such a spectacular woman.

Rough hands grabbed her by the shoulders, hauling her upright before the woman in black. Meredith stood considerably taller than her assailant but felt herself shrinking by the second beneath her harsh gaze. For once, words failed Meredith, but her attention was suddenly focused beyond her captor. She struggled not to laugh for there on the wall was a familiar, more friendly face. A pale, serene face that could not have contrasted more starkly to that of the one in front of her.

"Emily. What the hell are you doing here?"

"Take her away," snapped the Priestess. "I'll interrogate her later after I consult with the Prophets as to the reason she has violated this holy place. But I'll warn you, my child, I do not take kindly to such flagrant transgressions. Little girls like you need to be made an example of, there can be no exceptions."

Meredith wasn't even listening as she was dragged off for her eyes were locked firmly on the artwork depicting Emily, words now appearing on the wall beneath her. Words that sparked new hope, despite her present plight.

'The Tower. Skelly's Tower.'

∞ ∞ ∞

Emily's eyes shot open as she sat cross-legged, facing Harley in the cell. "Did you feel that? Did you feel it, Harley?"

Harley opened one eye and squinted back. "Was it a pop? I think I heard a pop."

"Exactly." Emily unfolded her legs and leaned across, sweeping Harley into a hug, which resulted in them both ending up in an undignified tangle on the floor. "That's the breakthrough, we did it, we got the message through." She kissed her bemused companion on the forehead before emitting a high-pitched squeal that left Harley wincing in discomfort.

"You mean, they heard us? They know where we are?" Harley pulled herself back up into a sitting position, all the while with one eye on the door expecting Maura or another of Skelly's goons to burst in and catch them red-handed in the act of interplanetary communication.

"Yes, they most certainly did," replied Emily, sounding most pleased with herself. She leaned back against Harley, a look of quiet determination on her angelic features. "Now, all we have to do is sit back and wait for our knights in shining armour to arrive."

∞ ∞ ∞

Deacon looked at his watch for the fifth time that minute before frowning and pressing the send button of his transmitter. They should have been back ten minutes ago. "Papa One to Foxtrot Seven, are you mobile? Over." There was a crackle of interference before a tinny voice responded in his earpiece. "Papa One. Confirmed. We are mobile. ETA 120. Over."

Deacon sighed and scanned the play area again, willing Tommy and Meredith to appear, but he was alone, and the window of opportunity was gone. To stay on this side of the river much longer was effectively signing your own death warrant if you were a Security Solutions operative. Deacon had hammered the message home to his troops often enough, so for him to disregard his own advice was the height of hypocrisy. He sighed and spoke into the transmitter.

"Roger that. Proceed to the RV point. Will meet you there. Out." He shook his head before turning his back on the play area.

"Sorry, guys. You're on your own now."

∞ ∞ ∞

"They've got her, haven't they?" Kirkwood felt his stomach drop into his ankles. If you asked him to explain, he wouldn't have been able to elaborate on how he came to that conclusion, but he knew, he just knew.

Giro screwed his face up, as if downwind of a particularly rank odour, before cocking his head to one side while tugging on an earlobe. "Bear with me, I'm trying to tune in to their essence. Meredith...there was an energy flare, something happened, it's dimmed again. She's out there near the Wall." His eyes misted over, and he dropped his head, unsuccessfully attempting to hide his emotions from Kirkwood.

"Giro, what is it? Tell me?" Kirkwood knew it was bad even as he spoke the words. Giro's crestfallen face said it all.

"It's Tommy. I can't sense him. He's gone."

∞ ∞ ∞

Skelly ran a finger along the razor-sharp seam of his trousers, pondering the options available to him. The game had suddenly opened up, and now was not the time for faint hearts. He had them on the ropes, but he was loath to wade in yet and deliver the knockout punch, tempting as that was. A cool head was required, and a steady hand.

"Softly softly, catchy monkey."

"Sir?" Maura stood in front of the old man, tentatively reminding him of her presence in the Study.

Skelly looked up irritably, his thinking disrupted by the flame-haired lieutenant. He composed himself and smiled at her. She was a personal favourite of his, had been since the first time he set eyes on her. Mad as a hatter, running to her death like that when she could have been halfway to Brussels and safety. All for the sake of a bloody man. Yet he had to admire her pluck, the manner in which she conducted herself when all around grown men were screaming for their mothers and soiling themselves. She died at his side, weapon in hand. French scum wouldn't even spare a woman such was their bloodlust at the end.

"Yes, my dear, what news?"

"We have her, sir. The one known to her kind as Meredith. The Priestess has taken her. All we have to do is bring her back."

"Ah, the Priestess. Now she's my kind of woman. Beautiful and ruthless." He paused, fully aware of the impact of his words on the young lady standing before him. "Oh come, come, Maura. No need to be jealous. Honestly, you Irish. So emotional."

"I'm not, sir, I..." The normally unflappable Maura stammered in front of her Commanding Officer.

"Stop your blubbering, woman. I'm all for equality. You keep bringing me good news, and a step up the ranks could be in order for you. I've always been an advocate for promoting on merit as opposed to privilege. Keep this up, and Rodriguez will be looking over his shoulder. He's hardly been setting the world on fire of late." He raised the never-empty tumbler to dry, cracked lips and sipped from its ruby-red contents. "Now, let's test your leadership credentials. What do you suggest I do next?"

"Me, sir? "Maura stared at the old man, hesitantly. This was a first, the Colonel never asked the opinion of anyone, such was his sure-footed decision making. The man was a legend, yet here he was asking her, a mere foot soldier, what the next course of action should be. It was either a fantastic opportunity or a cruel trap. She eyed him nervously, trying to figure out which, but his smirking visage gave nothing away. She swallowed hard and made her decision.

"They're separated, sir. No longer a single entity, which means The Presence cannot manifest itself against us. The Forsaken may rally, but without that, they cannot resist us. They may have closed the portal once, but next time there will be nothing to stop us laying claim to their plane."

Skelly nodded. "An astute summary. They're on their knees. What do I do? Strike while the iron is hot, deliver the coup de grace? Surely, it's a no brainer, a foregone conclusion?"

"No, sir, we don't." She gulped again, searching his bloated face for a clue as to how her daring statement had been received. She had witnessed colleagues reduced to piles of smoking ash for daring to challenge Augustus Skelly. She thanked all that was unholy when her audacious suggestion was greeted with a wicked smile.

"Excellent, Maura. Excellent. And your reasoning is?"

Maura spoke quicker this time, her confidence growing with each passing second. She was onto something here. "They'll expect that of us, sir. We have the White Witch and the cripple. The obvious next step is to claim the Street Urchin, the one known to her kind as Meredith Starc. But that would be playing into their hands. They will be gunning for her too. It could get messy if we play our hand too soon."

"Go on," urged Skelly. She was good, very good, and he was relishing the steps his latest protege was making towards what he had determined long ago. That oaf Rodriguez, if faced with the same scenario, would have waded in without a thought. He was a fearsome fighter, but when it came to strategy and tactics, his brains were in his boots. This one, though, she had potential. And so much more pleasing on the eye.

"We avoid confrontation, sir. Avoid New Jerusalem. The Priestess can take care of her for now." She risked a sly smile, warming to the task. "I say it's time Kirkwood Scott paid you a long-overdue visit. Make him an offer he can't refuse. But let him squirm a little first, soften him up."

Skelly clapped his hands, eyes alight. "Top quality, my dear. You and I really are cut from the same cloth. Yes, it's high time I had a chat with young Kirkwood. I wouldn't say absence makes the heart grow fonder, but I have missed our little meetings. Thank you, Maura. That will be all for now." He drained the contents of his tumbler, and when he looked again, she was gone.

"Ah, Kirkwood, how I've missed you. I do hate to see you suffer, but needs must."

CHAPTER 28 - THE PORTUGUESE PROPHET

Meredith gave as good as she got. Kicking and lashing out at every opportunity as she was dragged from the Wall to a battered white box van, that looked as old as the hills. She was bundled into the back of it, and the door slammed shut and bolted before she had a chance to turn and unleash a volley of expletives. Seconds passed before the van's engine grumbled to life. The vehicle jolted forward, throwing Meredith into the metal partition, separating her from the driver. She cannoned off it, falling on her side and lay there, desperately trying to control her breathing and channel rampant thoughts.

If she had learnt one thing in the last upside down, back to front week, it was not to panic. While her default setting was to catastrophise at the slightest setback, she recognised that even in their darkest hours, a flicker of hope had guided them safely through to the other side. What would Dobson do? What would Samuel do? What would Tommy...

She flinched as the image of Tommy's vacant stare filled her mind's eye. A rivulet of blood flowing idly from the single bullet hole adorning his forehead like a deadly bindi, the full stop on the plucky soldier's second life. She clenched her eyes shut and willed the death mask to vanish, allowing her to focus on how she was going to extricate herself from this latest pickle. Tommy was gone. The Priestess knew they were planeing in, it was an ambush which they were never going to escape. But how? How?

The van creaked to a halt as suddenly as it had started, and the back doors flew open. Piercing sunlight penetrated the murky interior causing Meredith to raise an arm to allow her eyes to adjust. Squinting against the glare, a large, silhouetted figure gradually came into focus. Her eyes were watering, a mixture of tears and exposure to the sun's rays, as she struggled to clear her vision sufficiently to make out who was now hauling her from the van by an ankle. She resisted vainly and within seconds landed painfully on the ground outside. She instinctively writhed and kicked out, determined to inflict at least one painful blow with her Doctor Martens.

It was then she heard the familiar booming laugh and froze. The same laughter which had mocked her as she attempted to evade his clutches at the bandstand in Botanic Gardens.

"Rodriguez?"

"The one and only, my sweet lady." Meredith looked up, her vision finally returned to normal, to be greeted by the toothy grin of Skelly's henchman. Dressed top to toe in designer black, he spread his arms out as if greeting a long lost relative. A jagged scar ran down one cheek before disappearing into the expanses of his glistening beard.

Meredith scrambled onto her backside in anticipation of a vicious kick, but none was forthcoming. The Portuguese giant pulled a hurt expression, dropping his arms disconsolately before speaking again.

"Oh, come now, senorita, this is no way to greet an old amigo. You and I go waaaay back." He dropped to one knee beside her with surprising agility for such a big man. "Besides," he whispered conspiratorially in her ear, "If it wasn't for me pleading your case back there, I fear you may have ended up like your brave friend. Such a shame." He pulled a pained expression. "But, I guess you know a little how I felt when you wiped out Gunther on the bridge."

Suddenly the jovial grin was gone, replaced by an unsettling leer. If she needed any reminding, Meredith realised Rodriguez was no friend of hers.

"What are you doing here?" was all she could muster. Their faces were mere inches apart. Meredith tensed, expecting any second for him to smash his forehead into her nose, shattering it like he had shattered her hopes of finding Emily and Harley. She felt further away from them than ever, a lost little girl entirely out of her depth against an enemy she couldn't even begin to comprehend.

Rodriguez, sensing her inner vulnerability, plastered a sickly, saccharine smile across his face. "Awh, poor little street urchin. Are you missing your friends? Your darling Emily?" He smirked, enjoying the anguish he was inflicting. "Such a pity you have no idea where she is...if she's even alive, that is." It took every fibre of self-control for Meredith to refrain from spitting in his smug, self-satisfied features.

"Where do you want her taken?" A stick insect of a man with feral features was leaning against the side of the van. He picked nervously at filthy fingernails in desperate need of a trim. "We don't want to keep Her Majesty waiting; she's not the most patient woman."

"Well, she will just have to wait until I'm ready," snapped Rodriguez, momentarily averting his attention to glare at the driver. The stick insect visibly withered and developed a sudden interest in the ground. Rodriguez turned his attention back to Meredith. She considered kicking him in the chest and making a run for it, but where to? She had no idea where she was, and in every direction, there was nothing but grey, nondescript buildings. She formulated a guess she was somewhere in the city's old harbour estate, such was the bland, anonymous landscape.

"Listen up, little one," snarled Rodriguez. "You and I are going to have to work together. You agree, and I get you out of here. You don't, and I'll leave you to rot on this plane. That's if the Priestess doesn't have other more interesting plans for you. I hear she likes her playthings." He jabbed a finger painfully into her clavicle to emphasise the point.

"Owwwww!" cried Meredith, clutching at the sore spot. Rodriguez raised his finger again. "Ok, ok, we'll do it your way. What do you want me to do, you big creep?"

"Much better," beamed Rodriguez. He straightened to his full, impressive height and held out a hand to Meredith, who reluctantly allowed to be pulled to her feet. "We are very shortly going to meet the crazy bitch you saw back at the wall. She runs this sad charade, calls herself The Priestess, thinks she's an apostle from God sent to prepare the way for the Second Coming. If only she knew the half of it." He shot another scathing look towards the driver who took the hint and climbed back into the van.

"She's crude but effective. The Colonel is quite taken by her, but he's a sucker for a pretty face. It will be the ruin of him one day."

"What any woman would see in a decrepit wreck like him is beyond me." Meredith expected a slap in the face for her insolence, but Rodriguez only guffawed a deeply unpleasant sound.

"Ha. Always have a smart answer, don't you, meu querido? But all I require when we court the Priestess is your silence. She thinks I am one of her Prophets, a messenger from God. And that's the way I want to keep it, so I'll be expecting you to keep that mouth of yours firmly shut. If you ever want to see your friends again, do I make myself clear?"

"Do I have any choice?" Meredith felt deflated, all out of options. The appearance of Rodriguez had knocked whatever fight was left out of her.

"None whatsoever."

"Then I'll play your game. For now."

Rodriguez threw his head back, and a thunderous laugh rolled across the deserted estate. "How I love your, how you say, pluck? You remind me of a young señorita I used to know back in my hometown. Before the British rolled in and I signed up."

"She had a lucky escape then," answered Meredith, unable to refrain from an opportunity to score points against her tormentor.

Rodriguez looked almost whimsical until he snorted derisively. "Just get in the back of the van. Or do I have to drag you there by the hair?"

Meredith's shoulders slumped. She meekly acceded to the instruction and climbed back into the rear of the van. Rodriguez leaned in and winked. "There's a good girl. See how easy it is when you do as you're told? I can tell you and I are going to get on very well now that we've established a few boundaries." He offered up a final wolfish grin before slamming the doors shut and plunging her into darkness. The van rattled into gear and started to bump and bounce to wherever their meeting with the Priestess was to take place.

Meredith sat down, cross-legged, and buried her face in her hands. Nobody heard her scream over the throb of the diesel engine. She was alone with her thoughts. Utterly alone.

Just as the first rampaging shiver coursed through her fragile frame.

CHAPTER 29 - JACK AND THE MAGIC SEED

Kirkwood opened his eyes, knowing the dice were there, even before his slumber coated vision adjusted to the dim light of Giro's room. Sitting on the desk just as they had sat on the desk of his little box room in Belfast. Calling him, goading him. They were back.

Two of them. No more, for that was all that was needed. The doorway to the 49 routines, which had blighted his existence for years. The chipped, dark blue four-sided die and it's more flamboyant, twenty-sided companion—two inseparable friends, hellbent on flattening his resistance and dragging him back to a hellish life governed by relentless compulsion. He realised he was coated in a sticky layer of sweat, nerve ends twitching as the first wave of unwanted thoughts crept effortlessly into his mind like a wisp of smoke floating across a previously unblemished sky.

Tommy gone, Meredith in a world of trouble, and now this.

Pick them up.

It was as simple, yet overwhelming, as that. Pick them up, feel their comforting coolness in his clammy hands. Roll them and perform the corresponding routine. Short term pain, long term gain. Perform the routine to the satisfaction of Skelly and watch the never-ending battery of shameful, disgusting thoughts vanish for another day. Experience a few hours of blessed tranquillity, time where he didn't have to avoid the news bulletins, knowing the latest tragedy was all his fault.

All his fault.

His hand reached out towards the dice. He watched, powerless, an unwelcome guest as his body betrayed him and reached for the deadbolt to allow the enemy to surge through and lay waste to what was left of his sanity.

"Don't do it." Giro's voice sliced through the darkness like a light sabre, severing the bond and snapping Kirkwood out of the mental malaise descending upon him. He peered beyond the dice to where the outline of Giro sat, until then a silent sentinel keeping watch over Kirkwood's body and soul.

"Giro. How long have you been awake? How did they get here?"

"I haven't slept, and I've no idea. All I saw was you reaching out, and there they were. But you're not going to pick them up, Kirkwood. I'm certain of that much."

Kirkwood swallowed hard, looking from the dice to Giro and back again to the two small orbs. "I have to. If I don't, stuff happens. People are going to die."

"No, they are not," replied Giro with surprising firmness. "This is Skelly seeking to control you through your weak spot, through the OCD. With Harley and Meredith gone, the Presence can no longer protect you from his advances. Which is where I come in."

Kirkwood sighed. "With the greatest respect, Giro, how are you going to stop him? How are you going to stop me?" He eyed the dice again, inanimate yet so tempting, so alluring.

"How do you feel?"

"What?"

"This very second. Tell me how you are feeling?"

Kirkwood paused before replying, struggling to verbalise emotions that had ruled his body for decades.

"Besides being worried sick about the girls? Grieving for Tommy? It's like there's this huge weight on my chest, an invisible anvil. Yet it's not solid, it's a dense ball of negative energy that races outwards, along my arms and legs. It sparks and fizzes, and I can't control it. The harder I try, the more it presses down, crushing me, consuming me."

"Consuming? Expand on that."

"What is this, an impromptu therapy session?"

Giro smiled, unseen by Kirkwood in the darkness. "Just humour me. This is important."

"Well. While the physical symptoms emanate from my chest, the anxiety, the worry, they all bounce around inside my head. It starts as a kernel, a seed, a thought flutters into my head and takes root. Then it just grows and grows and grows. Did you ever read Jack and the Beanstalk when you were a wee boy?"

"Yeah. Hasn't everyone?"

"Well, it's like that magic seed. It spirals and spreads, taking over my head. I can't focus on anything else, just the thought, over and over, an endless loop."

"That's the O in OCD, right?"

"Yup. It's everything. Nothing else matters. Work, family, friends. All logic and reason are washed away. That's when Skelly gets his claws locked into me. He's my gaoler, but he's the only person, if you can call him that, who holds the key, who offers relief. He's my tormentor and my saviour at the same time." Kirkwood groaned. "God, is any of this even making sense? I sound like a madman."

"Far from it," urged Giro gently. "Please, go on."

"That's when the dice come in, the '49.' When I'm at the breaking point. When I'm convinced the world is going to end and I'll have to live with the guilt and shame for the rest of my days. He offers me a way out, an escape."

"So, you roll the dice?"

"I roll the dice. I don't want to, I know what's coming, but I do it anyway. For anything is better than this monster rampaging through my brain. Like a drowning man clutching at straws, even if the straw is slick with poison."

"Samuel briefed me on the routines. They sound horrific."

"A man dying of thirst will crawl over hot coals for a sip of water. I'm desperate when the obsession takes hold, so I'll do anything—anything to be rid of it. It doesn't matter what I have to do. Run ten miles, charge up and down a street knocking doors, no matter how humiliating and embarrassing, I'll do it. Anything to quash the obsession."

"Which is what you want to do this very minute?"

Kirkwood paused before answering, his skin breaking out in goosebumps as if Skelly was dancing over his grave.

"Yes."

"And what will happen if you don't? What's the thought taking hold at the moment?"

Kirkwood clenched his eyes shut and gritted his teeth, fighting the growing urge to reach out, grasp the dice, and be taken to the Study. Anything to dispel the increasing anxiety which, at any moment, could explode into abject, utter panic. It took every ounce of self-control he had to reply, a fine film of sweat pooling on his upper lip.

"Meredith and Tommy. Harley and Emily. It's all because of me." He struggled to string the words together. "And the only way I can fix it is to perform a routine, comply with Skelly, maintain the status quo. Because if they die..." He stopped, the enormity of his present circumstances threatening to overwhelm him.

"You're not going back to that, Kirkwood. A rat doesn't deserve to live like that. But you *are* going back to the Study." Kirkwood looked on in amazement as his eyes adjusted to the poor lighting enough to capture Giro leaning forward and gathering up the two dice. The most unlikely member of the Forsaken fixed Kirkwood a determined look from under his bowl-cut fringe.

"Except this time, you're not going there alone."

"Incoming," a voice outside roared. Giro jumped to his feet before making towards the door. He stopped at the door and turned to face Kirkwood, who remained rooted to the spot.

"Come on. That's Deacon back. Your OCD will have to wait."

CHAPTER 30 - COLD TURKEY

By the time they reached the top of the escalator, Rodriguez was dragging her along. Meredith's legs were like water, her stomach wracked with cramps, which were increasing with disturbing frequency. A cold, oily sweat clung to her back, the cramps now accompanied by shivery spasms. Rodriguez grunted as he half led, half hauled her onto the mezzanine floor above the central concourse. Ahead of them, the Priestess sat atop her junkyard throne, a half dozen Maidens of Purity adorning the pallets at her feet. There was nobody else to be seen on the floor, although Rodriguez was confident the muscle was not far away if required.

"Remember, I'm your only way out of this, bambino," he warned, throwing her down at the base of the makeshift throne. "Your most Holy One," he simpered, accompanying the obsequious greeting with a theatrical bow. "I bring before you the interloper, the infidel who dared cross into your domain. As prophesied to you last night." He rose to his full height and folded two meaty forearms. One of the Maidens looked away, blushing furiously while a flutter of girlish giggles was exchanged amongst the others. Rodriguez smirked, well used to the attention of the opposite sex.

"Quiet," snapped the Priestess. "How dare you shame me before a prophet." The laughter stopped abruptly, and the Maidens collectively bowed their heads. Rodriguez turned his attention to the raven-haired woman on the throne.

"Indeed, Prophet. You have saved us once more from the Evil One's spies. We are indebted to you and our Lord. How may we repay your loyal service this time?"

Rodriguez opened his mouth to reply but was interrupted by Meredith emptying the watery contents of her stomach on the gleaming tiles by his feet. He frowned and inspected his boots for signs of vomit before speaking.

"I ask only that I have the pleasure of returning this one to where she came from. See how she cannot bear being in the presence of your perfection, most beautiful Priestess?" He nudged Meredith with the sole of his boot, sending her sprawling to the floor where she curled up into a tight ball, trembling and retching.

The Priestess allowed herself a twitch of a smile. "Evil cannot overcome good, that much is indeed true. But I, too, see a use for this wretch. Our monthly Communion is at dawn tomorrow, and I require one like her. Our Lord lay down his life and gave his blood and flesh on the Cross so that we could be cleansed of our sins."

Rodriguez inwardly groaned. If he had heard this deranged diatribe once, he had heard it a dozen times. The woman was quite mad. He maintained a poker face, though, giving nothing away of his contempt for the garbage spewing from her pretty lips.

"Yet the unworthy snubbed this ultimate sacrifice. They turned their backs on the truth and succumbed to the ways of this broken world. To leave us with this." She raised her hands, and on cue, murmurs of assent from the young women congregated at her feet resonated around the deserted mezzanine. The Priestess rested her chin on a cupped hand. "Tell me, Prophet. Why are you so interested in this one? Why should I consent to your wish when her blood and body could be given up for the atonement of us, the sinful and bereft?"

Rodriguez chose his words carefully, realising he was now on treacherous ground. One slip, one poorly constructed argument, and he would be returning to Skelly empty-handed. He could not afford another mistake, or the old man would have his head on a stick. That bitch Maura was skulking in the wings, waiting to capitalise on any further failure on his part. Losing the urchin at this delicate stage in proceedings would be unforgivable. It could signal the end of his rise through the Company's ranks.

"Look at her." He pointed at the sorry figure at his feet. "She is consumed by sin; her blood is impure and unworthy. Would you taint the souls of your believers with such foulness?" He paused to judge the reaction to his words, but the face atop the throne gave no indication as to how his argument was being received. "Let me remove the blemish that is her from this holy place. She is damned and must be punished, not rewarded for her misdemeanours."

"You hold the keys to hell, Prophet?"

"You know that I do, Priestess." Rodriguez sniffed an opportunity and forged ahead, keen to end the debate and seal the deal. "You have seen what I am capable of, the powers I have been granted by our Lord." He paused, allowing his words to settle unopposed. Was that a flicker of uncertainty crossing her normally icy exterior? Rodriguez clenched a fist by his side, for he had her.

"Very well," she replied, clearing her throat. For a second, she was exposed, vulnerable before the icy mask affixed itself again, and calm was restored. "Take her. I will not have New Jerusalem sullied by such filth. But I insist you stay with us and partake of the Communion. I would be honoured to have such a man of the Lord by my side for the event." An unspoken understanding passed between them, and Rodriguez broke into a trademark grin, shattering the tension. A ripple of laughter broke out again amongst the Maidens, and this time, their mistress allowed it.

"It would be my honour, my Priestess." Rodriguez bowed his head before addressing the source of his flattery with a sly smile. "And my pleasure."

She smiled back, a smile that held no joy or mirth, a smile fitting for the gallows. "Excellent. I'll expect you in my quarters before nightfall, where we can continue this conversation in more privacy." She rose from the throne, and the Maidens flocked to her side. From nowhere, two scruffy men appeared, both toting assault rifles. The Priestess turned to leave, her entourage behind her. "See to it that our guests are fed and watered. Until later, Prophet." Then she was gone, behind the throne, escorted by one of the men and her harem of young women. The other man gave Meredith a disgusted look before jerking his head for Rodriguez to follow them.

"My my, how the mighty have fallen," he sighed, bending down and effortlessly scooping her up and throwing her over his shoulder in a fireman's lift. Meredith's only response was a defeated grunt.

Rodriguez emitted a harsh laugh. "What's that? Cat got your tongue? Not so smart now, eh?" He proceeded to walk after the gun-toting guard back towards the inactive escalators. "But not to worry. Nothing a stiff drink won't fix." His laughter boomed around the complex as he strode down the escalator steps. Meredith could offer nothing in response as she drifted somewhere between consciousness and an unknown, darker place. For once, she agreed with the brute. Yes, she did need a drink. For the Presence was no longer there to protect her from a demon which had stalked her since Emily's death.

She needed a drink. So badly.

CHAPTER 31 - BAD NEWS DAY

Kirkwood and Giro were already waiting in the yard when the landrover roared through the gates, coming to a crunching halt beside them. An ashen-faced Deacon dismounted from the front passenger seat, rubbing his stubbled jaw in agitation.

"What happened?" Kirkwood searched the granite features of the old warrior for a glimmer of hope but was met with an expression that offered none. "Meredith. Is she?"

"It was a trap. Must have been. They planed in from the RV, I waited, but they didn't come back. Corbett," he barked to a passing soldier. "Get a drone up over NJ asap and find out what the hell is going on over there. I'll go in full-on if there's a chance we can get them back. Damn that bitch. We own this city, not her." Corbett nodded and hurried off towards the main building. When Deacon shouted *jump*, his soldiers responded *how high*.

Giro waited until his Commanding Officer unloaded his frustration before speaking. "Sir, certainly send the drone up, but I think I know what happened. And what's going to happen. If you would be so kind as to allow me to explain?"

"Tommy's gone, isn't he? He would have planed back otherwise."

"I'm sorry, sir. I can't sense him anymore."

"And the girl?"

"Somewhere in NJ. But I fear being held against her will."

"God damn it." Deacon pinched the bridge of his nose between thumb and forefinger. He gave a long, tired sigh before speaking next. "Is this the bit, Giro, where you hit me with a load of your cosmic mumbo jumbo, we argue for three hours, and I end up agreeing with everything you've said?" He looked at the techie in front of him, a hint of affection in his flinty eyes.

"Basically, sir, yes," smiled Giro, a twinkle in his own chocolate brown eyes. His charm was irresistible when adopting his best helpless expression.

"Very well," muttered Deacon. "Meet me in the briefing room in 60. I need some hot chow and a hotter shower." He trudged wearily towards the main building, a slight limp accentuated by heavy weariness. Kirkwood and Giro watched his slow progress across the yard.

"He really is a delightful man."

"His bark is worse than his bite, believe me," replied Giro. "He's hauled me out of hot water more times than I care to remember. He winked at Kirkwood. "I have a habit of getting into trouble. Occupational hazard."

"Tell me about it." Kirkwood tensed, another shiver running down his spine. He was now coated in a chilly sheen of sweat.

"How are you bearing up?" asked Giro, a concerned expression replacing his usual chirpy demeanour.

Kirkwood shrugged. "It's settled a bit since you took the dice from me, but he's still there, on the edges, hovering, waiting for an opportunity to drop a hand grenade into my head. It's taking all my willpower not to succumb. The guilt is eating me up. I can't help but think of Meredith, Harley, the others."

"He can't get to you as long as I keep my defences up," encouraged Giro. "Just hang in there until Deacon brings you up to speed, and then I'll reveal my plan. You're better than Skelly, Kirkwood. You can do this." He started to walk towards the main building and motioned for Kirkwood to join him.

"Is Meredith really still with us? Harley too?" Kirkwood needed a shard of hope to cling onto, no matter how small that might be.

"All I know is that they are still with us, unlike poor Tommy." He pushed open the emergency exit to the main building, the weight of the world seemingly on his shoulders. I've no idea where Emily and Harley are, but their energies are emitting strongly, and in unison, which suggests to me they are together."

"Well, that's something." Kirkwood struggled to keep abreast of Giro, who, despite his stout stature, was mounting the stairs like a gazelle. "And Meredith?"

Giro turned left on the first floor through a set of swinging double doors towards the mess. Kirkwood was rapidly learning food was never far from the thoughts of his rotund comrade.

"Oh, she's there. In New Jerusalem. But her energy is very faint. Barely more than a flicker and fading. It's crucial we get to her soon, if she's to have any hope."

"What's happened? Has she been hurt? Shot?"

Giro stopped outside the door to the mess. "Think, Kirkwood. When the three of you are separated, the Presence is diminished. Without it, Harley cannot walk, you cannot control your thoughts…"

"Oh, God." The answer struck Kirkwood like a wrecking ball tearing across his forehead. "The alcohol. She's going into withdrawal."

"Exactly. And if we don't get to her soon, she's going to be a gibbering mess. Putty in the hands of the Priestess or whoever else has got their claws into her."

"What do you mean, whoever else?" Kirkwood felt the hairs on the back of his neck rising as a fresh wave of panic coursed through him.

Giro removed his spectacles and nervously began cleaning them on the hem of his t-shirt before balancing them on the bridge of his nose again. "I didn't want to tell you this, but as well as sensing their energies, I've detected another darker presence, foreign to that part of the sector. A newcomer."

"A newcomer? What are you saying, Giro? Please, I need to know."

Giro pushed the door to the mess open and entered, followed by a frantic Kirkwood. He hadn't been particularly hungry to start with, but now food was the last thought on his mind. Giro grabbed two trays, handing one to him, before joining the line of weary soldiers queuing at the food hatch. Breakfast was being served, although the aromas filtering down the line were less than appetising.

"I'm afraid it's bad news, Kirkwood."

"Is there such a thing as good news anymore? If I didn't have bad luck, then I'd have none."

"The Company. They're here."

CHAPTER 32 - DRINKING TO FORGET

The door to the cramped storeroom opened, and the huge frame of Rodriguez filled it, blocking out the little light offered by the emergency lighting in the corridor outside. He bent onto one knee to study the shivering bundle in the corner. It took all her strength for Meredith to crack open an eyelid at his arrival.

"Here to brag, you big ugly ganch?"

Rodriguez smiled. "Ah, you're such a charmer, my dear. However, fond of you as I am, I'll admit I've seen you look better." He wrinkled his nose in disgust. "Have you been sick again?"

"Like you care." Meredith lacked the strength to partake in verbal jousting. "Why don't you just kill me now and be done with it? If this is all I have to look forward to, then I might as well be dead."

Rodriguez tutted in mock indignation. "You can be so theatrical at times, Miss Starc. You must have picked that up from your dead friend, the witch."

Meredith lunged for him with what little strength she had, wanting nothing more than to sink her fingers into his gloating eyes. She might as well have been trying to scale Everest. Rodriguez laughed as he wrapped his massive arms around her frame. He nuzzled her neck with his beard, before whispering in her ear.

"Good to see there's still a little fight left in you, urchin." He flung her roughly forward, and her cheek glanced off the hard wall, drawing blood. Meredith collapsed to her knees, winded. She had nothing left, nothing. If only she had a...

"Drink?" His voice was sly, dangerous yet enticing. She looked up to see him towering over her, a bottle in his outstretched hand. It was no peace offering, but she snatched it for peace of mind, or else her mind would be in pieces. Unscrewing the cap, Meredith guzzled greedily, all efforts to maintain her pride long since cast aside. The first deep mouthful caused her to wretch as the alcohol hit her empty stomach, yet she kept it down. The second mouthful, and the third, were easier as the familiar warmth began to spread through her tortured frame. She clutched the bottle protectively to her chest, dreading to make eye contact with her malignant benefactor.

"I'm sorry it's not your beloved Buckfast, but the wine cellar here offers more basic fare. Fermented potatoes, I believe, but looks like it's hitting the spot, nonetheless. I'm more of a dry Madeira man, myself, but each to their own. Beggars can't be choosers."

"Screw you, Rodriguez," screamed Meredith. She would have launched the bottle at him, were it not for its precious contents.

"Ha. How ungrateful. I bring you a gift, and this is how you thank me. Lucky for you, I have such a thick skin and forgiving nature. But it would serve you well to watch your tongue, my sweet Meredith. My patience is not limitless."

Meredith took a cautious sip from the bottle. She kept her mouth shut. She needed this bottle. Otherwise, her brittle body would shatter into a million pieces.

Rodriguez nodded. "Much better minha querida. That should get you through the night, but try to get some sleep, we have an early start tomorrow. The Priestess likes to hold Communion as the sun rises. She loves the spectacle, and we don't want to get on the wrong side of her."

He turned and left the storeroom, slamming the door behind. Meredith jumped, her nerve ends in tatters, as a key turned in the lock, leaving her alone, just her and the bottle. A lone tear tracked a meandering path down her grimy cheek. She wiped it away with the sleeve of her hooded top. Throwing her head back, she lifted the bottle to chapped lips and drank. Seeking nothing but temporary oblivion from the waking hell now dominating her every breath. This living death had no depths.

CHAPTER 33 - DESERT ISLAND FRY UP

Kirkwood prodded the greasy yolk of his fried egg and watched in horror as its turgid yellow contents spilled out, pooling around the lump of pink, processed meat that accompanied it on his plate. The yolk lapped against the meat like a toxic tide pummelling the rocks of the most unappealing desert island on Earth.

"In my day, this was called Spam. Nobody ate it, not even the students." He took a tentative bite from a slice of buttered toast and was relieved to discover that almost a century in passing hadn't significantly altered its taste and texture.

"You eat what you get in this dump and be grateful," grunted Deacon between mouthfuls of food. Head down, shovelling the breakfast into his mouth with all the finesse of a Ukrainian shot putter, he looked as downtrodden as ever despite allegedly having a shower.

"I've heard of this Spam you talk of," mused Giro, sipping from a glass of suspiciously cloudy water. "May contain traces of meat, right?"

"That's the one." Kirkwood smiled, even though his heart was aching. Much as he wanted to get the conversation round to rescuing

Meredith and the others, he was reluctant to come between Deacon and his meal. All around them, the mess hall bustled raucously as dozens of soldiers wolfed down their food, not knowing if it would be their last meal or not.

Finally, the cranky commander wiped the last of the yolk from his cracked plate with a slice of bread, before stuffing it into his mouth. He chewed noisily, smacking his lips together before a deafening belch signalled he was finished. Taking a considerable slug of bitter, lukewarm coffee, he began to talk.

"Okay, here's what we know. Thanks to the drone, we can confirm what Giro said. Your friend, Meredith, is alive. Our cameras picked her up being brought to the main complex, no doubt for an audience with that mad cow and her gang of ghouls."

"And Tommy?" asked Kirkwood tentatively.

Deacon paused, a deep sadness etched across his features. "He was a good man, but he knew the risks. He died a soldier's death."

Kirkwood bowed his head, words once more failing him. It was Giro who broke the silence, a hopeful voice amidst the desolation they all felt.

"We know where she is. What can we do, Major? Tommy wouldn't want us moping about feeling sorry for ourselves."

"You're right. I've had enough of this nonsense. We need to let that mad bitch across the river know I'm the sheriff of this town. I've given her a long leash for too long, and it's time to muzzle her. I'm proposing a raid tonight, two platoons with aerial cover. We go in hard, find your friend and back out quick. The Priestess won't know what's hit her skinny backside."

Giro coughed awkwardly and scratched an ear lobe, studiously avoiding eye contact with his Commanding Officer.

Deacon sighed and pushed back his chair in exasperation. "Okay, Giro. I get it. This is the bit where you completely disagree with me. Say your piece."

"Well, I wouldn't put it that way, sir. It's more..."

"Spit it out," growled Deacon, I'm in no mood for beating around the bush."

"It's an audacious plan. One cannot doubt your er...direct approach, but can I add a note of caution." He paused, expecting a volley of abuse from the older man, but Deacon only nodded for him to continue. Almost a year holed up with the bespectacled boffin had taught him Giro deserved to be heard when it came to strategies, given his unique set of skills.

"The Company are in there, sir. At least one of them, maybe more. Was the drone able to make out who was with Meredith when she was being taken to the complex?"

Deacon pulled a tatty notebook from the pocket of his fatigue trousers and flicked through several pages before arriving at the entry he was seeking. "Right, let's see. Two males, one driving. Front seat passenger escorted your friend into the complex. White male. Large build. Bearded. Dressed all in black. Scar on..."

"Rodriguez," shouted Kirkwood, earning stares from those seated at adjacent tables in the mess. "Giro, we've got to get her out of there. That guy's a lunatic. I..."

"Calm down, Kirkwood. Please." Giro raised his palms before turning to Deacon. "Major, if your intel is accurate, and I've no reason to doubt it, Meredith is with one of Skelly's most senior lieutenants. Sending your troops in there against the Priestess would be risky enough. With Rodriguez there, it's going to be a bloodbath."

"Fine," snapped Deacon, flinging the notebook onto the table in resignation. "What do you suggest then?"

"It's obvious Skelly is using Harley and Meredith as bartering chips. Otherwise, they'd be long dead. He's luring us in, it's a trap. And the prize he really seeks is sitting right here beside me."

"Me?" Kirkwood set down his mug of tea and stared incredulously at the two of them.

"Yes, you, Kirkwood. Skelly knows the power within the three of you when the Presence is activated. He saw that at Ardgallon when you closed the portal. Your plane is now closed to him. So, he must turn his attention elsewhere."

"He wants to claim this lump of dirt? He's welcome to it." Deacon downed the last of his coffee and pulled a face. "Rats teeth, this bilge doesn't get any easier to swallow."

"No, sir, this is merely a theatre of war for him, a stepping stone. He's thinking on a bigger scale."

"Another plane?" Kirkwood was struggling to keep up.

"Try planes. All the planes. If Skelly can harness the power of the Presence, then nothing will be able to stand in the path of the Scourge. They could lay waste to countless worlds and civilisations. You're the key to that, Kirkwood, the kingpin. He's using Meredith and the others to lure you in."

"So, what do you suggest? We just sit here on our hands and let the little runt get away with it?" Deacon's face was turning an alarming shade of puce, inaction not being part of his repertoire. "I'd rather die trying than do nothing."

"We'll do something alright, sir," replied Giro, leaning forward across the table, his face sparking with fierce intensity. "I want to crush them just as much as you do. The Scourge is a cancer, and Skelly needs stopped. And here's how we do it." He tossed the two polyhedral dice across the table towards Deacon. Kirkwood paled at the sight of them, and Giro placed a reassuring hand on his forearm. Fresh, unwanted thoughts bloomed into the young man's mind like rotten fruit dropping from the vine and splattering across his thinking.

"What, you want me to roll dice?" asked Deacon is disgust. "This isn't a game, Giro."

"Oh, but it is, Major. And this is how we're going to play it." He gave a knowing smile as Kirkwood shrunk further into himself, every bone in his body screaming to pick up the dice, roll, and be done with them. Anything to break free from the incessant, suffocating voice in his head.

You've killed Tommy.
You've killed them all.

CHAPTER 34 - OUTFLANKED

The cell door crashed open, and Maura stood facing them, the loathing in her eyes unmistakable. She burst into the room, without speaking, and grabbed Emily by the hair, pulling her along the floor towards the corridor. Emily screamed and began flailing and kicking out, her fists pummelling the legs of her assailant.

"Let me go, you bitch. Harley!"

Harley flung herself forward and clasped her friend's hand, momentarily halting Emily's slide towards the door. Maura stopped, twisting her hand and causing the ghost girl to wail in pain as the roots threatened to be ripped from her scalp.

"You let go of her now, or I'll break every knuckle on that hand." Her soft Irish brogue sat uneasily with the spiteful tone of her voice. She raised a heel towards Harley, indicating she was more than willing to carry out her threat.

Emily gave a slight, almost imperceptible shake of her head. "It's alright, Harley. I'll be fine. It will take more than this ginger hag to get the better of me." She was rewarded for her truculence by Maura tightening her grip on the knot of hair she had wrapped around her fist. Emily screamed a pitiful yelp that caused Harley to immediately release her grip of her friend's hand. "Where are you taking her? Don't you dare hurt her."

Maura laughed. "Don't worry, little one, I'll not hurt her. I have my orders." Her green eyes sparkled with malice. "Although nothing would give me more pleasure than to crush every bone in this tramp's miserable body."

"Charming, I love you too," sniped Emily, earning another tug on her hair, which reduced her to silence again.

"To answer your question, child, it's time you two spent a little time apart. Sharing a cell has served its purpose."

"What do you mean?" Harley would have given anything to launch herself at their tormentor, but her legs lay lifeless and unfeeling beneath her.

Maura rolled her eyes. "Do try and keep up, little one. Do you think we're stupid? We knew the minute you two were together, you would try and contact the others. Well, guess what, you succeeded. The cavalry has heard and is probably galloping over the hills towards you as we speak. Saint Kirkwood and his merry band."

Harley opened her mouth to respond, but the slightest shake of the head from Emily made her close it again.

"This was a setup?" Emily prodded at Maura's defences, eager to eke out the golden nugget that would give her the edge in this ongoing war of wits. Maura was powerful but overconfident, and the dead girl hedged her hopes on that cockiness being her undoing.

"You really are a bimbo, isn't that the word these days?" Maura relaxed her grip slightly, allowing Emily to twist onto her knees and make eye contact. "And don't give me those big sad eyes, it cuts no cloth here. The Colonel knew the second you two were together, you'd use what little power you possessed to send out a beacon. Which is exactly what he wants."

"What he wants?" Emily maintained the dumb demeanour as Harley looked on.

"Of course. When you become Three, you channel the most devastating force in the universe. Except you idiots haven't a clue how to harness it, to utilise the power to its full potential."

Suddenly the penny dropped. "You're luring Kirkwood and Meredith to us. It's a trap!"

Maura scoffed. "Duh. You two really were at the back of the queue when the brains were being dished out. Skelly was one of the most brilliant military strategists of his time. He could buy and sell you fools in the bat of an eyelid."

"Funny that. I don't remember any buying or selling on the bridge at Ardgallon," countered Harley, unable to resist the verbal bait dangling in front of her.

"Or at Waterloo," added Emily, earning a kick in the small of the back for her insolence.

"Silence," snarled Maura. "He should have been leading that army, not that coward Wellesley. Instead, he died in the mud a hero while the scum on that ridge earned the plaudits and promotions. I was there, I know." She realised her voice was rising and pulled back from the edge of exploding with anger. Emily sensed it was time to lower the temperature again if she was going to prise any more details from their flame-haired gaoler.

"Okay, cut to the chase, carrot top. Let's say Kirkwood and Meredith do fall for your lame trap, and Skelly gets the four of us under the same roof. What makes you think for a second any of us would give the evil old dog a smidgeon of the Presence? It's a force of purity, of goodness, not to be handed out willy nilly to every egomaniac who fancies a shiny new plaything."

"Never you worry your pretty little head, witch. The Colonel can be very persuasive when he needs to. Could charm the birds out of the trees."

"I'd rather die than let him use us." Harley met Maura's icy eyes and refused to flinch. "And the same goes for you, Emily, right?"

"Well, I'm already dead," pouted Emily. "But I appreciate the sentiment." She smiled, filling Harley's thumping heart with newfound courage.

"Enough of this prattle. On your feet, ghost girl. You're coming with me. I've a treat in store for you. This tower has many rooms, and I've just the one for you, my very special guest. She gave Emily's hair a final yank, pulling her upright and pushing her towards the door. "I'll bring you food and water later, cripple. Make the most of it, it's the last you'll get for a while." Affording Harley a final, vindictive stare, she closed the heavy wooden door behind her, condemning the terrified teenager to solitary confinement.

Harley sobbed silently, there was no point in crying out for there was nobody to hear her. Another massive explosion outside lit up the cell momentarily, reinforcing its cramped, dank confines. She curled into a ball as best she could and tried not to think, for thought was a rabbit hole which only led to despair.

CHAPTER 35 - TROJAN HORSE

"There's a time and a place for negotiations, and this isn't it." Deacon slammed the table, making the dice bounce before settling again. "If you go crawling cap in hand to the enemy now, it's only going to end in tears. We need to strike now, strike hard, and only consider talking when we have them where we want them. On the ropes with a bloody nose." He sat back and wrapped his hands around the back of his muscular neck. These civilians didn't have a clue when it came to strategy and tactics.

"I respectfully disagree, sir," Giro quietly replied. Kirkwood had to admire his tenacity. Others would have withered and backed down in the face of the surly old soldier's bluster, but Giro stuck to his guns. There was so much more to his new friend than met the eye. He unsuccessfully tried to avoid eye contact with the dice and the two numbers staring back at him.

"51."

"What?" snapped Deacon irritably, exposing Kirkwood to a glare that could have turned milk.

"A 3 and a 17. Routine 51." Kirkwood nodded at the dice, where the two numbers stared benignly back at them. "Just a bad memory, that's all."

"What in the name of all that is sacred is a 51?" Deacon fought the urge to storm out of the mess, jump in the first armoured vehicle he could find, and rumble through the front gates of New Jerusalem, letting his assault rifle do the talking. That's all the mad bitch understood, 450 rounds a minute, not this convoluted claptrap.

"You don't want to know, Major, believe me, you don't want to know. Please, tell me I don't have to do a 51, Giro?" Kirkwood was prepared to crawl over hot coals to save the girls, but the thought of the monster of all routines blanched his soul.

"No, Kirkwood. But you do need to roll the dice and perform the corresponding routine," replied Giro, swiftly picking up the dice and depositing them in a pocket, out of sight from the troubled young man sitting beside him. "It's the only way we can access the Study."

"Why in the name of good whiskey would you do such a thing?" asked Deacon incredulously. "That's playing straight into their hands. We need to regain the initiative."

"This *is* regaining the initiative, sir," replied Giro, removing his glasses and polishing them studiously on a stained handkerchief produced from nowhere. "Skelly wants Kirkwood, Meredith, and Harley for his own sick purposes. He covets the power they possess when together."

"This magic hocus pocus does my head in," rumbled Deacon.

"It's called, The Presence," Kirkwood quietly corrected.

"Past. Present. Future. Whatever. The only presence I trust is this." He patted the rifle by his side, affording it a look which verged on affection, or as affectionate as such a crusty campaigner like him would ever allow.

"You're a military man, Major. You know your history, the strategies, and tactics of the great commanders."

"All I know is pedal to the metal and never back down. Got me through three tours of Greenland. Don't see no point in changing now."

"Greenland?" Kirkwood was utterly lost now.

"Oil," explained Giro with a sigh. "It's a long and bloody story. I'll explain it another time." He turned his attention back to Deacon, sitting across the table. The mess was starting to empty out now as slightly less irritable soldiers returned to their duties with full bellies. "You've heard of the Trojan Horse, haven't you, sir?"

"Of course, I have," snapped Deacon. "Just cut to the chase, Giro. You're lucky I like you, or you would have been out of that window ten minutes ago with your endless riddles." He gestured over his shoulder to one of the grimy, grilled windows which lined the far wall of the mess. The little light they permitted suggested another equally grimy day in Hellfast.

"Well, that's exactly what I'm proposing we do here. Perseus offered up the horse as a gift to allow his troops to infiltrate the city. Then when they got inside... BAM." He slapped the table, causing Kirkwood to jump as Deacon threw another volley of daggers at the little Napoleon in their midst. A second later, the glower turned to a grin as the logic dawned on him.

"I get it now," he roared, causing the few remaining squaddies to eye him fearfully before collecting their belongings and beating a hasty exit from the mess. Everyone at Queen Street knew you didn't want to be in the vicinity when Deacon raised his voice. "Covert ops. Infiltrate and execute. Damn it, man, we'll make a soldier of you yet."

Giro returned his smile. "Not quite as brutal as that, sir, but you have the gist of it. Skelly wants to harness the Presence for his own purposes. Colleagues of mine are currently working hard to ascertain what those are, but as of yet, are making little progress. Skelly has his defences well and truly up. The only way we are going to find out what he wants is to deliver it in person wrapped up in a shiny bow." He placed a hand on Kirkwood's shoulder, remarkably pleased with his plan.

"Should I whinny or something?" muttered Kirkwood, his voice utterly devoid of humour. "For I'm guessing I'm the horse in question."

Giro extended his arm around the young man's shoulder. "I'm sorry, my friend, but it's the only way. We call Skelly's bluff, lay our cards on the table, and work out what he has up his sleeve. It's the only way we are going to see your companions again."

Kirkwood looked from Giro to a stern-faced Deacon and back again. He sighed in resignation, took a long slug of his now cold tea, and made his decision.

"Okay, Giro, let's do this."

CHAPTER 36 - THE GRAVEDIGGER

Samuel opened the front door of the cluttered cemetery gatehouse he called home and threw his jacket over the back of the battered armchair. Stuffing and springs protruded from several sections of it. He had sat on more comfortable barbed wire fences, but it had been Dobson's perch of choice whenever he called, demanding several bowls of Samuel's trademark broth, before launching into strategic debates which often left the younger man gasping at the tactical acumen of the old tramp. His first meeting with Cornelius Dobson taught him never to judge a book by its cover, a maxim which had served him well in the years to follow.

Samuel cleared a space on the workbench, a conglomeration of gardening equipment, and various other tools. Several bolts and a multi-coloured spool of wire fell to the floor. He kicked them under the bench before positioning his large frame, perched on its edge like an overgrown gnome.

"So, Cornelius, what would you do now?" He ran his hands through his greasy, unkempt mullet and squeezed both eyes shut. To any onlooker, he was a tired gravedigger, exhausted after another long day working the soil with shovel and barrow. His tiredness was more mental than physical, though. Indeed, he welcomed the fresh air and hard physical labour that the afternoon had provided, for it afforded the gentle giant an opportunity to process incomprehensible amounts of information at blinding speed. Although on the surface, he appeared a lumbering, slow-witted oaf, he had an IQ of 378. Nowhere near the levels of Dobson and his peers but nonetheless well above average for those of his kind.

The game was moving faster now, almost too fast for him to keep track of. Yet, he had to, for the mantle of responsibility lay heavily on his broad shoulders now that his old friend and mentor was no more. What would Dobson do? *What would Dobson do* was the only question that spun around his head like a figure skater on ice. He was finally grasping an understanding of the mental affliction which dogged young Kirkwood. The endless, torturous mental loop that never showed any sign of easing.

"What would you do, Cornelius?" He spoke the words aloud, half hoping the old tramp would respond, a voice from beyond the grave. Not that a grave was his final resting place, the Drummer Boy had put paid to that on the bridge. Samuel felt the raw anger which had dogged him since that day, rising within, and fought to push it back deep within his core. This was no time for rash action. He had learnt that, if nothing else, from Dobson. He could no longer afford to be a hothead. It had cost him his first life on that other bridge at the hands of the English. Almost 800 years ago now, but he could still taste the sharp, metallic rush of blood in his mouth as the sword breached his defences.

He tensed. It was time to sit down properly, a communication was coming through, and he needed to fully concentrate, no time for wistful daydreaming. He pushed his large frame off the bench and flexed his neck until rewarded with a satisfying crack. Sitting down in the busted armchair, he felt a welcome calm descend on him as if the old man was standing there, smiling and nodding, those mischievous eyes twinkling from within crumpled features. What mysteries and mayhem lay behind those eyes?

Samuel set his shoulders against the back of the chair and rested both palms against his tree-trunk thighs. "Go ahead."

To anyone present in the room, silence would have followed, but Samuel smiled and nodded, encouraged by the friendly, familiar face which formed in his mind's eye. He was reassured he still had so many good colleagues around him.

"It's good to hear from you again, friend. I, too, mourn at the passing of Tommy. He died a second death becoming of one of our kind. With honour and courage. He is no longer Forsaken." Samuel bowed his head, as if in prayer, and mouthed a few additional words which were for his ears only. When he raised it again, his eyes blazed with focused fury.

"Now, tell me of your plan, Giro."

CHAPTER 37 - COMMUNION OF BLOOD

"Wakey, wakey sleepy head. We have a big day ahead." The voice, and accompanying kick, roused Meredith from unconsciousness as opposed to restful sleep. She opened an eye to be greeted by a grinning Rodriguez standing over her. At the door, a heavy-set skinhead stared at her, a stocky revolver in one gloved fist. The hazy light within the room indicated it was morning. By her feet sat the bottle, her new best friend that had nursed her through the night. An inch of precious alcohol remained, and Meredith instinctively lunged for it, desperate to ward off the crippling hangover lurking just around the corner.

Rodriguez was too quick, squatting to lift it beyond her despairing reach. "Now, now," he tutted. "That's no way to start the day. We have a busy schedule ahead, and clear heads are required. I should be sticking your head in a bucket of water as opposed to letting you drink this poison." He held the bottle enticingly in front of her, watching as her tortured eyes took in the only relief to the living hell she was presently enduring.

"Never let it be said that I'm not a compassionate man, however. I always allowed the lads a double measure of rum on the day of a battle. Steadies the nerves, so I guess I could afford you the same luxury." He held the bottle towards her, then snatched it away before Meredith could lay hands on it. She groaned as her fingers grazed the glass. She needed it so badly, so badly, it overwhelmed the shame and guilt of her pathetic plight.

"Give it to me, you bastard," she screamed, the effort exhausting her. Tears began to track along both cheeks. The skinhead took a step into the room until a shake of the head from Rodriguez returned him to his original position. Meredith knew from his cruel expression he would think nothing of emptying the contents of his revolver into her body.

"Temper, temper," chastised Rodriguez, waggling the bottle at her. "What did I say last night?" He leaned in and gently brushed a lock of hair behind Meredith's ear before whispering so the watching skinhead could not hear. "We have an uneasy alliance with the Priestess, and our passage from this plane is by no means guaranteed. She is an unstable woman at the best of times, and it would not take much for you or me to outstay our welcome. Now, do you understand?" The sinister inflection convinced Meredith this was not the time for further histrionics. She nodded once before her attention was again consumed by the sweet, sweet alcohol held inches from her parched lips. Just one slug, to ease the mounting nausea swirling in the pit of her stomach.

"Please. I'll be good. Please." She almost choked on the words, as the last remnants of dignity surrendered to the lure of the liquor. If there was such a thing as rock bottom, Meredith Starc had just checked in for the foreseeable future.

Rodriguez smiled, like a proud father who had just watched his child walk across the room unaided for the first time. "Much better." He handed the bottle to Meredith, who raised it to her lips, gulping down the last dregs of the foul concoction. She gagged and covered her mouth, willing her reluctant body not to expel the poison onto the boots of her adversary. Squeezing both eyes so tightly shut, she thought they would burst, the sickness passed to be replaced by the warm glow of the alcohol seeping through her dry, aching body.

"Come on. Up on your feet. We are awaited." Rodriguez placed a meaty hand under the crook of Meredith's elbow and brought her to her feet in one seamless motion. She tottered unsteadily as the room spun around her at an alarming rate. "Just give me a minute, alright?" she muttered, the ongoing battle between gravity and her stomach contents continuing to rage inside.

"She's waiting," growled the skinhead, indicating with his handgun that he was in no mood for further delays. He turned and strode down a drab corridor, intermittently lit by flickering fluorescent tubes set in the ceiling. Rodriguez released his grip on her and swept an arm towards the door. "After you, little one."

"Where are you taking me?" slurred Meredith, the alcohol hitting hard now. She felt a serene calm settling on the jagged shards of panic previously cutting her apart. Was she walking to her freedom or death? Part of her didn't care anymore as a quickening realisation that she would never see her friends again took hold.

"Holy Communion." Rodriguez nudged her in the back as the guard halted up ahead of them to ensure they were following.

Meredith stumbled forward, simultaneously trying to stay upright while formulating the next question in her foggy mind.

"We're going to church?"

"Yes. Although it's not a form of church you or I will be accustomed to."

"What do you mean? I never did church. Full of interfering busybodies and sanctimonious hypocrites." She was surprised at the venomous tone of her voice. Where did that come from?

Up ahead, a rectangle of light burst onto her fragile eyelids, causing her to blink sharply and raise an arm to shield her face. The guard held the door open for them, and Meredith caught the waft of a bracing breeze, a welcome relief after the stuffy confines of the previous night. Her eyes slowly adjusted to the change in conditions as she slowly lowered her arm again, taking in her new surroundings. Behind her, Rodriguez stood, feet planted, an impassive expression on his rugged complexion.

"Welcome to heaven," he whispered in her ear. "Or hell. Depends what way you want to look at it."

They stood on a large expanse of waste ground, bordered by the stretch of water formerly known as Belfast Lough. Once, it had been a busy ferry route, but there were no vessels to be seen now. On both sides were congregated hundreds of stern faces, all focused on her. Meredith sensed the animosity resonating from the Red in waves. Fear and anger directed towards the stranger who had dared violate their most holy of sanctuaries. They were herded on either side by at least two dozen gun-toting guards, all with their backs to her and Rodriguez, scanning the crowd for the slightest hint of insurrection.

"What is this?" She risked a look over her shoulder at her captor, who merely nodded in front of them. Meredith followed his gaze as the crowd parted to reveal the Priestess walking through their midst, flanked on either side by several Maidens of Purity, their long flowing dresses juxtaposing sharply with her tight-fitting black jeans and t-shirt. In her left hand, she casually carried a wicked blade, two feet in length, with an ivory handle. The Maidens parted to reveal a flatbed truck reversing slowly behind them, it's hazard lights flashing. The absurdity of the driver adhering to road safety regulations within such a chaotic setting was not lost on Meredith.

"I need another drink," she commented drily. She was unaware of the smallest of smirks her words earned from Rodriguez.

The Priestess spoke, her voice loud and clear, carrying across the waste ground so everyone could hear. "My people. We gather again, as is our custom, to worship our most Holy Master. To thank him for delivering us from the hell of what was, what is, and what is yet to come."

"We thank him." The throng spoke as one, a choreographed monotone chant that earned them a sly smile from their leader. This chick loved the attention, thought Meredith. She would have given the Ashgrove selfie queens a run for their money back in the day.

"He died for us, he bled for us, he was broken for us, yet rose again to prepare for the time when he would come again." She paused, revelling in her adoring audience before continuing. "We are part of that preparation. We, his chosen people, for the time is here, the time is now."

"The time is now," they chanted as one, blank-eyed and bedraggled. As Promised Lands went, this wasn't a great advertisement. Meredith craned her neck to make out what was happening behind the Priestess. The truck driver had dismounted and was opening its rear doors. Another group of men were struggling with a cumbersome object, which they dragged slowly towards the van. Whatever they were up to, it was no doubt all part of this barmy pantomime she was being forced to endure.

"This land of theirs has been reduced to ruin as part of the coming vengeance. A just and pure vengeance, where all shall be judged. For centuries these fools have walked the crooked path, blinded by the ways of this tainted Earth. They have watered down the truth, ignored the one true way, the only way to salvation and eternal life, the ultimate prize that shall be ours."

"It shall be ours, it shall be ours."

Meredith closely watched the manic glee in her eyes as the Priestess built towards a shuddering climax. "She's good, I'll give her that. I could see her ending up on Coronation Street, or one of the other soaps." Her light-hearted words dripped with utter contempt for the woman in front of her, who now raised her hands and voice to the captivated audience.

"We have fought for many years to establish a foothold in this broken world, and are now being rewarded for our obedience. We have paid for it with our flesh and blood, our tears, and screams. But fear not, for it has not been in vain. He has listened and is coming soon to wreak a mighty vengeance on our enemies."

"He is coming, He is coming."

"Oh, please," sighed Meredith earning a sharp jab in the back from Rodriguez for her acidic aside.

"Be quiet. You want to get out of here in one piece, don't you?"

"I want another bottle of whatever it was you gave me last night, that's what I want." Meredith was aware The Priestess was talking again and sought to concentrate, her mind foggy, a muddled mire of fear and need.

"We cannot be complacent, my people, we cannot rest on our laurels. This is the time when we must redouble our efforts, work harder than ever before for the coming glory. No more wine. No more bread. He demands sacrifice. He demands more. We give him flesh and blood."

With a perfectly timed, theatrical flourish, she stood back to reveal the roller doors being flung upwards by a henchman. Meredith's mouth dropped open, and even Rodriguez puffed out his cheeks.

"Oh, God. No. Tommy."

Suspended by his heels from a hook attached to the roof of the van hung the body of Tommy, his arms hanging limply down. The Priestess swept her gaze around her fanatical followers and smiled serenely like butter wouldn't melt in her mouth. She allowed herself to be lifted into the back of the truck by two guards, her petite frame as light as a feather to them. Turning to face her audience as they edged towards the rear of the truck, she held the blade before them.

"My people, the veil shall be torn. The light will burst through. I promise you this by the blood of our sacrifice."

She turned and, in one graceful motion, raised the blade with both hands to her shoulders before bringing it forward, slicing across the throat of the dead man. There was a split second of terrible silence before the crowd roared in approval, and the blood began to trickle onto the floor of the truck, ruby red and viscous. An industrial metal bucket was produced from somewhere and placed beneath the bloody waterfall, collecting the thick, heavy flow. The Priestess looked on. A smug, self-satisfied leer on her face as the bucket filled to the roars of an audience verging on frenzy. Meredith could take no more and turned to flee, anywhere, just to get away from the abominable charade being played out in front of her. She was prevented from doing so by Rodriguez, his colossal biceps enveloping her within a cavernous embrace.

"I'm afraid I can't allow that to happen, little one." His voice verged on pity, if she hadn't known better. "I'm afraid this is only the curtain-raiser. The main act is yet to follow." He grabbed her chin roughly, forcing Meredith to meet his gaze.

"What do you mean?" she asked, desperately searching his eyes for some reprieve from the madness swirling all around. The bloodlust of the crowd was a deafening din, as the two of them stood within its eye, the most unlikely of allies.

"I'll get you that drink, but first, The Priestess insists upon our company at her table."

"Her table?"

"Yes. We must partake of her Communion." He allowed Meredith to turn, his hands on her shoulders, as The Priestess raised the full bucket to the adoring horde. She laughed loudly before lowering her full lips to it and drinking deeply. The crowd surged forward hysterically to the foot of the truck, only some roughshod tactics from the guards stopping them from mobbing their leader. She lowered the bucket and beamed, the blood staining her teeth and flowing freely down her chin. Bewitching, beautiful, utterly deranged.

"My people," she roared, her voice at its very limits. "We dine."

CHAPTER 38 - ROUTINE 33

The two little orbs bounced across the Formica table, followed by three sets of pensive eyes. Kirkwood inhaled, reluctant to breathe out again until they settled and sealed his fate, one way or another. It seemed an eternity as the surrounding drama and emotion were sucked irrevocably into the dice and their journey across the flat surface. Eventually, they came to rest, revealing the two numbers which would determine the next hour of his life.

Three and eleven.

"Thirty-three." Kirkwood exhaled loudly, placing his palms on the table. "That's a blast from the past."

"What the hell are you talking about?" Deacon's patience was being sorely tested by first Giro's vagaries and now this childish game. Time was ticking on, there were lives at stake, and they were currently getting nowhere fast.

"It's the number of the routine Kirkwood has to perform, sir," explained Giro, doing all in his power to rein in the explosive temper of his Commanding Officer. "What's it to be then, Kirkwood?" he added, turning to face the young man who sat beside him, a wry smile on his face.

"I haven't attempted this one in over a year," Kirkwood replied, scratching his messy mop of dark brown hair.

"Well, spit it out, boy," snapped Deacon, any pretence at tolerance rapidly dissolving.

"It's an eating routine," Kirkwood replied sheepishly. "I'm afraid I'm going to have to diminish the compound's rations somewhat."

Deacon threw his hands up despairingly. "Sure, knock yourself out. You're lucky I like you." Giro chuckled and pushed his chair back. "To the kitchen then, Kirkwood. You can explain when we get there."

Deacon led them out of the mess and down the corridor for a short distance before pushing open swing doors to reveal the bustle and clatter of the kitchen area, where half a dozen men were busy scrubbing pots, chopping vegetables, and preparing for the next hungry shift to descend upon them. A couple looked up to see who their visitors were, but once they clocked eyes on Deacon, redoubled their efforts.

"Okay, what do you need?" enquired Deacon, casting a hand around the kitchen. "You're in luck. We had a supply drop last week. It's not haute cuisine, but nobody starves on this base, that right team?" The kitchen staff answered "Sir" as one, before continuing with their allotted tasks.

"Biscuits," replied Kirkwood, his face a study in deadpan.

"I beg your pardon," spluttered Deacon. Even Giro raised an eyebrow at the request.

"I need biscuits," reiterated Kirkwood. "It doesn't matter what type, so long as there's plenty of them. Oh, and a glass of water, please."

Deacon scratched his chin before nodding at a subordinate who scurried off into the bowels of the kitchen. Cupboard doors could be heard opening and utensils clattering before he returned, clutching a battered metal tin to his chest.

"I'm sorry, but this is all we have, sir," he stammered, tentatively holding the tin out to the veteran. "Cook makes them himself on base. Nothing special, just plain oatmeal, but they taste alright dunked in a mug of tea." He stood awkwardly, shifting from foot to foot before Deacon dismissed him with a wave of the hand. He handed the tin to Kirkwood, sighing loudly as he did so.

"Would you care to explain the routine, Kirkwood?" asked Giro, keen to defuse the tension before Deacon exploded in exasperation.

"Yeah," replied Kirkwood, opening the tin and anxiously peering inside. "Routine 33. I need to consume ten biscuits in one minute, swallowed whole, in order to successfully complete the routine. Fail to do so, and I am permitted to retry again after a further minute has passed. This process will continue until the routine has been successfully completed."

"Are you kidding me?" blurted Deacon, unable to contain himself any longer. "There are lives at stake here, entire civilisations according to you two, and we are having a cookie eating contest?" His face had turned a peculiar shade of purple, and his eyes bulged like a constipated frog.

"Sir, please," reasoned Giro. "It's the only way, bizarre as it may seem. Kirkwood has Obsessive Compulsive Disorder. It manifests itself in a series of unwanted, intrusive thoughts. At the moment, he is convinced he is to blame for everything that has befallen him and his friends."

"All I can think of is I've killed Tommy. And Meredith and Harley are next". He lifted a dry, unappealing oval biscuit from the tin and eyed it dourly. "The only way to get rid of that thought is to eat ten of these in a minute."

"I've heard some strange tales, but this one well and truly takes the..."

"Biscuit," replied Kirkwood and Giro in unison before descending into fits of giggles. Try as he might, Deacon could not keep a straight face and chuckled deeply, earning astonished looks from the kitchen staff.

"Alright, alright, very funny," he said after several minutes, wiping a tear from his eye. "You eat the biscuits, then what? Puke up in a bucket? Pull a rabbit out of that tin?"

"It's how I connect with Skelly," replied Kirkwood, beating Giro to the verbal punch. "He can summon me at any time to his lair. It's called the Study. But the only time I can go there of my own accord is after I complete a routine. Not that I do very often. It's the last place on Earth, or wherever the hell it is, I want to go."

"But you can do it?" probed Giro, keen to ensure his plan was viable.

"Yes, I've done it in the past. To beg him to leave me be, to let me live a normal life. Fat lot of use that was. In the end, I stopped trying.

He summons me now and again, mostly to gloat at my expense, but for years I just plodded along with the routines. It almost became normal. I was too embarrassed to talk to anyone about it."

"I get that," nodded Giro. "I truly do. And I know the Study is probably the last place you want to go right now. But it's the only way we can find out what Skelly is up to. We have to front up to him. Sir, can you do the honours?"

"Eh?"

"Time Kirkwood. Oh, and have some water on standby."

Deacon nodded, and the three of them were soon standing by a worktop in the kitchen, ten oatmeal biscuits lined up in a line beside a glass of milky looking water. Kirkwood eyed it dubiously.

"Ready, sir?" said Giro, his voice strained and unusually serious.

"Ready." Deacon stood poised, his thumb and forefinger hovering over a battered watch on his left wrist. "Say the word, biscuit boy, and I'll start my stopwatch."

"Okay." Kirkwood flexed his arms once, before raising the biscuit to his mouth. The anxiety levels within threatened to overcome him, and his hand began to tremble, his legs wobbling beneath him. This was it, back on the OCD wagon.

"Go!"

The next sixty seconds were a cavalcade of flying crumbs and curses as Kirkwood crammed the dry biscuits into his mouth as fast as he possibly could while trying to simultaneously chew and swallow without choking. He stopped once to take a deep slug of water before returning to his task, eyes streaming and egged on by Giro and Deacon. On the verge of vomiting, he forced the last gooey mouthful down and slammed his fist on the worktop in triumph, before expectantly looking towards the surly timekeeper in front of him.

"Well?"

"64.2 seconds. Sorry, buddy."

Kirkwood hung his head before descending into a fit of hacking coughs. Giro stood sympathetically by him, a fresh glass of water in hand, until his friend recovered sufficiently to speak.

"Give me another few minutes, and I'll go again." He took the proffered glass and drained its contents in one gulp. His jaw ached, and his stomach registered its reluctance to continue with an alarmingly distended grumble. Kirkwood picked at his back molars with a forefinger where a mulch of partially masticated food remained.

"We've fifteen of these left," said Deacon, peering into the tin. "Do you want me to get the cook working on a fresh batch?"

"We don't have time," replied Giro, a little more sharply than he intended, causing Deacon to glare at him. "Sorry, sir, but I'm sensing negative energies from New Jerusalem. It's hard to specify, but whatever's going on over there at the minute, isn't good. We have to act now."

"I'm fine, I'm fine," insisted Kirkwood, flexing his jaw and wiping a trickle of sweat away, which threatened to overrun the defences of his left eyebrow. "I'm about to projectile vomit while having a full-blown mental breakdown, but I'm fine. Show me the biscuits."

The second routine was as frantic as the first. The kitchen staff gave up all pretence at working, their fascination at unfolding events negating their fear of their Commanding Officer.

"Thirty seconds," urged Deacon, alternating his eyes between the stopwatch and Kirkwood.

"Mmmmfffppppptttt."

"Come on, Kirkwood. You're over halfway. Do you need a drink?" Giro waved the glass in front of Kirkwood, who gestured in the negative. He reached for the tin, grabbed the remaining four biscuits, and forced them into his already bulging mouth. Bent over double, he rested both palms on his knees, eyes clenched tight, jaws working furiously to complete the routine within the allotted time.

"Fifteen."

Finally, he relented and signalled for the glass, which Giro promptly thrust into his outstretched hand.

"Ten."

Standing upright and tipping his head back, he guzzled the water like a thirsty marathon runner. Handing the empty receptacle back to Giro, Kirkwood continued to chew the residual mush in his mouth, desperately summoning the willpower to swallow.

"Five."

It wasn't happening. There was still too much, he was going to choke on it.

"Four"

There were no more biscuits. This was it.

"Three"

Harley...

"Two"

Emily…

"One."

Meredith…

Deacon clicked the button on his watch and looked up to see Kirkwood pointing frantically at his open mouth. His open, empty mouth. The kitchen hands broke into spontaneous applause, and even the old campaigner was forced to nod his head in appreciation.

"Fifty-nine seconds dead. Well I'll be, that's some serious chowing."

"Man v Food ain't got nothing on me," crowed Kirkwood.

Giro grabbed his arms, and the two danced a jig around the kitchen, oblivious to the bemused looks of the gathered military personnel.

"So, what now, Superman?" trilled Giro spinning wildly, his spectacles threatening to soar into orbit at any moment.

"What do you mean, *what now*?" replied Kirkwood. Giro started to slow, suddenly aware of the sombre tone in his friend's voice. Maybe the human merry-go-round wasn't such a good idea. Kirkwood had just consumed twenty biscuits, after all.

"When do we go visit that ancient freak, Skelly? Show him who's boss."

"Er…how about now?"

Giro realised Kirkwood had let go of his hands. He spun around to discover he was no longer in the kitchen at the Queen Street compound and found himself staring at a roaring fire set within a grandiose fireplace. Beside it sat the hunched figure of a balding man with spectacularly bad teeth. He knew they were bad as their decayed, yellowing finery was being exposed to him in a leering grin. The old man spoke, a velvet voice dripping with ill intent. Giro already knew where he was and who he was facing.

"Ah, you must be Giro," beamed Colonel Augustus Skelly. "Delighted to meet you. Welcome to my humble abode."

CHAPTER 39 - WINE TIME

Meredith allowed herself to be manhandled by Rodriguez towards the complex entrance. All around them, the crowd buzzed with anticipation, worked to a near frenzy by the words of the Priestess. Their eyes glistened with manic intensity, spurred on by the promise of fresh blood and a new world order in which they all would hold high office.

"Deluded religious freaks," slurred Meredith. "I can't do this, I can't." She shuddered at the image of the Priestess' stained lips, the blood of Tommy coating them. She would rather die than partake of this sick charade.

"You can and you will," whispered Rodriguez as they entered the complex and turned right, carried along by the human tide of acolytes, surrounded by gun-toting muscle. "You do want to see your friends again, don't you?"

Meredith groaned miserably as they passed through more doors into an oval arena, flanked by banks of seating on all sides. She recognised it, having attended concerts and ice hockey matches at the venue back when law and order held sway. The main floor was now filled by several long rows of tables, which stretched the length of the arena. The throng began to seat themselves as Rodriguez guided her towards a raised table at the far end.

"Come on, we are guests of honour. We get to sit at the top table."

Meredith looked up to see several young women, all dressed identically in flowing, white dresses busying themselves, setting the table. The clatter of plates and cutlery filled the huge space along with the squeak of chairs being pushed back and the excited chatter of several thousand people filing in. If she closed her eyes and knew no better, she could have been at a wedding reception or formal dinner, rather than the freak show of the century.

"You sit next to me and don't say a word, understand?" Rodriguez deposited Meredith on a plastic chair, reminiscent of her school days. Sitting beside her, Rodriguez smirked at two maidens, giggling as they set their spaces. Catching Meredith staring at him in disgust, he shrugged his shoulders, winking at the young women with a sleazy grin.

"What can I say? I'm their Prophet, they love me."

"You know, Rodriguez, there are times I almost warm to you before remembering what a complete and utter scumbag you are."

"Likewise, little one, likewise." The Portuguese giant leaned in closer before speaking again. "I don't expect you to be a fully signed up member of my fan club, but I do expect you to play along if we are to get out of here in one piece. Our hostess can be a touch unpredictable at times. We wouldn't be the first guests to end up with our heads being served up as the main course."

"Main course? What? They…"

"Let's just say they are getting their money's worth out of your Forsaken friend. He's providing the starter, main course and dessert on this menu."

Meredith paled as Rodriguez nodded knowingly and gestured towards the far end of the hall where four maidens were moving through the tables, distributing large wooden jugs. The volume increased as the revellers began to pour from them.

"Is that what I think it is?" asked Meredith, knowing she didn't want to hear the answer.

"Si. Lucky for you, it's not agreeable with my palate either." He clicked his fingers, and an auburn-haired Maiden appeared from behind them, brandishing a jug.

"Rodriguez, I can't, I just can't." The panic rose in Meredith's gut as the white-robed girl, who looked no more than sixteen, filled their glasses before placing her hand on the shoulder of Rodriguez and smiling shyly.

"Obrigado querida. Thank you." He placed a hand on Meredith's thigh beneath the table. "Relax, it's wine. And there's plenty more where that came from if you'll only keep calm and allow me to handle this. Fortunately for you, I've been here many times before and can call in a few favours." He raised his glass and tipped it towards a startled Meredith before taking a mouthful. "You see, ordinary wine. Not so dissimilar from your beloved Buckfast, non?"

He nodded towards Meredith's glass, and she slowly raised it to her nose, inhaling the familiar musty smell. Her eyes fixed on a smiling Rodriguez as she chanced a tiny sip, before sighing with relief and draining the remainder with a mixture of revulsion and relief.

No sooner had she set the glass down than the teenage Maiden was at her side, refilling it.

"Thank you," whispered Meredith. The girl bowed timidly before withdrawing sharply. Meredith followed her frightened expression as the Priestess paraded through the hall towards them, accepting the platitudes of her followers who raucously raised their glasses, roaring approval of their leader. She locked her snide gaze on Meredith some distance away and maintained it as she swept towards the front of the hall, her lithe frame gliding through the mass like a bloody knife through butter. Arriving at their table, she smiled and nodded towards Rodriguez.

"I hope my hospitality is to your liking, Prophet?"

"It is, Mistress," answered Rodriguez. "We are not worthy of this holy blood but accept it with gratitude. We are hopeless sinners in sore need of its cleansing properties."

"Indeed. None more so than this wretched soul." She looked Meredith up and down, causing the young woman to squirm uncomfortably in her seat. Part of her wanted to flee screaming from the hall rather than spend one more second under the sadistic spotlight of this clearly insane witch. But to do so would blow everything and any hope she had of escaping this sanatorium to be reunited with her friends. Trusting Rodriguez was a forlorn hope, but it was her only one at present.

"Well, speak child, are you a sinner? Do you desire the cleansing blood of righteousness?"

"I am," mumbled Meredith, lowering her head and taking a further sip. "Mistress." *Please don't let her twig it's wine*, she pleaded inwardly. Every fibre screaming that she was on the verge of being found out and gutted like poor Tommy.

The Priestess gave Meredith a final lingering look as if making an internal decision, before addressing Rodriguez again. "Are you sure you won't let me keep this one, Prophet? I bore easily and am in need of a new plaything." Her eyes twinkled with dark malice. "I've no doubt she could be transformed into a most virtuous Maiden under my careful tuition." She turned and winked at Meredith, whose blood turned to slush.

"Alas, Priestess, but this one is beyond even your pastoral care. I must return with her as she is destined for the flames." He frowned and bowed his head, as if in prayer while kicking Meredith's ankle at the same time, a silent warning that she play along. She bowed her head, suitably chastised and submissive.

"Such a shame, but so be it. Can I not persuade you to remain for the breaking of the bread?" If she noticed Meredith flinching at the words, then she chose to ignore her.

"We are honoured, Priestess, but alas, I must return to my Maker. There is much work yet to be completed in preparation for His return. Now, if you would excuse us, I bid you farewell until my next visit. I thank you as ever for your faithful obedience. You will be blessed abundantly in the New Age." He rose and stooped to caress her proffered hand with his lips. Grabbing the forearm of Meredith, he hauled her to her feet.

"Guards, escort the Prophet and his wench to the Wall." She shot one last lascivious look at Meredith before turning and walking back through the arena, flanked by a gaggle of Maidens.

"Does she really believe the utter drivel she's spouting?" Meredith could barely keep up as Rodriguez ate up the ground with his loping stride. They left the arena via an emergency exit onto what was once a car park, two guards keeping a respectful distance behind them.

"Every word of it. She's a madwoman but a devious, dangerous one at that. She serves a purpose for us on this plane, so we need to keep on the right side of her. And I'm just as susceptible to one of her bullets as your friend Tommy was. Now keep walking. We have people waiting to see us."

"Who?" Meredith was half jogging now as the graffiti coloured wall where Tommy met his end loomed in front of them. The guards stopped, unwilling to accompany them any farther, onto what they regarded as holy ground.

Rodriguez turned and clasped Meredith's hand. "All in good time, pequeno, all in good time. Thank you, gentlemen, that will be all." The guards shouldered their rifles and started to amble back towards the complex. Rodriguez held an oversized hand out towards Meredith.

"Time to depart this wretched plane, my dear. Shall we?"

CHAPTER 40 - STUDY STRATEGISTS

Skelly soaked up every drop of the heavy silence which descended upon the Study. Apart from the crackling of logs in the unnatural fireplace, there was no noise, as he and his newly arrived visitors eyed up one another. He licked his lips, savouring the waves of anxiety emanating from Kirkwood. This was nectar to Skelly, watching the young man squirm as he had so many times down the years. The smaller, bespectacled man was a different proposition, though. Calm, determined, no fear in his aura. He would break him, though, they all yielded eventually.

He unfolded his legs and stretched, oozing malignant charm. "Could I interest you in a drink, gentlemen?" He pointed towards the ever-present decanter on the table by his side. "It's New Jerusalem. 2099. A fine year I'm led to believe." He smirked at the look of horror, which took hold of Kirkwood, who remained rooted to the spot, eyes locked on the dark red liquid in the decanter. Giro merely wrinkled his nose in distaste, refusing to bite and rise to Skelly's bait.

Skelly shrugged, feigning hurt at their lack of interest in his offer. "Please yourselves. Now, let's get down to business. To what do I owe the pleasure of this most unexpected visit?" His upper lip curled, the suggestion of a snarl belying his pretence at hospitality.

"We thought it best we cut through the crap and lay our cards on the table," replied Giro, his voice relaxed and steady. "Our victory at Ardgallon obviously ruffled your feathers, and I'm sure it's not done any wonders for your career prospects." He paused, scanning Skelly's face for a clue as to whether he had scored a point against his wily adversary but was only greeted with a gruff laugh.

"Pah. A mere skirmish. The battle lines have yet to be drawn. If you for a second think that was a setback, then you are sadly mistaken. And from where I'm sitting, I'd say I have the upper hand now, don't you?"

"Where are they?" blurted Kirkwood, no longer able to contain his emotions. "What have you done with them?"

"Ah, Kirkwood, you speak. I thought you were sulking with me. So good to see you again, my dear boy. I've missed our little chats."

"I'll ask you one more time, you piece of dirt. Meredith. Harley. Emily. Where are they?"

"Oh, don't be so dramatic," tutted Skelly, folding his arms. "They're perfectly safe and well. Geneva Convention and all that, what type of animal do you take me for?"

"I think it best we don't answer that question in the interests of diplomacy." Giro's gaze never wavered for an instance.

"Touché," sneered Skelly. "Dobson taught you well. Pity he's not about anymore to reap the benefits."

"I could say the same about Gunther," shot back Kirkwood.

Skelly exploded with laughter, clapping his hands in delight. "My, my we are on form today, chaps. Splendid stuff. But let's get down to business. You have come to me under the white flag of parley and have my word I will honour that."

"As if that means anything," spat Kirkwood.

Skelly continued, choosing to ignore the latest jibe. "I have something that you need, or rather two young ladies, whom I'm sure you would like returned safe and sound. That can be arranged, all I ask for is a small favour in return."

"What sort of favour?" asked Giro, his curiosity piqued.

"Now, that's more like it. No point us being at loggerheads unnecessarily. As you know, our little disagreement at Ardgallon means the portal to your plane was closed to my employers. Let's just say they found that development a tad tiresome."

"You must be madder than even I took you for if you think we are going to reopen the portal and allow those monsters to kill billions of innocent people." Kirkwood made to step towards his tormentor, but as ever, when he visited the Study, his feet were welded to the spot.

"Oh, come, Kirkwood, I'm not a complete fool. I'm fully aware your little coven won't grant me that wish. What I ask for is a much more modest proposal."

"Go on," said Giro, glancing at Kirkwood to ensure he kept his powder dry.

"Your plane is but one of many we are interested in. You're a very small fish in a very large pond, Kirkwood Scott. If you were to be exposed to the full extent of the war being waged across the planes, then I fear your tiny brain would leak from your nostrils."

"Charming as ever." Kirkwood bit hard on his lower lip, wanting nothing more than to pummel Skelly to a pulp.

"17/4."

"What?"

"It's a plane, Kirkwood," explained Giro. "An unnamed and unoccupied plane. It's the fourth plane on the seventeenth circle from your Earth. What of it, Skelly? It's been utterly insignificant up to now. What possible interest do you have in it?"

"A staging post, nothing more and nothing less. It's a backwater, but we need a base from where we can conduct operations in the outer orbits. You know very well, Giro, that if you choose not to assist, we will simply find another way to claim it. This way just allows us to cut a few corners."

"We shouldn't give them an inch, Giro. I wouldn't trust him as far as I could throw him. Which isn't very far, the lump of lard that he is."

"Who's the charmer now?" beamed Skelly, oblivious to the abuse.

"He's right, though," said Giro. "This war has raged for millennia and will rage for countless more. We're only a small part of the bigger picture, a piece of a massive jigsaw, if that makes it easier for you to understand. 17/4 could be something, it could be nothing, it's a risk but one I'm willing to take to get your friends back."

"Exactly. It's refreshing to meet a fellow strategist," smarmed Skelly. "We are both fighting a long war here. You're not naive enough to imagine, Kirkwood, that Cornelius and I didn't come to such amicable arrangements before. No matter how vicious the conflict, a good general will always keep his communication channels open with the enemy."

"Samuel's good with this," encouraged Giro.

"Samuel? How does he...?"

"I can traverse the time/space continuum at will, Kirkwood. A little bit of telepathy isn't beyond me." Giro gave his young friend a tight smile. "It's your call, Kirkwood, your friends. I can only advise you."

"Okay, okay." Kirkwood massaged his temples and gathered his thoughts. "Let's just say I do agree to this. It could be the worst decision of my life, but let's just say I do. What I don't get is why you even need our help in the first place. If it's an unoccupied plane, then why don't you just steamroller in like you normally do?"

"Ah, well, there's the thing," replied Skelly, scratching an ear like a mischievous schoolboy caught playing truant. "17/4 has attracted a few unwelcome visitors of late."

CHAPTER 41 - CHANGE OF PLAN

Meredith stared at the graffiti coloured wall and blinked, before turning to look at a perplexed Rodriguez by her side.

"Well, that didn't go as I hoped."

"Why haven't we planed, you muppet? I thought this was one of the many strings in your big-headed bow?"

"It was...is. Something must be blocking us. It's..."

The click of a weapon being cocked interrupted their conversation. They turned cautiously to see half a dozen guards with their weapons trained on them. Two of the guards stepped aside to reveal a smiling Priestess, two Maidens flanking her. Meredith recognised one of them as the young, auburn-haired girl who had served her wine in the arena. The girl, head bowed, clearly wasn't enjoying the unfolding events.

"Change of plan, Prophet," purred the Priestess. "I've been thinking, maybe it's time I found a partner to share the responsibility of running this place. A throne can be a lonely place, and I desire company. I've prayed and fasted over this matter for some months, and the Lord spoke recently to me. He has chosen you to reign with me."

Meredith stared at her open-mouthed. "Are you for real?"

Rodriguez placed a calming hand on her arm before clearing his throat. "Much as I'm flattered, I fear you are mistaken. I am required elsewhere and can assure you, my master requires me to return to Him."

"Do you not desire me, Prophet? You have partaken of my Maidens. Am I to think I am beneath them in your favour?" She was toying with him, but every word was a potential land mine, given her hair-trigger temperament.

"Your beauty is breathtaking, these Maidens are nothing when compared with your majesty." Rodriguez studiously avoided eye contact with the other Maiden, older with blonde hair, who was glaring daggers at him. Meredith rolled her eyes. This ghost soldier couldn't keep it in his trousers. The industrial strength wine coursing through her veins provided the Dutch courage for her to step forward.

"Look, I don't know who you think you are, but dressing up like a reject from a Metallica video and brainwashing a load of starving, desperate people doesn't impress me. Nor does murdering my friend, imprisoning me, and then forcing me to drink his blood. So why don't you turn around and trot back to your temple of doom before I put my boot so far up your backside you'll be..."

"Excuse the wretch," blustered Rodriguez. "She will be punished severely for daring to besmirch your holy name. Let me take her to the eternal fire where she will burn for her transgressions."

The Priestess stepped forward, her eyes burning a hole in Meredith's forehead. She cupped her captive's chin in a bony hand, long nails digging into the younger woman's flesh. "Do you take me for a fool, girl? All I need to do is click my fingers, and your body will be riddled with bullets. Or perhaps you would prefer to go the way of your colleague? It would give me no pleasure, but I will slice open that pretty little throat of yours if I have to."

She released her grip, throwing Meredith's head back. Turning to Rodriguez, she stroked his beard, before running her hand down his wide chest. "Consider yourself mine now, my love. What is mine is yours. And before you even think about using one of your formidable powers on my people, know that you cannot. You are not the only one blessed with grace from above. She tapped his chest with her forefinger, and his sizeable frame was propelled through the air, slamming into the wall with such force that Rodriguez was unconscious before he ricocheted off onto the ground. A cloud of dust and debris encased his still form.

"Rodriguez," screamed Meredith. She took a step towards him but was hauled backwards by a guard who twisted her arm behind her back at an unnatural angle. Meredith groaned with pain, earning a harsh peal of laughter from the Priestess.

"Relax, child. You are spared the fire. I like your spirit. I see much of myself in you before I was chosen. Tara, Seren. Take her to your quarters and prepare her for me. I have transformed such waifs before and do so enjoy a challenge. Consider yourself blessed, child, and welcome to your new home."

Meredith sobbed, a broken, guttural sound as she was pushed forward by the guard towards the two Maidens. The younger girl reached out her hand. "Come with me," she said, her voice barely audible. "If you want to live, do exactly as you're told and don't say a word." She nodded at the other blonde-haired Maiden. "Come, Seren, we must ready our new sister for the mistress. Seren stared coldly at Meredith before taking her other hand.

Meredith allowed herself to be led away, numb with disbelief. She was farther away from her friends than ever, and even the uneasy alliance formed with Skelly's henchman was dead in the water. She had never felt so alone.

CHAPTER 42 - AN UNEASY ALLIANCE

"There was a little incident on your plane the other day. You probably won't have been aware of it, what with saving the universe and all that. Frontpage news everywhere, though." Skelly tapped the neatly folded broadsheet on the table by his armchair.

"What do you mean by *incident?*" asked Kirkwood cautiously.

"A little explosion. Well, a massive bomb to be honest. Some maniac planning to blow up a university. Frightful business."

"God, were there many people hurt?"

"Thankfully, no," gushed Skelly, reeking with insincerity. "The bomber was intercepted, and disaster averted. And by intercepted, I mean, he ended up on 17/4."

"You're kidding me. Does nobody actually die these days?" He looked at Giro, who could only shrug.

"Ah, death. Such a misunderstood subject." Skelly stroked a bushy sideburn thoughtfully. "There are many variations of it, some more finite than others. Anyway, this chap and his friends are proving to be a rather unwelcome distraction to our plans to occupy the plane."

"Friends?"

"Well, not so much friends. You see, crazy bomber chap was stopped by two gutsy young ladies. Seems they spiralled off this mortal coil with him. Now, all three are occupying 17/4 and refusing to budge, causing a bit of a logistical nightmare for my employers. Blocked up the portal, you know how it is."

"How on Earth did they end up on this 17/4? And how come your employers, as you so charmingly refer to them, can't simply reduce them to three little piles of dust?"

"You're not the only one with powers, young Kirkwood. Yes, only a select few can harness that blasted Presence on your plane, but there are others who possess special abilities. Turns out these three do and have formed their own version of it on 17/4. We need them removed and thought they might be more amenable to listening to others of their own kind. Deploying the Company would be a frightfully messy business, akin to using a sledgehammer to crack a nut."

"I can't believe I'm agreeing to work for you," sighed Kirkwood. "Okay, prove you're serious. Show me Harley and Emily. And what about Meredith? I can't do this on my own."

"Meredith will be joining us soon. I can assure you Rodriguez is taking very good care of her. As for the others..." Skelly clapped his weathered hands, and from nowhere, Maura strode into the Study, carrying an inert Harley over her shoulder.

"You? You're that bitch from my mum's house."

"Lovely to see you as well, lover boy," scoffed Maura. "Here's your little friend." She unceremoniously dumped the teenager at Kirkwood's feet, where she scuttled into a terrified ball. Kirkwood gave Skelly a pleading look.

"Oh, very well," sighed his ancient adversary. "You may move, but any funny business and I'll fling you in that fire." Kirkwood strained forward and found he could move his feet. He fell onto the opulent carpet and wrapped his arms around Harley. She huddled into him, her normally clear eyes, red-rimmed and bloodshot.

"Kirkwood. I'm sorry. I shouldn't have run off like that. This is all my fault. We should have stayed together."

"Shush, you eejit. It's alright. I wish I had an ounce of your bravery."

Giro knelt beside them, also free of the paralysis which Skelly inflicted upon all his guests. "Hi Harley, I'm Giro," he said kindly, smiling at the bedraggled young girl. "Love your hair."

"Thanks, I think." She looked towards Kirkwood for direction.

"It's okay, he's one of the good guys."

"You should be able to stand again, Harley, now that you and Kirkwood are together again."

Harley nervously flexed her legs and gasped before allowing Kirkwood to help her to her feet. He smiled at her. "Good as new, kid," and was rewarded with a bear hug, which almost knocked him off his feet.

"Oh, for the love of God, sir," groaned Maura. "Can't I just snap their miserable necks and be done with?"

Giro took a step towards her, his normally mild-mannered demeanour nowhere to be seen. "You touch a hair on their heads, camp follower, and I'll make sure your second death is even more unpleasant than the first."

"Children, children," pleaded Skelly, raising his voice to be heard. "This isn't getting us anywhere. Now, can we please return to the matters at hand. Maura, where's the witch? They need three for this to work."

"Emily?" Kirkwood felt his heart soar in his chest.

"At your service, kind sir." They turned as one to see Emily standing behind them. She performed a deep curtsey, daintily pinching the hems of her flimsy chiffon dress between thumb and forefinger.

Without any forethought, Harley launched herself at the platinum-haired girl. Kirkwood stood awkwardly by, not sure whether a hug was appropriate. Emily resolved his dilemma by playfully punching him on the shoulder. "Hey, Kirky, miss me?"

"Like a hole in the head. And you know fine well it's Kirkwood."

Skelly coughed, and they turned as one to see that Maura stood behind his armchair, her hand resting on the old man's shoulder. "If we've quite finished with the adorable patter, it's time to get down to work."

"Does this make us besties then, Augustus?" Emily stepped forward and folded her arms across her chest, her words dripping with sarcastic defiance.

Skelly leaned forward to meet the challenge, and Kirkwood noticed Maura's knuckles whiten as she tightened her grip on the back of the armchair. "Let me make myself quite clear," the old man hissed. "This is but a temporary arrangement. The war continues, and I won't rest until I'm drinking your blood from my glass as I watch your sorry little planet burn." His eyes glowed red with the reflection of the fire as its flames leapt and danced in concert with Skelly's words.

There was an ominous silence in the room before Harley spoke.

"Well, you can't get much clearer than that."

CHAPTER 43 - MEREDITH THE MAIDEN

Meredith closed her eyes, allowing the hot water to caress her head and body. She couldn't remember when she last showered, and despite the horrific circumstances, was grateful for the opportunity to avail of it. She stood alone in the shower block, an array of soaps and shampoos on the ledge in front of her. Lathering her tatty dark locks, she watched as the dirt that had encased her swirled down the plughole at her feet.

"Another couple of minutes and we need to go." Tara's voice disturbed her blissful solitude from the changing rooms outside, echoing around this otherwise empty part of the complex. They were directly beneath the arena, and Meredith surmised this was where the city's ice hockey team, the Giants, had once prepared for matches. She recalled her parents bringing her to a match once when she was no more than eight years old. She remembered the pizza slices, overpriced drinks, and an irrational fear she was going to be struck by a stray hockey puck despite the protective netting between the ice and crowd.

"Coming," replied Meredith, allowing the piping hot water to wash away the lather before reaching for a towel from an adjacent rail. Quickly wrapping herself in it, she stepped out to where Tara sat waiting. Meredith sensed a kindness emanating from the younger girl, a rarity in the New Jerusalem she had experienced so far. Her eyes hinted at great sadness, but also a quiet determination to survive, whatever the cost.

Tara nodded, pleased at what she saw. "There, that's much better. You don't look like you've been dragged through a hedge backwards now." Her accent was rural, certainly not from the city. Meredith wondered what her story was as she accepted a second towel and began to dry her hair.

"When we're done here, I'll take you to our quarters. Maidens have their own rooms, but because you're new, you'll share with me for the first few weeks."

"What have they done with Rodriguez?" While no fan of the oily thug, Meredith realised he was her only ticket out of this madhouse, the only way she would ever see her friends again.

"He will be in the private chambers of the Priestess. Don't worry, he's perfectly safe." Her eyes flickered with uncertainty. "Well, for now, anyway."

"For now?" Meredith sensed alarm bells ringing.

"So long as he pleases our mistress, he has nothing to fear. It's only if he causes problems..." She left the sentence unfinished, no words required to infer what disobedience to her leader would result in.

"And me? What happens to me?" Meredith bent over, wrapping the towel round her head, not sure she wanted to hear the answer. She needed as much information as possible, though, if she was going to formulate an escape plan. She was on her own now, no longer able to rely on Rodriguez. She had survived the best part of a year on the streets of Belfast, and she could survive this. All she needed was time to get her bearings and think.

"You might not agree with me, but you're incredibly fortunate," said Tara. "For whatever reason, our mistress has chosen to spare you. You are a Maiden now—there are only twelve of us. Well, thirteen now."

"Unlucky for me."

"No," exclaimed Tara, wide-eyed with fear as she warily scanned the changing room. "And be careful with your words. She has eyes and ears everywhere within the complex. You wouldn't be the first Maiden beaten to a pulp for insolence."

Meredith considered a pithy reply but bit her tongue and chose a different tack. She needed Tara on her side, and scaring the living daylights out of the young girl was not going to achieve that.

"Understood. And, thank you. For taking me under your wing."

Tara smiled shyly. "You're welcome. Although it's not as if I had a lot of say in the matter. Now put these on." She thrust a bundle of clothes into Meredith's still wet hands then coyly turned her back, allowing her privacy to change. It was a simple yet touching gesture, and Meredith found herself warming to her young mentor, another victim in this brutal, predatory world.

She changed quickly. Modest underwear, flat shoes, and a dowdy white dress, which made her feel like a cross between Miss Havisham from Great Expectations and an Amish grandmother. The coarse fabric itched against her skin, but otherwise, it was warm and comfortable. She coughed awkwardly when finished, and Tara turned, a broad grin adorning her delicate features.

"My, that's an improvement. How do you feel?"

"Ridiculous."

Tara tittered. "Meredith, what did I tell you about choosing your words carefully? Now, come along, I'll show you to our quarters." She turned and set off at a brisk pace, out of the changing area and along a series of identical-looking corridors, until they burst through another emergency exit door into daylight. The sun was manfully trying to break through a blanket of cloud lying low over the city. In the distance, a muffled explosion could be heard, followed by the rattle of automatic gunfire.

"Dirties," said Tara by way of explanation, crinkling her nose in disgust. "There but for the grace of God go I." They headed away from the arena along the side of the river through what had once been the city's Titanic Quarter, a Mecca for camera-toting tourists. To their left, half-submerged and riddled with rust, lay the SS Nomadic, the tender ship which had conveyed passengers to the Titanic before its one and only fateful voyage.

"Were you one of them?"

"Oh, no, I'm a country girl, from County Fermanagh. Or Sector 7 as they call it now. When they found the gold, things went downhill fast after that. We were starving, so my parents decided to risk it and head for Belfast. We were told there was a kinder regime up there where we would be safe. How wrong were we?"

"What happened?" asked Meredith. They were now heading towards the remains of the Titanic Museum, its angular structure jutting into the sky, imitating the prow of the great vessel itself. One side of it lay open, the building having caved in on itself.

"We managed to find refuge in a tower block at the back of Castle Court, but the SS raided it one night looking for troublemakers. They didn't really care who they took out—fired all round them.

"SS?"

"Security Solutions. My father was shot in the neck. I watched him bleed to death in my mother's arms, there was nothing we could do."

Meredith stopped. "Oh, my God, Tara, I'm so sorry. I know what it's like to lose a loved one suddenly." Tara nodded as a rough-looking, rake-thin man sporting a purple Mohican sped past on a scrambler bike, a rifle slung over his shoulder.

"It's alright," the younger girl replied sadly. "Mum and I got separated in the stampede from the flats. It was bedlam. I haven't seen her since. I've no idea how I survived, but I made my way across the river and ended up here. The Priestess has many faults, I'm not blind, but she took me in, fed me, clothed me. I've a lot to thank her for."

Meredith again chose to say nothing, allowing her fellow Maiden to reveal further layers of her story.

"She chooses us on a whim. We tend to all her needs: cooking, washing, cleaning, whatever is required. In return, we are well looked after and protected by her guards. This is us." She pointed at a red brick building to the side of the more modern museum, formerly a plush hotel that catered to visitors to the area. An armed guard at the main entrance grunted an acknowledgment, paying particular attention to the new Maiden, before stepping aside to allow them access to a deserted foyer.

"Urgggh," shuddered Meredith. "Those guys give me the creeps. That guard virtually undressed me. Did you see him? How do you put up with that every day?"

Tara shrugged. "Some of the girls are more...accommodating towards their approaches than others. It earns them extra benefits and privileges. The Priestess turns a blind eye as long as they are discrete. She also has her...favourites." She looked down, the mask slipping to reveal a deep melancholy.

Meredith could contain herself no longer, turning to confront Tara. "That's outrageous. You mean she presents you as vestal virgins, yet all along...she allows...she's?" Words failed her, a rare event, and she could only blurt out, "The hypocrisy is staggering. I've a good mind to..."

"Everything alright in there, ladies?" The guard poked his head through the door, a quizzical expression on his face.

"Yes, thank you. Meredith was just excited about her new dwelling place." The guard gave her a long, unconvinced stare before returning to his sentry duties outside. "You have to keep quiet, Meredith. Please."

"Fine, but it's disgusting."

"That may be, but from here on you will curb that temper, if you know what's good for you. I'll help you all I can, I truly will, but if you don't play the game, then you're not going to last very long around here. Come on, we have a master bedroom on the next floor."

She swivelled and started to ascend a sweeping staircase that wrapped itself around the rear of the foyer area on either side.

Meredith watched her ascend, weighing up her limited options, before rolling her eyes and following.

"Every cloud has a silver lining, I guess."

CHAPTER 44 - 17/4

The three of them stood facing one another, hands entwined. Beyond them, Giro paced anxiously, issuing instructions he had repeated at least three times since Skelly informed them of their mission less than an hour ago.

"I'll plane you in, and then it's over to you. Hopefully, these folks are reasonable, and we can talk to them, but if you have to, the Presence can be deployed in any way you see fit. We can't mess around here, it's the only way we're going to get Meredith and return you guys to your own time."

Kirkwood nodded. "Us Northern Irish are renowned for our tact and diplomacy. I'm sure we'll all get on like a house on fire." He hoped he sounded convincing, but the dejected look on Harley's face suggested otherwise.

"Are you okay, Harls?" asked Emily softly, squeezing the rainbow-haired girl's hand. "You can do this. Remember the bridge."

"Yeah, but look at the mess I made of things in Omagh."

"Can you spare me the post-mortem and get this over and done with." Maura entered the gloomy hallway they were congregated in. None of them had any idea of how they came to be there. One minute they were being lectured by Skelly in the Study, the next they were in this new section of the Tower.

"Who died and made you boss, ginger?" sniggered Emily, never missing an opportunity to goad the opposition.

"I represent the Colonel, which *makes* me boss, witch. Remember him? The one who drove you to slit your pretty little wrists in that bathtub. Tut, Tut, such a mess you left for your mother."

"Bitch," spat Emily.

"Ditto," replied Maura, a fake smile plastered across her face.

"Quit it, Emily, she's not worth it," urged Kirkwood. "The sooner we end this crappy arrangement and get back to killing each other, the better. Hurling catty insults isn't going to achieve anything."

Under the arctic glare of Maura, Emily snorted and flicked her hair back. "Okay, Giro, work your magic." The three of them took a step forward, tightening their circle while Giro closed his eyes, his face a mask of concentration. Kirkwood braced himself for the tell-tale sensation and didn't have long to wait as he was thrown upwards as if through a fireworks display on a clear November evening. A plethora of pinks and purples popped and fizzed past him at frightening speed. He felt Emily and Harley's grips tighten but could not see them as he reached the zenith of the ascent and started to plummet downwards, his stomach several seconds behind the rest of his body.

Then nothing.

He risked opening an eye to find himself in a familiar setting—rolling verdant lawns sweeping as far as he could see in all directions.

As before, the young woman with the blonde pixie hair cut was eyeing him wearily from a wooden bench.

"Took your time."

Kirkwood became aware of Emily and Harley beside him. Letting go of their hands, he took a cautious step towards the girl, her outrageous pink ballgown billowing in the balmy, gentle breeze.

"Last time, when I was here, how did you know my name?"

The girl flattened out her gown, picking a fleck of lint from it, before flicking it to the ground. She sighed. "Now, I've only been playing this game for a day or so, but your reputation precedes you. Kirkwood Scott and the mighty Presence. I see Emily, I see adorable little Harley. Hi, beautiful."

"Hi," replied Harley, raising a hand in greeting before a venomous look from Emily made her drop it again.

"Hi," replied the pink vision in front of them. "I'm Tess. Tess Cartwright. I think I'm dead."

Kirkwood arched an eyebrow. "Think you're dead?"

"Yeah. Now, isn't there someone missing. Megan...Madison?"

"Meredith, it's Meredith. Don't you concern yourself about her. I'm more interested in how you got to be..." Kirkwood held out a hand towards the endless green expanse, but further words eluded him.

"Here?" offered Tess helpfully. "I haven't a clue. I mean, one minute I was wrestling with that psychopath Adam and the next...voila." She spun on a pair of gleaming white, chunky trainers, performing a perfect pirouette.

"Adam? Who the frig is he?" Harley shot Emily a confused look, the ghost girl strangely quiet as she eyed up this new addition to their ranks.

"Oh, God, right, sorry. You guys have been a little preoccupied of late, haven't caught the news, I guess. Okay, quick history lesson. Does the Monksbridge Massacre ring any bells? Big terrorist bomb? Loads of people killed?"

"Everybody knows about Monksbridge. It was the town next to mine growing up. Biggest bomb in the history of the Troubles."

"Well, then you'll know the bomber, Declan O'Sullivan, was also killed in the explosion when the bomb detonated prematurely."

"Serves him bloody right," piped Harley. "All those poor innocent people. There were little toddlers killed and hurt by that maniac."

"Well, if you've heard of them, then you'll have heard of Bomb Girl."

Emily finally spoke. "The baby born on the day of the explosion. Her mother wheeled her out every anniversary. It was a bit of a pity party after a few years. Didn't the woman have all sorts of mental health problems?"

"She did and ended up in a psychiatric ward. By some miracle, though, her daughter turned out alright. Ariana Hennessy. Studied hard, got to university, became my best friend. Had a lot going for her."

"Modest little thing, aren't you?" sniped Emily.

Tess smiled sweetly before continuing. The clash of the alpha females was warming up nicely, thought Kirkwood with a wry smile.

"Well, they say the apple doesn't fall far from the tree, and that was certainly the case with Declan O'Sullivan's little boy, Adam."

"This guy Adam tried to blow you and Ariana Hennessy up? You're kidding." Kirkwood didn't like the way this puzzle was falling into place.

"Oh, just us and the entire campus. Thankfully, I got to them in time after he tried to wipe my memory with some weird mind control power he has."

"He killed you?" asked Harley, her eyes on stalks.

"Well, there's the thing," replied Tess, standing up. "I don't know. One minute I'm wrestling with him, the next Ariana screams, and...well, I'm here."

"Wowzers." It took a lot to silence the effervescent Harley, but Tess appeared to have succeeded.

"So, where are the others?" asked Emily suspiciously.

"We all landed here in a heap, and Adam took off. Ariana told me to stay here, and she chased after him. That was an age ago, it's just been me and my little bench ever since. Well, that's not strictly true, I've had a few visitors. You lot a while back and the big guy with the '80s haircut."

"Samuel? You've met Samuel?"

"Yes, Kirkwood. He's a lovely big lump, comes across as a bit slow but sharp as a tack. He told me all about you and that awful Skelly character. The Scourge, lots of stuff about planes, and the eternal struggle between good and evil, blah blah blah." She stifled a yawn much to the displeasure of Emily, who folded her arms across her chest, distinctly unimpressed with their new ally.

Kirkwood smiled. "Samuel and Giro. What a team. Cornelius would be very proud of them."

"Amen," added Harley sadly.

"So, I'm fully up to speed as to why you guys are here," said Tess, remarkably cheerful despite her predicament. "For whatever reason, Ariana, Adam, and I have bonded to create some kind of barrier which isn't allowing the demonic hordes to lay waste to this fair land. Although why they want to set up shop here, I've no idea. It's not as if it's got a lot going for it. Just grass, more grass, and this boring bench."

"Well, then you know why we're here," said Kirkwood. "For reasons way beyond my pay grade, we've got to get you guys out of here. I'm not quite sure how we're going to do that and where we're going to take you, but we'll cross that bridge when we come to it. For now, let's just figure out where Ariana and crazy guy are. What way did they head?"

Tess looked at him blankly. "Which way? Well..."

"You have no idea, do you?" sighed Emily.

"I wouldn't go that far, but..."

"Okay. I can see this is getting us nowhere. This place could be the size of Saturn for all we know, but we have to start somewhere. Harley, you're with me. Emily, you take Tess...."

"Must I?" whined Emily. "Can't I go with you, please? I promise to call you by your real name and not make fun of your haircut."

Kirkwood took a moment to compose himself. "Harley is the youngest, and with the utmost respect, I'm not leaving her with either of you prima donnas. There could be dinosaurs or giant zombie tarantulas over the next hill for all I know. Consider this an opportunity to get to know each other better. I'm sure you'll get on like a house on fire."

"I'd rather set her stupid dress on fire," muttered Emily under her breath.

"What was that?"

"Nothing."

"Okay, well, let's go then. Walk in a straight line for an hour, and if you find nothing, then come right back here, okay."

"Roger that," answered Tess, with a smart salute.

"There's just one slight problem."

"Yes, Emily," replied Kirkwood on the verge of losing the will to live.

"None of us are wearing watches."

Kirkwood gathered his composure before replying. "Well, then I will leave it up to you two ladies to estimate how long an hour is. Come along, Harley. This way."

"Laters haters," smirked Harley, before hurrying after her allotted partner, leaving Tess and Emily to warily eye one another. Eventually, Emily cracked. "Come on then," she said, flouncing off across the lawn. "The sooner I get off this sorry excuse for a back garden, the better."

Tess sneaked the slightest of smiles before following her newfound companion. If this was what death entailed, then she was going to have a whole world of fun. What better way to spend eternity than winding up spoilt little rich girls?

CHAPTER 45 - FIRST NIGHT NERVES

"Keep your head down, never look her in the eye, and only speak when you are spoken to. Got it?"

Tara hurried along the corridor, Meredith in her wake, a duck out of water in the suffocating dress and ill-fitting shoes. How she missed her hoodie, leggings, and Doctor Marten boots. And her beanie hat, she felt utterly naked without it.

"Got it...I think. Where are we going?"

Tara turned sharply right and started to ascend a flight of carpeted stairs. "We are tending to the Priestess tonight in her private quarters. She has specifically asked for you. A test, no doubt. You must be on your best behaviour."

Meredith, still coming to terms with her new job description, rolled her eyes and sighed. "Yes, yes, I'll be on my very best behaviour, I promise. I've seen what Her Majesty does to people who get on the wrong side of her. She killed my friend, remember? Whose blood you then drank." She tried but failed to contain the bitterness in her voice.

Tara stopped at the top of the stairs by the door, which led to the top floor of the hotel, where the Priestess resided. In the penthouse suite, offering panoramic views of the lough and ravaged city landscape. "I am very sorry about your friend. I don't enjoy what she makes us do, a lot of people here don't. But she is ruthless, and I can't go out there again. I just can't."

"Not even if I helped you find your mother?"

"It's in my past. I have to move on now, and so do you." Her eyes failed to conceal the heartbreak she could not speak of, and Meredith suddenly felt a deep sorrow for the girl. Sixteen years old, if even that, and destined for a life of abuse and slavery, forced to commit horrific acts in order to stay alive. All she could do was place what she hoped was a reassuring hand on Tara's shoulder and nod sadly.

"Let's do this then."

Tara smiled and pushed open the door leading onto a plushly carpeted corridor. It widened at its end into a reception area where a bored-looking Maiden sat on a chaise longue beside two oak panelled doors. Meredith recognised her as the ditzy blonde who had accompanied Tara at the Wall. A barrel bellied, balding man who looked as if he could eat his body weight in cheeseburgers stood by the door, the mandatory firearm strapped across his considerable chest.

"About time," pouted the blonde girl, who Meredith had formed an instant dislike towards. "She's in a foul mood. Has been asking where the new girl is. Although personally, I've no idea what all the fuss is about." She shot Meredith a filthy look before rising and stretching theatrically. "Her evening meal will be delivered in an hour, then it's just the usual routine. Have fun, girls. Night Arthur."

The guard grunted in response at the blonde's back as she sashayed down the corridor, all hips and attitude.

"What a lovely young woman," sneered Meredith, deeply unimpressed with the performance.

"That's Seren," replied Tara. "She's alright. There are worse than her."

"Really? Can't wait to meet them."

"The girls do what they have to do to get by. Come on." She turned, took a deep breath, and smiled at the guard. "Good evening, Arthur. We are ready to enter."

The guard looked Meredith up and down before stepping aside, opening the door for them in the process. Tara entered, head bowed, followed by Meredith, her heart threatening to burst from her chest. Meredith chanced a peek up to discover she was in a large room, dominated by a sumptuous four-poster bed adorned with dozens of plump cushions. Beneath the drapes reclined the Priestess, idly flicking through a fashion magazine. Seeing them, she tossed it aside and sat up, crossing her legs at the ankles. Meredith noticed what a tiny creature she was, no more than five feet tall in her bare feet. In any other setting, her slight frame wouldn't have proven the slightest threat, yet here, she was ruler of all she surveyed. Granted, a ragtag bag of survivors in a post-apocalyptic corner of Belfast, but impressive all the less. Despite her abhorrence at all she stood for, Meredith couldn't help but be grudgingly fascinated by this exotic, horrific woman. Where had she come from? What was her story?

"Ah, new girl. What am I to call you?"

"She has been blessed with the name of Meredith, Mistress."

The Priestess shimmied down the bed until she sat perched on the end, her legs not quite touching the floor. Meredith noted the edge of a tattoo starting at her left ankle, before snaking out of sight up her leg. What was it? A vine, some sort of flower motif? Classy, it was not.

"Mistress," mumbled Meredith, not knowing what else to say.

"A drink, if you would be so kind." Seeing Meredith's horrified expression, she threw back her head and laughed. A surprisingly girlish giggle that echoed around the vast suite.

"Oh, relax, I'll have a vodka and tonic. She pointed towards a mini-fridge situated to the right of the bed. "The blood of the unrighteous is reserved for special occasions."

Tara guided Meredith towards the fridge. Opening it, she found it well-stocked with all manner of spirits, wines, and mixers. Being a homicidal maniac must be thirsty work, thought Meredith, as she fumbled for the required bottles before pouring the drink in a tall, slim glass. One of half a dozen sat atop the fridge. She felt her stomach curl inwards as she watched the ice-cold vodka hit the bottom of the glass and curl seductively through the fizzing mixer.

"Pour one for yourself if you want." Meredith turned to find the Priestess smiling over her right shoulder towards her. "First night on the job, I'm sure you could do with one to settle the nerves. My husband-to-be has told me all about your little problem. Don't worry, it can be our secret." She unleashed a lascivious smile and tapped her nose. Beyond her, Tara stood, head bowed, awaiting further instructions.

Wanting nothing more than to seize the vodka bottle by its neck and drown her misery, it took every ounce of willpower Meredith had to resist its calling. "No, thank you, Mistress," she meekly replied, her legs like jelly, every nerve ending in her body on fire. No, for if she started, she didn't know if she would ever stop.

"No?" The Priestess shrugged and stretched again, a sleeked cat toying with her prey. "Please yourself, party pooper. You will eventually." She turned her attention to Tara, her tone suddenly sharper. "That will be all. You may wait outside until my evening meal is delivered. After that, I will have my bath prepared."

"As you wish, Mistress," nodded Tara. She began to back out of the room and gesticulated for Meredith to follow suit. She felt ridiculous but did as instructed, acutely aware that the Priestess was watching her every move with intense interest.

"After all, I must be looking my most radiant for when my fiancé visits later." She paused, scanning Meredith's body language for a reaction. When none was forthcoming, she lunged again, keen for her new acquisition to take the bait.

"I'm an old-fashioned girl at heart and know we should wait until our wedding night to consummate the relationship, but he's such a handsome specimen, I don't know if I'll be able to resist." She lifted her hand and casually began to inspect fingernails painted as black as her clothes—as black as her rancid heart. Meredith wanted nothing more than to throw herself at the bitch, to gouge at those green eyes until they ran red.

"As you wish, Mistress." Her voice a robotic monotone, Meredith shuffled to the door. She glanced at her tormentor and detected the slightest crinkle of an eyebrow, the merest hint of displeasure that her words hadn't garnered the expected reaction. I won't play your games, thought Meredith. I dealt with worse than you on the street. That said, she breathed a huge sigh of relief as she exited the suite, the guard swinging the door shut behind her. Joining Tara on the chaise longue, she leaned forward, burying her head in her hands. After a second, she felt the light touch of her newfound friend's hand on her back.

"You did well. She's testing you. She does it with all the new girls."

Meredith snorted. "Did well? Didn't feel that way. Who is that bitch?" She spoke quietly, aware that the guard was straining to catch their every word, no doubt on the instructions of his sadistic employer in the next room.

"I've no idea. All I know is I want to wake up tomorrow with my head attached to my shoulders. As should you. Forget about your friends, your family, forget about everything. All that matters now is getting through the next hour, the next day. Remember that, it's all you need to know about New Jerusalem."

Meredith sat back, struggling to curtail the nagging thought threatening to snuff out the flickering flame of hope within her, to quash her spirit once and for all.

You're trapped.

They aren't coming.

You're on your own.

It's over.

CHAPTER 46 - WHO CUTS THE GRASS AROUND HERE?

"Sooooo...this dead caper. What do I need to know?" Tess lagged a step or two behind Emily as they ambled slowly through an ocean of never-ending green. Above, the sun beat down on them, a scattering of clouds keeping it company in an otherwise brilliant blue sky. I wish I'd been wearing my sunglasses when I departed dear old planet Earth, she thought wistfully.

"What are you wittering on about now?" replied Emily irritably. The last fifteen minutes of Tess' company had done nothing to sway her first impressions that the girl had nothing but cotton wool between her ears. She sighed, the lawn ahead endless, with no discernible landmarks as to whether they were making any headway.

"Being dead. I mean, it's not as if I had the opportunity to attend an induction course or prepare in any way. I was alive one minute, gone the next. Any advice would be greatly appreciated. What's the accepted etiquette for the recently deceased? Can you teach me any tricks of the trade? Walking through walls? Haunting tips?"

Emily stopped abruptly and turned to face Tess, almost colliding with her. "Honestly, you'd make a good police officer, what with the constant questions. Do you ever stop to draw breath?"

"Is that a question?" The slightest smirk tugged at the corner of Tess' mouth.

"Don't push your luck, Wainwright."

"It's Cartwright. Tess Cartwright."

"Whatever. Doesn't make you any less annoying. Besides, you aren't dead."

"I beg your pardon?"

"You. Are. Not. Dead." Emily accentuated each word, her patience teetering on the brink. Why on earth had Kirkwood insisted on taking Harley under his wing? Hadn't she single-handedly taken care of her in Skelly's dungeons? Why were all men such chest-thumping masochists, and why did it bother her so much? The Emily O'Hara, who was used to both sexes melting in dewy-eyed puddles at her feet.

"Of course, I'm dead," scoffed Tess. "Suicidal maniac. High explosives. Blinding flash leading to this." She waved a hand in the direction of the grassy desert all around them. "I'm obviously in heaven. Or hell. Whatever you want to call it."

Emily blinked rapidly in incredulity. "I'll try and explain this in words of three syllables or less. This is neither heaven nor hell. It is a plane weirdly named 17/4. You are not dead. Trust me. From one who knows." She swirled around and continued her trek towards wherever it was she was meant to be going. "You don't look dead. You don't sound dead. You don't even smell dead."

"Smell dead?" exclaimed Tess, still rooted to the spot as Emily increased the distance between them. "How am I meant to smell? Rancid? Decaying? You don't."

"You're not bloody dead, Tess," bellowed Emily, raising a middle figure as she strode further away from her reluctant companion.

They walked in silence after that. Rolling hills gave way to a gradual, persistent ascent. Emily was lost in a whirlwind of worry, fretting over Meredith, wondering when it would all end. Was there ever any peace, any closure? Rest in peace? Fat chance. She was conscious of Tess behind her, dress rustling like a giant sweet wrapper. She knew she was being hard on the girl, but there was something about her that got right under Emily's skin, pushed her buttons, and rattled her cage. Suddenly it dawned on her. She spun around, startling Tess, who was several yards behind her.

"I know you."

"Eh?" Tess scrunched her face in confusion, eyes wary.

"You've got a younger sister, right?"

"Er, yeah. And what?"

"What age are you?"

"Twenty. Why?"

"And her? Your sister?"

"Who's the policewoman now?"

"Just answer me."

Tess drew a sharp breath before exhaling and answering.

"She's eighteen."

"Bingo. Beth Cartwright. You're Beth Cartwright's older sister. I knew there was something fishy the second I clamped eyes on you."

Tess stared at Emily for what seemed an eternity before her mouth dropped open in sudden realisation. "You're her. That girl. The one who..."

"Slit her wrists in the bath." She took a step towards Tess, who reacted by taking one back, to maintain the distance between them. "After six months of relentless bullying by Sasha Blackstock and her evil harpies. Davina Hudson...Samantha Allen...and the prim and proper, Deputy Head Girl, Beth Cartwright."

Tess' hand shot to her mouth. "Oh, my God. I had no idea it was you. I'm so sorry. It devastated Beth. She's been in bits ever since. The whole family. One of the reasons I was so glad to get away to uni."

"My heart bleeds for you and your darling sister." Emily stared towards the sky, as memories threatened to sweep her away. She had a choice. Throw a hissy fit and tear chunks out of the girl standing in front of her or cling to the bigger picture. The picture Dobson and the others had painted so carefully for her when she had passed over.

"You know, The Forsaken have a saying."

"Forsaken?"

"Samuel and his associates. They describe the likes of you and me as *ones known to our kind*. Known. Past tense."

Tess stared at Emily, not comprehending, but fearful of opening her mouth and earning the wrath of the dead girl standing in front of her.

"What I'm trying to say, Tess, is that as much as I want to kick you into the middle of next month, I'm not going to. For it's in the past. I wish I could go back in time and undo it all, but I'm dead. A stupid, spur of the moment decision I will always regret. But your sister, what happened, the whole sorry Ashgrove scene. It's gone, and we have to focus now on much bigger, more important matters."

"So, you and I are...good?" Tess arched an eyebrow hopefully and exaggeratedly fluttered her huge blue eyes. Emily sighed. It was like trying to pick a fight with the Andrex puppy.

"I'm not making any promises, but yes, we are good. But put one box-fresh trainer out of line, and I'll come down on you like a tonne of bricks, understand?" Tess nodded until Emily thought her head would drop off from overexertion. "Now, let's get a move on. Your friend needs us if this Adam O'Sullivan nutter is all he's cut up to be."

"Yeah," replied Tess, a serious expression making a rare visit to her features. "He's a bad one. I pleaded with Ariana not to go after him, but she said they had unfinished business. She can be a stubborn wee cow. Told me to wait for the cavalry to turn up. Then you guys did." She paused and frowned. "It was as if she knew."

Emily did her utmost to offer a sympathetic smile but was uncertain if she succeeded, so settled for words instead. "If you take in one piece of advice from me, then listen up. Take nothing as a given in your current situation. There are too many incalculables. Everything is a mystery wrapped up in a riddle. Seems Ariana is slightly ahead of the game than you are in that respect. Just watch, listen, and do your best to keep up. Now, come on, that's enough blathering, let's cover some ground and find her before it's too late."

She turned and started to climb the gradual ascent, which stretched ahead, no clue as to where it ended. As far as the eye could see was a swathe of green. Tess hitched up her ballgown and followed the ghost girl from her former school, in search of another girl, a girl whose powers Tess had only caught the briefest glimpse of.

"Mystery wrapped in a riddle," she grumbled. "First one I want answered is who cuts the grass around here?"

CHAPTER 47 - BOMB GIRL

"Are we there yet?" Harley asked for the fifteenth time since they separated from the others. She struggled to keep pace with Kirkwood's loping stride, which gobbled up the ground stretching before them.

"For someone who's spent the last year in a wheelchair, I would have thought a brisk stroll was right up your alley. I take it I was wrong."

"Yeah, a dander round the shops, sure. I wasn't planning on a three-day forced hike through the largest back garden in the universe. I'm wrecked." She sank to the grass as if taken out by a crack sniper armed with a high-powered rifle. Sprawling onto her back, she raised an arm to shield her eyes from the unrelenting sun. It was a warm but not unpleasant heat, aided by a slight breeze that cooled the sweat as it formed on their brows.

"The youth of today," tutted Kirkwood. "I thought you were never out of the gym when you were doing your rehab? Twenty-minute walk, and you're busted?"

"That was all strength and conditioning. My legs didn't work, remember? This is all new to me again. Duh." She stuck her tongue out at Kirkwood, who feigned a kick in her direction. "Ow, watch it. Bet I could beat you in an arm-wrestling contest."

Kirkwood laughed, reaching out a hand which she accepted reluctantly, and hauled her back onto her feet. "I've no doubt. I was always a bit of a wimp when it came to weights. I can barely raise a smile most days. But I can run a half marathon without stopping, thanks to good old Skelly and the OCD."

"Are...were all the routines about running?" They walked alongside one another at a gentler camber as they talked.

"No, not all of them. There are 49 in total. About half a dozen of them are running related. The rest are all over the shop. I've sort of accumulated them down the years. Some people collect stamps, I collect overwhelming, obsessive thoughts."

"So, is it Skelly, or do you really have OCD?"

"Oh, I have it alright," replied Kirkwood with a tight smile. "Since I was young, although it crept up on me at first. I thought it was just little quirks and idiosyncrasies. That's when dear old Skelly pounced. He realised it was my weakness and exploited it for all he was worth. If I was wrapped up in tortuous routines and drinking myself silly every weekend, then I wasn't a threat to him. I'd never have met you guys, the Presence would never have been activated, and the Scourge would be destroying the planet as we speak."

"I still can't get my head around why it's us. I mean, we're totally ordinary."

"Sometimes, that's where you find the extraordinary, Harley. It's been there staring you in the face all along. I've spent most of my life trying to work out why certain things happen, and others don't. In the end, you just give up trying to work it out, or it will melt your head. You go with the flow."

Harley mulled over his words. "Is that what we are doing here? Going with the..."

"Did you hear that?" Kirkwood's head whipped round towards a dip in the lawn to their left.

"What?"

He held out a hand, signalling Harley to be quiet and cocked his head to one side, straining to catch the sound again. What was it? Singing? Ten long seconds of silence dragged past before the weak strain carried on the breeze to them again. This time, Harley nodded enthusiastically, her eyes lighting with excitement.

"I heard it, I heard it."

With that, they were off. Freewheeling down the dip until they reached its trough before sprinting up a smaller incline towards a ridge. The voice grew stronger, and they were able to determine it was a female one.

"Things...can only get better..." It crossed Kirkwood's mind that it was not the most melodic rendition of the dance classic, but he cared not, it could only be one person.

Ariana Hennessy...

They crested the ridge together, and what little breath was left in Kirkwood's lungs from the pursuit whistled through his front teeth.

"Oh, my...."

"It's a freaking play park," shrieked Harley tumbling down the slope towards a toddler's paradise.

In the hollow below lay an assortment of slides, swings, and see-saws scattered across a spongey rubber surface. Kirkwood stopped at the top of the ridge, not quite believing what he was taking in. For it was a play park he knew intimately well. He marvelled at the breathtaking detail. The rusted suspended chains of the swings holding the rubber tyres in place, which he had spent hundreds of hours on as a young boy. The metallic slide which used to tower above him, daring little Kirkwood to scale its then terrifying heights. He was even certain the wooden hut Katie and him used to shelter within had his initials carved into its side.

"It's my play park," he mouthed as he slowly edged down the slope towards his childhood retreat, now nestled cosily in the middle of a bizarrely bland alternative universe. Most bizarre of all, however, was the young woman, wrapped in an immense hooded parka, gently swinging back and forward on one of the tyres. She stopped, grabbing the chains to halt her trajectory, aware her tuneless rendition of the '80s floor filler had an audience.

"Are you the Bomb Girl? The pixie's friend?" unloaded Harley, tactful as ever. Kirkwood inwardly cringed as he reached the bottom of the slope and began to cross the padded surface towards the swings. Thankfully, the young woman smiled in response. It didn't translate to her dark eyes, however, which looked as if they contained a lifetime of sad memories.

"Yes, I have been called that, Harley. But you can call me Ariana. Very pleased to meet you."

"How do you know my name?" It took a lot to quieten the younger girl, but Harley halted, uncertain how to proceed. She looked back towards Kirkwood for reassurance, but he could only shrug in response.

"I know lots of stuff," replied Ariana, letting go of the chains and propelling forward onto her feet. The chains squealed in protest, reluctant to part company with their occupant. "You're Harley Davison, and that's Kirkwood Scott behind you. Emily O'Hara has drawn the short straw and is two miles away, becoming frenemies with Tess. See, I know all sorts." She held out her hand in greeting to Harley, who considered the offer for several seconds before reciprocating the gesture.

"Impressive party trick," observed Kirkwood. "We were meant to be saving you from O'Sullivan, but seems you've got the situation under control. Where is he?" He scanned the hollow anxiously, expecting to be ambushed by a homicidal maniac at any second.

Ariana smirked knowingly. "Adam and I had a little chat as we had a few issues to thrash out. He's now six million miles over there." She pointed in the general direction of the solitary see-saw. "Give or take a mile or two. He won't be bothering us for a while."

"Equally impressive. Seems we're not the only ones with powers then?"

Ariana smiled shyly. "It was always Tess who gained the attention. Stunning looks, supernova personality, I preferred to keep a low profile. That's what a lifetime of being thrust into the spotlight does to you. Yet now, I'm the one that can…do stuff." She tailed off, uncertain of how to describe her recent experiences.

"Stuff?" Harley was straining at the leash for additional information, despite the reticence of the shy young woman before her.

"I just know stuff. And, by stuff, I mean pretty much everything. That's why I needed a bit of time on my own here until I went back to Tess. To learn how to control it, to filter what I need to know from the irrelevant. For example, I don't need to know that you're craving a Bargain Bucket, Harley, or that you're worried your socks need changed, Kirkwood."

"Wow. Cooooool," exclaimed Harley while Kirkwood became fascinated with a distant point on the horizon, his cheeks reddening.

"Sorry for leading you guys on a wild goose chase. But it's hard to come to terms with newly acquired superpowers when your best friend is rabbiting on about her chipped nails. Has she bored you about that yet?"

Kirkwood and Harley shook their heads in unison, causing Ariana to laugh and throw back the fur-lined hood of her parka. Her shoulder-length chestnut hair matched the colour of her eyes but was in serious need of a brushing. Full lips parted to reveal a sparkling set of teeth. The girl took care of her teeth, if not her tangled locks, thought Kirkwood. He could tell how she might have felt inadequate next to the soap star looks of Tess. He had felt the same way for most of his life, especially on the few occasions he frequented a testosterone-heavy gym environment. Yet, she had something about her, a sanguine serenity that permeated every pore of her frame. The girl was special, even if she didn't realise it yet.

"Adam and I had a little, shall we say, disagreement back on Terra Firma. And by disagreement, I mean beating me silly, and then trying to blow up half my university and me in memory of his sicko father."

"I guess you could call that grounds for an exchange of words," conceded Kirkwood.

Ariana giggled, a surprisingly refreshing sound for someone who had been through such recent trauma. Resilient as well as resourceful, thought Kirkwood. He was becoming more impressed the more time he spent in her company. He glanced at Harley, who was staring open-mouthed at Ariana in adulation. Seems he was no longer hero of the month.

"Yup. Seems I'm extra blessed or cursed whatever way you want to look at it. As well as reading thoughts, I can dispatch people through time and space on a whim."

"It's called planeing," said Harley, chest visibly puffing out with pride.

"Oh, really," laughed Ariana. "Planeing it is then, oh wise one."

Looking like the cat who had got the cream, Harley pressed on with her new best friend. "Well, if that's the case, can you plane us all back to Emily and Tess? My feet are killing me, thanks to this tyrant." She cocked a thumb towards Kirkwood.

"Hark at you, bossy-boots. You've only met her five minutes ago, don't be so forward." Kirkwood suddenly felt very old, laying down the law to his teenage charge.

"Sorry, Harley, but I'm still getting the hang of this planeing as you call it. I can do it pretty much at will, but I'm still fine-tuning my range and accuracy. There's a chance I could overshoot, and we could end up weeks from them. Besides, I quite fancy the walk, a chance to get to know you guys better. I've been sitting here for ages."

Harley nodded, her disappointment at having to cover more ground compensated by getting to hang out with her latest big sister. The three of them turned and began to climb out of the hollow. At the top, Kirkwood stopped to take one last wistful look at this fragment from a childhood long lost in the mists of time. Oh, to be back there now without a care in the world, messing about with his friends. Before he lost his father. Before that fateful day John Scott had taken his young lad to Mr. Bradley's Toy Shop. The day he brought home Skelly. The day it all started to go wrong.

"Everything okay?" asked Ariana, noticing he had not joined Harley and her on the descent down the other side. She already felt an affiliation to this sensitive, fragile young man. He was damaged like her—like they all were. Maybe having their worlds turned upside down is what's required to render them whole again?

"Yeah, just a memory. A memory from a time long ago."

"Hold onto it then." Ariana's soft voice caught Kirkwood unawares, and she was startled to discover a tear nestling on his cheek. "Save it for a rainy day. You never know when you might need it again."

The three of them set off across the eternal sea of green, leaving the playground behind, focused on uniting with Emily and Tess. Kirkwood felt more settled, but a dull ball of worry throbbed within his chest. Meredith was still missing and, until she was back safely within their grieving ranks, he could not rest.

CHAPTER 48 - A SPOT OF TROUBLE

Meredith groaned as another gust of nausea threatened to introduce the contents of her stomach into this mad, bad new world she now inhabited. It felt as if they had been sitting outside the Priestess' boudoir for hours, but her evening meal had only just been delivered and served. Tara had guided her carefully through the process of delivering the tray of food to the impressive oak table, which took up a considerable amount of space in the dining area to the right of the sleeping quarters. For all the grandiose plates and cutlery, the food itself was a sparse collection of salad accompanied by a sliver of roast chicken. The Priestess picked at it sparingly with all the enthusiasm of an anaemic sparrow. Much more interested in her glass, which Meredith frequently topped up with liberal splashes of vodka, diluted with tonic. She fantasised over lifting the bottle to her lips and allowing the harsh spirit to bathe the back of her throat.

"Are you alright?" asked Tara, concern in her voice. Through gritted teeth, Meredith thanked her lucky stars she had been paired up with one of the few examples of humanity left in this damned city.

"Yeah. I suppose there's no chance that bottle of vodka could be smuggled out of her lair for me?"

"The only bottle that leaves the Priestess is an empty one. She enjoys her evening drink."

"You're telling me," snarled Meredith. "She knew I was struggling in there and took great delight in necking that drink as if it was going out of fashion. Miserable cow. When do we get to finish here? I really need to see Rodriguez." She knew he was her only escape plan as the realisation that Kirkwood and the others weren't coming solidified with each passing moment. She didn't know what to do first, give up or throw up. It was a desperate, miserable situation, topping anything she had encountered during her time on the streets.

"We go when she releases us," replied Tara plainly. "As for your friend, Rodriguez, I think that can be organised. Our mistress has requested his company in her quarters later."

"Euuurghhhh." Meredith pulled a face as if she had trodden in something particularly unpleasant. "I shudder to think what that involves. When it comes to romance, I don't think either of them is at the top of the queue. They're hardly a match made in heaven. Hell is more like it."

"Do you want to see him or not?" whispered Tara, giving the ever-vigilant Arthur a butter wouldn't melt in her mouth smile. "I'll try and get you a few moments with him, but don't quote me on that."

"Thank you." It was all Meredith could manage, the snarky attitude draining from her by the second. Her stomach was cramping, and she was in desperate need of a visit to the bathroom — despotic tyrant or not in the next room. Her body was seized by a series of shivers, forcing her heavy head onto Tara's shoulder.

"You'll get through this, Meredith, you will," the auburn-haired girl said, gripping her hand reassuringly. "I've seen girls come in here in a worse state than you, and they're model citizens now."

Meredith sniffed, a running nose now complimenting the pounding headache. "I'm not sure I'm cut out to be a model citizen. Here, there, or anywhere. It's not in the Starc DNA. But, thank you, I am grateful." She squeezed Tara's hand, aware of the difference between the other girls' warm flesh and her own icy fingers. "Oh, the joys of alcohol withdrawal."

Arthur, who had been leaning against the oak doors, jerked to his not very full height, his belly jutting out in front, threatening to send the buttons of his ill-fitting shirt into orbit. Marching down the corridor towards them were two of his compatriots, manhandling a familiar figure between them. Although his face was caked with dried blood, the full, black beard and scarred cheek were unmistakable—*Rodriguez*.

"Dessert for, Her Majesty," jested one of the guards, shoving the Portuguese soldier to his knees. Meredith noticed his hands were tethered with coarse rope. He sprawled onto his face, unable to maintain balance, an act greeted with jeers by his two gaolers.

"You will address the Priestess with due deference," said Tara, her voice surprisingly loud and clear for one so normally timid. She rose to her full height of five-feet-not-very-much, and Meredith quietly admired her courage in the face of such thugs. She feared for the girl, though. If that's what the guards had reduced a man-mountain like Rodriguez to, then what hope was there for a Maiden who looked like a decent breeze would knock her over.

The first guard opened his mouth to speak again, but his colleague placed a hand on his arm to advise otherwise. At the same time, Arthur, who up until then had resembled a bored bystander, stepped forward.

"Don't think it would be the wisest career move hitting a Maiden now, would it, Jacko? Remember what happened to Harry O'Neill?"

Jacko looked from Tara to Arthur's rifle, then back before stopping and lowering his head. "I apologise, Maiden," he mumbled. "Please don't tell the Priestess. We bring the Prophet as requested." He shifted awkwardly from foot to foot like a schoolboy caught playing truant outside the principal's office.

"Consider yourself lucky our Mistress did not hear your disrespectful words, or it would be your blood we would be supping at next Communion. Leave the Prophet, we will take care of him from here."

Jacko nodded and turned on his heel, keen to get as far away from the quarters of the Priestess as possible. His companion shoved him roughly in the back and grunted an insult at him as they headed back down the corridor.

"Wow," said Meredith. "Proper kudos, girlfriend."

Tara allowed herself a tiny satisfied smile. "Some of the girls are more familiar with the guards than others, but there is a line, and they know they can't cross it. If the Priestess heard of one of us being insulted or abused, heads would roll. And by roll, I mean that, literally."

A groan diverted their attention to the prone figure on the floor. Meredith fell to one knee and shook his shoulder. "Rodriguez, it's me, Meredith. What the hell happened to you?"

The big man turned his face to look at her. Up close, he looked even worse than he had when first hauled down the corridor. His left eye was swollen and almost closed while his right iris was blood red. Meredith was no medical expert but would have put good money on the eye socket being fractured.

Rodriguez spat bloody saliva onto the floor, clearing his throat before replying. "For one who attended one of the most elite academic institutions in your city, you sure do ask some stupid questions, querida."

"You look like you've gone ten rounds with Mike Tyson."

Rodriguez looked confused before laughing hoarsely. "I do not know who this Tyson is. But the last time I took a beating like that was when I fought some Irish barbarian for the regimental boxing championship. I won a barrel of rum that night."

"We will take him to the adjoining rooms and prepare him for the Priestess. I don't think he's capable of standing, let alone escaping, so you can remain here." Arthur nodded. He was a man of few words, but his sneer told Meredith all she needed to know about his contempt for their newly arrived guest.

Between them, the two young women managed to get Rodriguez to his feet. He staggered wildly to the left, bouncing off the panelled corridor wall before Meredith grabbed his arm and helped him down another corridor from the one that led to the stairwell. Led by Tara, they stopped at a door no more than thirty feet from where the

Priestess resided. Opening it, Tara stepped aside to reveal another impressive suite, similar in decor but slightly smaller than the one next door. Rodriguez stumbled forward into the room, falling face down on the queen-size four-poster bed in front of them.

"I'll get the shower set up," said Tara, matter of factly, as if she had done this sort of thing countless times before. "You get him out of his clothes. The Priestess won't want him brought to her looking like that." She headed into the bathroom, followed swiftly by the sound of running water.

"Why do I always get the short straw," muttered Meredith. She looked at the inert lump of dead Napoleonic veteran on the bed. Where did you even begin? Tentatively, she attempted to unlace his boots, removing one then the other before rolling both socks from his feet. After much swearing and manoeuvring, she managed to haul the black designer pullover over his head, tugging at the arms before it finally slipped off, sending her tumbling onto her backside. The resounding thump brought Tara scurrying out of the bathroom through a cloud of steam. She took one look at Rodriguez, now snoring loudly, and Meredith scrambling back to her feet.

"Help me," said Tara curtly, stepping forward and unbuckling the belt of the prone man's trousers. "We need to get him showered, fed, and cleaned up." The routine way she set about the task forced Meredith to her feet out of grudging respect. They took a leg each and started to pull the trousers off the big man. Meredith was relieved to see he was wearing black boxer shorts underneath.

"Dead men wear underwear. Who knew?" she mumbled to herself as the trousers were removed with a final flourish.

"What?"

"Nothing. This isn't your first rodeo, is it?" She looked across to Tara, who smiled coyly as she went about her work.

"Our mistress has many gentleman callers, some of whom require more...encouragement than others. Your friend, the Prophet, is but one in a long line. I do as I am bid, without question or judgement."

"He's no friend of mine," sniffed Meredith. *Although he was my ticket out of here*, she added internally. "He may be one of many, but he must be different if she's viewing him as husband material."

"He is a Prophet, one from beyond the Wall, of course he is different." She continued to speak as she disappeared back into the bathroom. "The Priestess talks of expanding New Jerusalem far beyond this corner of the city. She wants all the lands." She returned with a glass of water which she emptied over the head of Rodriguez, causing him to start and flail out, before sliding off the bed. Thankfully the luxurious carpet provided a soft landing, not adding to the considerable injuries he had already accumulated.

"On your feet, Prophet," said Tara sternly. "The Priestess awaits you. Hurry, she is not a patient woman."

Rodriguez rolled onto his side and squinted up at the two young women standing over him. As his vision cleared and he became aware of his surroundings, he raised a hand to tentatively dab at his bloodshot eye. He winced before turning his attention to Meredith and her attire.

"I see you have changed your style, urchin. I cannot say it suits you. I prefer the grimier version of the one known to her kind as Meredith Starc."

"You will show respect to the Maidens of Purity, Prophet. You are not wed yet. She is to be addressed with deference. Meredith Starc is dead to this world."

Meredith showed no emotion as Rodriguez groggily raised his battered frame into a sitting position. "As you wish, my lady," he said. "I fear I'm not capable of challenging your people's etiquette at present. I suspect your overly enthusiastic guards may have tap-danced across my ribs a little too vigorously. They have somewhat knocked the wind out of me." He felt the left side of his body gingerly, a procession of bruises running down it.

"Nothing a hot shower and decent meal won't rectify. Come on, get up."

"Very well, take me to your leader." Rodriguez attempted to rise but sank immediately to one knee, sucking the air into his broken body. "A hand, if you will," he asked, in genuine pain. Tara secured an arm under one armpit and Meredith the other, between them hauling him to his feet. As he gathered himself, Rodriguez turned and whispered in the latter's ear.

"So pleased to see you again, little one. But I fear we are in a spot of trouble."

"Tell me something I don't know," Meredith spat back. "And if we don't come up with answers soon, it will be the last spot of trouble we'll ever find ourselves in."

CHAPTER 49 - BUYING TIME

"Damn it." Deacon slammed his fist on the desk before throwing his chair back and commencing another lap of the briefing room. "How long do you want me to wait? Every hour that passes is another nail in their coffins." He was a man of action, used to getting what he wanted, not sitting around twiddling his thumbs while others did the dirty work on the front line.

Giro counted quietly to ten before replying. He had been handed this posting largely because of his tact and diplomacy, but even *his* patience was being tested. It had been several hours since his return from Skelly's lair and still no contact from Kirkwood and the others. He had talked the options through with Samuel, and they both agreed. Agreeing to Skelly's request and handing him 17/4 was a risk but a manageable one, well worth taking if it ensured the Presence were reunited. But what If they'd got it horribly wrong?

"I'm as frustrated as you are, sir, believe me. But calm heads are called for now. The silence is to be expected. They will contact me when the time is right."

"Don't lecture me about timing." Deacon bored a hole into the back of Giro's head as he completed another circuit. It was just the two of them in the cramped room, its walls bedecked with maps and photographs of the city. Normally, this was the hub of the base, heaving with activity, but other soldiers were giving it a wide berth due to the foul mood of their Commanding Officer.

"Sorry, sir," replied Giro, well used to these outbursts. He knew Deacon would blow out as opposed to blow up, yet that made his current position in the older man's firing range no less pleasant.

"I don't know why I agree to these hare-brained schemes you dream up. You're fortunate you're in credit with me. Otherwise, I'd have you up on a charge and slung in a cell."

"Thank you for your vote of confidence, Major," replied Giro, half expecting a clip round the ear for his mild insolence. Deacon merely glared at him. "Believe it or not, Kirkwood and his companions are safer on 17/4 than they are here. Having reunited with Emily O'Hara, the Presence is intact again. They have more than enough in their arsenal to cope with whatever they encounter."

"And the Starc girl. Have we forgotten about her in the midst of this jolly jape?" It was a serious question, despite the heavy sarcasm.

"I can still detect her energy within New Jerusalem. It is strong, she is alive and well. I doubt she is having the most enjoyable of experiences over there, but she is still with us."

"So why the blazes don't we summon this Presence mumbo jumbo here, nuke the Priestess and be done with?" The exasperation in Deacon's voice was evident.

"Because Emily will not possess the same influence on this plane. She made a conscious decision to leave of her own free will. This world is forever closed to her now. She cannot be part of the Three on Earth."

"Who makes this stuff up?" Deacon groaned, utterly unimpressed with the laws of the universe.

"I'm afraid that's well above my pay grade, sir," laughed Giro, attempting to defuse the tension with his trademark gentle humour.

"Your kind are beyond me," sighed Deacon. "I sometimes rue the day you and Tommy turned up on my doorstep."

"One step at a time, sir. The only way to get Harley and Meredith back is, unfortunately, through cooperating with Skelly. It's an uneasy alliance, and it doesn't leave a pleasant taste in my mouth either."

"Pleasant taste? Frankly, it stinks." Deacon screwed his already wrinkled features until he resembled an octogenarian pug.

"I know, sir, I know. But please, a little more time." He looked pleadingly towards the old warhorse pacing in front of him.

Deacon stopped and stared up towards the cracked ceiling. It wasn't in his nature to prevaricate, but Giro had never let him down before. He owed him this one, in memory of Tommy, if nothing else. He stared at Giro long and hard, rubbing the sandpaper-rough stubble on his chin, before finally replying.

"I'm probably making one of the biggest mistakes of my career, but alright, we wait. For now. But if I don't hear anything soon, we are going in. I don't care if that mad bitch calls down every angel in heaven, we are going in. Understood?"

"Yes, sir." Giro watched as Deacon stalked out of the briefing room. He closed his eyes and cleared his mind. Concentrate, Giro, concentrate, home in on the source. Yes, there she is, strong and clear. Meredith's essence, vibrant, pulsating. There was fight in the girl, a steely edge. He was confident she was hanging in there. All she had to do was hang in there a little longer.

"Come on, Kirkwood. Time to keep your part of the bargain."

CHAPTER 50 - BURY YOUR DEAD

"EMILY."

"EMMMMMMM!"

"OVER HERE, YOU DONUT."

Harley's excited yells ruptured the otherwise idyllic silence of Plane 17/4, or Grassland as Ariana had christened it on their trek back to the bench. Emily turned, deep in conversation with Tess, and beamed with delight, as the younger girl barrelled towards her, arms outstretched in greeting. Upon reaching her, the two of them danced a circular jig, their laughter drifting over the endless expanse of green. Ariana and Tess hugged warmly as well, while Kirkwood stood awkwardly, not knowing what to do.

"Where's that nutter, O'Sullivan?" asked Tess breathlessly, breaking free from her friend. "Tell me you frazzled him to a crisp with your laser beam eyes?"

"We both know I don't have laser beam eyes," giggled Ariana. "He's gone, though. Far, far away and won't be bothering us again. We're safe, Tess."

Tess smiled and relaxed her shoulders before tensing again, a startled expression on her face. "You haven't, though, seriously. You know...?"

"No, I haven't killed him," exclaimed Ariana in mock outrage. "Although he deserves no less for what he did to us. I'm many things, but I'm not a murderer."

"You're not," agreed Tess. "You're the most wonderful creature alive." She hugged Ariana again before breaking free. "Ariana Hennessy, allow me to introduce you to Emily O'Hara. Turns out, Emily and I go way back. Fellow Ashgrove girl."

"Please don't hold that against me." Emily stepped forward and shook Ariana's hand, who exhaled sharply as she accepted the greeting. "Your hand, it's so..."

"Cold, yes. I'm dead," replied Emily, matter of factly.

"Oh."

"Then how come when I hug you, you're all warm and toasty?" blurted Harley.

"Seems Ariana has another string to her supernatural bow," explained Emily. "The ability to detect those of us who have passed over. Quite the special one, aren't you?"

"I get by," shrugged Ariana, not quite sure what to make of the slight, waifish creature in front of her.

"Well, now that we're all properly acquainted, I think it's high time we got off this plane and leave it for whatever Skelly has planned for it." Kirkwood scanned the group for signs of consent.

"Are you sure we're doing the right thing?" asked Harley. "He's the enemy, and we're helping him. It just doesn't sit comfortably with me."

"I agree, Harls, but he has us backed into a corner. This is the only way we were going to get you and Emily back. Plus, we've managed to rescue two people who otherwise could have been stuck here for the rest of their days." He gestured towards Ariana and Tess, who nodded in agreement.

"And left that rocket O'Sullivan to get acquainted with Skelly and his mob. I'm sure they will have lots of pleasant surprises lined up for him," added Tess, placing a protective arm around Ariana.

"Most definitely. All we need now is for Giro to plane us back to the Study, pick up Meredith, and skedaddle back to modern-day Belfast to protect the world from utter devastation, then live happily ever after." Emily let go of Harley's hands and clicked her fingers sharply at Kirkwood. "Come on, then. Beam us up, Scotty."

"I would if I had the slightest notion what to do. Giro didn't say anything about how we—"

His words were cut short as his stomach somersaulted, and eyes performed pirouettes, the now-familiar sensation of planeing hitting him with both barrels. Kirkwood squeezed his hands into tight fists and clenched his teeth, willing each endless second to pass as the worst fairground ride in the world bombarded every nerve ending in his body. It ended as suddenly as it began, and he opened his eyes to find himself standing in the horribly familiar confines of the Study once more. The equally familiar armchair was empty, and it took several seconds for him to realise Skelly was seated behind the grandiose oak table, poring over a sheaf of papers strewn across it. On either side of Kirkwood, his four fellow travellers were finding their bearings and adjusting to the new surroundings.

"I'm not bloody happy with this, not bloody happy at all," bellowed Skelly to no one in particular. His face was even redder than usual, and his bulbous, cratered nose looked as if it might explode at any moment. His visitors stood rooted to the spot, unable to move, all wondering if the old man was even aware of their presence. After an age, Skelly looked up from the papers and eyed them with barely-contained hostility.

"Well?"

"Well, what, grumpy drawers?" shot back Harley, sharp as a tack, earning disapproving looks from Kirkwood and Emily.

"Talk to me like that again, young lady, and it won't just be the power of your legs you'll be losing. Am I understood?"

"Yeah," muttered Harley reluctantly, fully aware the abomination in front of her was more than capable of carrying out the threat.

"And don't even think of invoking the Presence on me. This is my domain. Your powers mean nothing here."

Kirkwood straightened himself before addressing his childhood nightmare. "We've kept our part of the bargain, cleared 17/4 for you, now it's your turn. Where's Meredith?"

Skelly chuckled wryly, amused at some internal jest he wasn't prepared to share with the larger party. "Oh, I know exactly where she is, just having a few technical issues with my exit strategy, that's all."

"Problems? You don't bring us problems, Skelly, you bring us solutions. Get Meredith back here—now." Emily's soft voice contained an unusual edge. She wanted nothing more than to reclaim her best friend.

"Just like the solution to your problems was to slit your wrists in your parent's bath while they sat downstairs watching some godawful soap opera?" replied Skelly with venom. "Drip, drip, drip, wasn't that how they found out?"

Emily paled and bit down hard on her bottom lip, refusing to rise to his carefully laid bait. "Just keep to your side of the bargain, Skelly. Where is she?"

"Here." He jabbed his finger in the middle of a dog-eared map on the desk. "Bang in the middle of New Jerusalem, playing happy families with that idiot Rodriguez and the daft wench who runs it."

Tess made to open her mouth and speak, but a barely-noticeable shake of the head from Ariana convinced her to hold fire. The Bomb Girl was gathering information and considering options before throwing her hat into this most dangerous of rings.

"But," stammered Emily. "Can't you just zap her out of there? Surely the all-conquering Colonel Augustus Skelly isn't letting a woman get the better of him?"

"Touché, witch, touché. While my reputation precedes me, it would appear The Priestess has the ability to block our powers in her domain. So, I can't get in, and our friends can't get out. Damned inconvenient and I can't quite put my finger on it. She's not one of ours, although we do have an arrangement when passing through her plane. Some religious nonsense. Apparently, they think Rodriguez is a man of God. Couldn't be further from the truth."

"Then what are we supposed to do?" Kirkwood could feel the hairs rising on the back of his neck.

"I'm a pragmatist, Kirkwood, you know that. Sometimes one has to sit back, cut your losses, and fold. Lose the battle in order to win the war. I've suffered many reverses down the centuries. This is just one more to add to the list. You have your little harem back together with two shiny new additions, and I have 17/4. Not a bad day at the office. I suggest we retreat to our respective camps and prepare to bury our dead."

"And Meredith? Rodriguez?" Kirkwood was incredulous at the callous nature of Skelly's rationale.

"Every war has its casualties, my dear boy. War is hell. We will remember them at the going down of the sun, et cetera, et cetera, et cetera." Skelly began to fold the map before him. It was over in his warped mind; the cord had been cut.

Ariana could contain herself no more. "Colonel Skelly, my name is Ariana..."

"I'm quite aware of who you are, Ms. Hennessy. I've been following your career for some time now, and I must say I was terribly impressed with how you handled that thug, O'Sullivan. That would have been a frightfully messy business. Young Kirkwood here knows how devastating the effects of an explosion at close range on the human body are, isn't that right?" He smirked, revelling in his spiteful art.

"Even for you, that's low, Jabba." If Harley could have moved, she would have shoved the map down his foul throat.

"Sticks and stones," guffawed Skelly. "Now, if you'd be so kind, I have other business to attend to. I look forward to meeting you all again. Only next time, I can assure it won't be anywhere near as amicable."

He commenced shuffling the papers on his desk like an obscene newsreader at the end of their nightly bulletin. Kirkwood opened his mouth to speak, but there was nobody to speak to, nothing but the rollercoaster ride of planeing. Back to Belfast, 2099.

CHAPTER 51 - MEN ARE LIKE DOGS

Rodriguez shovelled the soup into his mouth, his loud slurping only punctuated by stopping to tear huge chunks out of a slice of crusty bread. Tara and Meredith stood watching him, the latter slightly aghast at the big man's lack of social fineries.

"Our Max back home has better table manners, and he's a four-year-old border terrier."

Tara whispered her reply so Rodriguez could not catch it. "Men and dogs have a lot in common. Eating and scratching themselves, it's all they seem interested in."

"I swear they would lick their bits and bobs if they could," giggled Meredith.

"Eww, gross. Is he really a Prophet?" Tara looked at Meredith with such wide-eyed innocence the other girl hadn't the heart to reveal the grisly truth.

"How can I put it. He's not of this world or rather he used to be, but he's not anymore. And he has powers much like your Priestess. So, if that meets your definition of a prophet, then I suppose he is."

"And you? Was he really taking you to the lake of fire?"

"Yeah. Something like that." Meredith returned her attention to Rodriguez, who was now gorging himself on a leg of roast chicken, stripping it clean—meat, skin, fat, nothing was being spared. He had emerged from the shower cleaner, but still sore and disoriented. Tara attempted to clean his wounds, but he brusquely refused, saying he healed quicker than most. He was now dressed in a pair of baggy track bottoms and a plain white t-shirt, a far cry from his usual designer attire.

Licking the chicken bone before tossing it onto the plate and starting on his fingers, he turned towards the two young women and smiled. "It's amazing what a clean body and full belly can do for a man. Now, take me to your leader so I can show her my appreciation."

"You really are the vilest individual." Meredith looked away in revulsion as Rodriguez unleashed a filthy laugh.

"When in Rome, querida. Or, in this instance, Belfast. Besides, I believe me keeping on the right side of the lady next door would be in both our interests. Do you follow me?"

Meredith looked hesitantly at Tara, who had wheeled away and was starting to clear the table of plates and cutlery. She turned back to Rodriguez and responded with a curt nod. He was right, there was still no sign of rescue. Her every move was watched by a heavily armed guard, and Tara provided only limited information. She was at rock bottom, desperate for another drink, and stacking her hopes on a dead Napoleonic soldier with a propensity for lying and extreme violence. The future did not look particularly bright from where she was standing.

Rodriguez rose, cracked his neck, and leaned forward to whisper in her ear. "Behave yourself, and I will bring some more of that special wine to your room tonight. After I have performed my duties. It's the only way either of us is going to get out of here in one piece. Let me work my magic. In a few days, that deluded bitch will think I'm the Son of God and be eating out of my hands."

He pulled back and fixed her with his dark, piercing eyes. "Do you trust me?"

Meredith snorted. "Trust? Hell no, but what other choice do I have?"

"You are learning fast, Meredith Starc. Trust no one. Now, young Maiden." He turned towards Tara, who was still busying herself around the table. "I am starting to feel remarkably better already. Lead me to your mistress so I may dazzle her with my wit and charm."

Meredith rolled her eyes, but he was the only ticket out of town. The cards were heavily stacked against her, but she was a survivor. Just hang in there, there was nothing else she could do. She began to count the seconds until Rodriguez would call to her quarters with the next bottle.

CHAPTER 52 - CRICKET IS A FIVE-DAY GAME

"You didn't really mean a word of that, did you?" Maura lazily ran a long, pale finger along the back of the armchair before resting it gently on Skelly's shoulder.

"Hmmm?" He lifted his gaze from the broadsheet and flicked it shut, folding it immaculately before setting it beside the decanter and tumbler next to him.

"That whole *you scratch my back, I'll scratch yours* nonsense. 17/4?" She felt confident in his presence, or as confident as any member of the Company could be. Maura had witnessed others feel the wrath of their Commanding Officer for even the mildest show of insolence. She knew she was favoured and could get away with more than most, but there was a line, and she always ensured she remained on the right side of it, the side where you kept breathing.

Skelly lifted a gnarled hand to his shoulder to take Maura's. The juxtaposition between his crooked, arthritic digits and her meticulously manicured fingernails could not have been greater. Skelly's liver-spotted skin turned her stomach, but she fought the urge to pull back as he patted her hand before returning his to his lap.

"Do you like cricket, my dear?"

"It's an English game, sir. I know nothing of it."

Skelly chuckled. "You bloody Irish. So uncivilised. Well, let me give you a short lesson in tactics. Cricket is traditionally a five-day game, a war of attrition, a test of both brains and brawn."

"Five days to play a game? I wouldn't have the patience for that, sir."

"Indeed. Many don't, especially as it can still end in a draw. Yet it is the purest, most magical form of the sport. Saturday afternoon at Lords in the Members Stand, a chilled gin and tonic in hand, two stout Englishmen out in the middle, giving the Aussies a sound thrashing and not a cloud in the sky. There's no better way to spend a day."

"If you say so, sir."

"It's an unpopular form of the game, though. People have no patience these days. Five-day cricket becomes three, then one, and now this horrendous 20/20 format. Blink and you miss it. Wham, bam, thank you, ma'am."

Maura maintained a respectful silence. Skelly loved to portray himself as a doddering old fool, but his mind was as sharp as the tip of a French lance. There was an important point being made here, in his inimitable meandering style, and her role was to listen and learn. Maura was keen to progress within the organisation and grasp every opportunity to gain leverage with the powers that be.

"Patience. A dying art. Yet an essential skill for any strategist worth his salt. No wonder jigsaws have been replaced by these damned computer games. All flashing lights and crashing sounds, turning the youth into a nation of zombies."

"Yes, sir."

"Ha," he snorted, turning his flabby neck to gaze up at her with sly, malicious eyes. "But you have the good sense to shut up and pin your ears back. You are wise, Maura Miller, wise and brave for one who passed over so young. I knew that the second I first set my eyes on you in the square. Too good for that barbarian you gave your life for."

She tensed slightly, pricked by his slur, before regaining her composure. "He was, and is, my love, sir. I gladly gave my life for him and would do so again." She braced herself for the old man's response.

"Pah, love. What poppycock. He died, you died, we all died. Love didn't save a blasted one of us. While Wellesley sat on the ridge and watched, the ink on our death warrants still wet on the page. Belittled and betrayed. Where was love, then?"

"Yes, sir. We were talking about cricket. Tactics?"

"Yes, yes, of course," blustered Skelly, regaining his train of thought. "Strategy requires forethought, vision, meticulous planning. That I have in bundles, as did Dobson. Samuel thinks he's smart, and yes, he is. He's two, maybe three steps ahead of the game. The thing is, Dobson was five, as am I. Samuel is learning on the job, which gives me the upper hand."

Maura's lip curled, a leering smile crossing her pale features. She was beautiful, but it was a cruel, raw beauty that left no doubt as to the blackness of her heart. "So, what are you saying, sir, we have them? I'd give anything to wipe that smug smile off the White Witch's face."

"Yes, my dear, we have. Hook, line, and sinker, I believe. The bait was dangled, and Samuel near took my arm off, gobbling it down. His emotions blind him, he dives in and doesn't fully grasp the bigger picture. You can't teach that instinct. Whereas I..." He clenched a leathered fist and grinned, exposing rancid, yellowing stumps masquerading as teeth.

"I see it all, Maura."

"What do you need me to do, sir, just name it?"

"He might have saved his little friends for now, but he doesn't realise he's just handed me the keys to that foul lump of rock they all value so much. Keys that will fling open the portal again and allow my employers to do what they please with dear old planet Earth. Yes, he's just handed me the jewel in their crown on a silver platter."

Skelly topped up his tumbler from the decanter and took a congratulatory swig. "I need you to pay a visit to 17/4, Maura. There's a package I need collected."

CHAPTER 53 - A QUIET NIGHT IN

It had been a perfect evening, but now Harley needed to pee. Badly. She rolled onto her side, switched on the bedside light, and dubiously eyed the waiting wheelchair. It had broken her heart to sit in it all night when all she wanted to do was leap to her feet and scream, "Mum, Dad. I can walk!" But rules were rules, and Giro had sternly warned that she was not to do anything to arouse suspicion during this too brief interlude with the Davison clan in Ardgallon, before returning to the fray of battling Skelly and the Scourge. They had each been given twenty-four precious, quicksilver hours.

A dinner of pizza, chicken goujons, and dough balls, washed down with several glasses of fizzy orange, was followed by movie night. The first Hunger Games film was chosen by Harley herself, much to the chagrin of younger brother Aidan, who wanted some brainless Jason Statham effort involving lots of big guns and pointless car chases. No, an evening with her hero Katniss Everdeen was much more Harley's cup of tea. She had allowed her father to assist in transferring her onto the sofa, wracked with guilt and bursting to tell them the truth. It would have to wait. Next time, Harley, next time, you can walk through the front door and prove all the doubting doctors wrong.

The rest of the night had been a happy haze of Pringles, M&Ms, and the love of the three people who meant most to her. Aidan and Harley fought like cat and dog but beneath the bravado, adored each other. He was her little brother but loved to play the protective elder sibling, even more so since she was mown down on the bridge by that drunk driver. All engineered by Skelly, who had sensed her presence in the sleepy village that hid a gateway to countless other worlds.

She really needed to pee. Without even thinking, Harley threw back the covers and swung a leg out of bed, her toes gripping the warm, welcoming carpet. It was a simple act, yet one she had craved for months. Her other foot followed, and before she realised it, Harley was out the bedroom door and shuffling sleepily up the hallway towards the ground floor bathroom. She rubbed her eyes, regretting opening that last tube of Pringles before colliding with a solid surface and stumbling back onto her bottom. She looked up in shock to see the lanky, bare-chested form of her brother, clad only in a pair of boxer shorts.

"What? How?"

"Sssshhh, Aidan. You wake Mum and Dad up, and I'll never talk to you as long as I live."

"But...you're walking...your wheelchair?"

"I mean it, blabbermouth. You breathe a word of this to anyone, and I'll put you in a wheelchair."

A calculated look replaced the previous stunned expression on his face. Her brother was a wheeler and dealer of epic proportions, and if he could mould a situation to his advantage, he would be on it in a flash. Harley waited for the opening gambit. She would have to think fast.

"Go on then, sister dearest. Explain yourself."

Harley clambered to her feet, mind whirring furiously to come up with a plausible reason for her miraculous recovery. Aidan waited, arms folded, his default cocky expression back in place. Let the negotiations begin.

"Well, you know it's mum's birthday next week?"

"Flip, is it? I'd forgotten. I'm going to have to get her chocolates or something."

"Wise up, she's got Type 2 diabetes. You'll get a clip round the ear if you hand her a box of Milk Tray."

Aidan frowned, before remembering he held the moral high ground. "You. Legs. Talk now."

"Okay, okay. It's like this. You know I've been killing myself in the gym and at physio?"

"Yeah." He stared suspiciously at her legs.

"Well, about a month ago, I started to get this weird tingling sensation in my legs. It intensified until I thought I was going to explode. Then one day, I was staring at my feet, willing it to stop when the big toe on my left foot twitched. At first, I thought I imagined it, but the more I focused and concentrated, the more toes started to respond over the next few days. Gradually, I've built up my strength until...well, this." She pointed at her legs, kicking out a foot, and hit Aidan with her cheesiest smile in the hope he would fall for this not so little white lie.

Her little brother, who towered almost a foot above her, pulled his most serious expression before bursting into a broad smile. "Oh, my God, Harley, that's incredible wait until I tell..."

"No, you plonker. I want to wait until Mum's birthday and surprise her. Just imagine. Me, standing up in front of her to cut the cake, it will be the best present ever. But I need you to keep your mouth shut. Please." She hoped the tug on his heartstrings would do the trick. Despite his tough-guy image, she knew Aidan was as soft as butter on the inside, a real mummy's boy.

An age passed before he spoke. "Okay, deal, but what's in it for me?"

"What do you mean, what's in it for you? Seeing your beloved mother's face light up with delight. What else do you want?"

"Twenty."

"Twenty?"

"Twenty pounds for my silence. Otherwise, I might let slip your devious wee secret."

"You absolute..."

"Now, now, Harls. You'll wake the parents." He smirked, confident he had his big sister in a corner she couldn't wriggle out of.

"Fine," fumed Harley, shooting him the middle finger, as she turned and stomped into the bathroom, the soft chuckles of her brother ringing in her ears.

She leaned back against the door, the urge to pee suddenly gone as the reality of her near-miss struck home. Straining to listen, she breathed a sigh of relief as creaking floorboards above indicated Aiden had returned to bed as opposed to rush into his parent's room to spill the beans. That was close. The giddy delight of a night with her family had almost backfired in spectacular fashion. Harley stepped forward to the washbasin and, turning the cold water tap on, liberally splashed her face. Staring into the mirror above the basin, she puffed her cheeks out. Saving the planet was one thing, but outwitting your younger brother was an entirely different matter.

"That was way too close, Harley," she chastised her pensive reflection. "Waaaaay too close."

CHAPTER 54 - THIS TROUBLED LAND OF OURS

Kirkwood buttoned up the toggles on his duffel coat and buried his frozen hands deep within its spacious pockets. Autumn in Northern Ireland was not for the faint-hearted, and the long stretch of Royal Avenue in the heart of Belfast's city centre seemed to channel the icy blast even more ferociously in his direction. It was dry, if nothing else, and a smattering of shoppers bustled about, making the most of the conditions. It could be snowing within the hour, or the sun could be splitting the rocks—that was his home country. Four seasons in one day.

Upon arriving back, he had tentatively reached out to Gerry via text message, suggesting they meet for a pint in the Montreal, their local hangout. At first, there had been radio silence, and the minutes dragged into several hours before his phone thankfully pinged, its screen lighting up.

Ok...

It was a start, if not the sturdiest of olive branches. Gerry was a miserable old git at the best of times, so Kirkwood recognised Herculean powers of persuasion would be required to bury the hatchet in the ground as opposed to the back of his head. He turned right onto High Street, the familiar sight of the Albert Clock towering ahead of him. It was Belfast's answer to Big Ben and brought back memories of his nocturnal stakeout of Meredith less than a week ago. It seemed more like a lifetime. So much had happened since then, the loss of Dobson aching most prominently in his bruised heart.

Kirkwood had considered inviting Grogan as well, to break the ice between Gerry and himself if nothing else, but decided against it. If he was going to properly smoke the peace pipe with the latter, then Grogan would prove an unnecessary distraction as opposed to intermediary. Firstly, he would turn up late when time was at a premium, and secondly would be more interested in chatting up the nearest available woman under fifty years old, as opposed to focusing on the needs of his feuding friends.

Kirkwood shuddered. In less than a century, this street would be a ravaged wasteland, testimony to the greed and hatred which gripped man time and time again. Their island was already soaked in enough blood to last an eternity, but it seemed future generations were not prepared to learn the lessons of their forefathers.

"This troubled land of ours, where will it end?" muttered Kirkwood, slightly taken aback by the melancholic words. He smiled, his spirits lifted by a familiar sight up ahead on his left. "The Montreal," his second home and so often refuge during the ups and mostly downs of life BM—Before Meredith.

He pushed the swing doors to the front bar open, inhaling the familiar odours of stale beer and staler moods into his lungs. Nothing had changed. Not remarkable really, as it was less than a week since he had stepped inside. It felt as though several lifetimes had passed, however.

Perched on a barstool by the door sat Big Mark, the ever-present, impassive doorman. He was well past pension age, but Kirkwood had watched him toss men half his age out of the bar when their unruly behaviour breached his unspoken code of conduct. He was the archetypal Belfast hard man, chiselled from the granite of Divis Mountain, but beneath the layers of knotted muscle was a kind heart and a solid moral compass.

"Alright, big man, what's the craic?" hailed Kirkwood, delighted to see the old warhorse in situ.

"Not too bad, son, yourself?"

"I'm grand. Is Brain of Britain here?"

"Your man, Gerry? Nah, he left ten minutes ago. Said he couldn't be annoyed waiting for you any longer." The bouncer considered Kirkwood's crestfallen face before erupting into laughter.

"I'm only messing. He's down in the lounge. Things must be serious. He's even got you a round in."

Kirkwood nodded in relief. "Thanks, Mark. Catch you later." Walking down the length of the bar, several sets of tired eyes followed him from the row of booths that lined one side. Opposite them, the proprietor, Francie, eyed Kirkwood warily as he pretended to dry a pint glass with a towel of dubious cleanliness. Despite having frequented the premises on countless occasions and filling his till with thousands of pounds, Francie still regarded Kirkwood, Gerry, and Grogan with an air of barely concealed contempt.

Kirkwood was determined to win the weasel over one day, but it would have to wait for now. Gerry was the priority.

"Francie."

"Kirkwood."

Pleasantries exchanged, Kirkwood exited the bar and proceeded along a short corridor that connected it to the lounge at the rear of the building. The toilets to the left greeted him with the unsettling aroma of overwhelming urine tempered by an undercurrent of bleach. Kirkwood was reassured the bar's abominable health and safety standards remained as low as ever.

A short flight of stairs took him into the bowels of the Montreal, a rarely frequented lounge that last saw sunlight around 1978. Kirkwood scanned the empty collection of tables and chairs, his eyes adjusting to the murky half-light. This was a place where dreams came to wither and die. To his right, a small, semi-circular bar was tended by a bored-looking woman of indeterminate age, and a face reminiscent of a heavily made-up prune. Kirkwood raised a hand in recognition.

"Afternoon, Tanya. Looking as radiant as ever."

He was rewarded with a withering smile before her attention returned to the crowning glory of the Montreal's social experience — a 50-inch high definition television mounted on a steel bracket on the far wall. Sky Sports News was reviewing the weekend's Premiership matches, and a panel of besuited pundits were arguing amongst themselves over a penalty decision in the United - City match. Kirkwood would once have been interested in such a debate, but today he had bigger fish to fry.

The fish in question was hunched over a barely touched pint at a table in the far corner. The worries of the world seemed piled on his slumped shoulders as Kirkwood edged towards him, uncertain as to his opening gambit. Humour? Reconciliation? The last time they spoke, it had almost come to blows over Kirkwood's growing obsession with the mysterious homeless girl he believed held the secret to Skelly and the OCD which ruled his life.

"Things must be bad if you're off your beer." Kirkwood stood over Gerry, uncertain if he should await an invitation to sit down. The older man looked as if he hadn't slept since their last encounter, sporting a heavy, dark stubble, flecked with grey. Greasy hair, stained clothing, and heavy, bloodshot eyes completed a look that wouldn't have been out of place in a homeless shelter. On second thought, that was a disservice to homeless people, thought Kirkwood.

"Sit down before I throw this pint over you," growled Gerry, a threat Kirkwood took seriously, quickly taking the seat opposite. He gestured towards a second pint. "Don't say I never buy you anything."

"Cheers." Kirkwood lifted the pint to his lips, taking a small sip. Its frothy head coated his upper lip, and the glass left his fingers damp from condensation. "But why did you get me a Guinness, you know I prefer lager?"

"Call it spite. Consider yourself lucky you're not getting a dig in the chops." He looked up and considered Kirkwood with bleary eyes. "So, what have you been up to? Still chasing wee girls round the town?"

"What, you're interested now? Last time we spoke, you stormed off. Thought you'd washed your hands of me?"

Gerry lifted his pint and swilled its contents, staring into its golden depths as if they held the answer to all his problems. Eventually, he downed the remainder of it in one sustained swallow, emitted a hearty belch, and slammed it back down on the sticky-surfaced table.

"You're one of the few friends I have, Kirkwood. Probably the only one, if you discount that deadweight Grogan. I might not agree with everything you say and do, nor you with me, but if I've learned nothing else in life, I've learnt this. Hang on to the people who matter. Life's miserable enough without having to live it on your own."

Kirkwood smiled and lifted his glass. "You really are a barroom philosopher, Gerry. Cheers."

The two clinked their glasses and sat in comfortable silence for a few moments, before ordering another round and picking up their friendship from where they had left off.

CHAPTER 55 - WE ARE WHO WE ARE

In the dream, Meredith was laughing. Belly aching, tears streaming down the face, proper laughing. They were sitting by a fire on a balmy beach, the crackling kindling shooting sparks up into the clear night sky where they danced like flirting fireflies, before disappearing into the vast starry expanse. Audible above it all was the surf crashing onto the shore and surging up the sand towards them, threatening to engulf all but falling yards short before sulkily retreating towards the unseen ocean.

Everyone was there. Harley, cross-legged and pulling daft faces, the light of the flames bouncing off her eyes, giddy with delight. Kirkwood, as ever the good-humoured butt of their jokes. Samuel, attempting to keep a straight face but failing. And perched on a log, presiding over the frivolity, sat Dobson. Sporting countless laughter lines on his tanned, bearded face. Meredith had never seen his eyes so clear. Gone was the fatigue which dogged him in the days leading up to his demise at Ardgallon.

Meredith felt her hand being squeezed and turned to see Emily beside her, an inquisitive expression on her features. Her best friend—the circle now complete. She had everyone and everything she desired.

"Happy?"

"Yeah, Ems, I'm really happy."

"Good, our work is almost done then."

"Almost? What do you mean?"

"Well, we still have to rescue you, don't we?" Emily reached forward and tucked a stray strand of Meredith's dark hair, caught by a mild breeze, behind an ear. "It's not as if I'm going to leave you with that caveman, Rodriguez, to drink yourself into oblivion."

"But, I'm safe, I'm happy, I'm with you guys."

The breeze picked up, bringing with it an icy blast that chilled Meredith to the core. She shivered, wrapping her arms around her midriff, before holding both palms out to eke extra heat from the fire. The flames danced higher and wilder as the laughter from her friends rose in tandem. Meredith howled with them, throwing her head back, her sides aching. She had no idea what she was laughing at, but it was so funny. So funny, yet so cold. She turned again to tell Emily but started upon realising she was alone. The fireplace deserted as the furnace continued to climb into the night sky. Her skin should have been scalded by her proximity to the pyre in front, but an icy chill permeated her bones, causing her to tremble uncontrollably.

She spun round, frantically scanning the sands for a sign of her friends. Calling their names, she ran from the fire, desperate for her cries to be answered. She ran this way, then that, until her foot caught a rock, flinging her face-first onto the beach. She threw out both hands to break the fall, and her fingers dug into the compact, damp sand. Sandcastle sand, as she and her friends had called it on long summer holidays up on Portrush Strand as a child.

Meredith had no idea how her disoriented dash had brought her so close to the waters, but before she had a chance to react, a wave washed over her hands and face, filling her mouth. She spat and blinked as seconds later, a more forceful wave immersed her head and upper body. Meredith started to flail, desperate for her limbs to find some purchase and regain an upright position.

"Wake up."

The voice was distant and vaguely familiar, barely audible above the crashing surf. A third surge, more powerful again, caught her totally unawares, sending her spinning onto her back like a crazed breakdancer. She started to panic, unable to distinguish up from down, as her lungs began to fill with water. Part of her wanted to let go, to succumb as her friends weren't coming back, and without them, what was the point carrying on?

"Wake up." More insistent this time, except why should she? Why not just let go and allow the sea to claim her for its own? Better to be fish food than alone in this world. It would be easy to breathe deep and let the saltwater take her to a better place. A safer place where Skelly and his legions could never harm her. Except, it wasn't saltwater...

"WAKE UP, MEREDITH!"

Meredith shot bolt upright as Tara emptied a third glass of water over her head. She was in their room at the hotel, the reality of her plight striking her like...well, a glass of icy-water over the head.

"You were laughing in your sleep. It's time to get up. We have morning duties to attend to."

Meredith stumbled out of bed and lurched towards the en suite bathroom. The comparative luxury of the exquisite suite did little to alleviate the air of apprehension that hung over her like a dank smog. The shower was hot and welcoming, a protective wall from which she could escape the constant supervision for a few blissful moments. She was still to work out where the electricity came from to permit luxuries such as power showers. Tara vaguely referred to generators but didn't entirely seem to know herself, when asked.

Eventually, she reluctantly stepped out, towelled, and dressed in her mandatory white attire. She sensed the beginnings of a monumental hangover starting to hover on the fringes of her awareness, but thankfully her blood/alcohol levels were still high enough to keep it at bay. She had no idea how Rodriguez fared with the Priestess, but true to his word, Arthur had arrived at her room before midnight with a bottle of the foul wine she now labelled, 'Jerusalem Juice.' Tara had shot her a disapproving look before turning onto her side and switching the light off, leaving Meredith in the adjacent bed to sip sullenly from its contents until unconsciousness finally claimed her.

Morning chores boiled down to washing, drying, and putting away a mountain of plates, glasses, and cutlery stacked haphazardly in the hotel kitchen. She tackled the task with relish. Grateful for the monotony, which allowed her to slip into autopilot and avoid the endless questions which pounded her psyche, eager for regress. The more she tried to convince herself that all was well and Kirkwood or

Emily or even Rodriguez would rescue her, the less convinced she became. The only silver lining to her morning was discovering half a bottle of whiskey on a dusty shelf in a walk-in pantry. She secreted it amongst the voluminous folds of her dress and took furtive nips whenever the opportunity arose, and none of the other kitchen workers were nearby. The warm glow of the alcohol soon started to spread from her stomach to aching limbs, casting a golden haze on her surroundings and circumstances. She caught herself whistling the tune to some nonsensical cartoon she used to watch as a child. So lost in her alcohol-induced thoughts that she was utterly unaware of Tara entering the kitchen.

"Well, you've cheered up."

Meredith jumped, dropping the plate she was soaking to the floor where it shattered.

"Quit sneaking up on people like that. You near gave me a heart attack."

"Well, at least you've finally woke up," replied the younger girl. "And you've fair rattled through those dishes. We are due our break. Do you fancy some fresh air?"

She led Meredith out of the kitchen and towards the main foyer of the hotel where two guards lounged on an opulent antique sofa, their firearms stacked against its side.

"Where do they get all this stuff?" whispered Meredith as they strolled through the main doors and down several steps to the outside world. It was an overcast day, and a faint drizzle hung in the air. She was glad of the fresh air and closed her eyes, allowing the gentle rain to coat her face.

"The Priestess tells us God provides for all our needs. Like the Israelites in the Wilderness before they were led to the Promised Land."

"I don't remember Moses being equipped with enough AK47s to arm a small country. I must have missed that Sunday at children's church."

Tara smiled as they walked past the ruined museum towards the river's edge. Across it, the city sat, sullen and silent. To her far-right, a plume of smoke was rising, but it was the silence that struck her. No traffic, no planes overhead—nothing but silence.

"What have we done?" Meredith's voice was small and desolate, her normally combative nature quashed by the devastation spread before her. Many of the buildings were smoke scarred, and the Old Custom House directly opposite was gutted out. The river itself was stagnant and still, coated with debris and slick with oil. Nothing could survive in there for very long. To her left, two ends of a bridge jutted towards one another, like lovers straining to grasp hands but never destined to do so, as the middle section had crumbled into the depths below. Everywhere she looked was ruin and wreckage, the rancid corpse of a once-proud city.

"We are who we are," Tara replied softly. "Fingers always hovering on the self-destruction button. Well, this time, we kept pressing until there was nothing left...but this." She placed an arm round Meredith's shoulder and pulled her into a tight embrace. The taller, dark-haired girl did not resist, grateful for any scrap of compassion when confronted by the enormity of her current plight.

"I don't belong here. I just want to go home and be with my friends." Meredith turned and buried her face in Tara's shoulder, muffling the guttural sobs which erupted from the pit of her being. Initially surprised, Tara froze before enveloping this strange young woman in her arms. She raised her eyes and looked towards the unwelcoming skies, wrestling with a decision to which she knew there was only one answer. Finally, her resolve steeled, she spoke.

"I know, Meredith, I know. That's why I'm going to get you out of here."

CHAPTER 56 - RETURN TO HELLFAST

Samuel looked at the three determined faces in turn, before speaking.

"Is all well with you?"

Harley spoke first. "Yeah, although it cost me £20 thanks to my deadbeat brother. But yeah, it was good. Thank you, Samuel."

Samuel nodded. "Kirkwood?"

"Well, I'm here," he replied. They were in the cemetery gatehouse where Samuel, in their absence, had made no discernible effort to tidy up. "Last time I saw Gerry, he was pouring himself into a taxi en route to another bar for a nightcap with Grogan."

"Sore head?" asked Samuel, concerned that a hungover saviour of the universe was of little use to him.

"No, I'm grand, actually. You would have been very proud of me. A few pints, and then I went on the water. Gerry was horrified, of course, but he settled down once I kept setting the drinks in front of him. Whatever happens now, me and him are sorted. I can die a happy man."

"Well, I intend to do everything in my power to ensure it doesn't come to that."

"Me too," added Emily. "The afterlife is bad enough without staring at your miserable face, 24/7." Kirkwood opened his mouth to issue a cutting rebuke, but a cough from Samuel indicated it was not the time for childish arguments. Behind the big man's back, Emily stuck her tongue out while Kirkwood silently fumed. The gatehouse was one of the few places on earth where she could take bodily form, an outpost for the Forsaken established by Dobson, and maintained by Samuel. It was on the planet, but not of it.

"I am glad you got to spend some time with your friends and family, but now we must focus on rescuing Meredith. Giro awaits my signal to plane the four of us to the Queen Street compound."

"Wonderful," groaned Kirkwood. "What better way to start the day than having your internal organs trampoline on your stomach."

Samuel continued, choosing to ignore the interruption. "When we get there, Major Deacon will brief us on how he plans to extract Meredith from New Jerusalem."

"Which no doubt will involve lots of gung-ho explosions and macho chest-thumping," snapped Emily.

"There are female soldiers in his unit, too," offered Kirkwood.

"Whatever, Kirky."

"I told you my name is..."

"Please." Samuel raised his voice several notches. "Like Giro, we defer to his orders. Bickering like this in front of him will do us no favours and likely end unpleasantly. Understood?"

"Sorry, Samuel." Kirkwood internally kicked himself. She was the most annoying girl he'd ever met, but there was a time and a place, and this wasn't it.

"Crystal," added Emily curtly.

"Thank you," sighed Samuel.

"What about Ariana and Tess?" asked Harley. "Where are they going to be when we go back to the future?"

"Don't worry about them. They will have plenty to keep them occupied while we are gone. I have left them with very clear instructions."

"Cool. They're our spin-off story. A bit like the Wolverine movies or The Hobbit."

"The Hobbit is not a spin-off, you goof. Tolkien wrote it before The Lord of the Rings; everybody knows that."

"Cool your jets, Kirkwood, I didn't. Some of us had a life when you were stuck in your bedroom playing Dragons & Dungeons. And anyway, who's this Talking character? Everybody knows it was directed by Peter Jackson."

"Give me strength." Kirkwood winced. "Okay, Samuel, let's get this over with. At least when I'm planeing, I don't have to listen to this drivel."

Samuel nodded and reached out his hands. The four of them formed a circle in the room. Then they were gone. They reappeared six miles across the city, eighty-seven years later, in the yard of the Queen Street station. Soldiers raced in all directions, equipment rattling as orders were barked over the hum of diesel engines. A row of six armoured landrovers sat backed up against the rear wall of the yard, several mounted with heavy-duty weaponry. Deacon leaned over the bonnet of one, poring over a map stretched across it. He seemed unaware of their arrival.

"Over here." They turned to see a familiar, friendly figure waving at them. Giro was seated on stone steps leading into the old entrance of the building. It was now bricked up and festooned with weeds on either side. They waved back and joined him. Giro hopped to his feet and warmly shook hands with his much larger colleague.

"Good to see you, Samuel."

"You too, my friend, it's been too long. How is life treating you on this plane?"

Giro swept an arm to take in the bustle of the yard. "Well, as you can see, there's never a dull moment in Hellfast. And it's about to step up another gear or two if old Deacon has anything to do with it. He's been chomping at the bit to have a pop at the Priestess. Now's his chance."

"Hmmm, so I see. Are you certain this is the only way? Have we exhausted all other options?"

Giro pushed his spectacles further up his nose so that he less resembled an errant professor haphazardly dumped in the middle of a war zone.

"I'm afraid so. She has some kind of force field in effect. Meaning our powers are largely inert within New Jerusalem. There's very little I can do other than assure you Meredith is still alive. As for Deacon's more, shall we say, direct methods, he's much more tactical than you might think. If you want to walk with me, I'll let him explain it all to you."

They began to cross the yard, weaving between scurrying soldiers, all working to a tight deadline. Deacon looked up from his map and grunted a greeting.

"Thanks for dropping by."

"Sir, let me introduce you to my other Commanding Officer. Samuel, this is Major Nathaniel Deacon, Security Solutions, Sector 8."

Deacon shook Samuel's hand warily, sizing up his opposite number. "Don't you lot have ranks? Or surnames for that matter?"

"Samuel will suffice, Major. Thank you for including us in your plans. For the purposes of this operation, I obviously bow to your greater knowledge and experience of the area."

"I should bloody well think so," grumbled Deacon returning his attention to the map. "I see you've brought an entourage with you. Well, make sure they all behave themselves. I won't be responsible for losing another teenage superhero on my watch."

"I'm not a..." started Kirkwood before a dark look from Samuel persuaded him to hold his tongue.

"Continue, please, sir," urged Giro, ever the peacemaker. "We're all ears."

Deacon regarded Giro dubiously before clearing his throat and jabbing a finger at the map. "New Jerusalem consists of an area of land which previously housed the city's Titanic Quarter and harbour area. The main access points are here and here." He indicated two random points on the far side of the river from them. "We control the bridges, but beyond them, it's largely a no-go zone. Our intelligence drones indicate the Priestess has two to three hundred armed men and up to three thousand people under her control. To date, we've left them be as we have enough on our hands, keeping tabs on the Dirties on this side of the city."

"So, if we go in over the bridges, it's going to be a bloodbath?" Kirkwood was no military strategist but grasped enough of Deacon's briefing to speak aloud what they were all thinking.

"Basically, yes." Deacon rose from the map and rubbed his eyes, suddenly looking extremely tired. Kirkwood wondered when he last slept. "We would probably win through in the end, but at what cost? It would be a hollow Pyrrhic victory, and your friend Meredith would be dead before we got anywhere near her."

"What are our options then?"

Deacon grinned, an unnerving sight, revealing uneven rows of tobacco-stained teeth. "I'm glad you asked that, young fella. It's time I called in a favour with an old associate of mine. Anyone fancy a shopping trip?"

CHAPTER 57 - WE ARE GODS

He swooped low over the city, probing and testing the newfound powers the old man had bestowed upon him. Skimming the tops of buildings and spiralling through low cloud cover, he was king of all he saw, intoxicated by the bracing wind whipping past his ears. To his right, the red-haired woman veered off to the right, swooping over the river towards her predetermined target. They were to rendezvous later on the ancient, foreboding hills which sloped down towards the lough.

The Hennessy bitch would have to wait for now, and the same went for her braindead sidekick as he'd bigger fish to fry at the moment. Skelly had seen to that. At first, he thought he was dreaming or in some kind of lucid coma. For all he knew, he was lying in some hospital bed being kept alive by all manner of machines. One minute he was on the cusp of greatness, about to redeem the honour of his martyred father, the next he was dumped in the middle of nowhere surrounded by nothing but grass.

He'd no idea how long he had wandered, but no matter how many miles he walked or what direction he chose, there was nothing, no landmarks or indication of habitation. The weather was unchanging, night never came, nor hunger or thirst. It was then that Adam

O'Sullivan concluded he was in hell, destined to spend eternity there. No sulphuric flames and little red men with pitchforks for him, but mind-numbing, unceasing monotony. There were no trees to hang himself from, no rivers to drown in, and even then, what was the point? He was dead anyway. It wasn't exactly what the priests had taught at school, but they were nothing but a bunch of drunks and deviants anyway. Now, he knew the truth, and it was far worse than anyone could have imagined.

He laughed, he cried, he pleaded and screamed but all to no avail. In the end, he lay down on the immaculately preserved lawns and stared at the sky, his mind untethered and adrift. That's when she appeared, standing over him, her pale features framed by an unruly tangle of russet curls that tumbled down her back. Was she an angel, a devil, a figment of an imagination stretched to breaking point? Adam didn't care. He sat up and listened, he listened to every word she spoke from those ruby red lips. Adam had no idea what love was, hell he didn't even know if he was capable of it, but the second he set eyes on Maura Miller was the closest he would ever come to it.

It was all nonsense, of course. She was quite mad, but he was dead and in hell, so why not make the most of a bad lot? If that meant listening to the ranting of the most beautiful woman he had ever set eyes on, then it was a small price to pay. He played along, oohing and aahing as she calmly informed him that she had died at the Battle of Waterloo nearly two hundred years ago with a bunch of other soldiers. Something about a square, whatever that was. Then she rambled on about losing the love of her life, her childhood sweetheart, but that was then, and this was now. Was she flirting with him? Was that allowed in hell?

Adam never had any trouble attracting attention from the opposite sex. He knew he was a good looking lad, but back then, there were more pressing matters. Girls were an unnecessary distraction. He was proud of his laser focus, it had brought him so far, right to the brink of infamy and justice for his father. Until that wee cow, the Bomb Girl intervened. Maura explained that she had powers, nothing was quite as it seemed, and she wanted to introduce him to a friend of hers. Some old guy called Scully. No, that was the FBI agent from the X-Files. Come to think of it, she had red hair as well, just like Maura.

Skelly. That was it—Skelly. Skelly was her boss and had croaked it at Waterloo as well. She said Adam and Skelly had a lot in common, that they were cut from the same cloth. Skelly could guarantee Adam a way out, and what's more, an opportunity for revenge. Revenge on goody two shoes Ariana Hennessy, her gormless mate, and the world that had turned its back on him. For Skelly understood. He knew what it was like to be cast aside, treated like the dirt on someone's shoe. The more Adam listened, the more he fell under the Irish woman's seductive lilt, the more he wanted to believe there was something to her crazy tale.

That's when he asked her to prove it.

That's why he was flying, yes flying, over Belfast. A Belfast in ruins, a Belfast on its knees, a city he liked very much, for he wanted it all to burn, the whole damn country to burn. This was insane, far surpassing his own plans to bomb the heart out of a university complex. This was the big league. This was what he had been born for. It was a shame he had to die in order to discover that.

He watched as Maura descended across the river, growing ever smaller until she was no more than a distant speck. What a woman, what a rush. She told him this was merely a taste of what was to come, a small sample of the riches and glory he would experience. She hinted she was part of that prize, and more would be revealed when he met Skelly. But first, a small task to prove he was worthy of initiation, a formality, nothing more.

Adam knew Belfast well. He had worked an electrical apprenticeship back when the city was a thriving, modern metropolis. Skills that served him well when it came to the tricky business of building a bomb. He flashed over the Castle Court shopping complex. Fires burned on its roof, and he saw figures huddled round, eking out what little warmth they could. He passed no more than a dozen feet over their heads and marvelled at how nobody had the slightest idea he was there, adding invisibility to his growing list of attributes. Onwards, across Mulberry Square, once a hub for lovers of fine food and ales, now a crumbling, cratered mess. He remembered drinking there when they had a big job in the city centre. Cold beer, and long, warm Friday afternoons. If only they could see him now.

Up ahead, there it was, the reinforced steel gates of the compound opening as a cavalcade of beat up police landrovers rolled out at speed. His targets were in it, allies of the Bomb Girl. Some bloke with a back to front name, a disabled girl who could now walk, and the ghost of some milly who had slit her wrists. Again, utter nonsense, but who was he to judge—the Invisible Flying Man from hell. Three, four, five, six vehicles swinging left, then right towards the back of Castle Court. The front and rear trucks had been adapted, heavy-duty machine guns welded to their roofs, operated by gunners hunched over with fingers poised on the triggers. If they could see him above them, the sky around would be filled with red hot lead.

He watched as gates containing the shopping centre's old docking bay were rolled back to allow the lead two landrovers through. The remaining four formed in a semi-circle outside, facing the gates which were closed on them. He watched as ant-like figures emerged from the shopping complex and moved towards the vehicles, where other equally tiny shapes were emerging from. Some kind of meeting, but about what he did not know nor particularly care. That information was well above his pay grade. His instructions had been to follow the convoy, find out where it was going, and then meet with the lovely Maura on the foreboding Cavehill to the north.

He soared upwards at will, arms tight to his side, fists clenched. He was like Ironman but without the accompanying armour. The ruler of the skies. As he levelled out and neared their meeting point, he saw her, standing on the highest promontory, the wind whipping her dazzling mane across her face. She smiled in recognition as he landed clumsily beyond her, stumbling on like a drunk paraglider until he found his footing. Turning, she spoke to him, and for Adam O'Sullivan, nothing else in this or any other world mattered.

"Did you follow them?"

"Yes. They went round the back of Castle Court. Seemed to be a meeting going on between the people inside and the guys in the landrovers. What are they, cops?"

"Something like that," purred Maura, walking towards him. She stroked the side of his cheek with a leather-gloved finger, sending chills shooting through his body. "You've done well, Adam, very well. The Colonel will be pleased."

"When do I get to meet him? You said it would be soon."

"And it will be, it will be. There's just a few more errands we need to run beforehand."

"Good. All I want is that bitch Ariana's head on a stick." He spat the words out, unable to contain his loathing.

"Channel that, Adam. Channel that hate. You will have your revenge—we all will. The Colonel has big plans for you. You're the key to unlocking a whole new world for us, a world where we will be gods."

"I like the sound of that," smirked Adam as Maura stood on her toes to place the gentlest of kisses on his cheek. "I like that very much indeed."

CHAPTER 58 - THE DEAD HEAL QUICKLY

"Are you kidding me?" Meredith stared across the broad waters of the Lagan and weighed up the options before her. She closed her eyes, swallowed hard, and turned to Tara. "It's disgusting, it's vile. I can't do that to you."

"It's the only way," begged Tara. "The guards patrol the outer perimeters throughout the night. They have four vehicles and work in shifts, two at a time. I can get you in the back of one of them, throw a bit of old tarpaulin over you, and you're out. You slip over the side when they slow down, and you're gone. Nobody will miss you until the next morning."

"But what about you? She will know you're involved somehow. You'll be flayed alive." The thought of sacrificing this sweet girl for the sake of her own freedom galled Meredith.

"I'm good. Arthur owes me a favour. We have an arrangement. I scratch his back, and he scratches mine from time to time."

"Oh no, please, Tara, tell me you don't..." Meredith screwed up her nose, appalled at the thought of that greasy sack of blubber pawing over her friend.

"Don't be ridiculous, I have my standards, unlike some of the others. I caught him once stealing tobacco from the stores. If the Priestess found out, she would have had his hand off, but I covered for him. He owes me."

"Right, well, okay then, but it still sounds incredibly risky." Meredith was grasping at straws but would never forgive herself for not speaking up. "Won't you come with me? I can't bear the thought of leaving you alone here."

"This is my place. It's not ideal, but I get three square meals a day, and I'm safe. I chose to come here, and I choose to remain. You, though, Meredith, I've no idea who you really are and how you came to be here, but you are not of this time and place. It's a risk I'm willing to take. Please, it's your only chance."

"But what about Rodriguez? He said he'd get me out of here."

"By all accounts, he has been persuaded otherwise by the Priestess. A night in her chambers was more than enough to convince him that a life as her partner was too good an opportunity to turn down."

"That dirty piece of lying..."

"Come, Meredith," announced Tara, lifting the hems of her dress. "Our break is over. We must return to our duties before we are missed." She started to scurry back towards the hotel, Meredith jogging behind her. "Tonight at 11. Be by the bins at the rear of the arena. Arthur will collect you. Do as he says, and God be with you."

Meredith could only nod in assent, humbled by the kindness she was being shown. She wasn't certain if God had any input in this, he had shown minimal interest in her life to date, but she would never forget this slight little girl in the oversized white dress.

∞ ∞ ∞

Rodriguez stretched and yawned in satisfaction, a big cat well-fed and watered. He could get used to this. Dozing on and off on the huge bed, wrapped in crisp, clean linen sheets. He estimated it was mid-morning, the woman having left several hours ago to do whatever she did. Something about an inspection of stores and fuel supplies. If he was going to be her escort, then such tiresome administrative tasks were not for him. A hearty breakfast had been brought to the room as she departed, bending to kiss him hungrily on the lips.

"I think you and I are going to get on famously, Prophet."

"I aim to please my lady."

"So far, you have exceeded my expectations. Enjoy your morning. Rest and avail of the facilities. I look forward to your company over lunch." She smirked and sashayed from the room, flanked by two Maidens, heads bowed, but faces beetroot red at the exchange they had just witnessed.

Placing his hands behind his head, he stared at the panelled ceiling, weighing up the pros and cons of his current predicament. Yes, she was insane but stunning at the same time. Last night proved he met all her physical needs and possessed what was required in that department. As for the rest, well, Martim Rodriguez was a survivor, if nothing else. Seven years with Wellington and two hundred with Skelly was a testament to that. Putting out fires, crushing resistance, doing everything that was asked of him and more.

Events at Ardgallon had left a sour taste in his mouth, however. The cowardice of the Drummer Boy, William, and the loss of Gunther, the closest thing he had to a friend in the Company sorely tested his loyalty to Skelly. Skelly, who he'd followed loyally to the grave and beyond, across countless planes and for what? Getting the blame for every mishap, the fall guy while others emerged unscathed with their reputations intact. And now, the Irish wench Maura, toadying up to the Colonel at every opportunity, seeking to ease Rodriguez out of the picture and undo decades of hard work. Why bow to them when he could have everything he desired here, where people bowed before him? Yes, she was mad, but he could manipulate her like he'd manipulated countless others. This city could be theirs.

Rodriguez turned onto his side and winced slightly. His eye socket still ached, but the dead healed quickly. By tomorrow, he would be fully recovered and able to properly inspect his new domain. For whatever reason, Skelly could not reach him here. Not by supernatural means anyway. There was some kind of barrier prohibiting his powers on this side of the river. He would get to the bottom of that in time, but the woman was certainly more than met the eye.

He smiled. Yes, everything seemed to be slotting into place for an extended stay. Free at last from the demands of the Company, he could grow fat and comfortable. And as for the girl Starc, well, he would keep to his word, keep her topped up with grog and ensure she wasn't manhandled too harshly by his newly beloved's goons. Rodriguez laughed out loud before biting into an apple from a platter of fruit on the breakfast tray. Things were indeed looking up.

CHAPTER 59 - TRADING WITH THE DIRTIES

"What can you see? What are they saying?" Emily whispered urgently as Kirkwood peered through the rear door of the landrover, having opened it an inch when Deacon and Giro climbed out of their respective vehicles.

"Shhhh. I'm trying to listen," he replied, shrugging off Emily's hand, which rested on his shoulder. Behind them, on the uncomfortable bench seat, Harley strained to see what was going on outside. "Where even are we?" she anxiously inquired. "You can't see a thing out of this rust bucket."

"I think we're round the back of Castle Court," explained Kirkwood. "It's a big shopping centre in the middle of..."

"Yes, I know what it is," she snapped. "I haven't lived under a rock, you know. Mum and I used to come up to Belfast all the time on shopping trips."

"Next thing you'll be telling us you have electricity and running water," teased Emily, earning a middle finger from the younger girl.

"Quiet," urged Kirkwood. "They're talking to some big guy. He looks like a biker. Bald head, beard, covered in tattoos." The discussion between Deacon and the bearded man appeared a heated one. The biker finally scowled and reluctantly accepted the offered handshake of the old soldier. Whatever they had been discussing, some form of agreement had been reached.

Deacon got into the front of their vehicle and, without speaking, tapped the dashboard, indicating for the driver to move off. The squeaking of unoiled hinges and the rumble of the vehicle's engine were the only sensory clues provided as Kirkwood lurched from side to side, gripping the bench to prevent being tossed across onto Emily and Harley who sat opposite him.

"Don't worry, Kirky, I'll catch you if you fall," smirked Emily with a cheeky wink.

After several minutes, they stopped. Doors opened and mumbled voices could be heard before the rear doors opened to reveal Deacon and Giro standing before them. Giro was carefully cleaning his glasses on his stained t-shirt, looking awkward in the flak jacket and helmet Deacon insisted they all wear. He looked up and smiled at the three nervous young people before him, his warm, oval eyes a reassuring sight.

"Okay," started Deacon. "We have good news. Our friends in the Castle have agreed to provide a distraction on the east side of the New Jerusalem perimeter tomorrow at dawn. It should buy us a little time for what we have to do."

"Friends? That big guy with the tattoos didn't look particularly friendly." Kirkwood was unconvinced by the soldier's explanation.

"I jest, of course," replied the grizzled veteran. "He would shoot me in the back as soon as look at me, but I've agreed to lay off them for a bit in exchange for this little job."

"Do they live in that shopping centre?" Harley was wide-eyed at the thought.

"If you can call it that. There are various loosely grouped gangs based in the city centre. The largest is based there. They call themselves the Kings of the Castle. Catchy, huh?"

"They're just thugs, really," added Giro. "Forever making our lives difficult. If they're not taking potshots at our patrols, then they're fighting each other. There's always some sort of feud rumbling."

"Stinking Dirties, they should all be round up and shot. I hate cutting deals with them."

"Unfortunately, we need them, sir. The plan, remember?"

Deacon grunted. "Well, it's done now, let's just hope they keep their word. I swear if that bearded buffoon double-crosses me, I'll…"

"Okay, what now?" interjected Kirkwood.

"Back to base. Rest up and prepare. We go in at dawn. Let's just hope your friend is still in one piece when we get there."

∞ ∞ ∞

"We've heard nothing from Rodriguez, sir. Not a peep." Maura struggled to keep the smug satisfaction from her voice as she delivered the briefing to Skelly. This didn't look good for the Portuguese brute but played straight into her hands. She watched the old man for signs of frustration and was immediately rewarded.

"I swear if that ugly lump has betrayed me, I'll have his guts for garters." The dark fury in his eyes was manna from heaven to her. She had always been envious of Rodriguez's position within the Company and thought she was superior to him in every possible department. Skelly had an illogical loyalty to him, though, always allowing him another chance even after the debacle at Ardgallon and that other farce in the graveyard with the Fitzpatrick idiots. Just because they trampled through Spain and France together 'giving it to the Frenchies.' Men were such pathetic creatures.

"I'm sure he hasn't, sir," she simpered. "Our powers are hampered within her lair. He's unable to communicate with us, most likely. Which is why we must do this."

"Hmmm," growled Skelly. "I hope you're right, for if he's had his head turned by that bitch, I'll boil his bones. Women always were his weakness, the damned dog."

Maura said nothing, the seed of suspicion now planted in Skelly's mind. All she had to do now was water it occasionally. Of course he'd had his head turned, Rodriguez never could keep it in his trousers.

"What about the boy, O'Sullivan?"

"All going to plan, sir. He has potential, and it goes without saying he's putty in my hands. Do we proceed as planned?"

"Yes." Skelly had regained his composure, the colour slowly draining from his cheeks, which were ruddy at the best of times. "Samuel's pitiful humanity is once again his undoing. He's so tied up reuniting his precious Presence that he's left the plane in the hands of two unproven novices. They think they're safe because they won that little skirmish at the bridge? Pah!"

"So, when do I brief him? He's chomping at the bit to get involved."

"Patience, dear. We will strike in unison. The Company is to focus on New Jerusalem. Keep Samuel, Scott, et al. occupied and find out what that clown Rodriguez is up to. Meanwhile, you can take our new recruit to pay Ms. Hennessy a little visit. The portal is closed to the Company and those of us who have passed over. But O'Sullivan, he's a different matter, our secret weapon. He gets his revenge, and we unlock the plane for our masters. The Scourge will have its prize, and you and I will be rewarded richly."

He raised a tumbler and toasted himself. "Yes, I've outdone myself this time, my girl."

Maura smiled. Cling on tight to his coattails girl, you've finally cracked it.

CHAPTER 60 - FOR MEREDITH

They waited.

The remainder of the day was spent rehearsing what would happen at dawn the next morning. Deacon drilled them mercilessly until they were able to regurgitate the plan back to him, word perfect. The landrovers were to take them to their side of the bridge under cover of darkness. Two motorised dinghies awaited them there, which would convoy them across the river to the New Jerusalem side. They would land and regroup by a disused drainage pipe before making their way up the bank to a section of steel link fencing. Two extraction teams would then deploy. The first would gain access to the compound, neutralise the perimeter guards, and hold the position while a second larger unit would make their way towards the building where the Priestess and her inner circle resided. Giro believed this was the most likely location where they would find Meredith.

Deacon had given Samuel a crash course on how to load and fire a pistol after the big man hinted at previous combat experience. A hushed conversation between the two of them had ensued, ending with the former walking off with a stunned expression muttering about still waters running deep. Satisfied that Samuel was competent after an impromptu training session in the basement firing range, Deacon announced Kirkwood, Emily, and Harley would be under Samuel's personal protection once they entered the compound.

"So, what are these messy people meant to do when Deacon is acting out his macho fantasies?" asked Harley, feet dangling from the top bunk in the room she had been allotted with Emily.

"They're called Dirties," corrected Emily. "Honestly, Harls, did you listen to anything he said?" She tugged playfully at the younger girl's ankle from where she sat beneath her on the lower bunk. Harley pulled her leg back before sitting cross-legged, tongue waggling at the dead girl below.

"The Kings of the Castle, if we're being specific," added Kirkwood, ever the stickler for detail.

"I wasn't, but don't let me ruin your fun. I know you're just bursting to play soldiers with the big boys." Emily rejoiced in winding up the sensitive young man. If only she had met him when she was alive, things could have been so different.

"They are creating a diversion. Crossing the river further up, lots of noise, screaming car tyres, shots in the air, enough to get the perimeter guards interested. That's when we will land, cut through the outer fence, and deploy."

"Deploy," spluttered Emily. "Hark at you, Action Man."

"I think you'll find that's the correct terminology," sniffed Kirkwood.

"So, we just sit about?" said Harley. "If there's a way I can help in there, I want to do it."

"You really weren't listening?" Kirkwood rolled his eyes. "As Samuel said..."

"Repeatedly," added Emily.

"...If me, you, and Meredith can be united, then maybe the Presence can activate. That's when we will come into a league of our own."

"I miss Meredith." Harley hung her head, and the atmosphere in the room darkened. "What if she doesn't make it out of there?"

"There's a chance none of us will make it out of there." Kirkwood rose from where he was seated opposite the bunk beds so he could look Harley in the eye, never having felt so protective of her as he did now. The girl who, without thought for her own safety, hurtled to the bridge at Ardgallon to risk life and limb for complete strangers after a visitation from Emily.

"I'm not bothered about myself. I just want Meredith out of there."

Emily stood and placed a hand on Harley's knee. "We are going to do everything we can to get her out of there, I promise. She means the world to all of us, not least me. She was the one who believed in me, who wrote all those letters when the rest of the world thought I was six feet under. If it wasn't for her, I wouldn't be standing here now. I gave up. Meredith taught me to start fighting back."

"It's time we all started fighting back," agreed Kirkwood. "Meredith deserves no less." He leaned forward into the two girls, and the three of them united in an awkward but heartfelt hug.

They spoke in unison, utterly unrehearsed, their voices raised in conviction.

"For Meredith."

CHAPTER 61 - DAMN THE COMPANY

She crouched low by the side of the industrial waste bins, scared to breathe in case it alerted the guards to her presence. Tara had somehow spirited her out of the hotel via a labyrinth of corridors, doubling back whenever they heard footsteps approaching. A quick hug when they emerged outside into the bitter night, and she was gone, back inside the hotel, leaving Meredith alone and afraid. She stuck to the walls and shadows, inching her way to the destined pick-up point. She ducked every time the sweep of a vehicle's headlights flooded the bins in light, terrified she would be discovered and hauled back to face whatever fate the Priestess dictated. The fear was such that it even forced her craving for a drink to the far recesses of her mind. Too scared to get drunk, she'd heard it all now.

Meredith thought back to her days on the streets of Belfast, the times she had skulked in alleys to avoid whoever was after her at any given time. It could be the police looking to move on rough sleepers or Danny's dealers seeking payment. Those experiences had made her an expert at becoming invisible at a second's notice. Disappearing into the background, an urban chameleon who lived by the skin of her teeth and the seat of her pants. Meredith prayed the same hard-won skills wouldn't desert her now when she needed them most. Just a few more moments and she would be free of this lunatic asylum.

The screech of tyres had her diving behind the bins again. She was still wearing the white dress that was the uniform of the Maidens, but Tara had somehow managed to retrieve her green parka and black beanie hat. Meredith felt more human with them on, her identity restored, telling her she was more than a commodity, a possession of the Priestess. She risked the smallest of peeks from behind the bins and saw a flatbed truck parked alongside; its engine idling. The driver cut the lights, and the opening of a door sent Meredith scrambling beneath the bin where she lay on her front, watching as a pair of dirty, scuffed boots approached. She was far from religious, but Meredith prayed with every bone in her body that whoever it was would go away.

"I know you're in there. If you're not out in the next ten seconds, I'm leaving without you. Tara or no Tara."

She recognised the gruff voice as belonging to Arthur, and breathing a sigh of relief, inched out from under her hidey-hole. Before she could rise, she was roughly hauled to her feet, where a waft of stale sweat underpinned by rolling tobacco threatened to send her to her knees again.

"Get in the back of the truck. No messing about, or you're on your own." He pushed her forward, and it took all her powers of balance not to crash chin first into the vehicle. Guardian angel, this man was not. She hauled herself onto the truck's flatbed, whereupon Arthur flung a stinking tarpaulin on top of her.

"We're going through the side gates. Not a peep out of you until I say so. I'm putting my neck on the line for you two."

She resisted the urge to bite back, burying her face in the crook of her arm. The truck's engine roared into life, and tiny vibrations coursed through her body as it lumbered forward. Upfront, Arthur whistled tunelessly as the truck reluctantly cranked through the gears, before veering right onto a smoother surface and picking up speed. Meredith started to choke, the tarpaulin reeking of oil, and was on the verge of tossing it back for a lungful of fresh air when the truck's threadbare brakes squealed, announcing they were nearing the side gate.

She cocked her ears, straining to catch what was being said, but other than the low mumble of male voices, could make nothing out. Seconds dragged into minutes before the truck chugged forward again. She stifled a scream, barely able to contain her glee at slipping her neck out of the noose of a life of servitude and misery. Not a care as to how she was going to negotiate the city centre back to Queen Street, as that could wait. Right now, she was free, and that was all that mattered.

Those hopes were short-lived as the truck slammed to a halt, flinging her painfully across the bed of the vehicle. Noise erupted all around her, raised voices, and the sound of feet pounding on gravel. Meredith jumped as a crack of gunfire filled the night, followed seconds later by two more in quick succession. She curled into a ball, hands over her ears, refusing to accept the inevitable. They had been rumbled, the game was up, and all her dreams were ruined. The tarpaulin was ripped away, and she was lifted from the truck by harsh hands, before being tossed to the ground like an unwanted cigarette butt.

She raised her head, the rough piece of ground they were on illuminated by the headlight beams of the truck. They swathed the inert body of Arthur, a dozen feet from her. A pool of blood was spreading outwards from what remained of his head. The silhouette of two armed men stood over him.

"Get her up," a deep voice bellowed. "Priestess wants this one brought back alive." The same calloused hands pulled her upright, nails digging into her upper arms. She blinked furiously, the lights blinding her as a towering figure approached. She tensed, expecting a stinging backhander, but what followed was even more shocking. A familiar voice that dashed what little hope she had of ever seeing her friends again.

"Oh querida, why must you insist on being so silly? It paints neither of us in a very positive light." Rodriguez feigned concern as he considered the young woman in front of him.

"You bastard," screamed Meredith. She struggled to break free and sink her nails into his smug, self-satisfied face but was held in a vice-like grip. "You said you would get me out of here. I trusted you."

Rodriguez threw back his head and laughed. "Ah, this one," he turned to the half dozen guards around him, wiping tears of mirth from his eyes. "She likes the wine a little too much, no? Doesn't know what she is saying half the time." He took a step towards Meredith and leaned forward to whisper in her ear. "Why couldn't you have behaved? We could have led good lives here. Why are you never happy?"

"Happy?" Meredith lashed out a foot, and the bearded brute had to hop back sharply to avoid the kick. "I'll never be happy until your rotting corpse is back in the ground where it belongs. Death isn't good enough for you, you piece of filth."

"Such a fiery temper, it will be the ruin of you. Now, you had your chance, more chances than you deserve. But I'm afraid I can protect you no more. You have betrayed the Priestess, snubbed her most generous offer to become a Maiden of Purity. For that, there must be consequences."

"Well then, do it," roared Meredith, her throat raw, eyes awash with tears, snot running from her nose. "Put a bullet in my head and be done with. But I swear I'll come back and haunt you until the end of your days."

Rodriguez pulled an offended look, raising his eyebrows and extending his arms outwards, a pathetic performance for his newfound colleagues. "What do you take us for, animals? New Jerusalem exists to restore social justice. We are a community seeking to rebuild, to create a new order from the chaos, to prepare the way for the coming of our Master."

"Do you think I came down in the last shower?" scoffed Meredith. "I know you don't buy into that for a second. You just know you're onto a good number with that mad cow. You're a leech. I hope Skelly finds out and burns you to a crisp, you lying scumbag."

A nerve was struck, and Meredith gasped for breath as Rodriguez struck out, grabbing her by the throat and slowly squeezing. His eyes glowed with hate as Meredith struggled for breath, her eyes bulging as he applied more pressure.

"Don't you dare question my loyalty, bitch." The bonhomie was gone now, his face a portrait of controlled anger. "I served that man for two hundred years. Died in the mud alongside him, thousands of miles from home, and my people. I gave everything for him and in return? I'm treated like dirt, the scapegoat every time his plans go awry. I deserve this. It's time I put me first." As Meredith's vision started to blur and darkness threatened to overcome her, he released his grip. She fell back gagging, coughing spittle, gasping for air.

"Take her away," ordered Rodriguez. "Tomorrow she can argue her case before the Priestess. Maybe she will wake up in a more magnanimous mood than the wretch deserves. But I wouldn't build my hopes up. Looks like the end of the road for you, little one." He strode away without another glance at her, and Meredith screamed again in frustration as the guards dragged her towards a waiting car. She squirmed and twisted, biting down hard on the hand of one of them, causing him to loosen his grip. Meredith strained to break free from the guard holding her other arm as his colleague turned away, gripping his punctured knuckles. Expletives and barked instructions filled the air as other guards ran towards her. Meredith looked up to see a raised rifle butt descending on her, followed by nothing.

As she slumped unconscious to the ground, Rodriguez climbed into the passenger seat of the car. He pulled at his ear lobe, annoyed he had allowed the urchin to get under his skin. He was not one to worry, but she had sneaked beneath his usual aura of supreme confidence. He was taking a risk, yes, and knew Skelly would come looking for him, sooner or later. But the decision was made, and his mind was made up. Life with the Priestess gave him everything he ever desired and more. So damn Skelly, damn the Company, and damn Meredith Starc.

He was done with them all.

CHAPTER 62 - IT MEANS NOTHING TO ME

Adam sat back, undoing the top button of his jeans. If he took another bite, he'd explode. The food was basic, yet the amount placed before him was enough to feed a small army. All washed down with several glasses of iced beer, which loosened his tongue and provided the Dutch courage for his audience with this Skelly character. He pushed back his chair, belched loudly, and smiled across the table at Maura, who sipped her beer, eyes continually flitting to and from his plate.

"Is that you filled up? For a while there, I thought you had hollow legs." She smirked at Adam, now utterly under her spell. Men were such vain creatures. All you had to do was fill their bellies and flutter your eyelashes, and they were yours for the taking. Except for her James, they broke the mould when they made him. How she missed him and ached to be in his arms again.

She blinked hard, dispelling the thought from her mind. This was no time for weakness, and the only reason she was babysitting this ingrate was to build a better future for her and her beloved. To rise within the Company to positions worthy of their talents. Until then, she had to focus. As did James, wherever he was and whatever murky task Skelly had allotted to him. They both knew and understood that the job came first. For now.

"I'm busted," groaned Adam, patting his stomach. "Couldn't eat another bite. Now, when do we meet this Skelly fella?"

"You will address him as Sir or Colonel," advised Maura. "You will not impress him with shows of insolence." He was a handsome lad but so full of himself, a trait she did not like in a man. They didn't make them like her James anymore, quietly confident, humble yet assured in his own ability.

"I don't care what he thinks of me so long as he gives me a chance to see to my unfinished business." Flying about in the future and the best roast chicken dinner he'd had in years was all well and good, but those two bitches were never far from the forefront of his thoughts. His Dad never backed down, never forgot, and neither would he. They were on borrowed time.

Maura nodded, keen to harness the hate within him. If she could pull this one off and gain access through the portal, Skelly would finally see sense and promote her. Gunther was gone, and the Drummer Boy's copybook was blotted. There was no better time to reinforce her credentials to the old man. Especially as her main competition, Rodriguez was presently missing in action.

"Very well. No time like the present, then." She casually clicked her fingers, and they were in the Study.

Adam swayed in shock, his eyes adjusting to the dimmer lighting and change in surroundings. Sitting before him in a padded armchair by an open fire was an old man, ugly as sin with ruddy cheeks and wild, unkempt gunmetal grey sideburns. He looked like he belonged in a nursing home, his jowls pouring over a shirt collar, which looked several sizes too tight. Adam's initial impression was one of disappointment until the man looked away from the flames to study him. His eyes burrowed into his very soul. There was nothing in them but death and hatred. Adam suddenly felt horribly out of his depth. He turned to Maura, whose eyes were fixed front and centre on the obese figure before them. For a second, his nerve faltered, and he turned to run, only to discover his legs were immobile as if set in concrete.

"No need to panic, Mr. O'Sullivan." A clipped, upper-class English accent forced him to turn back towards the old man. "We are all friends here, and Maura has been telling me great things about you. It seems we are like-minded gentlemen."

"I don't know about you," drawled Adam, desperately trying to maintain a stoic front, "but I ain't no gentleman." He sensed Maura shooting daggers at him. "General, sir."

"Ha," roared Skelly, clapping his hands. "You're bloody right, boy. I would have been if it wasn't for that dog, Wellesley. My one regret in life was not challenging him to a duel when we were your age. I should have blown his brains out when I had the chance." His hearty chuckle degenerated into a phlegmy wheeze.

"All I want are Ariana Hennessy's brains blown out. Just tell me how I get to her."

Skelly smiled, revealing rotten teeth to match his rotten heart. "Excellent, a man after my own thinking. No time for small talk, straight down to business, I like that. I'll let Maura fill you in on the plan." He gestured for the redhead to continue.

"Thank you, sir." She turned her head to address Adam. "We have a mutual interest in Ariana Hennessy. Let's just say it suits our needs as well if she is eradicated."

"I like the sound of that. Eradicated." He allowed the word to roll over his tongue. "But why's she so important to you? She's nothing but a wee tramp who's made a living off the back of my dead father."

"I'll answer your question with a question," interrupted Skelly. "How much do you hate her?"

"With all my heart."

"And what would you do to gain revenge? Avenge your father's death?"

"Anything."

"Even if it meant the destruction of your planet?"

"It means nothing to me. They can all go to hell." The venom in Adam's voice was undeniable. Maura's heart started to pound—this was dynamite. If they could channel the latent negative energy within him, they would set the planet on fire, a fire from which it would never recover.

"When the Purge lay waste to their miserable plane, they'll be begging for hell." Skelly licked his lips with ghoulish glee. "All that stands between it and them is your little friend, Ariana. She's fallen into league with our enemies, and we need her removed. Would such a proposition interest you?"

"Hell yeah."

"Excellent. Maura will accompany you. Do well here, boy, and we can talk about a more permanent business arrangement between us.

You have a unique set of skills I believe would interest my employers."

Adam considered the offer. For a young man who had spent most of his life with nothing, it was a mouth-watering prospect. He looked down to see Maura holding his hand. She winked at him. "Well, handsome. What do you say?"

He winked back, before turning to address a beaming Skelly. "I'm in, boss. Where do I sign?"

CHAPTER 63 - MY LITTLE ARIANA

Ariana opened the door to her room in the university's halls of residence to reveal an impatient Tess, resplendent in a studded leather jacket, white t-shirt, and ripped denim jeans. Ariana, as ever, felt woefully inadequate, still wearing her pyjamas and dressing gown. Tess raised an eyebrow before brushing past her into the room.

"You're a twenty-year-old woman, and you're wearing a unicorn dressing gown?" sniggered Tess, bouncing onto Ariana's unmade bed.

"It's My Little Pony, actually," huffed Ariana, pulling the gown around her body to hide the High School Musical pyjamas beneath. "And I'm not a walking clothes horse like you. Do you ever wear the same outfit twice?"

"Don't be ridiculous, I have a reputation to maintain." She adopted a cross-legged position and rested her chin in her hands. "So, you've been cooped up in here all night. Are you going to tell me what Samuel needs us to do? The suspense is killing me here."

Ariana took a seat at her study desk, facing her best friend. "It's a bit of a mind melt. I'm still trying to get my head round a lot of it.

But the gist is, we have to defend the world from the powers of darkness until he returns. It's called the Scourge, and this Skelly is part of it."

"Oh, is that all?" Tess buried her face in her hands. "Piece of cake, really. We can have that done and still make this afternoon's Shakespeare seminar. What is it? How You Like It? The one with the ghost?"

"It's *As You Like It*," groaned Ariana, stunned by her friend's lack of knowledge. "And there are no ghosts in it. Have you even read it?"

"Possibly...not," squirmed Tess, before changing the subject, bored by the thought of studies. "Anyway, I haven't time for that nonsense, not now I'm a superhero's sidekick. You're like Supergirl and Wonder Woman all rolled into one, Ariana."

"Hardly."

"Are you kidding me? One minute we were on the verge of being blown into a million pieces by that lunatic, Adam. The next, we're standing on the other side of the galaxy. Or is it cosmos? Universe? Whatever, you saved our lives, Ariana—you saved *my* life."

"Wise up, Tess." Ariana began to blush and bowed her head, shielding the embarrassment with her mop of tangled brown hair.

"I will not. The fact is you did, and for that, I will always be grateful. Now tell me what I can do. I'll even put on a cape and wear my tights outside my big girl pants if you want." She laughed; an easy, warm expression of the Tess Cartwright Ariana loved so much. Always using humour to lift her from her own default melancholic setting.

Ariana giggled, lifting her head to address the blonde-haired bundle of positivity sitting opposite her. "Believe me, there's no requirement for that. I saw the shape of you at the Freshers Fancy Dress Ball. You looked like an anaemic Kardashian."

"My Morticia Adams was a triumph I'll have you know. Everyone was talking about it."

"Yeah, for all the wrong reasons." Ariana turned, grabbing a notebook from her desk. "I scribbled down some notes. There's a lot of stuff about Kirkwood and the others, this Presence force they can activate, and how Samuel and his kind act as guardians against the Scourge."

"Like angels and demons?" asked Tess incredulously.

"Funny, I mentioned that to him, and he didn't really give me a straight answer. Just smiled enigmatically and said it was complicated. He's a man of few words."

"I noticed. Kind of hunky, though. But in serious need of a haircut from this decade."

"Well, he seems to be the big cheese. The others all look up to him, so we need to trust him as well."

"Shouldn't we be doing something, though, instead of sitting about chewing the fat?"

"Apparently not." Ariana pushed herself off the chair, reaching for her bag. "He said continue as normal. When I asked how we would know if this plane was being attacked, he just said we would. The only provisos are that we don't separate..."

"Excellent," shrieked Tess, clapping her hands in delight. "Sleepover at my pad."

"And no alcohol. We need to keep our wits about us."

"Awk, for flip's sake," Tess replied, her bubble burst. "That's a bridge too far, girl. Whoever heard of a girlie sleepover without a couple of cheeky glasses of vino?"

"Sorry, Tess, I'm not going to face the Scourge with you four sheets to the wind. We do this, we do it by the book. Soft drinks and pizza tonight. I'm sure your exorbitant bank balance can stretch to that." She slung her bag over her shoulder and made towards the door, gesturing for Tess to follow suit.

"Where are you going?" she replied, reluctantly rising from the bed.

"To the library. Samuel says he should be back tomorrow, our time, at the latest. Until then, we are to behave as normal. If we need to act, and he said it's unlikely we will, it doesn't matter where we are. They will come to us."

"They?" Tess gulped, folding her arms as if the temperature in the room had plummeted.

"The Company. Skelly's foot soldiers."

"Well, let them come. They shall not pass," she bellowed, enunciating each word by stamping her feet.

"Was that meant to be Gandalf?" Ariana looked deeply unimpressed.

"Yeah. I'm just trying to tune in to your geeky side."

"Try harder."

Ariana stood aside, letting Tess flounce out into the corridor, a cheesy grin on her face. She wished she could tell her friend more, for there was much more. Samuel had talked long with her, preparing for what lay ahead. She shuddered as she closed the door, linking arms as they stepped down the corridor. Tess was tough and brave, she knew that, a true friend who ran unflinchingly to her aid when her life hung by a thread at the hands of Adam O'Sullivan. But that was small fry compared to what was coming. Maybe, she was being naive, or maybe she was acting selfishly by just wanting one last day of normality before everything changed.

"You okay? You're quiet," asked Tess as they walked out of the halls towards the main university building.

"Yeah," replied Ariana, tapping her friend's hand. "Let's just enjoy the day. Everything is fine."

"Apart from the fact you're still wearing your pyjamas and dressing gown?"

Ariana halted and groaned, before shrugging and continuing down the corridor. "Whatever. If the student masses can stomach you in a pink ballgown, then they can put up with my jim jams for an hour or two."

CHAPTER 64 - HELL TO PAY

Meredith awoke to a splitting headache. She winced and instinctively raised a hand to her forehead. The pain intensified, and she pulled it away to discover her hand was coated with a warm, sticky layer of blood. She dreaded think of what she looked like, but such vain thoughts were not a priority at present. Attempting to rise from the concrete floor, she was forced to lie down again as a wall of nausea struck her like a baseball bat. She collapsed onto her side.

"Oh, dear God, get me out of here."

A single, stark light bulb illuminated what looked like a storeroom with floor to wall shelving containing all manner of cleaning products. She guessed she was in the main complex, but the eerie quiet all around gave no indication as to her exact whereabouts or how long she'd been out cold. All she knew was that the game was up. The cavalry wasn't coming, and her last hope went up in smoke the moment Arthur's lifeless body hit the ground. It was over.

Meredith fought an internal battle to keep the tears at bay. If this was it, she wasn't going to allow the narcissistic Rodriguez to feed off her misery. She'd been an idiot to place her hopes in him, the beast was rotten to the core and only interested in satisfying his own base urges. Wine, women, and song. He would get his fill of all three in New Jerusalem.

"You're an idiot, Starc," she sourly muttered.

A rattling noise at the door indicated she had visitors. It creaked open, and two guards entered, one with a plastic tray while the other covered him with the obligatory rifle. The first guard approached her warily, never taking his eyes off Meredith as he kneeled and placed the tray in front of her.

"The prisoner's last meal," he growled, before rising and backing towards the door again.

"What's going to happen to me?" blurted Meredith, unable to hold her nerve any longer.

"You'll be judged," he grunted back. "If it was me, I'd have just thrown up the rope and let you swing, but the Priestess is of a kindlier disposition."

"Judged. In a court? But I haven't done anything wrong."

"Not for me to say. Although I don't fancy your chances. The mistress doesn't take kindly to having her hospitality flung back in her face. You should have made the most of your lot like the rest of us instead of trying to escape."

"Please, help me," pleaded Meredith. "They killed your friend...Arthur. Doesn't that show you how ruthless they are? You could be next."

"And don't I know it," replied the guard, beginning to grow tired of the exchange. "Which is why I keep my head down, follow orders, and say nothing. Arthur was stupid and paid the price. He was no friend of mine. It pays not to build close friendships in this place. Now shut up and eat your breakfast."

He slammed the door shut, leaving Meredith staring at the paltry offerings masquerading as breakfast. Despite her dire situation, she was hungry. A small bottle of water accompanied a bread roll, which was as hard as a hockey ball when she bit into it. Rounding off the miserable meal was a blackened banana—as black as her hopes of seeing tomorrow.

She winced again as another shard of pain shot through her forehead. She smiled wryly. At least she wouldn't have to worry about it leaving a scar. Pushing herself gingerly into a seated position against the wall, she uncapped the water bottle and guzzled greedily from it, the sight of it awakening a deep thirst. Draining half of it in one mouthful, she stared at the water, struggling to capture a thought that had suddenly drifted into her mind. Something important, something very, very important, screaming for her attention.

Then it hit her.

The water. It wasn't wine. In fact, the thought of wine or any other alcoholic beverage, for that matter, hadn't occurred to her since regaining consciousness. She looked at the bottle again and took another sip.

"But that means...they must be close."

For almost a year sleeping rough in Belfast, every morning, her first waking thought was a craving for alcohol. Until Kirkwood Scott tracked her down—a sorry, sodden mess begging for loose change outside the Ulster Hall. Until the day the Presence was ignited within them. A faltering, flickering flame that erupted into a ferocious blaze when Harley Davison joined them on the bridge at Ardgallon. It was irresistible, infectious, sweeping everything in its path. When the three of them were together, nothing could withstand its healing, cleansing power. Not Skelly, the Company, Harley's disability, Kirkwood's OCD, or ...

"I don't want a drink. I don't want a frigging drink!"

Meredith jumped to her feet and started to pace circles around the cramped storeroom. Suddenly, the nasty gash on her forehead was forgotten. For her friends hadn't forgotten her. They were coming, and all she had to do was hang in there, buy a little time, and somehow stay alive.

A rattling of keys outside caused her to jolt and spin round. The door opened, and the same two guards as before entered.

"Come on," said the talkative one. "It's time for your fifteen minutes of fame."

"But I haven't finished my breakfast yet. And aren't I entitled to representation? To prepare a defence?"

"You're lucky your head is still on your shoulders. Now move, I haven't time for your nonsense, girly." He stepped forward and grabbed Meredith by the wrist, yanking her roughly towards the door. She cried out but complied, not wanting another war wound to add to her growing collection. As they shoved her down the corridor, Meredith walked with new hope in her heart. Her friends were coming, and when they were reunited, there would be hell to pay. Rodriguez and his psycho lover were going to learn the hard way.

Just hurry, guys, please hurry.

CHAPTER 65 - ONE NIL TO THE GOOD GUYS

The sleek craft ghosted across the dark waters and cut their engines as they neared the far bank of the river. Kirkwood watched it come into view, rising above them, beyond which lay the perimeter fencing of New Jerusalem. The city was quiet, and thankfully, dense banks of cloud cover ensured there was no moonlight to announce their covert arrival. Behind him sat Harley and Emily, hands joined, both of them unusually quiet. At the prow of the boat knelt Samuel, pistol in hand. A modern-day Washington crossing the Delaware. Four of Deacon's troops, three men and a woman armed to the teeth, completed the vessel's complement. To their left and slightly ahead, a second vessel carried Deacon and another seven soldiers. They neared the bank in perfect synchronisation, communicating with one another via a series of whistles and hand gestures.

The landrovers had convoyed them from the Queen Street compound to where the motorised dinghies, moored to the base of the bridge, awaited them. Bar a couple of stones clattering against the side of the armoured vehicles, a traditional Dirties greeting for Sector 8 patrols, the journey was uneventful. The atmosphere in the rear was tense, and Kirkwood thanked his lucky stars Harley was close, the Presence strong enough to keep intrusive thoughts at bay. His OCD was triggered by stressful situations, and currently, his levels were through the roof. He looked across at Emily, who smiled back reassuringly. The one Skelly called 'the witch' was a rock, and he was falling increasingly under her spell.

As they neared the rocky bank, grappling hooks were thrown from the crafts, gaining purchase and allowing them to be tethered. The party silently disembarked and started to scale the bank, one soldier remaining behind to guard the vessels. Deacon was the first to poke his head above the bank, the whites of his eyes in stark contrast with his black combat attire and camouflaged face. Harley had stifled a giggle when she first saw him, his appearance reminiscent of her brother Aidan's toy soldiers.

Ahead of them stretched several hundred yards of waste ground leading to the steel perimeter fence, standing twenty feet high. Beyond that, more barren land before the lights of New Jerusalem lit up the night sky. The Odyssey Complex and Titanic Museum stood silhouetted. Silent sentries mourning the madness which had enveloped this part of the city.

Deacon checked his wristwatch before turning to speak to the party on the slope beneath him. "Thirty seconds."

Kirkwood nodded. "You guys okay?" Harley responded with a fearless nod; the girl was utterly nerveless.

"I'm peachy," smiled Emily. "What's the worst they can do, kill me again?" Kirkwood smirked, unable to argue with her logic. He rotated stiffly, his ankles creaking, to address Deacon, but the crackle of automatic gunfire awakened the night far to his left. Rough voices sprang up, startled by the noise, and silhouetted figures could be seen scurrying in the distance as a hefty explosion announced the arrival of the Kings of the Castle.

"Go, Go, Go!" shouted Deacon.

As one, the party rose and ran at a crouch towards the fencing. The soldiers fanned out on either side, countless hours of training kicking in as they covered every possible angle with their rifle sights. Kirkwood marvelled at the almost telepathic symmetry of their movements. A deadly ballet that did not bode well for any opponent who dared challenge their progress.

Upon reaching the wire, a soldier produced a bulky set of bolt cutters from his backpack and began to cut the heavy fencing like a hot knife through butter. A colleague covered him, peering down the sights of her rifle, her face a mask of concentration. A gun battle had commenced to the left as the New Jerusalem forces sought to come to terms with the incursion of the Dirties. A shriek filled the air as the first casualty of the night was felled. Kirkwood sensed they would be the first of many.

A rattle reverted his attention to the fence as the bolt cutters completed their job, the wire peeled back to afford access to the compound. Two guards ducked through and took up holding positions on the other side, then another two, until within seconds, the first team was inside and in position.

"You follow me, no stopping for anything. You fall behind, it's not my problem. I've no room for passengers on this one. Good luck." Deacon lowered his head and slipped through the gap in the fence, shadowed by two soldiers. Samuel indicated with his pistol for the others to follow suit, content to form the rear guard, his eyes sparkling with intensity.

"Take my hands," said Kirkwood, holding them out for Emily and Harley to grasp. "We don't get split up whatever happens, alright?" He felt their hands in his, the juxtaposition between Harley's warm, clammy palm and Emily's cool skin oddly comforting. The two girls were as different as could be yet united in their objective of rescuing Meredith. The three of them shadowed Deacon, Kirkwood's eyes never straying from the back of the old soldier's head. He zig-zagged ahead of them, displaying surprising speed and agility for a man of his years. As tough as old boots, thought Kirkwood, as several flashes to his left, were met with a volley of automatic gunfire from the soldiers at his side. Kirkwood heard a grunt in the distance and caught a glimpse of a shadowy figure keeling over. 1-0 to the good guys.

They reached the cover of a lone storage container, the sole cover between them and the museum. Soldiers crouched at either side of it, exchanging fire with an unseen enemy. The gun battle involving the Dirties seemed to be dying down, the gunfire less frequent. They had been asked to provide a temporary distraction, and their work done, were now falling back towards their own side of the river. Kirkwood realised they were on their own now, and the full force of the Priestess' army would be brought to bear against them. Deacon turned to address them, a manic glint in his eye, shouting to be heard above the cacophony around them.

"Buckle up kids, that was the easy part. The real fun starts now."

CHAPTER 66 - HOME TO ROOST

James Miller was a man of few words, even before seven pounds of French shot lifted his head from the rest of his body on 18 June 1815. He had seen it coming from several hundred yards away. Watched it land in the mud before the square and then bounce into the densely packed British ranks, smashing bone and crushing organs. At least his was a clean, instant death. Unlike others who lay in their own filth for days afterwards, their intestines scooped into their hands, slowly going mad with pain, shock, and dehydration. Men crying like babies, begging to be put out of their misery. His only regret was that his Maura had not been with him at the end instead of halfway along the road to Brussels with the rest of the regiment's camp followers.

Except she hadn't. Bloody woman never listened to him, so why change the habit of a lifetime. She snuck away from the baggage train, and somehow made her way through the reserve regiments, down the slope, and into the square. He was already dead by then, but his heart soared with pride every time he thought of his woman giving up her life to be with him. Some of the other fellows, who lasted longer than him, recounted how she picked up a musket and fought like the best of them, by the Colonel's side. He thought back to that lazy Sunday when the regiment was billeted in a tiny village, and he had taught her how to load and fire a musket. Brown Bess and Red Maura, a potent combination.

James cracked his neck, letting out a satisfying sigh as the permanent dull ache eased slightly. Whoever said death meant the end to suffering was sorely mistaken as his war wound had persisted beyond the grave. He sat alone in the modest quarters that he and Maura had been allotted within the Tower. Not that they saw much of each other these days. Maura had caught Skelly's eye and was being fast-tracked, so was rarely in their bed at night. They had talked about it, and he reluctantly agreed to support her more ambitious nature. He was a foot soldier, he did what he was told and had no aspirations for rank. The only motivation he held was putting the crooked nose of an old foe further out of joint...

Martim Rodriguez.

The two had never seen eye to eye. James had been the regimental boxing champion until that damned foreigner signed up. On a bitterly cold night south of Marseilles, they had fought bare-knuckle for seventy rounds until the challenger floored him with a devastating uppercut. James woke up several hours later in their tent, Maura tending to his shattered jaw. The injury took forever to heal, and one side of his face was left disfigured and without feeling. This was something Rodriguez took great delight in regaling all and sundry about at every opportunity. Since that day, James had watched the Portuguese braggart's star rise within the regiment, to the point where he wore three stripes on his arm. A *foreigner* leading them into battle. It stuck in his throat every time he thought about it.

James was a patient man, however, in life and in death. His grandfather once told him that a patient man would be rewarded in the next life, and the sly old fox was right. Rodriguez was bound to trip up over his ego eventually. It was only a matter of time, and that time was now. The fool could never keep it in his trousers and now appeared to be looking to break from the Company. Well, he was an utter fool if he thought he could outrun the old man. Skelly was gunning for the rat, and when James was offered the mission, he had almost taken the Colonel's hand off.

The only downside was that Maura, as ever, was unavailable to accompany him. Her being off on another of Skelly's top-secret missions where she was sworn to secrecy.

James stood and started to button his regulation tunic, which he wore open over his undershirt. Others had succumbed to modern-day garb, but he was proud to wear the regimental uniform. You could cut your finger on the crease in his breeches, and his boots were polished within an inch of their lives. Yes, it helped he no longer had to rely upon an unreliable and wildly inaccurate musket when in battle, but he still felt special wearing the colours he had sworn allegiance to—for King and Country.

An exaggerated knock on his door announced the arrival of the clown who would be accompanying him to New Jerusalem. Their objective to bring Rodriguez back to his rightful place by whatever means necessary. Dead or alive, and this time it would be James Miller delivering the knockout punch. If only his beautiful, resourceful wife was at his side instead of the puffed-up buffoon on the other side of the door.

"Come in if you must."

"Delighted to be working with you as well, Private." The thick French accent accentuated the last word, a deliberate attempt to evoke a reaction from him.

"Your rank doesn't impress me, Captain." James put as much bile as he could into the last word, keen to return the serve with interest.

"The feeling is entirely mutual," replied the slight man in front of him, a full foot shorter than the muscular Irishman. Pierre LaPointe was as blue-blooded as they came, purporting his lineage could be traced back to Louis X. A natural opportunist, he had used his family background to secure a commission in Les Coeurs Bleu. A crack light French regiment, which was part of Bonaparte's last throw of the dice to break the Allied lines before the arrival of Blucher's Prussian forces. The myth propagated by the British press after the battle was that no Allied square was broken by French cavalry. As with many aspects of the battle, they had lied.

The volley fire had been devastating, raking through the front line of his colleagues, taking down man and horse alike. The screams were horrific, the wreckage of human and equine form cruel and complete. LaPointe was many things: arrogant, aloof, entitled—yes, but also fuelled by a reckless bravery which carried him to the edge of the square, somehow unscathed. Spurring on his mount, he arrived just as it began to give way, caving in on itself. The bodies of British and French lay thick on the ground, united in death to create a ghoulish stairway that LaPointe urged his mount over. A stairway to hell.

Atop the mound of corpses, LaPointe's lance was dragged from his hands. He pulled his sabre free from its scabbard and began to slash wildly around him as his steed reached the summit of bodies and descended into the square. Before him, planted in the mud, lay the ultimate prize—the enemy colours. Seizing them was the supreme accolade, a guaranteed pathway to promotion and plaudits. All that stood in his way were an old officer and, bizarrely, a red-haired woman. What the hell was she doing there?

Undaunted, LaPointe kicked his heels into the flanks of his horse, encouraging it to push on. It responded, but from the periphery of his vision, he caught a glint of steel before he was catapulted to the ground. Landing winded, he scrambled to his feet only to be sent stumbling onto his back, a blazing pain searing through his side. He looked down as a circle of red spread outwards across his midriff, where the blade had pierced him. Blood bubbled from between his lips, and he gazed upwards at his killer. A brute of a man, beard as black as his now dead horse, a deranged grin plastered against his soot smeared face.

"Mercy, please," croaked LaPointe, although he knew in his rapidly slowing heart, it was the end. There was no mercy in the eyes of his killer.

"Non." The blade skewered into Pierre LaPointe, and the darkness consumed him. Seconds later, the square collapsed as the Old Guard trundled over it, like a bulldozer levelling a teetering building. Onwards, over it, onto the ridge and upwards towards their own demise at the hands of the hidden mass of Allied troops beyond it. Like British accounts of the battle, French histories made no reference to the 49th Somerset Regiment under Colonel Augustus Skelly. The family of Pierre LaPointe was informed he died with honour at the front of the final French offensive with no further details provided. His body was never recovered, having been stripped and plundered by the human magpies who did not distinguish between friend and foe when it came to material gain. Buried in a mass grave, mistaken for a member of the regiment, Pierre lay in the cold, unforgiving earth with the man who killed him.

LaPointe straightened before the tall, muscular Irishman, Miller. He was the black sheep of the Company, an outsider who didn't belong. But he had proven his worth to Skelly many times before, accepting his lot and earning the grudging respect of the old man and his new comrades. Behind the foppish, vain exterior was a steely will, chipping away at the prejudices and barriers thrown in his path. He knew he would get there in the end, and this was a gilt-edged opportunity. A chance at the day, he would finally take revenge against the brute who extinguished his life on that grey day outside Brussels.

"Let us clear the air, mon ami." LaPointe stepped forward, his closely cropped grey hair and sharp features giving him the appearance of an aggressive rodent. "You do not like me, nor do I particularly care for you. But the Colonel has chosen us for the one characteristic we have in common, not the many we do not."

"Our hatred of Rodriguez?" James tensed at the very mention of his name, veins throbbing on his thick neck.

"Oui. This is our chance to be rid of him once and for all. I don't know what he's been up to, but it's thrown enough doubt in the

Colonel's mind to get us involved. You heard what he said. It's open season. We take Rodriguez out now, and our honour is satisfied. Plus, it clears the way for your beloved to take her rightful place at Skelly's right hand."

James completed buttoning his tunic, looking LaPointe up and down with disdain. The navy-blue suit, white fitted shirt, and pencil-thin tie were all from an age he wanted no part of, but Pierre was right. This was the day the birds came home to roost for Martim Rodriguez.

"You don't have to convince me, Frenchman. I know what's at stake here. By any means necessary, the Colonel said. And if we were to discover that Rodriguez betrayed the Company and subsequently had a little accident. Well, I'm sure the old man would understand."

"Exactly," smirked LaPointe. "So, we forget our differences and do this. Agreed?" He extended a soft, manicured hand which, after considering for a second, James shook with his much larger, calloused palm.

"Agreed. Let's do this, Frenchie."

CHAPTER 67 - INJUSTICE FOR ALL

They brought Meredith to the mezzanine floor, where she had been first presented to the Priestess. Much was as before, the leader of New Jerusalem perched upon her junkyard throne, surrounded by an array of Maidens and heavily armed guards. On either side, hundreds of inquisitive eyes followed her entrance, kicking and screaming every inch of the way. Meredith scanned the white-robed young women at the foot of the plinth, but Tara was nowhere to be seen.

The guards pushed her unceremoniously onto her knees. Meredith knew better than to attempt to rise, so she settled instead on glaring at the Priestess who looked down on her, the suggestion of a smile playing on her lips.

"So, this is how you repay me?"

"Screw you, bitch."

"Charming. I bring you in, feed you, clothe you, elevate you to Maidenhood, and it's all thrown back in my face. Such a shame, I had high hopes for you, Meredith."

"Whatever."

"Silence." The voice of the Priestess echoed around the cavernous confines of the complex. "You will not speak unless spoken to. Your insolence tires me. Consider yourself fortunate I place such high value on justice for all. Otherwise, I would be supping your blood from my cup."

Meredith resisted the urge to answer back—her head bowed and fixed on the floor. She sensed the others ever closer, the crippling hangover dissipating, her mind and body clearing of the effects of her drinking binge. All she had to do was hang on for a little while longer.

A ripple in the crowd formed to her left as bodies shifted to allow someone through. The Priestess stood, almost on tiptoe, a sly smile forming, as Rodriguez forced his way to the front of the throng. Meredith glowered at him as he bowed before the throne, winking when sure nobody but her could see him.

"Dickhead," muttered Meredith in greeting.

The Priestess turned her attention to the wider audience, flicking her mass of dark hair over a shoulder. "My Prophet will act as prosecutor for this hearing. The wench will be given an opportunity to argue her case once all the evidence has been heard. Never let it be said that I am not a fair ruler. Then you, my people, will decide the fate of the accused. I pray that you exercise the wisdom of Solomon in your judgement."

"Fair," sniggered Rodriguez. "I'm afraid for you, querida, this is..." He paused before continuing, his voice low so only Meredith could hear him... "a four-gun conclusion."

"That's foregone, you cretin."

"As you will. For you, the race is run." He stood to his full height, muscles rippling beneath a plain black t-shirt which matched that worn by the slight, pale woman atop the platform.

"I am ready, my Priestess," he leered.

"Proceed, my love," she replied, rewarding Rodriguez with a salacious grin.

"Pass me a bucket, I think I'm going to be sick," mocked Meredith, earning a kick in the thigh from the guard behind her.

"The case against this sinner is simple," began Rodriguez in a strong, clear voice. He turned as he spoke, revelling in the attention. "I intended to consign the defendant to the lake of fire for crimes that I will not burden your pure minds and hearts with this morning. Your Priestess, as is her wont, displayed mercy and offered the wench a second chance. She welcomed her, cared for her, placed her within the Maidenhood, a position only a fortunate few may occupy. She was a mother to this girl."

Meredith sat on her knees, digesting the nonsense coming from his lips. She knew there was no chance of a reprieve, this so-called trial was a mockery. All around her, the Red murmured in assent as Rodriguez continued with his risible performance.

"And in return, that mercy was tossed back in her face. This wench has conspired and plotted against our Priestess and you, her people." He extended both arms to include everyone in the audience who hung on his every word. "She has deceived a fellow Maiden. Tempted her innocent, pure soul down the path of unrighteousness."

"What have you done with—" Meredith was cut short by a stinging slap in the face from the guard standing over her, sending her reeling to the floor. She tasted fresh blood in her mouth, a fat, split lip to add to her other injuries.

Rodriguez continued, unperturbed by the interruption. "They have, between them, used their feminine wiles to deceive one of our most respected and trusted warriors. Sadly, he has paid the ultimate price for his indiscretion. I only dread to think what disgusting, carnal acts they indulged in to convince him to take part in this despicable plot."

"Guilty." A voice, somewhere in the throng, piped up, causing Rodriguez to raise a palm in protest. "Patience, my friend, you will have your say in good time." He paused for dramatic effect before continuing, soaking up the adulation, feeding off the rising tension. "In summary, I see no redeeming features in this wicked child before us. She has brazenly flaunted the helping hand of New Jerusalem and renounced the values we most cherish. As your Prophet and consort of the most-high Priestess, I strongly urge a guilty verdict be delivered by you, her most holy people.

Bedlam ensued as cries of "Guilty" resonated around the building. Guards struggled to hold back the crowd as red-clothed followers surged forward, intent on taking retribution into their own hands. Rodriguez had whipped them into a feeding frenzy with his inflammatory oration. He stepped back, a sheepish grin plastered over his face as he shrugged both shoulders. Meredith would have shot him dead right there if she had access to a gun.

"Quiet," roared the Priestess over the melee, as gradually the guards brought the agitated mass under control. She waited until order was restored, before speaking again. A dropping pin would have reverberated around the walls, such was the silent reverence of the crowd.

"You have heard from The Prophet. Does anyone in this gathering offer any defence for the girl or mitigating factors that might excuse her behaviour?" The total silence that followed surprised no one, least of all Meredith. She knew she was friendless, eyes boring into her from all angles. They wanted their pound of flesh with interest.

The Priestess, satisfied with the silence, turned her attention to Meredith, stepping down from her throne, aided by a Maiden on either side. Meredith recognised Seren, who glared back at her with total contempt.

"So, Meredith Starc," the Priestess purred, taking the extended arm of Rodriguez, the Portuguese cat who got the cream. "Do you have anything to say for yourself before my people pass judgement on you?"

"Yes," replied Meredith, the defiance evident in her voice. "I have something to say."

"Very well." The Priestess seemed slightly disgruntled but regained her composure quickly, aware that the pretence of justice had to be maintained. "Guards. Let her stand." The two heavies on either side of Meredith took a step back, their eyes never leaving her. There was no point making a run for it, as she wouldn't get ten feet before a bullet was lodged in her back.

Meredith rose slowly, eking every last second out of the situation. She felt strong and steady, her mind clear of the alcohol-fuelled fog which had descended upon it in recent days. She opened her mouth to speak, knowing she had to make every word count. It would need to be the performance of her life. Drawing on every last crumb of pathos old Mrs. Wilson had instilled upon her when she attended Ashgrove's Debating Society, she began.

"You might look upon me as a hopeless sinner, and yes, you would be correct. I've made many mistakes in my life, mistakes which have brought me here today. I stand before you broken, at rock bottom. I have taken the kindness and mercy shown by your great leader and thrown it back in her face. She offered me a lifeline, and I foolishly cast it aside."

The Priestess stared through Meredith stony-faced while Rodriguez, unbeknownst to her, winked at Seren, who looked away, blushing furiously. The watching crowd was quiet, but Meredith caught a fragment of movement off to her left, which also drew the attention of a vigilant guard. He started to push past people towards the source of the activity. Meredith continued, knowing time was running out. The others had to be close now, they just had to be, she could feel the edifying force of the Presence beginning to course through her battered body.

"All I ask is that you take pity on the mess I have made of my life. Forgive me for my transgressions, allow me one more chance, and I promise I will repay your faith. I promise I will..."

"Get on with it," hissed the Priestess, her patience running perilously low. Rodriguez had stopped flirting and was now looking towards the disturbance at the back of the crowd. People were starting to push forward, and a raised voice could be heard, which then turned into a strangled grunt.

Meredith dropped to her knees again, wringing her hands for dramatic effect. If the Priestess could do hammy overacting, then so could she. "I beg of you, in the name of the Father, the Son, and the Holy Spirit. May angels descend from above and strike me down if..."

The guard who had set off into the crowd to investigate the disturbance landed with a crunching slam inches from Meredith's knees. She recoiled in shock, the guards either side of her raising their rifles and sweeping the air above to determine where he had fallen from. Meredith looked again at the body before her—a body with no head.

"Miller," roared Rodriguez, at the same time as the Priestess shrieked and was dragged backwards, a curved dagger resting on her exposed throat.

"Nothing fancy, Sergeant," the owner of the knife warned, manoeuvring the Priestess away from Rodriguez and the guards who now had their weapons trained on him. LaPointe applied more pressure to the blade, and a thin crimson line trickled down the side of her neck. "And none of your fancy magic tricks, madam, or I'll slice that elegant throat of yours open. Now tell your men to back off."

"Do as he says," wheezed the Priestess, barely able to draw breath. The guards reluctantly complied, and the crowd parted to reveal a tall, muscular man with a mop of unkempt curls forging a path through it. He also carried a curved blade, although this one was coated in a slick red veneer. Meredith didn't have to be Agatha Christie to solve the mysterious case of the decapitated guard.

"Put the knife down, and let's sort this out man to man. I'll knock you on your backside just like I did back in 1813." Rodriguez leered at his old foe, but Meredith sensed a tension in his voice that hadn't been there before.

"Times have changed, Rodriguez," replied James Miller, casually wiping the blade clean on the sleeve of his tunic. "I don't have to play by your rules anymore."

"Who are these intruders, Prophet?" asked the Priestess, her voice no more than a strangled croak. LaPointe maintained a vice-like grip on her, his eyes never leaving the Portuguese hulk in front of him. "Oh, Sergeant Rodriguez and we go way back, madam. Aren't you going to introduce us to your new lady friend, Martim?"

"Your issue is with me, not her. The three of us can walk out of here in one piece, and I'll explain everything to the Colonel."

"I'm afraid it's a bit late for that," snarled James.

"Yes," continued LaPointe, adopting an expression of fake concern. "So sorry, Colonel. We tried to talk to him, but he wouldn't listen. Attacked us. In the end, we had no choice but to..." He left the words unspoken, a wicked grin on his face.

"I've killed you once La Pointe, and I'll have no hesitation in doing so again, you pampered clown. Now put the knife down, Miller, and we'll let our fists do the talking."

"I don't think so," replied Miller, edging ever closer. He lunged, without warning, and only for his quick reflexes, Rodriguez would have been watching his intestines splatter on the floor at his feet. LaPointe maintained his grip on the Priestess, blade at her throat, to ensure no guards could intervene. Miller struck out again but overextended slightly, allowing Rodriguez a tiny opening. It was all the hardened brawler needed. He swung his right leg in a roundhouse kick that connected with the knife, sending it sailing out of the Irishman's grasp and clattering across the tiled floor.

In a shot, Rodriguez followed up the kick by barrelling into the midriff of Miller, the two men landing heavily on the ground with the Portuguese soldier on top of his opponent. Rodriguez rose, straddling his opponent, and began to rain blows down upon his foe, who wriggled in vain to break free from the ferocious counterattack.

An explosion rocked the building, and the sound of automatic gunfire rattled in its wake. Within seconds, any remaining semblance of order evaporated as people started to run in all directions, desperate to escape the growing chaos. Guards began running towards the sound of the explosion, while others attempted to herd together the Maidens, several of whom were screaming in terror. LaPointe was momentarily distracted, and the Priestess needed no second invitation, sinking her elbow into his stomach before spinning and ramming her knee into his groin. The diminutive Frenchman groaned and sank to the ground, the knife falling from his hand.

"Guards, with me," shrieked the Priestess, scurrying behind the throne. LaPointe watched, blinking tears from his eyes, as a few feet away, Rodriguez and Miller rolled on the floor, exchanging punches. The noise of gunfire drew nearer and at the top of the broken escalators, which led to the ground floor, two guards crouched firing at an unseen enemy. One toppled over and lay motionless as raised voices could be heard from below, barking orders. LaPointe winced and turned onto his side, reaching for the knife which lay just beyond his grasp.

"Too slow, loser." He screamed in pain as Meredith slammed her foot down onto his outstretched knuckles, before bending to retrieve the knife and run towards the platform, intent on taking cover behind the throne. She hurdled Rodriguez and Miller, who oblivious to all, continued their personal battle on the ground.

"Meredith!"

She froze in her tracks and spun round to see a sight which brought tears to her eyes but an unmitigated joy to her heart. Standing at the top of the escalators were half a dozen Security Solution soldiers, their weapons trained on LaPointe who rose unsteadily to his feet, hands raised in surrender. Rodriguez and James stopped trading punches and followed suit. The latter was bleeding heavily from his nose while a lump the size of a golf ball was forming above the left eye of Rodriguez. None of this, however, was what Meredith was focused on as, from behind the soldiers, three familiar figures emerged.

She dropped the knife, and half ran, half staggered into the waiting arms of Emily and Harley, who smothered their friend in tears and kisses. Kirkwood, several paces behind, stopped short, uncertain as to whether he should join the embrace. Breaking temporarily free, Meredith saw his awkward pose and rolled her eyes, gesturing for him to join them.

"Come here, you numpty," she laughed. He needed no further prompt and joined them, burying his face into Meredith's hair, inhaling her scent as if it was the last smell he would ever experience.

"I knew you were coming, I just knew," she whispered in his ear. "I'll never leave you, Meredith. Ever."

CHAPTER 68 - SMELLY PANTS

The next hour was a blissful blur for Meredith. Deacon's men escorted them back to the boats. There were isolated firefights, but the Priestess and her followers had largely vanished, retreating deeper into the harbour estate to count their losses. She batted off a blizzard of questions from her companions as they recrossed the river, followed by an uneventful journey back to the safety of the Queen Street compound. Once inside, she was tended to by a medic who cleaned her wounds and deftly applied several stitches to the gash on her forehead.

"Don't worry, it should heal just fine. I doubt you'll even have a scar," smiled the medic, packing her kit and leaving Meredith alone with Emily and Harley. They looked at each other, stunned as if it was the first time they'd set eyes upon each other. The silence, though, was a comfortable one, the type decade-old friends lapsed into, content to enjoy each other's company without the need for words for the sake of words. It was Harley who eventually spoke.

"What's going to happen now? Are we staying here? That Priestess cow is still on the loose."

"I don't know about you, but I see a long, hot shower and a visit to the kitchen in my immediate future," murmured Meredith. "I'm starving, and I stink."

"You said it," sniffed Emily, pinching her nose in fake disgust.

"Shut it, O'Hara," laughed Meredith. "What are they going to do with Rodriguez and those other two psychopaths?"

"Deacon has them down in the cells. Samuel and Giro are debriefing them, whatever that means. The Priestess and her rabble are being left to their own devices. All we were interested in was getting you back."

"So, can we please go home?" pleaded Harley. "I've had enough excitement to do me a lifetime. The Presence is united again, let's get out of here and back to protecting our own plane."

"Ariana and Tess are taking care of that, relax. Can't I spend a bit of time with you guys before you go back? You know I can't return with you."

"Sorry, Em, I forgot. That was selfish of me," said Harley sheepishly.

"Don't be such a silly girl. I'm the selfish one. It's my own fault I can't go back, and I'll just have to live with that. Well, maybe not live, but you know what I mean." She shrugged in exasperation at her own poor choice of words.

"Oh, stop with the pity party, you two," snorted Meredith, bouncing to her feet. "I'm off for that shower. Meet me in an hour in the canteen. Deacon says it's curry and rice tonight."

"Yeah, rat curry, probably." Emily wrinkled her nose in distaste. The combat environment was certainly not her favourite scene.

"I'm that famished I'd probably still eat it. One hour." She waved farewell and returned to her room to collect towels and basic toiletries before making her way towards the shower block on the floor below. Her entire body ached, and she could sleep for a week, but it was nothing compared to what it should have been. The Presence working its magic again, she surmised. Best of all, the urge to drink was gone. For the first time in days, Meredith felt clean.

She passed Kirkwood's room, the door slightly ajar. Much as she craved the piping hot water and lathered soap of the shower, she stopped and politely knocked before poking her head into the room. "You decent?"

"As decent as I'll ever be." Kirkwood was lying on the top bunk, his arms crossed behind his head, staring at the ceiling. "How are you feeling?"

"Sore. Hungry. But I'll live. You?" She leaned against the door frame, studying the young man who continued to turn her world upside down and back to front at every available opportunity.

"Just trying to take it in. Less than a week ago, you and I were sitting in Burger King in the city centre trying to work each other out."

"If it's any help, I thought you were a weirdo then, and I still think you're a weirdo now." She smiled to let him know she was only teasing. He had a habit of taking things at face value and wore his heart on his sleeve, an endearing but, at times, infuriating quality.

"Har, har," replied Kirkwood, taking the joke as it was intended. "The first time we properly met you stank of dog pee, and by the looks of you, things haven't improved much."

"Charming as ever, Kirky." Her brow furrowed. "Are you alright, you took yourself off when we got back to the compound. I thought we would have all been together, celebrating. I've waited so long to hug my Emily. We have the Presence again and won't mess it up next time. Skelly is toast."

Kirkwood leaned on an elbow to face her. "Sorry, I've been a sad sack, I know. I'm just worried. Skelly is going to be furious at this latest setback, it's like prodding a nest of vipers with a stick. As far as the Company goes, we've only scratched the surface."

"Those two back at New Jerusalem. The French guy and the one who almost ripped Rodriguez in two. Did you recognise them? From your childhood?"

"That's the worry. I didn't. The squares at Waterloo were comprised of hundreds of soldiers. I didn't even have a quarter that many toys. Then, when you take into account camp followers like Maura, and the French dead, God only knows how many perished there that day. He will just keep hurling them at us, and I'm not sure how long we can withstand his attacks."

"You really are a sour puss, aren't you? You seem to forget it's not just the three of us. We've got Emily, Samuel, Giro and there are others. Them aside, we've got each other. As long as we stay strong and believe in the Presence, Skelly can huff and puff all he wants. Not forgetting Ariana and Tess. I can't wait to hook up with them. It's not all doom and gloom now, is it?"

"I guess not." Kirkwood swung his legs outwards and jumped from the bunk. "Okay, I promise to cheer up if you promise to have that shower, smelly pants." He playfully punched her in the forearm, instantly regretting it when Meredith winced in pain. "Oh God, sorry, I forgot you've been in the wars."

"It's alright. I'll live. I'm meeting the others in the canteen in an hour for something to eat. Be there or be square." Meredith turned and left him standing there, marvelling at her resilience and courage. Kirkwood thanked his lucky stars Meredith, and Harley had been the ones chosen to carry this heavy burden with him, for he knew he couldn't have done it alone. Then there was Emily, who drove him mad yet turned his stomach into a butterfly garden in equal measure. He didn't know where to even start with her. He thought he'd been in love with Natasha, he thought he knew its twists and turns, but this ethereal, whimsical young woman was something else. Love, obsession, there was a fine line between them, and he wasn't sure which side he was on. It was a time for focus, not fawning over a dead girl with relationship prospects somewhere between six feet under and zero.

CHAPTER 69 - A VERY CHARMING IDIOT

He found them in the middle of a chaotic canteen scene. Curry day, whatever the dubious meat of origin, was a popular event at Queen Street, and any soldier not on duty was busy piling their plate high from the serving hatch. Harassed kitchen staff barked orders, and the clatter from behind the hatch indicated they were stretched to the limit. Despite the tempting aroma, Kirkwood could not stomach food presently, and instead, made a beeline for a table in the far corner of the canteen. Meredith and Harley were huddled over heaped plates, shovelling curry and rice into their mouths as fast as they could. Emily looked on in mild disgust.

"I see this is where the zombie feeding frenzy is at," he quipped, taking a seat next to Meredith, who merely grunted in response, unwilling to be distracted from the serious business of eating.

"That's an insult to us recently deceased with impeccable table manners," gasped Emily in mock outrage, before a warm smile replaced it.

"Wharybs harrthhhingh Kertkwroood," spluttered Harley, her chin dripping with curry. Kirkwood had seen less happy pigs in mud.

"Oh, nothing much, just coming down to earth after this morning's high drama. How are you feeling now, Starc?"

Meredith gave a thumbs-up sign without averting her attention from the food in front of her.

"Hungry work being a superhero," offered Emily to an unimpressed Kirkwood.

"I swear that girl has hollow legs," he offered meekly, turning his attention to the ethereal, silver-haired young woman opposite him. The finality of what he was going to say sat in his stomach like a concrete breeze block.

"You can't come back with us, can you?"

Emily smiled sadly before replying. "You know I can't, Kirkwood. Not beyond the gatehouse at the cemetery. At least not in this form anyway."

"Jeez, this is serious stuff. You called me by my real name. Is there no way? Some sort of supernatural loophole we can manipulate."

"It almost sounds as if you're going to miss me." Emily leaned back in her seat, eyeing Kirkwood with a knowing smile.

"No, it's just, well, Meredith will be devastated...and....and... Harley. You're like a big sister to her...and..." He stopped, withering beneath her gaze, as she feigned innocence and wrung out his embarrassment.

"And?"

Kirkwood flapped like a hooked fish on the deck of a fishing boat. "Yeah. Well, I've got used to having you around as well. Properly around. Not popping up in dreams or cryptic graffiti."

Emily's smile softened, tinted with sadness. "Well, I'm honoured, kind sir. I've gotten used to being part of your little gang as well. But the Presence is three. We are three, yet we are one, remember? You don't need me, even if I could return to our plane in physical form."

"So, what do we...I mean, what are you going to do?" Kirkwood inwardly berated himself, earning a peal of laughter from Emily.

"What are those two waffling on about?" enquired Meredith, lifting her eyes momentarily from her plate. She studied the diminishing queue at the serving hatch, contemplating going up for a second helping.

"Search me," replied Harley. "Wanna see if they're doing dessert today?" She pushed back her chair and was halfway to the hatch before Meredith knew it. "You guys want anything?" she asked, shrugging her shoulders and following Harley when both Kirkwood and Emily replied in the negative.

Emily watched them make their way to the hatch. "Samuel has plans for me on other planes, he's keen for me to sign up and fight the Scourge. I've said yes, it's not as if I've much else to do. Now that the Presence is united again and the portal sealed, I'm sure you can slip away now and again to pay me a visit. You've got Ariana and her annoying friend to hold the fort if need be as well. You and I are going to see plenty of each other."

"Promise?" Kirkwood swallowed hard. He really was laying his cards on the table here, scared and excited in equal measure. She was dead but also entirely out of his league.

"I promise," replied Emily, leaning forward, her most serious expression burrowing a hole in his heart. "Besides, I want to see just as much of Meredith and Harley as I do of you, you great steaming wet blanket of gloom."

"Oh...right, of course, yes." Kirkwood's face reddened instantly, causing Emily to burst out laughing. Meredith nudged Harley in the queue, and the two of them peered suspiciously at the goings-on at the table.

"You really are clueless, Kirkwood Scott," whispered Emily, aware their every move was being watched. "Seems like I'm going to have to spell it out. I. Like. You. Three words. One syllable each. Does that help lessen the impenetrable wall of angst and doubt currently swirling around that excuse for a brain you have?"

"Oh." Kirkwood leaned back and blinked several times in quick succession before a goofy grin took hold.

"Typical clueless man."

"It goes without saying I like you as well," he added quickly. "A lot...when you're not driving me insane, of course." He paused, uncertain if he'd shot himself in the foot again. This was completely new territory for him, especially when stone-cold sober. Throughout his chequered interactions with the opposite sex, the large majority of his romantic declarations had been uttered after copious amounts of alcohol. He felt as if he was edging across a vast lake, coated with a thin covering of ice that barely held his weight.

"The Presence comes first, agreed? Meredith, Harley, the others. We protect them from Skelly, no matter what. Everything else must take second place. I deserted Meredith once, I'm never going to let her down again, now that I've been given a second chance."

"Agreed, absolutely," he replied, nodding his head idiotically like one of those dogs that people set in the back window of their cars.

"I'm not even sure how it works, what with me being...well, dead and everything. Consider it a long-distance relationship."

"Relationship?" Kirkwood gulped. This was serious.

"Oh, Kirky," she sighed. "Why must you analyse every word and inflection in such microscopic detail?"

"Because I'm an idiot?"

Emily laughed brightly, easing the tension between them. "Yes, indeed. That you are. But a very charming idiot."

"Interrupting something, am I?" Meredith stood over them, eyebrow raised beneath her beanie hat. Harley peered out from behind, an impish grin lighting up her face.

"No, not at all," blurted Kirkwood, a fraction louder than was necessary.

"Hmmm," replied Meredith unconvinced. "We've had to take a rain check on dessert. Samuel wants us in the briefing room in ten minutes. Apparently, there have been developments." She raised her hands and waggled her middle fingers to accentuate the last word.

"Developments?" Kirkwood and Emily spoke simultaneously, faces creased with concern.

"Yup. Don't ask me what, because I don't know. But I'll bet my last dollar our friend Senor Rodriguez is at the bottom of it."

"Come on then, Kirky," said Emily, rising to her feet. "No rest for the wicked." Her eyes twinkled with unspoken promise.

Kirkwood groaned and rose wearily. No rest whatsoever.

CHAPTER 70 - AN UNPALATABLE OFFER

"What are you going to tell them?"

It was a simple question, yet one of the hardest Samuel would ever answer, which Giro knew when he asked it. The problem wrapped within that question was the elephant in the room, and no amount of sugar-coating would stop its trumpeting calls for a response.

Samuel turned away from the spot on the bare wall that he was studying intensely to find his loyal lieutenant facing him. The two of them, accompanied by Deacon, had spent several hours in the cell block upon their return to the compound, grilling their captives. The big Irishman had remained impassively quiet while his slippery colleague, LaPointe, had waxed lyrical about all manner of topics without revealing anything significant. Skelly had his troops well drilled in counter interrogation techniques. When it came to these two, they weren't spilling a bean as to their mission or their leader's next step.

"I tell them the truth, of course. What other answer is there?"

"You'll never make a politician, Samuel Huddlestone. Far too honest for your own good. Cornelius knew how to twist the truth into a format that suited his needs." Giro smiled fondly, remembering his old friend.

"Cornelius was a rascal of the highest order," answered Samuel. "How he got away with half the stuff he did, I'll never know. I prefer the direct approach. I know no other way." He shrugged at Giro, unsure as to what else he could say."

"What about our friends in the cells, then?"

"Deacon has kindly offered to host Miller and LaPointe for the foreseeable future. I've ensured their powers are defunct on this plane. They'll be moved to a Sector 1 high-security correction facility in the morning. They won't be bothering us for a very long time."

"And what about the talkative one?"

"Rodriguez? Yes, even I wasn't expecting that." Samuel leaned back in his chair, balancing on its back legs. It creaked, straining to hold his sizable frame until he relented and leaned forward again, rubbing his jaw. "How can I be certain he's telling the truth? And what do I make of his offer?"

"In Ireland during their Troubles, they referred to his type as a snitch, a tout, a grass. They can be invaluable commodities or the road to ruin. It's your call, my friend, all I can do is offer my counsel."

"Which is?" Samuel looked towards the diminutive man, hopefully. "I've always valued your advice."

Giro pondered his answer before replying. "No war can be won without taking risks. Rodriguez is a reptile of the highest order, but there's a ring of truth in what he says. Yes, he's desperate to save his own skin, but that works in our favour. He's well and truly burnt his bridges with the Company now. We're his only straw, and he's clutching to us like any drowning man would. I say we go for it."

"I agree," nodded Samuel, "but it's good to know we are on the same wavelength. Thank you." He stretched his arms, revealing a considerable wingspan, stifling an imminent yawn at the same time. "Well, best bring them in then. Let's get this over with."

Giro nodded and left the room, returning a few moments later with Kirkwood and Emily. Behind them, Meredith and Harley jostled each other, stifling giggles when they saw the stern expression on Samuel's face. "Uh oh, I don't like the look of this," muttered Harley beneath her breath as they took their seats facing Samuel, and then Giro, who joined him on the other side of the briefing table.

"I know," replied Meredith. "Now I know how the contestants on The Apprentice feel when they enter the boardroom."

"How are you all?" asked Samuel. "Fully recovered from your exertions, Meredith?"

"Just about," she replied. "It's amazing what a supernatural life force and a few sticky plasters can achieve."

"Good. Because I have some news for you."

"Please, let it be good," groaned Kirkwood. "Or at least something that doesn't involve us putting our lives in mortal danger for a day or two."

"Rodriguez has agreed to assist us."

"What?" shrieked Harley.

"Are you for real?" roared Meredith leaping to her feet. Kirkwood and Emily attempted to restrain her, but she was having none of it. "That low life piece of dirt stabbed me in the back and left me hanging out to dry. If he had his way, I'd be on the evening menu at New Jerusalem right now. I wouldn't trust him as far as I could throw him," she fumed. Having said her piece, she reluctantly sat down again at the gentle insistence of Emily, the latter placing a protective arm around her best friend's shoulder.

"I appreciate this is difficult news for you to take in," said Samuel, his powers of diplomacy being tested to the limit.

"That's an understatement and a half," remarked Kirkwood.

Giro sniggered, earning a silent, but stern, rebuke from Samuel.

"I've always been honest with you all, and I've no intention of stopping now. There is a rift in the Skelly camp. It appears Rodriguez decided to jump ship and live the good life in New Jerusalem. This is why he betrayed Meredith, and his former comrades were dispatched to return him to the fold. He now finds himself out of the frying pan and into the fire. He's cornered, and like any other bully, has folded like a deck of cards when the underdog stands up to him."

"There truly is no honour amongst thieves. Or dead Napoleonic psychopaths."

"But how can we trust him?" pleaded Meredith, yet to be convinced as to the validity of Samuel's plan.

"We can't," replied Samuel plainly. "But that's a risk I'm willing to take and manage. What he has told us, if true, has the potential to undo everything we have achieved to date. Skelly has used New Jerusalem as a distraction and is now attempting to outflank us. We have no other choice."

There was silence for what seemed forever as they mulled over the unpalatable proposal Samuel was placing before him. Finally, it was the youngest member of the party who spoke.

"I'm in. It's not as if I'd anything else planned for this weekend. Tell me what I need to do."

Kirkwood looked at Meredith, then Emily, who nodded their tacit assent. Turning back to Samuel and Giro, he gave a thumbs-up sign. "You heard what the young lady said. Talk to us."

Samuel talked.

CHAPTER 71 - THE MAN WHO HATED MANKIND

"This place stinks."

"Slurry. It's the natural aroma of the Irish countryside. You're a country girl. You should be well used to it." Adam exaggerated filling his lungs and breathing out again as he strode through the ankle-deep grass, taking care to avoid the smattering of cow pats dotted about the field.

"Not the slurry, although it is foul. I mean this plane. When you pass over but then come back, it's vile." Maura shielded her nostrils with a raised forearm, half a step ahead of Adam. "There it is, up ahead."

Adam peered through the darkness at the silhouette of the unremarkable stone bridge coming into view above the hawthorn hedge ahead of them. So, this was it, the portal to countless parallel worlds and universes. He was far from impressed, having expected something a little more spectacular.

"That's it? The famous bridge at Ardgallon? Looks like the first half-decent gale would bring it tumbling down. It's hardly a wonder of the world."

"You mock, but this is where it all begins or ends. We open this portal, and everything changes forever." Maura stopped and placed a hand on Adam's forearm causing him to stop and look down into her bewitching green eyes. They sparkled with an intensity that dispatched any cynicism to the farthest reaches of his mind. He would crawl over hot coals, broken glass, whatever was thrown in front of him for Maura Miller.

"We do this tonight, Adam, and you and I will see riches beyond our wildest dreams." She raised a hand and stroked the side of his face with a pale, bony finger. The fool was putty in her hands. She swallowed the ball of revulsion rising in her throat and thought of James, wherever he was, doing Skelly's dirty work. This was all for her brave, handsome man, not this pitiful boy.

Adam leaned in to kiss her, and she pulled back, hands planted firmly on his shoulders. "I want to as well, but we have to concentrate, Adam. Stick to the plan. Soon, though, soon." She forced another dazzling smile while inside her stomach churned in disgust. The sooner the portal was open, and she was back in the strong arms of her husband, the better. As for Adam O'Sullivan? He would have served his purpose, and Skelly could do with him as he saw fit.

"Very well," he sulked, the frustration evident in his tone. Men never really grew up, did they? It was akin to being a kindergarten teacher. Maura inwardly counted to ten before smiling sweetly and continuing towards the bridge.

"The Presence is at its most active on this plane in centuries. So much so that Dobson, and now Samuel, struggle to contain it. The

White Witch passing over also disturbed the equilibrium, Dobson having to incorporate the one known to her kind as Harley in order to maintain the Three. It is an unpredictable power, and that has provided us with this window of opportunity. The Bomb Girl has somehow been blessed or cursed by it in addition to the Three. The trauma of her birth and the events surrounding it somehow drew the Presence to take up residence within her and those most directly affected by her. Her dumb little friend..."

"And me." Adam finished the sentence. "Her and her daft mother made my life a misery, but I'm finally getting my just reward."

"Exactly, my dear." They reached the hedgerow and effortlessly levitated over it onto the road, at the foot of the narrow, humpbacked bridge. "Voila." Maura extended a manicured hand towards its brow. "This is the only place on the planet where our masters can gain access to your world."

"Those mutant dragons you told me about?"

"I'm not sure they would take kindly to such a description, but yes. They are higher sentinel beings who seek to take possession of this and other planes. The only barrier to them is the Presence. Kirkwood Scott and his friends. Until now, that is."

"So, what do I need to do?" Adam was growing impatient. Enough of the explanation, he had the ability, that was enough for him.

"Now? We wait. They are coming. And when they do, you will be the conduit whereby they will breach the portal and enter this plane. Once through, the Scourge will do the rest. It will be the greatest show the world has ever seen. And the last."

Adam leaned back against the stone wall of the bridge and smiled. This was going to knock the Monksbridge Massacre into a cocked hat.

∞ ∞ ∞

Augustus Skelly was not one to rest on his laurels too long or indulge in self-congratulatory platitudes. You were only as good as your last battle, and centuries of relentless campaigning had taught him the hard truth of that. That said, he allowed himself a slight smile as he mulled over recent developments from the comfort of his armchair. Not since Salamanca had he pulled off such a dazzling feint leaving the enemy tied up in knots, not knowing whether they were coming or going.

"Yes, Augustus. Not bad, not bad at all."

The loss of Miller and LaPointe did not concern him, there were plenty more where they came from. He would have to manage a distraught Maura when she learnt of the capture of her beloved, but certain promotion within the Company would help to ease her grief. He would not forget the treachery of Rodriguez, but revenge was a dish best served cold, and he could wait. Let the coward think he'd gotten away with it then chop him down in the long grass. No, Skelly had a new feather in his cap. Adam O'Sullivan.

Who would have thought a resurgent Presence would have worked in his favour? Dobson had worked tirelessly to channel it in good and worthy souls, but it was like herding cats. The Presence had somehow touched the dark, damaged heart of O'Sullivan, a young man whose hatred of humanity impressed even Skelly. Broken by the murderous past of his father, his childhood had been unrelentingly miserable, ferried from one loveless foster home to the next. Abandoned by humanity, Adam had allowed the countless slurs and snubs to fester within, a ripe breeding ground for the hatred and callousness Skelly now required.

"The man who hated mankind," grinned Skelly. "Poised now to unleash a power which will rid the earth of its cancerous growth forever." He sat back in his chair and positively purred with pleasure.

"On my command, young man...unleash hell."

CHAPTER 72 - TIME IS RUNNING OUT

Kirkwood edged down the narrow stairway behind Samuel and Deacon, the old soldier rattling ahead of them, a set of clunky keys attached to his belt. He stopped at a foreboding grey steel door, opening it with a key selected from the bunch. Swinging inwards, it revealed a further four doors set in one wall of a rectangular room. On the opposite wall was a desk and several chairs, where two slumped soldiers jolted upright at the unexpected sight of their Commanding Officer.

"Easy lads, I'm not here to catch you out. Just need a chat with our bearded friend. All quiet?"

"Yes, sir," replied a lean, angular recruit with several days stubble on his chin. "The little one stopped singing an hour ago. Couldn't make out a word he was saying. The other one hasn't uttered a squeak. Just lies on the bed with his back to us. The big guy, he just grins every time we check on him like he hasn't a care in the world. Is there something we should know?"

"That's restricted information, Caldwell. Strictly need to know basis, and you don't need to know," replied Deacon curtly. "Go and take a break, lads. We'll cover for you. Back in an hour, alright?"

The guards didn't need to be told twice, leaping to their feet and bolting out the door, the lure of curry night too much to resist. Deacon shook his head at them before turning to Samuel and Kirkwood. "You know the deal, so stick to the script. He's agreed to tell us more if we meet his demands. I think we have some leverage here, so no silly stuff. He's a slippery customer, so be careful. He likes to play mind games."

"Tell me about it," sighed Kirkwood, remembering his previous dealings with Skelly's henchman.

"We understand, Major," replied Samuel. "Please, proceed."

Deacon nodded, leading them to the far cell. He pulled the metal hatch to one side. "Rise and shine, Sergeant, you've visitors." Kirkwood peered round his shoulder as a familiar bearded face appeared at the hatch, breaking into a sparkling smile as he recognised the people on the other side of the door.

"Well, look who it is, how kind of you to drop by. I'd let you in, but I'm afraid I'm not prepared for company. How have you been, Kirkwood?"

"Oh, I'm just grand, big man. I hear you've parted company with your boss?"

"I am an opportunist, my friend. The Colonel and I arrived at a fork in the road, so I decided to move on and accept a new position."

"Yet, look where it has landed you," said Samuel. "Skelly won't take kindly to being double-crossed. Seems an awfully big risk to me."

"I'm willing to take my chances," replied Rodriguez, the cheesy grin replaced by a scowl.

"Which brings us to our ongoing negotiations, Sergeant. I've briefed Samuel and the others about what you've disclosed so far—a new offensive against the plane our young friends hail from."

"Indeed," replied Rodriguez, his smile returning. "How are the girls? Little Harley and the delightful Meredith. Aren't they joining us?"

"Just talk," snapped Kirkwood, his patience already starting to wear thin.

"Temper, temper." Rodriguez was enjoying holding a trump card. "The terms are simple. I tell you what I know, and you return me to New Jerusalem unharmed. I see out the remainder of my days on their side of the river, and our paths need never cross again. Agreed?" A sly expression crossed his swarthy features as he sniffed the sweet scent of freedom.

"And what about Skelly?"

"I'll take my chances with the Priestess. She's a formidable woman. The Company will do well to give us a wide berth if they know what's good for them."

Deacon looked at Samuel. "Your call," he said, an edge to his voice. The quietly spoken giant considered the prisoner for several seconds before inclining his head. "Agreed. Now, what is Skelly planning?"

Rodriguez visibly relaxed and cricked his neck before replying. "He's going back to the bridge."

"What?" exclaimed Kirkwood. "Ardgallon? But the portal is sealed by the Presence. There's no way for the Scourge to break through."

"Correct. The portal has been sealed by the Presence. Nothing can re-open it...except for the Presence."

"O'Sullivan." Samuel hung his head as if a death sentence had been proclaimed on him. "He's using Adam O'Sullivan."

"What? I don't understand?" Kirkwood turned to Dobson's successor, desperate for an explanation.

"The Presence has expanded to combat the threat posed by the Scourge. When Emily passed over, Dobson channelled it through Harley to maintain the Three. But it has continued to spit and fizzle, spreading to Ariana and those closest to her spirit. Tess...and Adam O'Sullivan. The man whose father was the architect of the Monksbridge Massacre, who grew up hating the baby girl born the day her town was blown to pieces, the Bomb Girl."

Rodriguez chuckled. "Big shoes to fill, aren't they, Samuel?"

Samuel ignored the taunt. Yes, it was a steep learning curve, Dobson had warned him of that. Skelly was as devious as they came, but his old mentor also taught him to respond to setbacks with a positive mentality. "Dear boy, you will make mistakes, Lord knows I made thousands, but the true mark of a champion is to bounce off the ropes and come back swinging."

"Just tell us when."

"You let me out, and I'll happily disclose the details." Rodriguez had them exactly where he wanted. Now, it was time to swing the axe. Samuel looked glumly at Deacon, whose shoulders slumped. "This doesn't sit well with me at all," he grumbled, selecting another key, opening the cell door, and standing back to allow the prisoner out.

The Portuguese soldier emerged, proud as a peacock, strutting before Samuel and Kirkwood, desperate for a reaction. Kirkwood stared at him with contempt but remained silent, his respect for Samuel too great to stoop to such levels.

"Much better," gloated Rodriguez. "Now, if you'd be so kind, Major, could one of your armoured cars convey me back across the river to my people? When I'm safely across, you will have the information you require."

"You'll burn for this, you dog. Skelly will have your guts for garters." A deep, Irish brogue roared from the adjacent cell.

"I'll take my chances, James. Anyway, the only garters the Colonel is interested in belong to your pretty wife. Pity you're not currently available to defend her honour."

"The minute I get out of here, I'm coming for you, you bastard," snarled Miller. "Run back to your painted whore. I'll find you. I'll..."

"Yeah, Yeah. I look forward to it." Rodriguez was already out of the cellblock and starting to scale the stairs. "Keep up, gentlemen. Time is running out for you and your little world. We wouldn't want young Adam to get a head start on you all."

His laughter echoed back down the stairs leaving Kirkwood, Samuel, and Deacon with no choice but to exchange worried glances and follow in his destructive wake.

CHAPTER 73 - GETTING AHEAD IN THE AFTERLIFE

Ariana grabbed the wrists of Tess and squeezed them tightly to gain the attention of her near-hysterical friend. Tess squirmed to free herself, but Ariana maintained her grip until she settled sufficiently to allow a coherent conversation to commence. They were back in Ariana's room at the halls of residence, having failed spectacularly to concentrate on their studies in the library.

"Oh, my God, oh, my God, oh, my God," gasped Tess, to the extent where Ariana considered scouring the room for something for her freaked out friend to breathe into. "He's here, Tess. He's back."

"Where, Tess, where?" asked Ariana as calmly as she could, despite her own heart threatening to burst through her chest. When Adam O'Sullivan attempted to turn her into a human bomb, Tess had somehow been able to track her down. At the time, it had been an utter mystery, but given their understanding of the Presence now, and how it functioned, they realised exactly how it could happen. Tess Cartwright, party girl extraordinaire, was a diviner. Wherever Ariana or anyone else touched by the Presence ventured, Tess could track them down to within inches.

"West to the west, it's Northern Ireland definitely. But in the sticks. Get me a map, quick, your phone."

Ariana handed her mobile over without thinking and watched as Tess googled a satellite image of the island of Ireland, taken on one of the rare days it wasn't shrouded by cloud.

Tess furrowed her brow, sucking on a bottom lip, a picture of concentration. Finally, she jabbed a finger at the centre of the map. "There." Triumphantly she maximised the image before thrusting the screen under her friend's nose. Ariana squinted uncomprehendingly at it before the stark truth stared her in the face.

"Ardgallon."

"Ard what?"

"He's in Ardgallon."

"What's that got to do with the price of fish? Come on, girl, the suspense is killing me here."

"It's where the portal is, the only place on the planet where Skelly's creepy dragons can enter."

"What's he doing there?"

"I don't know," replied Ariana. "But it's not good. We've got to get there asap. Hold out your hand, I'll plane us in there."

"Woah, hold your horses. It's the dead of night out there, and you're going to fire us into the back end of beyond? Where the psychopath of the year awaits us? Shouldn't we think this through first?"

"There's no time, Tess. Now, are you taking my hand, or am I going to have to do this on my own? Either way, this train is leaving the platform in exactly thirty seconds."

"Fine," pouted Tess. "But these are £200 shoes. If you dump me into the middle of some boggy field, there will be hell to pay."

She grasped Ariana's outstretched hand, and within a millisecond, their surroundings exploded into a smorgasbord of noise and colour.

∞ ∞ ∞

"Incoming." Adam peered into the clear, starry sky, the moon casting an eerie light over the deserted bridge.

"I sense them," agreed Maura. "How long have we?"

"Two, maybe three minutes."

"And what about the others? The one known to his kind as Kirkwood?"

"Nothing...yet. I guess they're still tied up with those Company guys Skelly sent to New Jerusalem. Who are they anyway? How many of your lot are there?"

"I don't know," she lied. As far as he was concerned, she was besotted with him, no need to mention her beloved husband until the job was done. She was certain James was ripping up trees on the other plane, and hopefully, that included the head of Martim Rodriguez. Decapitation was his signature move, a little in-joke between them, considering the nature of his own demise. What a divine man he was, worth a hundred of Adam O'Sullivan.

She turned to face him, the moonlight lighting up his perfectly contoured face, rippling physique, and melted chocolate eyes. He meant nothing to her.

"As for their number, they are many, and that is all that should concern you. I will buy you more time with this Bomb Girl, just focus on opening the portal." She caught the rawness in her voice and swallowed hard, forcing a saccharine smile and slipping into character once more.

"I'm sorry to snap, my dear, it's just this is our one chance. Succeed here, and we will accumulate incredible riches and power. We must not fail."

"Don't worry," replied Adam, lapping up the attention. "This is a piece of piss. Don't you worry your pretty little head about a thing."

Maura stood on her tiptoes and kissed him gently on the cheek, all eyelashes and parted lips, before turning her attention to the threatening skies above. "Patronising arsehole," she muttered under her breath. The things a girl had to do to get ahead in the afterlife these days.

CHAPTER 74 - BRIDGE OVER TROUBLED WATERS

The truck engine cut out, and a few seconds later, the rear doors were unbolted and opened to reveal the silhouetted frame of Deacon. "Out, laughing boy. We're here." Rodriguez awkwardly shuffled his huge bulk along the bench, both wrists bound by plastic ties. From the opposite bench, Samuel watched his every move. Deacon reached in and used a hand to guide their prisoner onto the rear step of the landrover and then the bridge. They were on the far side of the river, and to one side, the lights of New Jerusalem blazed defiantly at them.

Taking an arm each, Samuel and Deacon guided Rodriguez the last few yards to the end of the bridge, two of Deacon's team covering them with rifles. Ahead, a welcoming party awaited, in its midst, the Priestess flanked by two Maidens and several edgy looking guards. It would only take one wrong word for the uneasy truce to evaporate and a firefight to light up the night sky.

"Prophet, how I have missed you," opened the Priestess. "I knew you would find a way to return to me."

"Nothing could keep me from you, my love." He looked towards Deacon and indicated his cuffs. "Now, if you would be so kind as to undo these, Major. I wish to return to my people."

"Not before you keep your end of the bargain," answered Samuel sternly.

"You know, Samuel," sighed Rodriguez, turning to his adversary. "You really need to work on your people skills. I know you take all this saving the world business very seriously, but so did Dobson, yet he possessed a certain charm and style that you sorely lack. You bore me with your bland sincerity. Is it any wonder I chose a darker path after passing over?"

Samuel took a step towards Rodriguez, never taking his eyes off his foe until their noses were almost touching. Rodriguez tensed, acutely aware that the other man was an imposing proposition, especially given his hands were still tied. The already fraught atmosphere crackled with tension as both sides watched the two men, poised to erupt into conflict. It was Samuel who spoke next.

"I may not have the personality of Cornelius, but I can assure you I do not lack his desire to wipe out the likes of you. I swear I will avenge his passing, and you will see then how bland I can be." The threat in his voice was unmistakable, and the two eyeballed one another, the only sound the waters below lapping against the base of the bridge. Tellingly, it was the bearded man who looked away first, licking his lips before spitting at the feet of Samuel.

"I suggest you spare me the monologue and concentrate on events at Ardgallon."

"When?" Samuel rarely raised his voice but did now, his patience rapidly wearing thin.

"Just tell them, Prophet. This war they fight does not concern me. Speak and be free of them forever." The Priestess folded her arms, her pale skin in the milky moonlight almost translucent.

"Very well." Rodriguez took a step back, a move reciprocated by Samuel. "I suggest you get back to your plane as fast as you can, Forsaken. The portal will be opened within the hour. And unless your precious Presence is there to combat it, I fear the Scourge will be unopposed. Such a shame for all those billions of unsuspecting people."

"O'Sullivan couldn't do this on his own. Who's with him?"

"Why, the delectable Maura Miller no less. No doubt swooning at his every word while her husband rots in your cell, Major. Now untie me."

Deacon produced a short-bladed knife from a pocket of his cargo trousers, slicing the ties. Rodriguez rubbed his wrists and swaggered past Samuel towards the Priestess, who greeted him with a lingering, passionate kiss. Samuel would not have seen it, for he was already running towards the landrover, closely followed by Deacon and the other soldiers. Once inside, the vehicle screamed in reverse along the length of the bridge before swinging round and powering back into the city.

The Priestess watched it disappear out of sight before taking the hand of Rodriguez and staring up into his dark, malevolent eyes. "Will they get there on time?"

"Maybe, maybe not," he shrugged. "Either way, it no longer concerns me." He took her hand, and they turned back towards the other side of the bridge, where a sleek, black 4x4 awaited to return them to his new home.

"You've rattled a few cages, though, dear. Won't Samuel be baying for your blood?"

"Samuel is all talk. He has more than enough to keep him occupied without worrying about me. If he has any sense, he'll let sleeping dogs lie." He stopped at the 4x4 and opened the rear door, offering a hand to the Priestess who climbed in, before joining her. Its gruff diesel engine roared into life, and soon they were headed back towards the main gates.

"And this, Skelly? Who is he? A god, a demon?"

"That's a very good question, my love. One I've never quite got to the bottom of. A bit of both, I suspect." He leaned back and yawned, draping an arm across her shoulders.

"You're not a prophet at all, are you?" she smirked, drawing into his chest and resting a hand on his thigh.

Rodriguez laughed before lowering his voice so the two guards in the front couldn't hear. "I'm as much a prophet as you are a messenger of God preparing for the second coming." He raised an eyebrow before kissing her fully on the lips.

Drawing back, she considered him for a moment before replying. "Be careful what you say, Martim. I am a generous lover, but there is much you do not know about me. You have witnessed my powers—I pray I never need to use them against you."

The smirk left Rodriguez's face replaced by an expression of uncertainty. It was a temporary lapse, but enough to assure the Priestess she maintained the upper hand in their relationship. Squeezing his hand, she looked straight ahead as the 4x4 swept through the heavily defended gates of New Jerusalem.

"Take us straight to my chambers," she instructed the driver. "The Prophet and I have much to catch up on."

CHAPTER 75 - A TERRIBLE BEAUTY

The gates to the station were already opening as the lead truck careered around the corner, throwing its occupants from side to side. It swung right into the compound and crunched to a halt. Samuel jumped from the back as Deacon did likewise from the front of the vehicle. They raced through the main doors of the old police station and took the stairs two at a time to the briefing room on the first floor. Giro greeted them at the door, a worried expression on his normally cheery face.

"It's not good, is it?" he said, taking in the fraught expressions of the two men as they barrelled past him into the room.

"Try bloody awful," barked Deacon.

"Gather the others, Giro, as quickly as you can," said Samuel, slightly more composed than his moody colleague. "We have little time."

Giro knew when to curb his witty asides and merely nodded, wheeling round and leaving the room. Within five minutes, Kirkwood, Meredith, Harley, and Emily were seated with him on one side of the huge rectangular table, which took up half the room.

Nobody spoke, waiting for Samuel and Deacon, seated opposite them, to update them on the handover of Rodriguez.

"The good news," started Samuel. "Is that he's told us what Skelly's next step is. There's going to be another attempt to breach the portal to your plane."

"But that's impossible," cried Meredith, never one to hold back her thoughts. "We sealed it at Ardgallon with the Presence. They can't open it."

"Unless they have access to the Presence themselves," interrupted Kirkwood. "Which they now do."

"What?" It was now Harley's turn to join the verbal fray, an expression of utter incomprehension on her youthful features.

"The Presence has become unpredictable, given the upsurge in activity by the Scourge. It has spilled out, touching others with its power."

"You mean Ariana and Tess?" muttered Emily. "I knew there was a reason I didn't like that slimy, little, bottle blonde..."

"No, Emily." Kirkwood struggled to contain the rising emotion amongst his friends. "Tess and Ariana are on our side, which is why Samuel has trusted them to remain on our plane."

"Then who is it?" interrupted Meredith, desperate for an answer.

Samuel provided it. "Adam O'Sullivan. When Skelly struck the deal on 17/4, it was O'Sullivan he was after. I was too slow to realise he also was a conduit for the Presence. For that, I take full responsibility. I have failed you, and I am sorry." The big man hung his head, the enormity of the mantle inherited from Dobson hanging heavily on his broad shoulders.

"You are too hard on yourself, my friend," said Giro softly. "If it were not for you, we would all be dead many times over. You have our full support." The others nodded in unison, endorsing a resounding vote of confidence in their leader.

"He's right," added Deacon. "No leader is immune from mistakes. I've made more than I care to remember down the years. The most important thing is to learn from them and move on. Now, tell us what we need to do to neutralise this little rat."

"Yeah," shouted Harley. "Let's kick his cowardly backside to Timbuktu and back. Wherever that is."

"I think you'll find it's in Africa," offered Giro kindly, before an icy glare from Deacon sent him scampering back into his shell of silence.

"Hang on a minute." A lightbulb popped in Meredith's head, causing her to turn and face Kirkwood. "You know about O'Sullivan? Oh, I get it, that's why you and your girlfriend were whispering sweet nothings in the corner of the canteen earlier."

"Watch it, Starc." Emily's ordinarily placid eyes filled with a gathering fury. "I knew nothing about it either, and less of the sweet nothings crap, you jealous little…"

"Me? Jealous? Of him?" Meredith's face was a picture of outraged horror as she pointed at Kirkwood. "I've scraped a few barrels in my time, but…"

"QUIETTTTT!" roared Deacon, jumping to his feet and letting off a round from his revolver into the concrete ceiling. The roar of the discharge reverberated around the room, and they all ducked, clutching their ears as a fine coating of dust and debris rained down upon them. A brace of soldiers walked past and paid no heed to events inside the room. It seemed Deacon's unique style of conversation management was well known within the compound.

"Thank you," said the veteran campaigner, holstering the weapon and resuming his seat between Giro and Samuel. "Now, please, Samuel, if you would be so kind as to continue." He smiled as if offering a refill of tea at an afternoon garden party.

"Er, yes, thank you, Major Deacon. As I was saying, we knew O'Sullivan was being used to try and re-open the portal. I swore Kirkwood to secrecy, so there's no point haranguing him. If anybody still has an issue with that or my way of doing business, then speak now or hold your tongues until I finish."

Harley slumped back into her chair, the archetypal moody teenager, rolling her eyes, while Emily and Meredith exchanged awkward glances monitored by an unimpressed Kirkwood. Samuel studied each of them in turn for signs of further rebellion before continuing, satisfied he would be allowed to speak uninterrupted.

"As I said, the good news is, we now know Skelly's intentions. The bad news…" He paused, his heart heavy at the information he was about to impart to his young colleagues. What he was about to say would place them in terrible danger again, but he was left with little choice. "It is happening imminently."

He stopped, expecting another barrage of protests and questions, but was greeted by silence. The inevitability of their situation, the realisation that there was no other option, that they were the only option struck them both individually and collectively.

"When do we go?" Kirkwood was the one to break the ice.

"Now," said Samuel. "Giro will plane the three of you to Ardgallon. Major Deacon, we cannot thank you and your unit enough for your assistance. It will never be forgotten."

The two men stood and shook hands. "Anytime, friend," the old soldier replied. "Now go, before I change my mind and have the lot of you chucked in the cells." A wry grin crossed his face as he ushered them out. "Get the hell out of my briefing room. I've a city to run."

Samuel led them out into the main yard, where Giro embraced each of his young companions like an over-affectionate puppy. "I'll get you as close as I can to the bridge, but it's very turbulent down there at the minute. The Scourge and the Presence are vying for dominance."

"Ariana and Tess will do what they can, but it's vital you get there as soon as possible. Emily, stay here for now. Giro and I will look after you."

Emily nodded at Samuel and exchanged brief, tight hugs with Harley, then Meredith. "Be careful, you numpty," she whispered in the latter girl's ear.

"You too," replied Meredith tearfully, before forcing herself to turn away as emotion got the better of her.

"Laters, Kirky," smiled Emily sadly. "Don't you dare let that Tess Cartwright turn your head."

"I won't. Looking after one Ashgrove reprobate is more than enough for me." He returned the smile even though he was dying inside. *Get a grip, Scott, you great big soppy lump. Moping over a* girl when the universe is about to implode. Gerry and Grogan would have a field day over such shameful weakness.

"You ready, Kirkwood?" asked Giro. Kirkwood nodded and joined hands with Meredith and Harley. Emily looked on, her chest bursting with a mixture of sadness and pride. Sadness at her friends once more risking their lives while she stood helplessly by and did nothing; pride at the selfless, unquestioning way they got on with it. Emily O'Hara, you truly were the most selfish little rich girl that ever lived. And now you're dead.

She turned and walked away, flinching only slightly at the dull thud and flash of light, which signalled Giro had planed them back to the year after she took her life. The year it all began.

∞ ∞ ∞

They re-entered in near darkness. The last light of the day slipping over the western horizon, a streak of orange fighting a losing battle against the darkening skies. Kirkwood lifted a boot and grimaced. They were in the middle of a sodden ditch which flanked a narrow, country lane. Grass sprouted from it, indicating it was a rarely used thoroughfare. He took a step back, lost his balance, and landed with an undignified squelch on the verge, unceremoniously bringing Meredith crashing down on top of him. Harley clambered out of the ditch onto the lane and frantically attempted to gain her bearings.

"There," she pointed towards a distant huddle of lights. "That's the village. Which means..." She rotated, surveying the murky landscape carefully as Kirkwood and Meredith crawled out of the ditch in a tangled heap. "There," shouted Harley, pointing towards a distant destination which neither of them could make out. "It's that way. The bridge. Come on, let's go." She set off at a jog, her boots splashing through a series of muddy puddles. Kirkwood hauled Meredith to her feet, and they set off in pursuit. A cracking noise from above lit up the sky, causing them all to crane their necks skywards. A distant flash heralded a chilling sight as high above, a swirling vortex was illuminated, containing dozens of tiny specks within it.

"Hurry!" roared Harley, breaking into a sprint as the wind around them picked up, accompanied by a smattering of fat, heavy raindrops. "They're coming!" she yelled above the strengthening squall, struggling to maintain her forward momentum.

Kirkwood lowered his head into the headwind and pumped his legs forward, pulling Meredith after him. Running largely blind, they ploughed along the potholed track, transformed into a series of mini lakes by the freak conditions. Ahead of them, the faint outline of Harley provided the only discernible landmark. He risked looking up and was dismayed to see the vortex descending steadily, the specks now larger and their features coming into focus—withered, malformed bodies upon which sat giant angular heads with wicked, snapping beaks. Their wings flapped in a frenzy, massive webbed extensions of their frames, which only added to the terrifying spectacle. The Scourge had returned, and the battle for control of the portal was to begin afresh.

"Left, left!" screamed Harley, battling to be heard above the deafening din all around them. The rain was battering down, stinging their faces, each drop a painful missile of foreboding. Kirkwood was as much following Harley's voice now as visibility reduced to almost zero. He plundered on, the heat from Meredith's hand warming his own, praying they weren't already too late.

∞ ∞ ∞

Six hundred yards away, the world was ending.

"Ariana!" screamed Tess, on her hands and knees at the foot of the bridge. She looked up, squinting through the deluge, towards the brow of the little stone bridge where her enemy stood, oblivious to their arrival. There, stood Adam O'Sullivan, face raised to the heavens, or rather hell, he was summoning ever closer. He was soaked to the bone but glowed with an inner heat that lit up the area on either side of him.

Beneath him, Ariana staggered like a three-day drunk, inching up the incline towards her nemesis. Her feet felt like they were in wet concrete, and every muscle of her body ached as if she had run a marathon to reach the bridge, as opposed to the short walk from where she had planed from the halls. Every inch of her body was coated in a clammy film of sweat, and her teeth chattered involuntarily from an inner cold that chilled her very core. Above her, the swirling vortex was almost upon them. Demonic creatures cawing and clawing in malevolent delight, seconds from breaking through the portal and wreaking devastation.

Ariana flung every ounce of what she now knew to be the Presence towards O'Sullivan in an effort to bounce him from the top of the bridge. She had no time to fine-tune her efforts, not caring where it took him. His knees buckled, and he swayed to one side as if caught by an invisible uppercut, before regaining his balance and grinning at her, his eyes mad, utterly devoid of humanity.

"Is that the best you can do, Bomb Girl? I've been practicing hard since our swords last crossed. Think you'll find I've come on a fair bit since then."

"Are you completely insane? You're going to kill us all, every last one of us. Do you hate me that much?" His momentary lapse in concentration allowed her to inch a few feet closer. However, the effort involved was making her nauseous with exhaustion.

Adam reverted his focus to the maelstrom, an expression of childhood wonder on his features, like a five-year-old meeting Father Christmas, for the first time. When he spoke next, his voice was softer, verging on peaceful, and Ariana had to strain to make out the words.

"It's funny how it's all worked out. There was me, with my sights set on blowing the heart out of a campus when all along, I was destined to blow the heart out of the whole bloody world. An outsider all my life, and now I stand before you, a god in waiting."

"Is that what you really want? Is that what your father would have wanted? You say this is all to avenge him, but would he really have wanted this? Destroying an island, he fought all his life to free?

Destroying a planet?" Ariana hinged her last faltering hope on connecting with some remaining shred of decency within the damaged young man turned monster before her.

"Oh, my bleeding heart," scoffed Adam. "Do you really think I give a toss about any of that when I have this power? When I have the most beautiful woman who ever walked this damned Earth on my arm, soon to be in my bed?"

Ariana watched in horror as a figure emerged from the other side of the bridge to stand by O'Sullivan's side, and indeed, she was breathtakingly beautiful. A terrible beauty, her billowing flame-red locks framing the flawless face of an angel. An angel thrown from heaven and now full of searing evil, locked behind devastating, emerald eyes. Before she could react, the woman spread out her arms, sending Ariana tumbling backwards, her hard-won yards gone in the blink of an eye. She clattered into Tess with a sickening crunch, their groans bringing a sadistic smirk to Maura Miller's face.

"Are we done here, my love?" The woman looked towards O'Sullivan, who was transfixed again by the horrific events unfolding above them.

"Yes," he replied, slightly irritated by the intrusion. "Finish them."

"With pleasure." Maura raised her hands and walked towards the two prone bodies lying below her. "Say goodbye to your miserable little lives, ladies."

"Nooooo!" screamed Harley as she rounded the bend and hurled a wave of raw energy towards the bridge. A heartbeat behind her came Kirkwood and Meredith, the three of them fanning out across the road as the barely visible wave crashed into Maura, knocking her off her feet. Ariana grabbed Tess and dragged her to one side as their rescuers homed in on their targets.

"We are Three, but we are One. We are Three, but we..."

An ear-splitting scream split the night as the first creature burst out of the vortex. A colossal pterodactyl-like being with gleaming black scales and devilish eyes that burned with a callous intelligence. It was soon joined by a second, then the floodgates opened, and a stream of others followed. The first stretched until its wingspan covered the bridge, standing almost three metres high on spindly, stunted legs. O'Sullivan stepped back, a creepy half-smile on his lips as Maura regained her senses and rose to her feet alongside him.

"It is done," she whispered. "They are through." She slipped an arm through O'Sullivan's, and the two of them vanished in an albescent light, as the creatures began to take flight and beat their powerful wings towards the unsuspecting village. The first beast paid no heed to them, its attention still drawn to the five human forms who gaped at it, and it's brood, in open-mouthed shock.

Tess crouched on one knee, helpless before the beast. "If you're going to wave that magic wand of yours, I suggest you do it soon," she hissed in Ariana's ear. The creature cocked its head to one side as if listening to their conversation as it considered its options.

"I'll be bouncing blindly. We could end up anywhere. I'm still getting the hang of it." Her eyes remained locked on the monster in front of them, unwilling to move a muscle for fear it provoked a deadly reaction.

"Anywhere is better than our current circumstances, just do it."

As if the creature knew their intentions, it stood on its haunches and beat its wings in and then out, repeating the motion as if winding itself up like a clockwork toy. Ariana yelped and looked down at her throbbing wrist, where Tess had just pinched it.

"Now, Ariana!"

Channelling her fractured thoughts, she battled to summon the power she knew lay within her. She gradually sensed it forming and rising, a kinetic core within, that replaced the fear and worry gripping her body. Rising, rising, she thought of nothing but the five of them elsewhere and out of danger, united and safe.

"We are Three, but we are One." Her concentration was shattered by a crazed shriek, and she looked up to see two shards of green lightning shoot from the inverted wings of the beast towards where she and Tess crouched. By right, they should have been no more than a smouldering pile of ashes, but somehow the bolts stopped less than a foot from them, suspended in mid-air. She turned to see Kirkwood, Meredith, and Harley standing behind them, hands outstretched in a semi-circle, the Presence forming a protective shield around them.

The beast threw back its angular head in frustration, an elongated beak opening to reveal several rows of serrated, savage teeth. Teeth designed for the shredding and cutting of flesh. The shimmering energy field between it and them was all that was saving Ariana from a grisly end.

"Hurry up, Ariana, we can't hold this much longer," gasped Kirkwood, the effort being expended obvious by his pale demeanour. Meredith and Harley were equally drained, every ounce of their being focused on stopping the beast from breaking through the field.

One slip in concentration, and it was over for all of them. Ariana needed no further encouragement. Looking at the two shards as they inched towards her face, pushing the field slowly inwards on itself, she fumbled within her frazzled mind, finally locating the switch she needed to flick.

The beast flapped its wings one last time as the green bolts were finally unleashed, striking the road in front of it. All that remained was a deep, smoking crater. There would be no early feast, it's prey no longer there. It wheeled away, no longer interested, it's ravenous mind only concerned with locating its first feed. It soared effortlessly into the sky, climbing swiftly as it joined the horde still pouring from the vortex and spreading out across the land. In the near distance, the village of Ardgallon was already ablaze as a murderous green shower fell upon it. The beasts swept lower, their hungry cries drowning out the screams of the dead and dying.

It was a bloodbath, and it was only the beginning.

CHAPTER 76 - SAVING SKELLY

The back of Ariana's head bounced off the ground with a resounding thump. She stared at the grey, bleak sky above informing her it was daylight where she had landed, but offering little else. Before she had time to gather her bearings, she was grabbed by an ankle and awkwardly dragged along the rough surface on her back. She opened her mouth to complain but was interrupted by the unmistakable sound of gunfire. The ground next to her exploded as she was showered with a fine coating of grit and loose stones.

"Stay down," a voice above ordered. She felt her body being swung around in concert with the squealing of metal and bolts being slammed into place. She flipped onto her side to face the main gates of the Queen Street compound, two soldiers securing them in place. Looking up, she was met with the imposing figure of Deacon staring down at her.

"And then there were five," he grunted before turning and loping across the yard. "Come on, the others are waiting for us." He left Ariana to find her feet and scamper after him. She was still developing her planeing skills but suppressed a smile at extracting her friends to where she intended them to go, even if she missed her own landing spot by a few feet.

Dusting herself down, she scaled the stairs behind Deacon to be greeted by an apoplectic Tess, who hugged her so tightly Ariana feared her eyeballs would pop out of their sockets. Inside sat the other three survivors from the bridge, flanked by a relieved Samuel, a poised Emily, and a grinning Giro.

"Ariana, please, be seated," said Samuel. "We are truly grateful for your bravery at Ardgallon. If it were not for you and Tess, all would be lost. He rounded the table and enveloped her in an awkward hug, the big man towering over a foot above her.

"It doesn't feel that way," she replied, extricating herself from his suffocating grasp. "I failed. The portal is open. Everything and everyone is gone. Our families, friends..." She tailed off, and a sadness fell upon the room, each of them cocooned in their own bubbles of grief. It was Samuel who broke the silence.

"Yes, there has been a breach, but that does not mean we give up. We fight on, there is no other choice. Your plane is the hinge, the crucial domino. Now that the Scourge has secured it, the others will fall quicker. It is at the heart of the entire system, a one-in-a-billion world. We are all on borrowed time, so must act now or accept our fate."

"But why is our world so important? It's nothing special. I saw enough on the streets to put me off the human race for the rest of my life." Meredith shrugged her shoulders and shrunk back into her chair.

"I accept your people are tainted," said Samuel. "But your world is blessed with everything your race needs to live happy, long, and productive lives. Somewhere along the line, unfortunately, something went badly wrong. It doesn't take much. Think of a drop of ink in a glass of water."

"But what can we do?" asked Kirkwood. "The Scourge is through, Skelly has won, game over, the end. And nobody lives happily ever after." He looked around the room in resignation to see other heads nodding in agreement.

Except for Giro. "Not quite. There is a way. The only way to kill a weed is to pull it out by its roots. Cutting a few leaves here are there won't achieve anything. We strike at the core, sever the head from the body, and no matter how strong, it will fall."

"Those monsters back at Ardgallon? Are you mad?" Tess was mortified at the thought of ever getting close to one of the winged abominations again.

"No," replied Samuel plainly. "We must strike at the general on the hill, overseeing the carnage below."

"Skelly? But he always takes great pleasure in saying he's middle management. A mere cog in the machine." Kirkwood was far from convinced with Samuel's rationale.

"Yet Skelly is of this Earth. He was a man once, flesh and bone, just like us." Emily's eyes opened wide as if a penny had dropped, revealing all to her.

"Exactly, Emily." Giro boarded Samuel's train of thought and stoked the fires further. "The Earth lies at the heart of this whole crazy cosmic war, one that has been waged for aeons between foes that barely understand themselves, let alone each other. Yet, the one constant, the tipping point, has always been the Earth. It is the jewel in the crown, but the Scourge can only access it by those who have been born into it. Much like the Presence can only be activated by those who have been born into it."

"O'Sullivan was used to open the portal. I get that," reasoned Meredith. "But, Skelly?"

"Adam O'Sullivan was the key. But the locksmith is Colonel Augustus Skelly, and they have what turns it, the men and women who died with him at Waterloo on 18 June 1815."

"My toy soldiers. The Company." Kirkwood was barely audible as he mouthed the words.

"Those buggers sure aren't toys." Deacon sat apart from the others, oiling his rifle like a first-time father caring for his newborn child.

"We stop Skelly, and we stop the Scourge. It's as simple as that," concluded Samuel. "The Scourge cannot succeed without him."

"Oh, so we just swan into the Study, chop off his head, and home in time for tea and cakes?" The sarcasm in Kirkwood's words was an outlet of his frustration and sense of helplessness.

"No, you numpty, think laterally." Emily took his hands into hers, an action that did not go unnoticed amongst the others. "Where is he at his weakest, where can we fly undetected under his radar, finish him once and for all?"

Kirkwood looked at her blankly, struggling to think, acutely conscious that all eyes were on the two of them. If squirming were an Olympic sport, he would have attained the qualifying standard there and then. It was Harley who rescued him from the embarrassing predicament.

"Waterloo! That's it. We find him at Waterloo."

"Whaaa?" was all Kirkwood could manage in response.

"We get Skelly before he became, well... Skelly. He died at Waterloo because he and some other soldier had a big fall out, and Skelly got wiped out because of it."

"You mean, Sir Arthur Wellesley, the Duke of Wellington and the demise of the 49th Somerset Regiment?" offered Giro.

"That's the one," grinned Harley, like a kid who had answered all their maths questions correctly and been propelled to the top of the class.

"Here's what we do," said Samuel leaning forward, a rare smile on his face. "If we can plane back to before the battle and somehow prevent the decimation of Skelly and the square, then we remove the hatred and spite which the Scourge have exploited to turn him into the monster he has become."

"We save Skelly?" The words hung in the air for some time after Meredith spoke them, each of them wrestling with such an unpalatable concept. Samuel allowed the dust to settle before speaking again.

"We save the planet, Meredith. If we can achieve that, there will be no need for any of this. Skelly will survive Waterloo, live as normal a life as he ever could, and never materialise into the guise we now know."

"Let's do it, then," whooped Harley, never one to back down from a challenge.

Kirkwood looked at Emily and Meredith, in turn, who both nodded their assent. "Okay, Samuel, but I have two questions. First, how do we stop Skelly from sending the Company after us at

Waterloo? He's not just going to sit back and let us do this. And secondly, how on Earth are we meant to survive five seconds when we plane into the middle of one of the bloodiest battles the world has ever seen?"

Samuel fidgeted slightly in his chair, clearing his throat before answering. "I have answers to both those questions. But I don't think you are going to particularly like them."

CHAPTER 77 - THE STREETS RUN RED

Gerry contemplated the dregs of his pint before raising the glass to his lips and downing its contents.

"Fancy another one?" he asked.

"Well, thank you, Gerard, I think I will. Thanks very much for offering."

"No problem, mate."

He scanned the deserted room before hopping off the stool he was perched on and sauntering behind the bar. An act which would normally have resulted in his feet not touching the ground as Big Mark removed him from the premises.

Taking in the array of optics before him, he settled on the most expensive whiskey and helped himself to a very generous double topped off with a cube of ice.

"Might as well go out in style." He leaned against the bar, surveying the empty booths and stools, several of which had been knocked over in the rush when the news was confirmed. Initial reports had been met with the jaded cynicism that the Montreal's regulars greeted all such bulletins.

"What a pile of crap."

"Next thing, they'll be saying the Chinese are behind it."

"Is it April Fool's Day? Stick the racing on. I've a bet on the next one at Fairyhouse."

Then the first-hand accounts started to filter through as news crews scrambled to the west of the country to capture the first barely believable images. Towns and villages ablaze, bodies lying piled in the streets, the skies black with a swirling, swooping mass of death and destruction. That's when people started to take notice, and the horse racing was forgotten about. Everything was forgotten bar the need to vacate, find loved ones, and somehow survive what was descending on Belfast. Gerry sipped his whiskey and smiled ruefully. It was an exceptional malt, far too good for a dive like this.

He had nowhere to run to and nobody to call. Kirkwood and Grogan would be sorting out their own affairs. Kirkwood had family in New Zealand, and for all his bragging about being a man about town, Grogan still lived with his parents. The last thing they needed was Gerry hogging their final few moments in the land of the living. Besides, eight pints of Carlsberg before the news broke somehow hindered his conversational skills at that moment in time.

No, he intended to face his death as he had lived his life. As drunk as possible. He downed the remainder of the whiskey and topped it up again. The television screen mounted in the far corner of the bar displayed nothing but static. He could have tried to change the channel, but what was the point, it wasn't as if anything was going to change. Outside, the initial clamour and screams had died down to the occasional hollow fall of footsteps. In the distance, he could hear a window shattering and the wail of sirens. Just another quiet Saturday in Belfast.

Gerry hadn't batted an eyelid when faced with the news that hundreds of thousands of flying beasts were laying waste to Counties Tyrone and Fermanagh. He was a lover of conspiracy theories and often lectured anyone unfortunate enough to be within earshot that one day a zombie virus or alien invasion would finish them all off once and for all. The moon landings were fake, The Loch Ness Monster was alive and well, and Elvis was running a bar in the Canary Islands. It was only a matter of time before something like this happened, so Gerry was more prepared than most for Armageddon hitting his homeland.

An explosion rocked the bar and brought several rows of glasses crashing to the floor all around him. He barely flinched, instead removing the whiskey bottle from the optic to ensure it didn't meet a similar fate. It was much too delicious a malt to end up all over Francey's filthy floor. He suspected the winged fiends were close now, for although it had been a bright afternoon, the light filtering into the bar was diminishing minute by minute. A distant hum was also gradually building. Gerry recalled the stories his Granny McAleese used to tell him when he was a wee boy about the sound of the German bombers over the city during the Blitz. The feeling of helplessness, knowing what was coming before you saw it but being utterly powerless to do anything. You just waited and took what came, praying you would survive the deluge of high explosives falling from the skies.

He had spent many a happy hour in this bar, and one or two unhappy ones as well. Those that he could remember, anyway. But the time to be happy was no more. Never again would he cross its threshold on a payday Friday. His wallet full of cash and his heart full of laughter, cracking jokes with Kirkwood and Grogan. Gerry lifted the bottle and walked back round the counter and across the bar towards the entrance where Big Mark maintained order. The gentle giant who had disappeared the second the news reports were confirmed to spend his last hours with his daughters and grandchildren.

"You were right all along, big lad," remarked Gerry fondly, tracing a figure along the barstool where the kind-hearted bouncer perched most evenings. "There's wiser eating grass than me."

He opened the bar door and turned left towards High Street. To his right, two youths were stepping through the shattered display window of an electronics retailer, shouldering a widescreen television between them. They eyed Gerry warily before deducing he wasn't a threat and skulking off in the opposite direction. Gerry shrugged and took a long slug from the neck of the bottle, the whiskey burning his throat.

"Enjoy it while it lasts, boys."

He emerged onto High Street and proceeded towards the river, casually taking in the ensuing chaos. A handful of people were in the vicinity, some running with purpose, others wandering with tearful or dazed expressions. Like him, they had accepted their fate. To the west, a black, shifting cloud neared the city. An explosion ahead caught Gerry's attention, and he looked up to see the Albert Clock erupt into a ball of flame. Its foundations rocked before the top half accepted defeat and crumbled in a shower of masonry onto the streets below.

"There goes the neighbourhood." Gerry continued to stare at the unfolding melee above him. Shapes started to break away from the central cloud and swoop down over the city, revealing their true horrific identities. Sharp claws and beaks tore into soft flesh as those on the ground tried and failed to escape their grasp. A feeding frenzy developed, and the streets ran red just as the heavens exploded. Buildings all around him burst into flame as bolts of garish green light shot from the wings of those creatures who remained above.

Gerry took one last mouthful of whiskey before placing the bottle beside him and lying back on the pavement, a warm, comforting glow spreading outwards from his stomach. He closed his eyes and waited for the agonising, but mercifully quick end. His one regret was not believing Kirkwood and his insane insistence that a homeless girl sketching a picture held the key to unlocking his own trauma. Insane, yes, but no more insane than this. One regret from a lifetime of missed opportunities and broken promises, not a bad end return, he reasoned.

"Sorry, Kirkwood. Hope it works out for you wherever you are, mate."

CHAPTER 78 - EVEN THE DEAD NEED REST

Rodriguez had never screamed in his life, not even at the moment of his death, but he screamed now, awakening in a sweaty tangle of sheets. He flailed at an imaginary enemy, wide-eyed and disoriented, initially unaware as to where he was. It took the Priestess several minutes to convince him it was all a dream, he was safe in her chambers with two armed guards permanently outside their door, and the perimeter watch doubled. There had been an influx of new waifs and strays once word spread she was to wed a powerful prophet with powers beyond their comprehension. Eggs were being placed in baskets all over the ravaged city, and many were viewing New Jerusalem as the only option when it came to a protracted lifespan.

When she asked what the dream was about, he fobbed her off, saying he couldn't remember. This was a lie, of course, for he would never forget the visions which had visited him in his sleep. Images of blood and slaughter the likes of which even a battle-hardened campaigner like Martim Rodriguez had never witnessed before. New Jerusalem ablaze as the Scourge laid waste to all within it, his body being torn apart by several of the winged demons. He could still feel each excruciating tear, the never to be forgotten sound of his flesh being ripped from bone and greedily gobbled down. Drowning in his own blood, he had gagged and choked, watching as his life spurted and pooled from an ever-growing collection of scarlet wounds. And standing over him, savouring every last second of his demise was Augustus Skelly, leaning in to whisper in his ear before the killer blow was struck.

"This is what happens when you cross me, Martim. I'm a loyal ally, but a terrible foe. You will find that out for yourself, the hard way."

The Priestess quickly fell asleep again. Rodriguez listened to his own still rampant heartbeat compete with the change in her breathing pattern. He stared at the ceiling, occasionally swathed in light as a patrol swept by the hotel. While they hadn't spoken directly about it, she seemed to sense his discomfort and had implemented additional security measures to place him at ease. It hadn't worked. He tossed and turned, but no matter how hard he tried, sleep eluded him. It was probably a good thing, as he had no desire to return to the horrors of his slumber.

A scratching noise across the chambers made him sit bolt upright in bed, peering into the gloom. Was it the guards? No, they wouldn't dare enter uninvited and face the wrath of their less than understanding leader. Rodriguez slowly slid from under the sheets, at the same time reaching for a pistol he had secreted under the mattress. Firearms were expressly banned from the chambers, but his new conquest turned a blind eye to his indiscretion. The woman was well and truly under the famous Rodriguez charm, or so he thought.

Rodriguez felt for and secured the plush carpet underneath, his toes digging into it as he rose from a crouch, cocking the hammer of the pistol as quietly as he could. It wasn't anywhere near quiet enough.

"Oh, put it away, you cretin," a soft but sour voice echoed from the opposite side of the room. Rodriguez froze, not sure if he'd imagined the voice as the Priestess continued to snore lightly, her back turned to him.

"She won't wake up, Martim. In fact, neither of you will. This is a dream, so please put it away. And I don't just mean the gun. For God's sake, put some pants on, man."

Rodriguez suddenly realised he was naked and wrapped a sheet around his midriff. "Show yourself," he hissed through gritted teeth. "Or I'll blow you away." He reinforced his intent by pointing the firearm in the general direction of the voice.

"Oh, please." He heard a palpable sigh before the voice, that of a woman, spoke again. "Your bullets don't bother me. The only thing you'll be shooting up will be your new girlfriend's swish pad."

Rodriguez squinted as a faint emerald green glow grew before his eyes, a slim, silver-haired young woman stepping from it as if through a looking glass.

"Witch," he whispered in almost reverential tones.

"I prefer White Witch if you have to stick to silly nicknames," said Emily, painting her most bored expression. The unnatural lighting accentuated her pale skin and delicate bone structure, giving her the appearance of a painstakingly painted ceramic doll. "You've certainly landed on your feet with this gig. Talk about nine lives, you must be down to your last couple by now."

"What do you want, ghost?"

"Charming," sniffed Emily. "Well, it takes one to know one." She took a step closer to him, the folds of her dress rustling. Rodriguez set the pistol on the bed but maintained eye contact with her.

"I have a proposition," she said brightly. "From Samuel."

"I want nothing to do with your war," he growled, regaining a degree of his usual cocky composure. "I'm retired now, living a quiet life in this beautiful city of yours. There is nothing Samuel can offer that would persuade me otherwise."

"Yeah, right," snorted Emily derisively. "Been having any bad dreams lately, have we? Face from the past keep popping up in them?"

Try as he might, Rodriguez could not contain his surprise. "How do you know of this? You set one foot inside my head, and I'll..."

"You'll do what? Kill me. Wise up, Martim. Now cut the crap and listen to me. You've jumped ship, bailed from the Company, and that takes some nerve, I'll give you that. I'd almost be impressed if you weren't such an utter hallion."

"Hallion?" He furrowed his brows in confusion. "You think I am a horse?"

"Oh Lord," sighed Emily. "Hallion. Thug. Scoundrel. Undesirable."

Rodriguez shrugged. "I've been called a lot worse."

Emily decided it was time to lay her cards on the table. "We both know, Sergeant Rodriguez, that Skelly does not take kindly to being double-crossed. So, if you think you're going to live happily ever after in your ivory tower with your freaky fairytale princess, then I'm afraid you're very much mistaken. You are a marked man, living on borrowed time."

"I know what I've done, witch," he replied after an uncharacteristic pause. "But I'm prepared to take my chances. I have everything I need here. Let the Colonel come, he has no power in this place. My bride will ensure that." He motioned towards the bare back of the Priestess, her midnight mane cascading down it. He was still none the wiser to the source of her strength but grateful, nonetheless.

"You can't hide here forever," countered Emily. "Is that how you're going to spend the rest of your days? Clinging to a few grubby acres of wasteland in this wreck of a city? A man who used to traverse planes at will, who saw so much. You're a warrior, a traveller, you need to be free, not prowling up and down a cramped cage, the pampered pet of a bored psychopath."

"You know nothing of her and me," he replied, his hackles raised. There was a pause as he considered his options. Emily waited. Men were so basic, all you had to do was identify and appeal to their basic needs, push the right buttons, and voila, they collapsed like a deck of cards. But she had to tread warily, he was as slippery as an oiled piglet. She had piqued his interest, she was certain of that, but one false move now and he'd wriggle off the hook, never to be seen again.

"I know you're sick of Skelly, sick of the Company. For all your disgusting attributes, I believe you when you say you want to step away from all that. But they won't forget your treachery, won't let it lie, and they'll be gunning for you. The Priestess, for all her powers, is mortal. She won't be around forever to hold your hand and fight your battles. That's when they will come for you. That's when you'll wish you'd never been born."

Before he spoke next, she knew the lock within him had been sprung, the bare reality of his situation exposed. Emily resisted the urge to click her heels in delight and retained her deadpan expression, watching his every move. She had him, she had him. His next words confirmed that.

"Your proposition? What does it involve?" It was the subtlest of capitulations, but he knew in his black, still heart that she was right. He was free but would be looking over his shoulder every second of every day. He knew very well the fate of those who fell foul of the Company. It was not a pleasant sight. Martim Rodriguez was a survivor, and survivors fought under many flags of convenience. It left a bitter taste, but he had eaten much less palatable meals in his time.

"Samuel would like to speak to you and the Priestess. Face to face. Tomorrow at noon on the bridge. Don't be late." With that, she was gone, and the big man was left alone in the dark once more. He lay back onto the bed and allowed his head to sink into the plush pillows. It was an age since he had slept in such comfort. He was tired, and his bones ached. Death did not ease the niggle of old wounds. Let the Scourge and the Forsaken knock each other senseless for the rest of eternity, he was done with them all. He would meet Samuel and hear what he had to offer.

Leaning across the bed, he placed a tanned, calloused hand on the smooth, milky white shoulder of the Priestess.

"Wake up, my love. There is something I must tell you."

CHAPTER 79 - I DESTROYED THE WORLD TODAY

"What happens to us?" LaPointe peered through the hatch in his cell door, more interested in events outside than the breakfast tray on his bed. The guard delivering it stepped back, allowing Samuel and Deacon to fill his limited field of vision. The diminutive Frenchman took half a step back, temporarily startled, before gathering his resolve and repeating the question. "Are we to rot in this hole forever? I can help you, Forsaken one. I was Skelly's right-hand man. He confided everything in me."

Deacon guffawed loudly. "We both know that's not true. I wouldn't trust you to take my dog for a walk, let alone run an army." LaPointe ignored the snub and instead reverted his attention to the quieter of the two men, the more powerful one. He could tell from his aura, it surged from him in waves, as white and pure as Skelly's was black and rancid.

"Your offer is most kind, and I'll certainly consider it. But for now, I have no need of your services. Major Deacon will provide you with three meals a day, fresh water, and clean sheets for the foreseeable future, which is more than you deserve. We will speak again, but for now, I have more pressing matters to attend to. LaPointe's shoulders slumped, his disappointment visible as Samuel turned to leave the cellblock. His eye caught a flicker of movement from the adjacent cell. It seemed LaPointe's comrade in arms was finally willing to talk to them.

"I always knew that Dago was a wrong 'un," The soft Irish brogue failed to conceal its contempt for Rodriguez. "Well, he's burnt his bridges now. The Colonel will see him fry for this."

"He beat you in a fistfight almost three centuries ago. Surely it's time to let bygones be bygones." Samuel skilfully returned the serve to the brooding Irishman, keen to deduce where his loyalties now lay.

"Some wounds never heal, they just fester and stink. He and I will never be friends. My loyalty is to the Colonel."

"The same Colonel who chucked you into New Jerusalem like a lamb to the slaughter. He doesn't care about you, James. You died, Rodriguez died, he doesn't care who dies so long as he feathers his own nest. He got you killed at Waterloo and was quite prepared to do the same yesterday. You're cannon fodder, nothing more."

Miller looked away, a pained expression on his face. Samuel saw it as an opportunity to press home the advantage now that he was under his captive's skin. "And what about your lovely young wife? A little bird told me she is a rising star in the Company's ranks. Skelly's darling. Haven't you stopped and thought where that leaves you? Now that Rodriguez is out in the cold, she could step right into his shoes. How do you feel about that?"

Miller grunted. "Maura would never desert me. She ran from the ridge to be with me at the end. No man can ever come between us. Especially an old man."

"Oh, haven't you heard?" replied Samuel casually. "She's got a new sidekick, now. Handsome young chap by all accounts. The two of them have been quite the item, I'm told. Skelly has brought him into the ranks, building a new, young leadership around him. While old-timers like LaPointe and you are thrown to the wolves."

"Go to hell, Forsaken. I know my woman, she would never betray me. She will come for me like she did in the square." He wheeled away from the hatch and lay down on the bunk, his back to the door. "I'll wait as long as it takes. You can shove any slippery deal you might be planning; I'll not be having any of it."

"Very well." Samuel nodded at Deacon, and the two of them left the cell block, climbing the stairs from the basement of the old police station. Deacon cast a glance at the imposing figure by his side.

"So, we go with Plan B then?"

Samuel nodded. "Yes, Deacon. I only hope Emily has managed to charm her way into his dreams. I can't have them going back to 1815 on their own. They need a guide, someone who was there— who knows what to expect. He's the best of an awful bunch, but beggars can't be choosers. We go with what we have. Time is not on our side."

"It never is, Samuel. It never is."

∞ ∞ ∞

Maura's scowl was not what a jubilant O'Sullivan had expected. He sat in the kitchen area where she had first taken him, again not sure how he had come to be there. His recent experiences had left him exhausted and disoriented, and all he craved was a warm bed and a night's uninterrupted sleep. Maura had left him with a cold beer, and while it temporarily revived him, he could feel his eyes growing heavy and closing with each passing moment. She eventually returned, a concerned expression adorning her flawless features as she slid onto the bench beside him.

"Pour me a glass of that ale, I need a drink."

"Everything okay?" asked Adam, a wary tone to his voice as he obliged, pouring from the iced jug that Maura had initially magicked from nowhere.

"Thank you." She lifted the glass to her lips and drained it in one gulp, before belching and indicating she required a refill.

"What?" Her green eyes blazed as she became aware of Adam's incredulous expression.

"Nothing," he replied, quickly topping up her glass. "It's just I become more impressed with you the more time we spend together."

She forced a thin smile. "You ain't seen nothing yet."

Adam sensed an edge to her voice and took her hand in his. The flinch was minimal, and she hoped he hadn't felt it. The last thing she needed was undoing all her good work with him.

"Are you alright?" his voice verged on kind; the boy really was a pathetic specimen. Skelly owed her big time. Especially as he insisted that she keep the facade up after the news he'd imparted upon their return from Ardgallon. James was missing, with no indication as to his current whereabouts. Skelly was furious, convinced now Rodriguez had double-crossed him. Maura maintained a steely, dignified front while in the Study as to give the slightest indication of weakness would be frowned upon. Once outside, however, it was a different story. She crumpled to the floor, laid low by the thought she would never see her beloved again. James was her everything, the reason she crawled and simpered around Skelly, swallowing her pride and entertaining his skin crawling attention. Without him, she was a hollow, clanging vessel. She tore her thoughts from him back to the present, aware of O'Sullivan squeezing her hand.

"Yes, I'm sorry, it's been a long day, and I'm tired. Do you need me to show you where your quarters are again?"

"No, but I thought we could..."

She leaned forward, coyly pecking him on the cheek. "Soon, my dear. We have a big day ahead of us tomorrow, and I must sleep. When this is all over, we will have forever together."

She slipped off the bench again and left him alone with his frustration. Lifting the jug, he refilled the glass and took a rueful sip of beer.

"A big day? I destroyed the world today. It doesn't get much bigger than that."

He would learn.

CHAPTER 80 - AND SO IT BEGINS

Kirkwood was sick of bridges. Yet, here he was again, standing with Samuel and Deacon as they faced the Priestess and Rodriguez. Both sides were bolstered by dozens of high-powered rifles, twitching fingers only needing the slightest encouragement to open up on the enemy.

Deacon sensed the tension and spoke first, eager to strike a deal and get back on his own side of the river. "Rodriguez, I believe you've had a visitor who has delivered our offer to you. There's no room for manoeuvre or negotiation. You're either with us or you're not. It's a simple yes or no. You know the terms."

Rodriguez scratched his bearded chin and looked at his new partner, whose sullen expression confirmed words had been exchanged between the two of them when he told her of Emily's offer. He had talked her around, but it had taken every drop of his oily charm. She was confident Skelly could not breach her mysterious defences and told him so in the firmest of terms, but Rodriguez knew Skelly. He had seen men melt into puddles of visceral gunge at his feet, nothing more than a pile of teeth and bones.

No, if he wanted to make the break, it would have to be total. Skelly would have to be neutralised, one way or another.

"Speak, Forsaken. What are your terms?"

Samuel took a step forward. He spoke clearly and calmly. "We share a problem—Skelly. The Scourge has broken through, and the planet known as Earth is lost. You know it's significance, Sergeant. Once it has fallen, it is only a matter of time before all other planes follow suit. You know I speak the truth."

The Priestess looked towards Rodriguez, concern clouding her features. "What is he talking about, Prophet? The man speaks in riddles."

"He speaks the truth," replied Rodriguez bluntly. He nodded for Samuel to continue.

We don't know the timescale. It could be five minutes, it could be five years, but the Scourge will take this plane." He directed his attention towards the Priestess. "You may think you can defend your territory, but you will be swept aside like ashes in the breeze. They will purge this land of all life."

"So, what do you want of my Prophet?" She jutted out her chin, determined not to be muscled out of the negotiations on her home patch.

"I need to borrow him. As a guide on a mission."

"A guide? My man is a warrior. Find another to perform such a menial task." She sneered at Samuel and made to turn away, but Rodriguez placed a hand on her wrist. The two of them exchanged a series of urgent whispers before the Priestess returned to his side, her body language screaming discomfort at the unfolding events.

"It's Waterloo, isn't it? You want me to return there?"

Samuel arched an eyebrow. "Impressive Sergeant. Some of Skelly's tactical acumen must have washed off on you after all. The only way we can stop Skelly is to get to him before he became the abomination he is now."

"Before he entered the square," added Kirkwood, forcing himself to be part of the conversation. A natural introvert, a large part of him felt hopelessly out of his depth, content to keep to the background. Samuel, Deacon, and Rodriguez were all huge personalities, how could he possibly compete with them in terms of experience and knowledge? Yet, he was the one the Presence burned brightest within; he was the one bizarrely chosen to carry it in defence of all existence. He needed to step up to the mark even though a significant part of him wanted to be back in Belfast, hiding under the bed covers, wishing all this was just a bad dream.

"He speaks," jeered Rodriguez. "I take it you are the one whose backside I'll be cleaning if I agree to these terms?"

"I seem to remember it was your backside we kicked at Ardgallon," countered Kirkwood, refusing to be cowed by the bullying tactics of his adversary.

"You'll be with all three of them," interrupted Samuel, keen to keep the discussion flowing. "Kirkwood, Meredith, and Harley. They are all required for the Presence to function to its full potential. Giro will plane you in before the battle, he will do everything he can to get you as near to Skelly as he can. Then the rest is up to you. But by whatever means necessary, he cannot be allowed to die in the square. You have to save him, and the 49th Somerset or we are doomed."

He had seized the verbal baton again, desperate to secure the consent of Rodriguez. His bearded, scarred features gave no indication as to what he was thinking, but the Priestess remained suspicious and on edge. One wrong word and their fragile negotiations would be dead in the water.

"I fought with the Colonel for seven years. All the way from Portugal, through Spain and France. Good times, hard times. I know what happened." Rodriguez spoke quietly, his thoughts elsewhere, recalling the trail of blood and devastation the 49th left as it wound its way through the Continent. Hot on the heels of the retreating French.

"Which is why we need you," stressed Samuel, pandering to his opponent's ego. "You know Skelly, and you know what happened between Wellington and him."

"Hah," laughed Rodriguez. "I know for sure. Two spoilt brats who never grew up. Couldn't put their personal differences behind them. Got the lot of us killed."

"You also know the terrain," said Deacon. "These kids wouldn't last five minutes out there. No disrespect, Kirkwood," he added hastily.

"None taken. I don't know one end of a gun from the other."

"We fired muskets," replied Rodriguez pointedly. "Brown Bess muskets. Highly inaccurate but when deployed in volley fire at close range incredibly effective. We were the best-drilled regiment in the British Army—had never been breached by cavalry before

Waterloo." The colour left his cheeks as he recalled those final frantic moments when the square collapsed inwards and years of training dissolved into a panicked rout. "I'll teach you what you need to know, boy. You have a deal."

"Are you sure?" The Priestess tugged at his sleeve, trying to regain her lover's attention from the hell he was reliving.

Rodriguez looked down at his arm and then her, an expression nearing fondness on his rugged features. "We have no choice, my queen. If I do this and succeed, we are free of him. Let me do this, and we can live no longer in fear of this mongrel. *Please*." The final word was a mostly unused one within his vocabulary, and he had to force it from between his lips.

She studied his face with a withering intensity which would have broken the will of many, but he returned it, his expression impassive. Finally, she sighed and nodded.

"So be it. When will this happen, Samuel of the Forsaken?"

"Now," replied Samuel. "There is no more time to lose."

Rodriguez lowered his face to hers and kissed her lightly on the lips before spreading his arms out and greeting Kirkwood and the others with a trademark movie-star grin. "I'm all yours, mes amigos. Lead the way." Two guards raised their rifles and warily eyed him through their sights as Deacon led him to the rear doors of the front landrover. Kirkwood gave the Priestess one last look before climbing into his. He was greeted with an icy stare, confirming that this was the most uneasy of alliances. She turned on her heels and stormed back towards her end of the bridge. All the while covered by several of her men.

Kirkwood closed his eyes and swallowed hard. "And so, it begins."

CHAPTER 81 - AMBUSH AT THE BLACK HOUSE

"Are you sure he's secure in there?" Kirkwood pointed through the cracked, grimy windscreen at the vehicle in front of them, which bounced along the rubble-strewn streets of the city centre, heading back towards the Queen Street base.

"He moves a muscle, and my guys have orders to put a bullet between his eyes. Waterloo or no Waterloo," replied Deacon. Kirkwood was wedged between the gruff Captain and their driver in the front of the vehicle. The latter was hunched over the steering wheel, all his concentration devoted to avoiding the numerous potholes and lumps of debris on the road ahead. They could have been conversing in Mandarin, and he wouldn't have noticed.

"Thank you, Major Deacon. For everything."

"All in a day's work, young man. Besides, I don't like the sound of this Scourge landing on my doorstep any time soon. I've enough on my plate dealing with the Dirties and that crazy bitch across the river." A crackle of radio static in the earpiece of his helmet temporarily distracted him. He scrunched his nose before replying. "Roger that. We'll come in via Route 67. That's six seven. Over." He leaned across Kirkwood, tapping the driver on the shoulder.

"Did you get that, Stockdale? 67, alright?" The driver nodded in response without taking his eyes off the road. Up ahead, the front landrover slowed and turned left onto what was once Royal Avenue, the main shopping thoroughfare in the city. Behind them, the rear vehicle followed suit, all three vehicles closely bunched. Kirkwood sensed an edge to Deacon's voice, and the knuckles of the driver were almost translucent, so tightly was he clinging to the steering wheel.

Deacon stirred from his thoughts. "There's activity up ahead. Dirties have blocked the road. They're not from the Castle, seem to have drifted in from the west, around two dozen of them. We're just going the long way as a precaution. I haven't the time to get involved in a scrap with them."

"Right-oh," replied Kirkwood, trying to sound more relaxed than he actually was. All he wanted was to get back to the compound and spend some time with his friends before he was plunged into the latest chapter of his increasingly bizarre new life. The convoy rattled along Royal Avenue past deserted shop fronts, their windows boarded and adorned with crude, multi-coloured graffiti. Up ahead, the once magnificent City Hall was now a burnt-out husk. Noticing Kirkwood's startled expression, Deacon pointed towards it. "They call it the Black House now," he chuckled.

"At least they don't have to worry about what colour of flag is flying above it anymore." Deacon chortled again, and Kirkwood felt good at making the grumpy old soldier laugh. He looked up at the remains of the City Hall's dome, finding it hard to believe these were once the streets he had strolled along several lifetimes ago. It was as if...

"WHAT THE FU—!"

The landrover in front swerved violently right as a huge slab of masonry bounced off its bonnet before landing in front of the vehicle Kirkwood was in. Thankfully, their eagle-eyed driver saw it as well and ploughed onto the brakes, the jeep coming to a shuddering halt only inches from where the slab lay embedded in the already ruined tarmac. There was a surreal second of silence before two figures dashed from a shop front and pulled open the front vehicle's passenger door, dragging a female soldier out by her helmet strap. She fell to the ground under a flurry of kicks and punches.

"Stay in the truck. Do not move," roared Deacon, opening his door while simultaneously reaching for his revolver. He had taken no more than three steps towards his stricken colleague when a crossbow bolt thudded into his left shoulder. He performed an awkward pirouette before going down on one knee, reaching for the open door of the landrover to steady himself.

"This is Papa One to Base. We are under attack. Repeat. Under attack at the Black House. Troops down. Urgent assistance required. Repeat, urgent..." The opposite door was flung open, and a hand thrust a blade into the side of Stockdale's neck. Thick, dark blood pumped out onto the face of his assailant who cackled madly before dragging the driver onto the ground and out of sight. The bloodied attacker, a mess of dirty, matted hair and rotten teeth, grinned gleefully at Kirkwood until a crack knocked him backwards off his feet, a red dot appearing on his left cheek. Kirkwood spun round in his seat to see Deacon, revolver in outstretched hand, clinging to the landrover door. The bolt protruded from his shoulder at a crooked angle as he used his good arm to haul himself up into the vehicle.

"Budge up. You're driving. Next right."

"What?" yelled Kirkwood in disbelief. He jumped as another bolt glanced off the armoured bonnet of the landrover. Gunfire crackled from behind as soldiers in the rear truck disembarked and fired off rounds in the general direction of the archer above. All around them, figures surrounded their vehicle, which began to rock from side to side.

"Well, you hardly expect me to chauffeur you around the city with this sticking out of me," bellowed Deacon, pointing at the bolt before a spasm of pain doubled him over. "Just go."

Kirkwood studied the gearstick in horror before cranking it into first gear and releasing the handbrake. He toed the accelerator, and the truck jumped forward a few feet before stalling. Their assailants, now numbering around a dozen, temporarily pulled back before renewing their assault. Ominously, the gunfire from behind had stopped.

"Move it. We're being overrun here," urged Deacon. In the distance, a siren could be heard, but it seemed woefully far away. Kirkwood turned the ignition key and breathed silent thanks as the engine spluttered into life again. A young boy, no more than sixteen, was on the bonnet swinging wildly at the windscreen with a lump of wood. More cracks began to appear, dancing a crazy pattern across the glass. Beads of icy sweat began to trickle down Kirkwood's back as he struggled to find first gear, his hand slipping, and his left leg trembling as it pressed down on the clutch.

"I can't get the bloody thing in gear," he yelled, panic threatening to overwhelm him. A second figure clambered onto the bonnet before continuing to the roof. The truck lurched sickeningly to one side, rising onto two wheels before crashing back onto all four.

"You get it in gear now, or we are dead men!" yelled Deacon.

A shot rang out, and the figure on the roof fell forward, colliding with the youth on the bonnet, and sending them both crashing onto the road. Kirkwood peered through the crazy paving of the windscreen to see Rodriguez standing, arms outstretched towards them, revolver in hand. He grinned and then strode towards Kirkwood's side of the vehicle, firing all the time. Grunts and gasps of pain filled the air, and more gunfire sounded on the other side of the landrover. A hand slammed against Deacon's window, and he turned to see Samuel standing there, breathing heavily. He indicated for the old campaigner to open the door, which the latter did with some difficulty. A patch of blood was spreading outwards from where the bolt sat nestled in his shoulder. The five o'clock shadow which dominated his chin was more pronounced against his grey, clammy skin.

"Open the rear doors, Major. I suggest we get out of here fast before more unwelcome guests arrive."

Deacon grunted in agreement, and a few seconds later, the rear doors opened. Samuel climbed into the back with a still grinning Rodriguez. "Drive, Kirkwood," urged Samuel. "It's just us." Kirkwood looked in his wing mirror to see a pile of bodies behind them, a mix of military uniforms and dirty, ragged clothing. He blinked before finding first gear and eased the landrover slowly forward. After a few feet, the truck veered upwards before righting itself again. Kirkwood did not dwell on what he had just driven over.

"Base. This is Papa One. We have neutralised the contact and are coming in. 67. We have casualties. Medics on standby. Out." He pulled out his earpiece and leaned back, struggling for breath. "Right, then second right at the old library. I'll guide you in from there." Kirkwood nodded, risking second gear as they crawled past the City Hall, it's ruined edifice a silent testimony to the wreck of a city he was driving through.

"I'm starting to enjoy my new role already, Major," beamed Rodriguez from the rear. "Although it doesn't say much about your troops that I'm already saving your neck from the locals."

"What happened back there, Deacon?" asked Samuel, ignoring the Portuguese soldier.

"I'm not sure," winced Deacon through gritted teeth. "They were Wild Westies, but it's rare to see them in the city, they usually keep to their own patch. The Kings don't take kindly to incursions, so it's a worrying sign. I'll speak to our intel guys when I get back and see what they can come up with. Right here, Kirkwood."

Kirkwood nodded without taking his eyes off the road as he complied with the instruction. Up ahead to his left, he saw the fortified observation posts of the Queen Street station dominating the skyline. He wiped his brow and risked squeezing the accelerator, wanting nothing more than to be safely behind its thick concrete walls. The front gates inched open as they neared, and a convoy of six trucks raced past in the direction of the Black House.

"Body recovery," explained Deacon darkly. "We leave nobody out there. There's all sorts of talk as to what the Dirties do with our dead. Mutilation...and worse." Kirkwood swallowed hard and carefully turned left into the compound. He gratefully drew alongside the main building. No sooner had he applied the handbrake and turned off the engine, two medics were at the vehicle tending to Deacon, who reluctantly allowed them to inspect his injury before being helped from the truck. Kirkwood dismounted as well and stood in the yard, his legs like jelly. He watched as Rodriguez ambled past towards the main building, warily escorted by two troopers. He looked up at the darkening sky and puffed out both cheeks, the enormity of the last thirty minutes now hitting him like a freight train.

"You did well out there."

Kirkwood sensed Samuel standing beside him, also looking towards the sky. They stood together in silence for a minute, oblivious to the bustle all around them in the yard, content to savour another oasis of calm before the coming storm consumed them once more.

"I don't know how much more of this I can do." Kirkwood finally broke the quiet between them, his voice raw and croaky. "We could all have been killed out there because of me. If I can't even put a rusty landrover into first gear properly, how am I going to survive Waterloo? I'm going to get us all killed."

"You saved lives out there, Kirkwood, my own included. Look at how far you have come, what you have achieved. Stop viewing the glass as half empty when yours is overflowing. Dobson chose you for a reason. You must believe in yourself as he believed in you. You owe him that."

"I know, Samuel, I know." Tears began to well in Kirkwood's eyes and, try as he might, they escaped onto his cheeks. "But it's so hard. I've spent all my life being beaten down. By the OCD telling me, I'm worthless. A weak, pathetic mess who will amount to nothing. Why do you think I hid myself away in a dead-end job with loser mates?"

Samuel placed a muscular arm around the young man's shoulders. "The time for hiding is over, my friend. You have proven yourself to me and the others. We believe in you, now you must believe in yourself. Allow the Presence to become part of you, do not fear it. Embrace who you were created to be, Kirkwood Scott. For that time is now."

Kirkwood shrugged, responding with a sheepish smile. "If you say so, big man. Now, come on, let's go save the world...again."

CHAPTER 82 - THE REGIMENT THAT NEVER WAS

The others were waiting for them in the briefing room. Hurried greetings were exchanged, and Kirkwood studiously avoided eye contact with a perplexed Emily, for fear the tears would flow again. Meredith and Harley babbled incessantly, but it was largely nerves. A sombre cloud hung over the young friends as they prepared for the next stage in this breakneck journey they'd been flung together to embark on. Tess tried and failed to wind up Emily, as Ariana tried to rein in her friend's gentle teasing. Giro eventually restored order and gathered them around the table. Kirkwood sipped a piping hot cup of sugary tea, rustled from the kitchens in order to restore some colour to his cheeks.

"How's Deacon?" he enquired, the old soldier's absence a notable hole in their ranks. They had all grown fond of the grumpy major and were eager to know his condition.

"He won't be leading out a patrol any time soon, but he will live," replied Giro. "Our medics have removed the bolt and cleaned the wound. He's being pumped full of antibiotics and hating every second of it. Once he's stable, he will be heli-vaced out of the sector to one of our main medical centres. I pity his doctors, they're in for a rough ride with the old goat."

"And Rodriguez?"

"He's being briefed by Samuel. Although, it's in his best interest to comply with everything we're asking of him. Beneath the bluster and bravado, he recognises he needs us as much as we need him. It's the last throw of the dice for all of us."

"Dice." Kirkwood smiled, but there was little warmth to it. "I've had enough of dice to do me a lifetime."

"And I've had enough of waking up with stinking hangovers," said Meredith, a rare vulnerability in her voice. "We all have the same demon, Kirkwood. Skelly. It's just he has many strings to his bow. This time we finish it, once and for all."

"Yup," added Harley. "No more OCD, no more bottles of cheap wine, and most definitely no more wheelchairs. Agreed?" They all nodded, a quiet determination evident on their faces.

"Excellent." Giro was proud of the young people gathered around him. "Now, pin your ears back kids, for I'm about to give you a crash course on early nineteenth-century history. That all came to a head one day in June 1815 near a sleepy little Belgian town called Waterloo."

∞ ∞ ∞

"You do realise, if you try to cross me, Skelly will be the least of your worries." Samuel sat back in his chair, fixing Rodriguez with an icy expression. The Portuguese man smiled and took a sip of water, savouring the mental tug of war that was about to commence.

"You need not worry. What's the saying you have? About the buttering of the bread? I know which side I'm on, and I know the consequences if Skelly is not vanquished once and for all."

"So long as we are clear," warned Samuel. "These three young people are our last hope. Their destiny is in your hands."

"You need to learn to relax a little more." Rodriguez chuckled, stroking his thick beard. "Dobson knew how to enjoy himself. You two are cut from a very different cloth. I would have thought two knights of the realm would have had more in common."

Samuel glared across the table at his smiling inquisitor. "I do not like to talk about my past life. Yes, we took oaths to the same Crown, but Cornelius and I lived in very different times. He had his style, and I have mine. I will say no more on the matter."

"Very well," smirked Rodriguez. "I'll probe no more. Now, tell me what your plan is, and I'll tell you if it's feasible."

Samuel relaxed slightly, glad the subject was being changed. His life and death were deeply personal matters to him and not for discussion with the likes of Rodriguez. The only person who knew his full story was Dobson, and he was no more now. Given that, his past was now a closed book and would stay that way. His ghosts would remain that—ghosts never to see the light of this new existence.

"It would be suicide to plane them into the battle itself."

"I won't disagree with you on that one."

"They need time. Time to get to Skelly and to somehow influence events so that the 49th is not sent like lambs to the slaughter down that ridge."

Rodriguez nodded thoughtfully. "We need a day at least. For that's when it all started. The day before the battle. Wellington and Skelly always had, shall we say, a healthy rivalry. They schooled together, rose through the ranks together, yet old Hooky always seemed to have the edge. He was always one step ahead of dear Augustus. Be that war, wine...or women." He paused before the final word for dramatic effect, and only an idiot would not have picked up on the significance of it. Samuel was no idiot.

"Women. You mean this unholy mess we're in at the minute is all over some childish argument over a woman?" It took a lot to annoy Samuel, but he could feel heat rising in his cheeks. This was ridiculous.

"Perhaps," shrugged Rodriguez. "But in this case, quite a woman, I'm told."

Samuel bit his lip, containing the growing anger within him. "Go on."

"Sienna Melrose, daughter of the Duke of Abervale. The darling of the Brussels social scene. Half their age and then some, but that didn't stop Skelly. He was besotted with her. He was an old friend of the Duke, and the rumour was, that a gentleman's agreement had been made. The lovely Sienna would be betrothed to Skelly after Napoleon was put to the sword. The Duchess had other plans, though."

Samuel took a deep breath. This was descending into a sordid soap opera, and he was already dreading his decision to send Kirkwood and the others back in time into such a cesspit. "What do you mean, other plans?"

"She was insanely ambitious, desperate to clamber up the social ladder, no matter the cost. Even if it meant bartering off her only daughter to the highest bidder. Unbeknownst to her husband, she was plotting behind the scenes against Skelly so that Sienna would be wed to Wellington—war hero and future Prime Minister."

"So, Skelly and his regiment were sent to their deaths for the sake of a young woman?"

"Young Sienna played no part in it. She despised both of them. She found Skelly obscene, a dirty old man who would drool and fawn over her at every possible opportunity. He made her skin crawl. As for Wellington, well, he was cold and aloof to her, she was nothing more than a trinket to him, a trophy wife. All part of the game."

"Enough of a game to send Skelly and the 49th to their deaths?"

"Wellington had it all. Yet he couldn't stand to see Skelly get one up on him at anything. Be it billiards, cards, or the hand of a beautiful young heiress. When it came down to filling the breach in the Allied line during the final French advance, he knew it was a suicide mission, a forlorn hope. He could have sacrificed one of the foreign regiments, but instead, he sent the 49th. They saved the day and secured his legend forever. Plus, he got rid of Skelly, therefore killing two birds with one stone."

"And his influence afterwards ensured the 49th were effectively written out of the official records of the battle."

"Exactly. Everyone knows the victors write the history books. Until now. Skelly has returned to rewrite them one final time."

Samuel rubbed his eyes. He was exhausted and required sleep. Yet this new information needed to be appropriately handled, and his plans amended accordingly. He leaned forward on his elbows and stared across the table at a smug Rodriguez.

"Alright, Sergeant. That's the background. Now, all we have to do is figure out how we get this done and be rid of Skelly once and for all."

Rodriguez leaned forward himself so that only a few feet separated the two big men. "I thought you'd never ask, Samuel. I just happen to have a plan."

CHAPTER 83 - HELL HATH NO FURY

The guard's finger snapped with frightening ease, like a dry twig before being tossed into a red-hot fire of agony. The gag over his mouth stifled the scream, but Maura savoured the twitching body in her grasp before it slumped once more into a sobbing heap.

"Three."

"Is this going to take much longer?" O'Sullivan was bored. Why they were back in this futuristic dump was beyond him, but Maura insisted Skelly wanted them to retrieve the two members of the Company who had messed up their mission to locate Rodriguez. She had been quite vague on the details, and he'd went along like a lovestruck puppy, but his mind was on other things—Arianna. Tess. Vengeance.

"It will take as long as it takes, my dear," replied Maura, struggling to conceal her revulsion of this vain, vacuous fool. Not much longer, though, and she would be reunited with her beloved James. Returning her attention to the simpering guard, she spoke, her words full of malicious intent.

"Unless you tell me where they are, I'm going to break every one of them. Then I'm going to start on your toes. The choice is yours."

She cocked her head inquisitively at the guard, who nodded in painful resignation as she loosened the gag, allowing him to speak.

"They were taken. By Security Solutions, Deacon, and his soldiers. They're probably across the river now, in their compound." Maura smiled sweetly at the man on his knees before wrenching his neck savagely to one side. She released her grip, and the lifeless body crumpled to the ground like a sack of potatoes.

"There, that wasn't so hard now, was it?" She stared at the dead guard, before reverting her attention to O'Sullivan. "Come along, Adam, time to fly."

"I don't see what the big deal is," he huffed. "Since when did Skelly become so interested in the welfare of his foot soldiers? It's only two, I thought the Company was hundreds strong? Let them rot over there, I say, we've more than enough to be getting on with."

It took every ounce of self-control she possessed not to snap his miserable neck and send him the same way as the guard. She bit her lip until the metallic taste of blood mixed with the bile rising from her roiling stomach.

"We leave no one behind, my dear. Even the lowliest members are looked after. The Colonel views it as a matter of regimental pride. Now, let's go before our friend here is discovered."

She rose into the air and circled O'Sullivan, who followed suit less steadily, still coming to terms with his newfound powers. Soon, however, they were sweeping low over the river, before rising and banking left. Adam raised a hand to shield his eyes as the sun peeked from behind a bank of clouds, causing his eyes to water. Maura slowed and pointed down towards the Queen Street compound far below, where ant-like figures scurried back and forth, unaware of the threat above.

"That's where they are," she pointed. "You ready to go have some fun?"

Adam's lip curled into a chilling smile. They angled downwards, gathering speed, the wind buffeting their skin as the ground rose to meet them.

∞ ∞ ∞

"LaPointe. Wake up, you useless buffoon." Miller pounded the concrete wall separating their respective cells. "Can you feel that?"

"What?" A groggy French accent responded. "Isn't it bad enough we are holed up here, can't I even sleep without your persistent whining? You'd wake the dead."

"We are the dead, you cretin. Listen."

There was silence for several seconds before LaPointe spoke again. "Mon dieu. They come."

Miller leaned against the wall, a rare smile creeping across his normally dour features. He knew she wouldn't forget about him.

"Hell hath no fury..." he whispered, cracking his knuckles as he waited for the show to start.

∞ ∞ ∞

The dual blades whipped in unison as the ancient helicopter wobbled from the helipad on top of the old police station's main building and rose jerkily into the air. Having refused to be stretchered off his base, Deacon sat staring darkly at the disappearing compound while a medic fussed over his shoulder, one arm strapped tightly to his chest.

"Would you leave me alone, man? I'm not an invalid. It's a flesh wound, you would think I was on my last legs."

"Sorry, sir," replied the medic, beating a hasty retreat to the other side of the cabin. Up front, the pilot and co-pilot were oblivious to their irritable cargo, focused on clearing the city rooftops before swinging west over the green countryside towards the medical facility. Deacon looked down at the city as the helicopter continued to rise, guilty he was deserting his post at this crucial juncture. He would rather be out there with one good arm than being poked and prodded by a bunch of clueless quacks. Three weeks off the front line, they had told him. Screw that, he'd be back in three days.

The sun filtered through his window, and he blinked as a flurry of multi-coloured bubbles temporarily swam across his vision. He blinked again but not before two flashes sped past the helicopter, perilously close to striking it. The pilot veered, and the helicopter dipped momentarily before she regained control and began to climb again. Deacon turned to follow the streaks, ignoring the shooting pain which accompanied the manoeuvre. He felt the stitches in his shoulder straining where the sadistic medic had removed the bolt and sewn him up. He gritted his teeth, watching in disbelief as he realised the flashes were not comets or missiles, but two figures now slowing, setting foot inside the confines of the compound. Before he could raise the alarm, a row of landrovers lined along the perimeter wall exploded. Bodies staggered across the yard, ablaze, before collapsing at the feet of the two forms.

"Queen Street is under attack. Turn back, we need to go back," roared Deacon at the pilot in front of him.

"Calm down, sir," reasoned the medic. "You're going to open up those sutures."

"I don't give a damn. Get me back down there now. That's an order." He started to unbuckle his belt, and the medic wrestled to subdue him.

"I'm sorry, sir," replied the pilot via her headset. "I have strict orders to deliver you to the medical facility. From the very top." She returned her attention to the panel of lights and instruments in front of them.

Deacon watched helplessly as further explosions from below rocked the air around them. He squeezed his eyes shut, never having cried in all his career, even the darkest moments of the Greenland campaigns. But try as he might they came, coursing a track down his scarred, pitted face.

"Those poor kids," he groaned. "God, help them all."

∞ ∞ ∞

And all the while, Skelly laughed. A callous, manic laugh that filled the Study. Flames shot from the fireplace in concert with each explosion from a Belfast, that was days from succumbing to the same evil presently stripping plane after plane of all life. In the meantime, Maura and her new plaything would exact his revenge on Kirkwood Scott and his motley collection of allies, including the traitor, Rodriguez. He felt no pity, no remorse, just the need to kill and kill and kill again. It was his calling—it was his destiny.

"Farewell, dear boy. It was fun while it lasted."

CHAPTER 84 - BACK TO THE BATTLE

The first explosion rocked the briefing room, throwing its occupants about like sweet wrappers on a windy day. Giro was the first to react, bounding out into the corridor where he returned after a rushed conversation with a gaggle of soldiers making their way to the stairs which led down to the main yard. He returned, face full of concern.

"We're under attack. They're not sure if it's a missile or something else. It's chaos out there, and we've taken casualties."

"Did Deacon get away?" asked Kirkwood, his first thought about the injured veteran who was due to fly out of the base.

"Barely, but they're up and away. He will be pulling his hair out up there."

"It's Skelly," said Samuel calmly.

"What?" Meredith's face drained of colour at the mention of his name.

"You have to go. Now. Giro, how long do you need?"

The little man scratched the fringe of his pudding bowl haircut, his face a mask of concentration as he internally computed the permutations. The sound of sporadic gunfire from below did nothing to aid his thinking.

"I could wing it now, but I'd be taking a chance with the coordinates. I could get them to Waterloo, but it could be 1715 as likely as 1815. Can you buy me five minutes?"

They were interrupted by a breathless Corporal poking his head into the room. "You're not going to believe this, sir," he panted at Giro. "It's a woman and man, as if they fell from the sky. They're tearing the yard apart with some type of incendiary devices. We're taking heavy casualties." He disappeared as quickly as he'd appeared, as another explosion brought dust raining upon them from above.

"Maura Miller, come to rescue her beloved husband."

"That red-haired cow who kidnapped me? The guy in the cell is her husband?" Harley rose from her chair and made towards the corridor before Emily grabbed her wrist and hauled her back to the table.

"Leave them to it, my little firecracker. You need to plane. Come on, ladies. Let's show that bitch the true meaning of girl power."

"Finally, we agree on something," said Tess, rolling her eyes. "Come on, Ariana, time to play. Good luck you guys, I know you've got this."

Ariana reluctantly joined her friend in rising from the table. "I won't let you down, I promise," she said, looking earnestly at each of them in turn.

"We know. Now show them what you're capable of, Bomb Girl." Harley high fived her newfound friend.

"God, I hate that name, but you're forgiven this time," laughed Ariana. She joined Emily and Tess at the door. Emily stopped and shot one last look at a stricken Kirkwood before they disappeared down the corridor.

"They will be fine," said Samuel, sensing the worry in the room. "Once you have planed, I will take care of them. I've taken on bigger than the Millers in my time and dispatched them to their graves." The normally quiet man bristled with aggression at the very mention of their names. There was steely intent behind his words, and it did much to allay the concerns of his young friends.

"Let's get this show on the road then," said Giro, breezily rubbing his hands together. The four of you. Form a circle and hold hands."

"I'd much rather be dispatching Miller to the hereafter, but if I must," grunted Rodriguez. "For your information, Samuel, he's got a decent uppercut." He rubbed his beard, painful memories evoked.

"Hang on." Meredith looked at Samuel in disbelief. "You're just casually lobbing us into the battle of Waterloo. Don't we kind of stick out like a sore thumb?" She indicated her modern clothing. "Plus, I'm an eighteen-year-old, skinny-assed girl. I'm no military historian, but I'm pretty sure there weren't many of them kicking about the battlefield."

"You'd be surprised," replied Rodriguez mysteriously to nobody in particular.

"Yeah, and if anyone hasn't noticed," added Harley. "My hair is six different colours. Do you not think that might raise a few eyebrows?"

"A nice hat?" offered Kirkwood.

"We were planning to brief you on such matters," explained Samuel. "But there's no time now. Rodriguez will explain all on the other side. Needless to say, I have attempted to provide for every eventuality, but I agree, it's not ideal. Now hurry, please." As if to accentuate his plea, shots were accompanied by panicked shouts in the corridor outside.

Kirkwood, Meredith, and Harley exchanged worried looks before joining hands. Rodriguez completed the circle, although Meredith grimaced when he gripped her palm. "This is the one and only time I let you touch me, dirtbag," she muttered. The Portuguese hulk merely chuckled in response. Behind them, Giro set his palms on the shoulders of Kirkwood and Harley, closing his eyes and incanting quietly to himself. Samuel took a step back and watched as the four figures vanished from the room, leaving an exhausted Giro panting for breath.

"Did you get them close."

"Close enough."

"It will have to do. Now, come on. We've a base to save."

CHAPTER 85 - BROKENHEARTED

Miller craned his neck, but the hatch offered only a limited view of the outside environment. After the initial explosion, the two soldiers guarding them had quickly conferred before one bounded up the steps from the basement cell block. That was five minutes ago, and the intervening period had been punctuated by explosions and gunfire, which diminished as the seconds passed. The remaining guard stood nervously by their cells, clutching his revolver like a security blanket.

"I think it's night-night time for you, mon ami," goaded LaPointe from the adjacent cell. "Why don't you be a good chap and liberate us? If you do, our friends might let you live."

"Shut it," screamed the guard, his face basked in sweat. He looked no more than twenty and was clearly terrified. Miller almost felt sorry for him, he had seen many such young men with equally haunted expressions in the ranks.

"If you're thinking about running, then I suggest this is the time to do it," he added darkly.

The young man looked from one cell door to the other, torn by the duty to stand his ground and fight versus a growing urge to desert his post and survive this developing nightmare. In the end, the latter option prevailed. He bolted from the room, to be hurled back into it seconds later. He landed on the floor, his neck at a sickening angle, eyes wide and vacant. Eyes that did not see Maura and Adam sweep into the room, a path of devastation in their wake. Maura bent down and removed a set of keys from the dead guard's belt, much to the delight of a cackling LaPointe who watched the proceedings gleefully.

"Bonjour, Madame Miller. Comment allez vous? We were beginning to think the Colonel had forgotten about us."

"Save the small talk for later, Pierre. We aren't out of the woods yet." She selected a key and unlocked the door to his cell, the Frenchman strutting from captivity like a preening peacock.

"And who is our other guardian angel? Such a dashing fellow?" enquired LaPointe, a twinkle in his eye.

"That's Adam. Adam O'Sullivan. He helped me open the portal at Ardgallon," replied Maura absent-mindedly, her attention now focused on the occupant of the remaining cell.

"Helped?" Adam could not conceal the hurt and disappointment in his voice.

LaPointe bowed theatrically to his rescuer. "Pierre LaPointe at your service, young sir. If there is anything at all I can do to thank you for your valour, then you need only ask." He winked at Adam as he returned to an upright position, causing the latter's skin to creep like a herd of elephants had stampeded over his grave.

A jangling of metal and Maura flung open the other cell door before flinging herself into the arms of the bear of a man who emerged from it. Adam's face dropped like a lead balloon as their embrace developed into a kiss, which left little to the imagination as to the nature of their relationship.

"What's going on?" was the best he could manage as anger and shock battled for supremacy of his body. Maura whirled to face him, her arm around the waist of the man, a sly smile hinting he wasn't going to like her answer.

"Adam, this is my husband, James. While I enjoyed our time together, I'm afraid we are going to have to call an end to our dalliance." She considered her words before barking harshly. "On second thought, I think you deserve the truth. I hated every second of it and couldn't wait to be rid of you. You served your purpose to us by opening the portal, but it's time to part ways now."

"Are you kidding me? After everything you promised me." He struggled to control the rising acidic tide threatening to flood his mouth. The room suddenly was uncomfortably warm, and his skin started to break out in a prickling rash.

"Oh, dear," purred LaPointe. "Spurned love, how tragic. Well, I'm happy to step into the breach and show you the ropes," he added. "I think we would make a wonderful team. What say you, mon cherie?"

"You take a step nearer me, and I'll stick your head through that wall," spat an appalled Adam. "But Maura," he bleated, a pathetic shadow of his former cocky self as he fumbled for the words to describe the pain now coursing through him.

"Needs must, I'm afraid." Maura mimicked her most sympathetic expression while gazing up into the eyes of her betrothed. "The

Colonel is happy to retain you in a freelance role, should you wish, as he envisions your unique skills may come in handy. He's taken quite a shine to you."

"It's a generous offer," conceded LaPointe.

"Freelance? But you said we were going to run the Company for Skelly. You and me. Together."

"I'm tired of this." Miller unhooked himself from Maura's clutches and took a menacing step towards Adam. "You seem to be having some problems with all this, so let me simplify it for you. You turn around, walk out that door and never bother my wife again. Or I rip that thick head from your shoulders and kick it up and down the street outside."

"And he would," winced LaPointe. "He literally would. I suggest you accept his generous offer. It would be such a shame to see that pretty head of yours being defiled in such a manner."

Adam looked at the three of them in turn, weighing up whether he could take them on. In the end, wisdom prevailed, and he backed towards the door, slowly shaking his head. "This isn't over, you whore."

"Sticks and stones," replied Maura, picking at a fingernail. "Now, run along little boy, before you get yourself hurt."

Adam turned and took the steps two at a time, not wanting to give them the satisfaction of witnessing the tears well in his eyes. He had been played, well and truly conned, and how it hurt being on the receiving end for once. He reached the top of the steps and ran towards the exit, the corridor deserted, bar for a handful of bodies in military uniform. Men and women he had killed, and for what? A stupid schoolboy crush which had left him a laughing stock? Well, they would all pay.

As he skulked through the front door of the dilapidated police station and down the steps that led to the main gates, he casually flicked a wrist, throwing them open. A female soldier, hunched behind a pile of wooden pallets, raised her rifle to take a pot shot, but the bullet dropped to the ground several feet from its intended target. She stared at her weapon, and then O'Sullivan, in astonishment before thinking better of it and taking more substantial cover behind the pallets. A later roll call would reveal she'd lost twenty-one of her colleagues, with dozens more injured. It was the single largest loss the Queen Street base would ever suffer. She had no desire to be number twenty-two.

Adam contemplated reducing her to an oily puddle but decided against it. Somebody else could do Skelly's dirty work from now on. He strode through the main gates, not knowing where he was going or what he was going to do. He was certain of one thing, though, he would be back, and Maura Miller and her knucklehead husband would regret the day they ever crossed his path. Of that, he was sure.

"Should we go after him?" asked Tess, peering from behind one of the few vehicles in the yard that was still intact.

"No," replied Emily. "There are others still here. We must clear the base of them. Deacon would expect no less of us. Adam O'Sullivan can wait, for now, agreed?"

Ariana nodded tersely. "If we must. But he and I are far from finished. Enjoy it while it lasts, Adam."

CHAPTER 86 - THE ROAD TO BRUSSELS

Meredith flapped and flailed, desperate for something to cling onto, her lungs screaming for oxygen. The first insane, irrational thought to cross her addled brain was that she'd got it horribly wrong, and Waterloo was a naval battle. The conviction she was drowning vanished as she opened both eyes and surveyed her surroundings. Coughing up a mouthful of straw, she took in the haystack she was perilously perched atop, one of dozens stretching as far as she could see across a sleepy rural landscape. Low, graphite skies carried the threat of imminent rain, and a series of dull thuds in the distance signalled thunder rumbling her way.

"Meredith. Down here," hissed a familiar voice, fraught with nerves. She rolled over to see Kirkwood standing beneath her, none the worse for wear. To his right, Rodriguez was studiously picking ears of wheat from his designer overcoat.

"Here, give me your hand," Kirkwood whispered. She accepted his offer and slid down the side of the stack onto the ground. The surrounding terrain was flat and featureless. "Where's Harley?" she mouthed before quickly adding, "and why are we whispering?"

"Oh, my God," bellowed a voice from the other side of the stack. Harley waddled into view like a pregnant duck, her trainers caked with the remnants of the world's largest cowpat. "Euuuuughhh, this is beyond gross, guys. I need a shower. Immediately."

"I'm afraid you will have to get used to a bit of dirt for the foreseeable future," laughed Rodriguez, immensely amused at her predicament. "We're in the middle of a war zone. Staying alive takes precedence over cleanliness.

"War?" sniffed Harley. "Where are all the tanks and guns then?" She folded her arms and arched an eyebrow at Rodriguez, confident she had seized the upper hand in the conversation.

"Er, the modern tank won't be invented for another century yet, Harls." Kirkwood looked to Rodriguez for further direction.

"Your war is approximately twelve miles that way," he replied, pointing in the general direction of a wooded area at the edge of the field.

"I take it that's not thunder then?" asked Meredith, already fairly certain as to what the answer would be.

"That, Miss Starc, is the sound of the Allied and French artillery testing each other out. For your information, it's the morning of 16 June 1815, and we are less than an hour away from the start of the Quatre Bras engagement."

"Quatre Bras?" tutted Meredith. "We're meant to be at Waterloo. I knew Giro looked a bit ropey when he was planeing us in. He's only gone and sent us to the wrong bloody battle."

"All battles are bloody," growled Rodriguez, distinctly unimpressed with his companion's grasp of Napoleonic military history.

"Sorry to be the class geek again," interrupted Kirkwood. "But Quatre Bras was fought two days before Waterloo, wasn't it? Largely between the French and the Prussians?"

"Yes," replied Rodriguez. "A brutal affair. Old Gunther's regiment got a kicking at it. Hell, anyone there got a kicking."

"Do we have to go there?" asked Harley cautiously. Her anxiety levels were already sky-high without having to contend with a second battle.

"Thankfully, no. For we are going that way." He pointed across the field in the opposite direction from the trees.

"Which is where exactly, oh wise one?" asked Meredith sarcastically.

"Brussels. We have business to attend to in the city this evening before the battle. It's best you don't know too much at the minute. All will be revealed when we get there."

"I don't like you holding all the cards, Rodriguez," said Kirkwood warily. "If we weren't in such desperate straits, I'd be washing my hands of this whole plan, Samuel or no Samuel."

"Snap," said Meredith.

"Hell yeah," added Harley, sticking her chin out defiantly.

Rodriguez placed both hands over his chest in faux concern. "You insult me, my young friends," he pouted before it was replaced by a snarl. "Believe me, I would much rather be under the sheets with my Priestess and a bottle of good red than babysitting you brats through the horrors that await us. But, we both find ourselves in the one boat, without a paddle, and having sprung a leak. Now, you play this my way, or we hand everything we hold dear to Skelly. Do you understand me?" He was met with wary nods and silent assent.

"Good, now follow me. We have several fields to cross before we hit the main road. From there, we can follow it to the city along with every refugee within fifty miles of here." He set off at a brisk pace, his coat flapping in a brisk breeze that had picked up. Kirkwood shrugged at Meredith, who rolled her eyes before they both set off in the big man's wake. Harley brought up the rear, one last question bubbling within her.

"Don't you think people might notice we're a bit...well...different. Hair? Clothes? Et cetera, et cetera, et cetera?"

"Ha," rasped Rodriguez. "Allow me to introduce you to the ancient art of glamour, mes amigos."

∞ ∞ ∞

"Wow," gasped Harley. "I'm a bloke."

The four of them stood in a row, staring at their reflections in the muddy brook, which separated the two fields. Across the far field, rows of wagons could be made out backed up as far as the eye could see. Harsh cries and the panicked whinnying of horses added to the chaotic scene. The sound of cannon fire in the distance providing a permanent reminder to those on the road that they couldn't get to the comparative safety of the city quickly enough.

Staring back at them from the murky waters were four dishevelled British infantrymen in red tunics, muddied white breeches, and faded black boots. Atop their heads were impressive caps, which added several inches to their height. Rodriguez was as he would have been in 1815, all toothy grin, bushy beard, and three stripes proudly emblazoned on his arm. The others were unrecognisable to themselves, however.

Meredith peered at their wavy reflections before looking at Kirkwood and Harley. When I look at you two, I see you. Harley with her funky hair and Kirkwood with his...hair?"

"Thanks," muttered Kirkwood. "It's a good job I'm not self-conscious about my appearance."

"But when I look in the water," continued Meredith, ignoring him. "I see two grimy old guys with bad teeth and skin, dressed in toy soldier uniforms."

"Likewise," giggled Harley, nerves getting the better of her. "Meredith looks like a smelly old tramp." She continued to chortle until daggers directed at her by the older girl cut short the merriment.

"Exactly," said Rodriguez. "You look like average British infantrymen. Bedraggled, malnourished, and stinking to high heaven. You'll fit right in. Nobody will bat an eyelid when they see us on the main road. We're just four soldiers on our way to Brussels. Delivering a message to our Commanding Officer, one Colonel Augustus Skelly of the 49th Somerset Regiment. The beauty of the glamour. One of Giro's more impressive party tricks, even if I do say so myself."

"Thank God I don't actually have to wear that uniform," said Meredith, scrunching her nose in disgust at the reflected image. "It looks rank."

"The British infantryman was not known for his personal hygiene. But, by God, they could fight." He stared fondly into the waters, a glint of pride in his eyes.

"Are we actually delivering a message to him? Won't he see through the glamour?" Harley was still struggling to work out the mechanics of their current plight.

"The Augustus Skelly of 16 June 1815 is merely that. A career soldier who has yet to die, who has yet to form the Company, and pledge his allegiance to the Scourge. He is still a man, not a very nice man, but a man nonetheless. The demon lurking within him has yet to show its true colours. It took Wellington to ensure that." He took a few steps back before clearing the brook in a running leap. "Come on, time is passing us by."

The others followed suit despite Harley's efforts to topple into the stream in an unseemly heap. Soon, they were working their way through a muddy morass towards a hedgerow full of gaps that bordered the rapidly deteriorating road. It was starting to rain. Potholes filling and making the conditions even more treacherous for man and beast alike. Stopping by the bank, he turned to address his young companions, who formed a semi-circle around him.

"Tonight, the Duke and Duchess of Abervale will host a special supper for all the brave, foolhardy officers willing to sacrifice their lives in order to save Europe from La Enfant Terrible. It will be a who's who of Brussels high society, all auctioning off their desirable daughters to the highest bidder. And the belle of the ball will be..."

"Sienna Melrose," the three friends echoed in unison.

"Correct. The feud between Skelly and Wellington has been simmering for years, but the blue touch paper will be well and truly lit tonight when Sienna must choose which of the two gallant gentlemen accompanies her for the first dance of the evening. The whole ballroom will get to see who triumphs over the other. It would be an unparalleled slight, were she to rebuke the advances of the Duke. He was a notorious womaniser and used to getting his own way."

"Sexist pig," muttered Meredith. "Some things never change no matter what century you're in."

"So, we have to make sure she chooses Wellington," said Kirkwood, putting the pieces together. "If she dances with Skelly, it effectively signs his death warrant on the ridge."

"For mortals, you three are quick learners," scoffed Rodriguez. "Now come on. We need to get to Skelly before the ball begins and persuade him that he's required back with the 49th." He turned and clambered up the bank, through a gap in the hedgerow, and onto the packed road.

"This is nuts," sighed Harley before following suit. "Come on, you two."

"Why did I ever agree to go for that Burger King with you?" sighed Meredith.

"Because you're a greedy cow," laughed Kirkwood. He tentatively began to edge up the bank, reaching a hand out to

Meredith. She grabbed it, and they squeezed through the gap, lost in the arterial surge of horse and human towards the Belgian capital.

CHAPTER 87 - A COMMON FOE

"Something isn't right, why are we still here?" Miller tugged at Maura's wrist, impatient for an explanation, LaPointe completing their circle in the compound yard. The flame-haired woman opened her eyes and scanned the carnage around them—twisted bodies and burning metallic wrecks. They should have been back at the Tower but hadn't budged an inch. Her emerald eyes flared with indignation as she witnessed the reason for the delay striding across the yard towards them.

"Forsaken."

"You didn't think I'd let you slip away so easily, Mrs. Miller?" said Samuel, stopping a dozen yards away and folding his arms. "You've made quite the mess here. The least you can do is help me clean up."

"Turn around now, Forsaken, and I'll let you live. It is over. The Scourge is rampaging through the planes as we speak, and you are powerless to stop them. Do you think acting the hero now will make a pittance of difference?"

"I'm no hero," replied Samuel, unfazed by the threat. "Now, are we going to cease the chest-thumping and get down to business?"

"Three against one? I like those odds I must say," sneered LaPointe. "Breaking the mighty Samuel will go down very well with the Colonel." He glanced towards Maura and Miller for validation, but their eyes were firmly locked on their opponent.

"Why don't you pick on someone your own size, little man," shouted Giro, emerging from behind Samuel. Ariana and Emily stepped out from behind the landrover, pulling a reluctant Tess by the wrist.

"What's this, a party now?" LaPointe's tone was less cocky than before as the odds were no longer in his favour. The three young women joined Giro, slightly behind Samuel, who simply nodded his appreciation at their presence.

LaPointe was the first to crack, shooting upwards into the sky, followed a heartbeat later by Giro. Ariana and Emily reacted by stepping forward to either side of Samuel, as Miller flung out a hand, the air shimmering between them. They looked away as a wall of heat passed over their faces before the jeep behind them flipped onto its roof and burst into flames. Samuel remained impassive before them, both arms outstretched, palms pointed outwards.

"You can't keep that up all day, Forsaken." Miller closed the gap between Samuel and himself, but it was as if he was walking into a gale, his stride lessening with each step. His face reddened with the strain, rivulets of sweat running down his face, the veins on his neck throbbing with exertion. Less than six feet from Samuel, he dropped to one knee, no longer able to sustain his approach. Maura circled, edging around Samuel as she worked herself ever nearer an anxious Tess.

"I think it's time you did your Bomb Girl thing."

"Would you stop calling me that Tess, you know I don't work well under pressure." Ariana's eyes never left Maura, who stalked her prey like a ravenous big cat.

"Not so brave now you haven't got your little Chinese friend, are you girls?" she taunted.

"He's Northern Irish, actually. Don't push your luck carrot top," snapped Emily

"You think you can provoke me with your childish taunts, witch."

"Seems to be working."

"Shut up," screamed Maura.

"Or what, Fanta Pants?"

Maura screamed and rushed at Ariana, both hands flung outwards, all her energies channelled towards the forcefield Samuel had created to protect them. It was an uncoordinated and reckless attack. Ariana watched, fascinated that she could make out the contours of the energy as it flowed from her adversary—every nuance, every contour...and every gap.

Closing her eyes, Ariana rushed forward, slicing through the dead woman's defences, the palm of her hand striking Maura's shoulder with all the power she could summon. She winced as the shock of the contact raced up her arm, her nerve endings tingling from the impact. The next thing she knew, she was sprawled on the ground, Tess by her side.

"You flipping did it, girl. The ginger psychopath is no more." Tess beamed with delight.

"No more?"

"Well, to be precise, she's in Cretaceous-era North America, about 65 million years B.C. Impressive, Ariana."

"Hopefully, she'll make a tasty snack for some Tyrannosaurus Rex." She pulled herself into a seated position, aided by Emily, to watch as Samuel hauled a barely conscious Miller to his feet. A handful of surviving soldiers began to emerge from the nooks and crannies they'd taken refuge in when they realised their weapons were no match for the intruders.

"Take this one back to the cells," ordered Samuel, pushing Miller towards two bewildered guards. "He shouldn't give you too many problems anymore." Miller staggered forward and had to be held between the guards as they led him back to the main building.

"Your powers are growing," he congratulated Ariana and Tess. "You barely needed me here." The big man was the colour of milk and looked almost as unsteady on his feet as Miller did.

"You need to sit down, Samuel, you look awful," advised Emily.

"I will rest in due course. Until then, my main concern is what happened to..."

A shrill shriek from above cut him off, and they all looked skyward as a tiny speck spiralled downwards, gradually coming into view, seconds before crash landing at the far end of the yard. Ariana and Tess watched in stunned silence as Giro rose to his feet, dusted himself down, and adjusted his glasses before rewarding them with a cheery wave.

"Sorry about that. I'm alright taking off but need to work on my landing technique."

"You're telling me," gasped Tess. "Nil points for style and grace. Are you okay? That was a hell of a tumble."

"I'm perfectly fine," he replied, giving them a thumbs-up sign. "Except for my bruised pride. That horrible man escaped me in the low cloud. I nearly had him as well."

"He's no doubt already back in the Study, spilling his guts to Skelly. I'll interrogate James Miller later, but I doubt we will get much out of him. At least we won't be seeing his awful wife anytime soon."

"But what about Adam?" asked Ariana, her voice fearful again. "We can't rest on our laurels as long as he's still out there."

"He will have to wait for now." Samuel pulled a deep breath and took in the devastation around him, before turning to Giro and stiffly saluting him. "Giro. As Acting Base Commander, can I offer my sincere condolences at the loss of your colleagues? I know many brave men and women fought and died here today against our common foe. I offer whatever service myself and my colleagues can provide in honouring your dead."

"Thank you, Samuel," replied an unusually subdued Giro. Turning to Ariana, Emily, and Tess, he bowed slightly. "Your assistance is greatly appreciated. Our casualties need to be evacuated, and replacement troops brought in. Although the Scourge may be with us soon, I also have a duty to keep this powder keg of a city under control. But first, if you will excuse me, I have an unfortunate message to pass on to Major Deacon." He turned and walked with heavy steps towards the doors of the old station. About him, the grisly clean-up operation was already underway.

"Sorry, Samuel. That was insensitive of me," mumbled Ariana as she bowed.

"Don't be sorry," he replied kindly. "We have all been under a great amount of stress. If I feel it, I dread to imagine what you are going through."

"Yeah, don't beat yourself up," added Tess. "I'm the Queen of foot-in-mouth, and if I wallowed in self-pity every time I pulled a howler, then I'd never get anything done. Cheer up, sad sack." She placed an arm around her friend's shoulders and ruffled her hair. "My friend and I are at your disposal, Samuel of the Forsaken."

"No need to be so formal, Miss Cartwright. Now let's see what we can do to help these poor people."

CHAPTER 88 - SARCASM HASN'T REACHED PARIS YET

"The day I allowed a Frenchie into the Company was the worst bloody day of my life," bellowed Skelly as a contrite LaPointe trembled before him in the Study.

"I am sorry, sir. I wish I could bring you better news, but I only escaped by the skin of my teeth."

"Indeed," fumed Skelly. "James Miller remains a prisoner, his wife is only God knows where, and the boy, O'Sullivan, is wandering around that blasted city, no doubt getting into all sorts of trouble." He drummed his bent, arthritis-riddled fingers on the arm of his chair, before fixing LaPointe with a withering glare. "Yet here you stand before me, LaPointe. The silver lining in my cloud."

"Thank you, sir. I appreciate your kind..."

"SHUT UP, YOU CRETIN. HASN'T SARCASM REACHED PARIS YET?"

"I'm from outside Marseilles, actually. A little village..."

"SILENCE!" Skelly closed his eyes and inhaled deeply through his nostrils, leaving LaPointe to dangle on the hook, not knowing whether he had spoken his last words. An eternity seemed to pass before he opened them again and studied the quivering wreck in front of him.

"Give me one good reason why I shouldn't send you for recycling, garlic breath. Hmmm?"

As straws went, it was a fragile one. LaPointe grabbed it as if his continued existence depended on it. Which, of course, it did.

"Intelligence, sir?"

"Something you have a distinct lack of," muttered Skelly, refreshing his glass from the decanter by his side.

"Very good, sir," simpered LaPointe. "But I obtained information while in captivity, which may be of some interest to you."

"I'm tired, LaPointe. Very tired. This had better be good."

"I can assure you it is, sir. What if I were to tell you the Forsaken and Rodriquez are up to something?"

Skelly arched an eyebrow, his interest piqued. "Continue," he said, taking a sip from his glass.

"While in my cell, I overheard talk. The one known as Samuel has offered Rodriguez a deal. His freedom in exchange for returning to Waterloo on some sort of scouting mission. I, of course, would have rejected such an offer outright, such is my loyalty to the Company."

"Of course you would, Pierre. Such loyalty," replied Skelly, far from convinced. "Return to Waterloo, though, now that is interesting. I wonder what he's up to?" He set the glass down and stared into the roaring fire, brows furrowed, before clicking his fingers and hooting with delight. "By God, I've got it."

"You have, sir?" replied LaPointe, partly puzzled, but primarily relieved at the upturn in his employer's mood.

"And there was me, thinking young Samuel didn't have the brains to match his undoubted brawn. Seems I was mistaken. Hats off to you, Cornelius, you appear to have chosen wisely after all."

"I'm sorry, sir, I don't follow you."

"I wouldn't expect you to, you Gallic fool. I had to earn my commission, not have it handed to me on a silver platter like you."

"Sorry, most sorry, Colonel."

"Oh, stop grovelling, LaPointe, I'm not going to dispense of your services. Not yet anyway," he added darkly. LaPointe wisely opted for silence, content to allow his Commanding Officer to further verbalise his train of thought.

"It's a flanking manoeuvre. Desperate, highly unlikely to succeed, but clever, I'll give him that. He can't defeat me face to face, so he's opted for a more subtle tactic. Attack me at my weakest before I became who I am today." Skelly steepled his fingers and rested a multitude of chins upon them.

"He's going back to 1815 to kill you? I don't understand." LaPointe was miles off the intellectual pace, but Skelly was too wrapped up in his own thoughts to further rebuke the Frenchman.

"Not at all. In fact, the complete opposite," replied Skelly, his mind elsewhere as he recalled the terrible glory of the last day of his life.

"He's trying to save me."

CHAPTER 89 - MESS OF A GIRL

Emily O'Hara felt useless. Worse than useless, she felt hopeless. A gloomy blanket had settled over her since Kirkwood's departure, and try as she might, she could not escape its suffocating embrace. While the others had busied themselves about the Queen Street station, under the watchful eye of Giro, she was left kicking her heels in the largely deserted canteen. Just her and a couple of kitchen staff preparing for the evening meal. She knew there was something she could be doing, which doubled the guilty thoughts, circling her head.

"You're a stupid, spoilt, selfish brat," she scolded herself, the admonishment doing nothing to improve her mood.

Guilt was a constant emotion in Emily's life. Beneath the glamorous, carefree, confident exterior was a mess of a girl. Or rather, mess of a dead girl. For that's where the guilt stemmed from, that's where it burned brightest, a molten ball of revulsion and despair. Her decision to take her own life, to step into that bath after half a bottle of vodka and a handful of Mummy's anti-depressants, topped off with the slice of the knife against her slim, pale wrists.

Selfish girl, putting herself first as usual. Yes, she was bullied at Ashgrove, mercilessly trolled online, but she fought them every inch of the way. She carried her head high, ignoring their sly asides and venomous stares in the corridors, always ready with a witty comeback or devastating putdown. They wouldn't break her. That's what she told Meredith every day, her beloved Meredith, who she left alone and broken. Meredith, who couldn't cope with the loss, succumbing to a hellish year on the streets with alcohol—her only friend.

She groaned and buried her head in her hands, earning a curious glance from a staff member cleaning a nearby table. "Are you okay, Miss?" he asked, stopping from his task to enquire of the peculiar young woman, encamped in the corner of the canteen.

"Yes," smiled Emily sadly, lifting her head. "I'm just having a moment, that's all. It's been a tough day."

"Is there anything I can get you? Dinner isn't for another hour, but I could fix you up a sandwich and a drink?"

"No, I'm fine, thank you," replied Emily.

"If it's any consolation, we all lost people we cared about today. Two of my graduation class died, and another is being flown out for emergency surgery. They're hopeful they can save her leg."

"Wow...I'm...sorry." It was all she could manage, tears pricking her sad, wide eyes.

"It's okay, Miss. Nobody forced any of us to sign up. I'm just angry I wasn't out there myself to help them. Been stuck on menial duties since I got my knee rearranged by a Dirty with a baseball bat." Emily looked down, for the first time, noticing the orthopaedic brace on the man's left knee. She also saw his face for the first time, looking beyond the bland uniform all the soldiers wore. He was fresh-faced, not much younger than herself, a good-looking boy.

"Yeah," he smiled shyly, tapping the brace when he noticed her staring at it. "Surgery went well, but I'll need to keep this on for another few weeks. Then I'll hit the gym big time and get myself back in shape. I'm hoping I'll be back out there in a few months. The guys need me, and I miss them. Until then, I help out how I can. There's no way I'm leaving the zone until the unit's tour is up."

"You're an inspiration," said Emily. "You put the likes of me to shame."

"Pardon me, Miss, but I beg to differ. I don't know a lot about you or your friends, Major Deacon insists it's highly classified and strictly need-to-know. But the guys say if it hadn't been for your friends, then a lot more of us would have been wiped out today. We will always be grateful. Everyone has their bit to do out there." He nodded and finished wiping the table down before turning and making his way back to the kitchens, a slight limp evident in his gait.

Emily watched him leave, touched by the quiet courage and respect the young man had displayed. Yet, here she was, wallowing in misery at her own misgivings and the fact she was missing her friends. Friends who were in grave danger again, yet still very much alive. Alive and fighting for all they were worth against an evil which would stop at nothing to destroy them.

"Wise up, Emily, get a grip." She pinched her wrist and wiped the tears from reddened eyes with the back of a hand. Taking a deep breath, she rose, just as Tess poked her head around the door of the canteen.

"Yo, dead girl, Samuel wants us all to meet in the briefing room in half an hour. That good for you?"

"Yeah, I'll be there." Tess nodded and made to leave before Emily forced herself to speak again.

"Tess?"

"Yeah," she replied warily. To date, Emily had shown little interest in membership of the Tess Cartwright Fan Club.

"Would you like to sit down and keep me company for a bit?"

"Er, sure." Tess edged forward and hesitantly took a seat at the table. "Are you feeling alright? Or did the body snatchers get to you when we were fighting Mr. and Mrs. Looney Toons out in the yard?"

The ice was broken. Emily erupted into peals of laughter, and try as she might, Tess could not help but join her. The tension between them evaporated like a morning fog touched by the first rays of the sun. After that, they babbled like two long lost friends catching up after years apart. Ashgrove anecdotes were exchanged, and memories revisited of cranky teachers and odious classmates. Before they knew it, it was time to join the others in the briefing room.

"Feeling better?" the kitchen hand enquired as they passed him on their way out of the canteen.

"Much better," smiled Emily. And thank you...I'm sorry...I don't your name."

"It's Private Muldoon, Miss."

"No, your first name."

"Oh, it's Matthew. Matt to my friends," he replied, cheeks reddening at the familiarity.

"Well, I shall call you Matt then. Thank you, Matt."

"You're welcome, Miss." He paused. "What for?"

"Come on, Emily," urged Tess, holding the canteen door open. "They're waiting for us."

Emily stopped at the open door. "For teaching me there's more to life than the death of Emily O'Hara." With that, she was gone. Matt Muldoon, in later years to become a much-decorated war hero, would never forget his encounter with the strange young woman in the canteen at Queen Street Police Station.

CHAPTER 90 - PIG UGLY SOLDIERS

The road to Brussels was barely that. A narrow potholed track, where every step forward out of the cloying mud was a torrid victory. Rodriguez kept them close to the hedgerow to avoid the majority of traffic, but before long, their clothes were splattered with mud and their boots filling with water. They trudged on, heads down, just four nondescript soldiers caught up in the unrelenting flow to and from the city.

The French advance had led to a hurried exodus from the outlying villages and countryside. Wagons inched forward, equine muscle straining to make progress in the appalling conditions. Their owners urged the poor animals forward with expletives and harsh blows to their flanks. Animal rights were an unheard phenomenon in this day and age.

"If he hits that horse one more time, I'm going to knock his block off," said Meredith, a little too loudly for the liking of Rodriguez. He grabbed her by the forearm and spun her around to face him. "You'll do no such thing. We're not to draw attention to ourselves, understand?"

She stared defiantly into his scarred, bearded face before shaking free of his grip and plodding on behind Kirkwood and Harley. The road ahead was packed. Hundreds of voices struggling to be heard above the clatter of wagons and distant rumble of cannon fire. It was a tinder box of raw human emotion, requiring only a spark to burst into flames.

Harley sneezed. "Wonderful. I time travel to the nineteenth century, and all I got was a lousy cold. Is it much further, Rodriguez? My feet are soaked."

"That's Sergeant Rodriguez to you, brat. Talking back to a higher rank like that is a sure-fire way to the lash." He looked around, concerned their conversation would attract unwanted attention, but their fellow travellers were too wrapped up in their own worries to notice.

"Well, pardon me for having an opinion," huffed Harley.

"Opinions aren't allowed in the army. You follow my orders. Now shut up and walk." They trudged on, a persistent drizzle doing nothing to lift their spirits. Families lucky enough to have wagons and livestock to pull them trundled ahead, the welcome lights of the capital still tantalisingly out of reach. Others less fortunate carried what they could when the cry had gone up that the French were coming. Children dressed in rags huddled close to their mother's legs, their wide, blank expressions summing up the horror of the war that was sweeping this once peaceful land.

Kirkwood took it all in, not quite believing what his eyes were seeing. He looked down and watched his feet shuffling forward, his mind detached from the actions of his body, thinking he was going to wake up any moment with a raging hangover. Harley stumbled in front of him, and he watched as Meredith reached out to steady her. No, this was real, and up ahead, Skelly awaited him. He dreaded staring into those cold, dead eyes, but he knew he had no choice. It was either end it now, or it would end them. It would end everything that ever was.

A young girl sat crying at the side of the road. The colour of her dress indistinguishable because of the mud. Harley instinctively dropped to one knee beside her, taking hold of her tiny hand. "Hey, little one, where are your parents?" Her heart broke for the child, paralysed by fear at being separated from her family. The girl stared at Harley, her huge brown eyes like chocolate saucers, before emitting a high-pitched wail that could have woken the dead. Staggering back in shock at the reaction of the child, she would have landed on her backside in the mire, had the considerable hand of Rodriguez not intervened, and hauled her up by the scruff of the neck.

"Keep walking, you idiot. You'll attract attention." Heads were already turning amidst the throng on the road as others sought out the source of the screaming.

"Get your hands off me," yelled Harley. "I'm only trying to help the wee thing. She's scared stiff."

"Yes, of you, you fool. All she sees is a smelly, pig-ugly British soldier."

They hurried their step, a sullen Harley muttering all the while, her face no doubt the colour of the red tunic she wore that all but them could see. Kirkwood glanced anxiously over his shoulder towards the hub of the commotion. A woman had emerged from the crowd and plucked the young girl up, her raised voice a mixture of anger and relief. While cross the little girl had wandered off, she was equally glad to have found her. A solitary good news story on a road that would lead to so many unhappy endings.

"Kirkwood! Eyes front and centre. Before Sergeant Grumpy Drawers catches you showing a shred of humanity." Meredith tugged at his arm and angled her head towards Rodriguez, who still glared at an unrepentant Harley.

"This is nuts, Meredith. I've never thrown a punch in my life, and now I'm expected to fight Napoleon Bloody Bonaparte as well as Skelly and his merry band of psychopaths."

"I know, but try and stay cool. As long as the three of us stick together, we'll be grand. The Presence versus Napoleon, no contest, right?"

"If you say so."

"Is it much farther?" groaned Harley, struggling to keep pace with Rodriguez, whose loping stride ate up the sodden ground.

"You people. So lazy, with your cars and flying machines. The 49th was famous for being able to march twenty-five miles a day in perfect formation. All while carrying a seventy-pound pack and with nothing to eat but what we could forage." Rodriguez screwed his nose up in disgust. "Brussels is less than ten miles. Now shut up and walk."

"Yes, sir, no, sir, three bags full, sir." Kirkwood shot Rodriguez a mock salute and turned his attention to avoiding the numerous obstacles on the road ahead. The rain was increasing in its intensity, and he became aware of how badly the nineteenth century smelt. Men and women openly urinated on the verges, and the stench of animal faeces, sweat, and God knows what else threatened to overwhelm him. Meredith and Harley were similarly affected, and all three walked with their forearms covering their nostrils for fear of what horrendous aroma would assail them next. Rodriguez was unperturbed, leading the way with only the occasional glance behind to ensure they were keeping up.

A man carrying a wooden crate under his arm shoved past them, causing Meredith to reel back in pain.

"Frig sake, something just bit me." She swivelled to be confronted by an angry-looking goose, it's head protruding from the crate. "Here, mister, keep your pets under control. I'll need a tetanus shot when this is all over." The man waved his arm at her and continued on his way, muttering under his breath.

"Sergeant Rodriguez," a rich, melodic voice roared above the babble. "You're going the wrong way. The action is going to be back down the road."

A huge grin broke across Rodriguez's face, and he turned just in time to be consumed in a meaty embrace by a soldier sporting the colours of the 49th. Rodriguez erupted into laughter, and the two men slapped each other's backs as the human tide slipped either side of them.

"I could say the same about you, Wesley. It's not like you to duck out of a fight."

"No chance. Captain Grant has sent me back to hurry up the supply wagons. Word is, the Frenchies have Blucher on the run, and we're next for the high jump. Old Hooky means to make a stand tomorrow. The Colonel wants the boys fed and watered if there's going to be a scrap." Wesley stood slightly shorter than Rodriguez, but the breadth of his shoulders and muscular frame indicated there would be little between them in terms of physicality. A shaved, shining head, and flawless ebony complexion made him further stand out in the sea of pale, grimy faces all around them.

Meredith nudged Harley and smirked. "Check out the eye candy, Harls." The younger girl blushed but nonetheless could not pull her eyes from the impressive figure in front of them.

"A fight, eh? Well, I'll be sure to be back for that. When have you known me to ever miss one? Just delivering a message up to Brussels. Brought these greenhorns with me as I don't trust them left to their own devices. They'd be halfway to their mother's apron strings if I left them."

Wesley studied each of his friend's travelling companions in turn, seemingly unimpressed by the pained expression on his face. "Fresh meat? Well, talk about a baptism of fire. They're saying this is the big one. Boney is going to throw everything at us. Best you greenhorns stick close to your Sergeant, he'll keep you right."

"You're too kind, Corporal. Care to keep us company this fine summers day?"

"Aye, why not. You can tell me what you've been up to these last few weeks. Last time I saw you was the night you knocked that thick Cockney out in the prize fight. You won me a few shillings that night, my friend."

"Ha," laughed Rodriguez, slipping an arm around his comrade's shoulder. "He was thick alright, any man with sense would have stayed down after the first knockdown. But he kept getting back up." The two men roared with laughter and slipped into each other's company like a pair of well-worn slippers. Behind them, Kirkwood, Meredith, and Harley trudged in their wake, all three united in their misery.

"I've been on a few crappy road trips in my time, but this one takes the biscuit," griped Meredith, her black hair now matted to her cheeks by the worsening deluge.

"Why did you have to mention food," moaned Harley. "I'd kill for a chocolate digestive, I'm starving."

Kirkwood said nothing, focused on the back of Rodriguez's head and placing one foot in front of the other. For every step was a step nearer Skelly and a step nearer getting out of this deepening nightmare. A step nearer a normal life or as normal as his could ever be again. A step nearer a quiet life with his family, friends—old and new, and a dead girl named Emily. He had no idea what the future held for him, but he knew he wanted her to be a part of it.

CHAPTER 91 - TEARS FOR A STOLEN CHILDHOOD

"Deacon sends his regards. Well, maybe regards isn't the right word. But he's swearing at the hospital staff a lot and wanting hourly updates about the situation in his city." Giro waggled his fingers to highlight the last two words. "Expect a lot of helicopter action over the next day or so, they will be ferrying new troops in and taking our injured out."

"Along with twenty-plus body bags," added Samuel grimly.

"Any word from Kirkwood and the girls?" inquired Emily, eager to change the subject to anything other than death.

"I can tell where they are and that they're all alive, but other than that, nothing," replied Tess.

"And I could take you to them and probably take out half the French army with my bare hands, but I'm not allowed to," added Ariana, more than a little exasperated.

"We have had this conversation, Miss Hennessy," scolded Samuel gently. "What Kirkwood and the others are trying to achieve requires subtlety and precision. Changing the outcome of the battle in the manner you desire could cause irrevocable damage to millennia of work."

"Are you really that old?" asked Tess. "For if you are, can I get the number of your personal trainer?"

Samuel laughed shyly. "I am neither young nor old for my kind. Giro and I are no longer defined by such parameters."

"Ever the riddler," sighed Emily. "Now, please, can you tell us how we can help? I've had my pity party, and I'm ready to rumble again."

"The universe thanks you," grinned Giro.

"Sod off, geek boy," sniggered the ghost girl.

"Well, I'm glad to hear we are all singing off the same hymn sheet and willing to roll up our sleeves. While events hinge on Kirkwood and the others, there is much we can be getting on with." Samuel eyed each of them in turn. "Are you ready to hear what your next missions are?"

"Missions. I like it," laughed Tess. "Makes us sound like secret agents."

"Go on," said Ariana, her interest piqued.

"Very well then, but don't say I didn't warn you. I'm about to place you all in considerable danger."

"Tell me something I don't know." Emily rolled her eyes while every inch of her skin prickled with excitement. It was good to be back.

∞ ∞ ∞

Adam O'Sullivan also wished he was back. Back home. He was done with this ridiculous war, that bitch Maura made sure of that. Now, he was wandering through what was once Belfast city centre. Hungry, cold, and clueless as to what he was going to do. There was no Plan B, hell, there hadn't really been a Plan A to start with.

He first became aware of them after leaving Queen Street and turning right into the city. There were three, little more than kids, following him, not hiding, but at the same time maintaining a respectable distance. He'd ignored them at first, so caught up in his own thoughts, but as he reached Royal Avenue, the city's main thoroughfare, they began to close the gap, jogging now, crouched low and tight to the surrounding buildings. Upon reaching the junction, he saw two other groups approaching from separate directions.

Nothing worked. First of all, it was mind control, something he could normally do without even thinking. He focused on the youths, willing them to go away and leave him alone. They should have moulded immediately to his suggestion and turned tail, but they kept coming. Next, he tried to hurl a wall of bone-shattering energy at them, like Maura had taught him, but again, nothing. In the end, he sought to take flight, to sail high above the cursed city and its inhabitants. He couldn't lift himself an inch. That's when Adam started to panic. Whatever powers he once had were gone.

They were herding him, he realised, as he broke into a trot down the only street left open. He jumped as a rock landed several feet to his left, sending up shards of fine granite. Then another, bigger this time, narrowly missing his head. He ducked instinctively, raising his hands over his head and breaking into a zig-zag run, desperate to find some cover. Footsteps sounded behind him, and the third stone found its mark, striking him on the crown of his head. He stumbled and almost fell, somehow retaining his balance as the sporadic stoning became a hail of missiles. The ache in his shoulder was forgotten as another stone struck the back of his trailing leg, this time felling him. He attempted to get back up, but the coup de grace was a glancing blow to the head, drawing blood and dazing him.

His vision blurred as a group of shadowy figures approached. So, this was it, the great crusade to avenge his father's death ending in some futuristic wasteland at the hands of a group of teenage hooligans. Part of him wanted to stand and fight to his last breath, part of him didn't care anymore. He'd been outwitted by Ariana Hennessy and Maura Miller, he didn't deserve to live even if he had something to live for, which he didn't.

"Hurry up then, you dicks, get it over and done with."

He lay back, content to watch the low clouds drift by above as they deliberated over which of the closing pack was going to deliver the killer blow. He blinked, his vision filling with red, the cut on his head flowing freely. He thought he heard his mother's voice, calling to him like she used to when his dinner was ready, and he was out playing football with his mates.

"Adam.

"Coming, ma. What's for tea tonight?"

"Adam O'Sullivan?"

"Awwwch wise up, ma, you know my name."

"Yeah, it's him. Light it up, boys."

Gunfire erupted all around him, and the shadowy figures danced like broken marionettes, spinning and falling. Adam laughed until he cried, tears for a childhood stolen from him. Tears for what might have been, tears for how it had all fallen apart. A great sadness weighed down upon him until the noise stopped, and blessed darkness claimed him.

CHAPTER 92 - SLEEPING THROUGH THE APOCALYPSE

"Get up."

"Why should I? It's the end of the world, and I'm entitled to die as I want."

"Stop being an eejet and get up, Gerry."

"How do you know my name?"

"I know lots about you, Gerry. About how you have a crappy job, stomach pains you tell nobody about, how you still owe Kirkwood £20 from last Christmas for that taxi fare."

"What? He was as drunk as a skunk. He couldn't possibly have remembered..."

Gerry opened an eye expecting to be surrounded by dozens of ravenous prehistoric beasts ready to tear him limb from limb. He was slightly disoriented to find himself staring into the face of a young woman, a knowing smile adorning otherwise angelic features. Huge dark eyes juxtaposed a head of silver hair that hung almost to her waist. Given that it was the end of the world and raining monsters, she was dressed entirely inappropriately in a slip of a dress and dainty shoes, which probably cost more than he earned in a month.

"Do I know you?" He risked opening the other eye. They were alone on High Street, the sun blazing from a cloudless sky, devoid of demonic beings. "Have I missed something? Isn't this meant to be the end of the world?"

"Don't worry," she replied breezily. "You won't miss a thing. You've passed out. That's what happens when you neck a bottle of whiskey in record time. Not forgetting the numerous pints beforehand."

Gerry forced his aching body into a sitting position. Beside him on the kerb sat the incriminating evidence of a near-empty bottle of spirits. "Am I dead?"

"Not yet, but if you keep up with the endless questions, that's a distinct possibility. Now shut up and listen."

Gerry shook his head in disbelief but indicated for the strange girl to continue. It wasn't as if his day could get any weirder.

"My name is Emily. I'm a friend of Kirkwood."

"Kirkwood? What? I..."

"I said shut it," snapped Emily. Gerry nodded meekly like a chastised schoolboy. "We've no time. Yes, the end of the world is happening, and no, you haven't imagined the events of the last hour. The world as you know it, it's over, finito."

"Got it. Finito."

"Better. When you wake up, you're going to get up and go back to that smelly bar you spent half your life in. You're going to walk to the till, remove the key underneath it, then go to the door next to those god-awful toilets."

"The door to the cellars?" Gerry stared in awe at Emily as if she was referring to the Holy Grail. "Francey doesn't allow anybody down there. Not even Mrs. Francey."

"Well, consider this your lucky day, Gerard." She leaned down and wagged a finger in his face. "But if you mess this up, I'll personally drag you back onto this street for the first passing beastie to devour. Are we clear on that?"

"Crystal." Gerry had never been more motivated to stay sober.

"Good. You'll remain there until I come for you. Whatever you hear, whatever you see, you don't leave the cellar. You'll be safe as long as you remain there."

"So, you want me to hide out in a cellar stocked to the gills with free drink?"

"Exactly," beamed Emily. "Consider it Christmas come early for you this year."

"I guess I can do that," Gerry replied warily. "Dare I ask why, though, and what Kirkwood's got to do with all this?"

"Kirkwood Scott is going to save the world, Gerry. This world and many others. But I need to buy him some time by stalling our friends for a while. I can only do that through somebody's dreams. I'm dead, you see."

"Of course, you are," intoned Gerry sagely. "That makes perfect sense."

"Cut the sarcasm, or I'll leave you to the birdies. I can't walk this world, only in the dreams of others. For your sins, Samuel has deemed you an appropriate channel for me. I think he feels a bit sorry for you. Either that or you're the one person prepared to sleep through the apocalypse."

"Fair point," mused Gerry. "Who's Samuel?"

"No need for you to worry about that. He's a friend, and he's on our side, that's all you need to know. A very powerful friend. Once you're in that cellar, he'll ensure your safety when your little party is in full swing. Then, I'll pop in and see you later when you're having forty winks. Sorted?"

"If you say so. Although I'm pretty certain I'm already dead. I didn't expect hell to contain lock-ins, free drink, and pretty girls."

"Kirkwood's told me a bit about you, Gerry. How you always land on your feet. Consider this one of your nine lives. Now go, before this pretty girl changes her mind and shows you what hell really looks like."

Gerry watched as the dream girl melted before his eyes, like a warm breeze taking petals from a cherry blossom tree. His vision was replaced by a swirling mass congregating around the remains of Albert Clock. One by one, figures began to break off from it and descend into the city, distant screams replacing the calm of Emily's visit. He needed no further encouragement. Scrambling to his feet, he ran the fastest hundred metres of his life, propelling his horribly unfit body back up the street towards the Montreal. Crashing through its door into the bar, he wildly groped beneath the till, at any moment expecting Big Mark to clamp a hand on his shoulder and throw him out on his ear.

"Bullseye." Gerry held the metal key triumphantly before his eyes, and hands shaking, fumbled at the lock to the cellar door. The noise outside was growing all the time. The lighting in the bar dimmed as huge figures swooped past. At any moment, he expected the windows to crash inwards and be torn to pieces by razor-sharp beaks and claws.

"Come on, open, open." He turned the key again and groaned with relief as the lock clicked, and he forced down the handle, his weight and momentum carrying him inwards, almost falling down the narrow flight of steps to the cellar floor. Closing the door and locking it behind him, he surveyed the promised land below. A complex system of kegs and pipes illuminated by two bare light bulbs dangling from the pockmarked ceiling. Edging down the stairs, he perched on a keg and ripped open a cardboard box, removing another bottle of Francie's finest whiskey. Twisting the cap, he took a long slug from it, relishing the burning sensation as it hit the back of his throat.

"Well, Kirkwood, this is another fine mess you've gotten me into." Gerry was many things, but he always kept his word, and when he started a job, he saw it through to the finish. If saving the planet meant drinking himself into a stupor on top-grade spirits, then who was he to argue?

CHAPTER 93 - FIGHTING TALK

Emily breezed into the briefing room and leaned against a wall opposite the others, eminently pleased with herself. "Mission accomplished. Kirkwood's little friend is all signed up and guzzling down the grog as we speak. I now have full access to all areas of *Scourgefest*, and am at your disposal, Samuel." She bowed as Ariana and Tess broke into applause. Giro joined in by enthusiastically banging the table, and even Samuel smiled.

"Good job, Emily. Gerry is safe for now, I've taken care of that. And don't worry, I've got another little job for you that I'm hoping will buy Kirkwood and the others some time. The longer we can disrupt the Scourge in present-day Belfast, the longer it will take them to occupy the other planes. They will fall, that much is inevitable, but we can fight a rearguard campaign, make them fight for every inch."

"And O'Sullivan?" Ariana raised the thorny issue, which still niggled at her.

"He is not your concern anymore, Ariana," said Giro softly. "I know how much he hurt you, but we must focus now on other matters. Forget about him."

"I can't," gasped Ariana, fighting back the tears. "You don't understand the things he did to me. I need..."

"Closure," finished Samuel. He leaned forward and took Ariana's hands, dwarfing them within his own. "There's no point me saying I understand as I don't. I didn't go through what you did. But I know what it's like to be deprived of your freedom, to be mentally and physically tortured. Believe me, I know." She looked into his dark eyes and believed every word he said. They contained a sadness that connected the two of them at this moment in their lives. For that moment, nothing else mattered to either of them but their shared bond.

It was Tess who broke the silence. "If I was to tell you where he currently is, Samuel, would that change your thinking?" Her tone was without its usual positivity, and Samuel was unsure he wanted to hear the information she was about to impart. Still, he had to ask the question. Leadership was leaping from one fire to the next, he was learning that fast.

"Go on, Tess."

Her face draining as she spoke the words, Tess tossed the hand grenade into their midst. "Mr. O'Sullivan is currently inside the New Jerusalem complex." She bit her bottom lip before continuing. "To be precise, the private chambers of the Priestess."

"Well," said Samuel, sitting back and running a hand through his mullet. "That certainly changes everything."

"Indeed, it does," agreed Ariana, her face set in steely resolution. "Tess. I do believe we've found something to keep us occupied until the others get back."

∞ ∞ ∞

She eyed him like a lioness about to devour her evening meal. Adam shifted awkwardly, the comfort of the chaise longue he was sat upon doing little to ease jangling nerves. The silence stretched until he could stand it no more, blurting out words before he'd even properly thought about what he was going to say.

"Are you one of them?"

"One of them?" Her lip curled into a smile, seemingly amused by the question. She leaned back, relishing the terror she instilled in the young man. "And who might *they* be?"

"That crazy red-haired bitch and the dirty old bugger she works for. She led me up the garden path, made a complete bloody fool of me. You've got what you wanted, can't you just leave me alone now?"

The Priestess flicked her dark hair over a bare shoulder, dressed plainly in a black vest and jeans. "Oh, I assure you I'm not one of them, Adam."

Adam eyed her warily. "How do you know my name? Where am I?"

"You're safe, Adam. Well, safer than you were out there, about to be stoned to death by the locals."

"Who are you?"

"You may call me the Priestess," she replied, extending her arms to take in their surroundings. "And this is New Jerusalem. You're welcome to stay and join us. I can assure you I'm no friend of your former colleagues."

"You know them?"

"Oh, yes. Well, one of them in particular. He and I knew each other very well." She giggled, accentuating the latter two words, leaving him under no illusions as to the nature of the relationship.

"What happened?" Despite his caution, he was eager to learn more, especially as she seemed the only show in town at that time.

"Your enemies took him away from me. All my life I've waited for the man who would be my equal, then I find him, and five minutes later he's snatched from me again. Packed off to most probably die a brutal death for the second time. Well, I'm not taking that sitting down, and you can help me if you want."

"You're mad if you think you can take on that lot. They've got serious firepower."

"You think that's impressive? Well, you haven't seen anything yet. I've been keeping my powder dry up until now. They think they can turn up here, kill my people, take the love of my life from me, destroy the empire I've spent years building. Well, if they think I'm going to take all that lying down, they've got another thing coming. It's high time I showed them what I'm capable of—put them in their box once and for all. Including your little pet project, Ariana Hennessy."

"Fighting talk," replied Adam. "Hope you can back it up. I've seen those boys and girls in action. They mean business."

"As do I, Adam. Skelly and that oaf Samuel think they hold all the cards. They don't know what they've started. But I'll finish it. I'll finish them all for daring to cross my path."

Adam smiled and relaxed a little. What did he have to lose? "Keep talking. I'm listening."

CHAPTER 94 - WAR STORIES

"Then there was that time at Salamanca he stormed a French battery single-handed. The cowards took one look at him, turned, spiked their guns, and fled the field. Got you your second stripe that one, didn't it Martim?"

"Third actually," said Rodriguez, tapping his upper arm smugly.

"Ha, one more than I have," roared Wesley.

"You've only yourself to blame for that," bellowed Rodriguez, slapping him heartily on the back. "How many times did you make Corporal only to balls it up. Twice?"

"Three, actually," replied the big Jamaican. "Stripped off me the first time for being drunk on duty. Then the misunderstanding with the 95th Rifles at that tavern outside Marseilles..."

"Put three of them in the infirmary, I heard."

"And finally, my temporary absence from the regiment before Tavalero."

"Temporary? I heard it was a week."

"Almost two, actually. I always meant to return. But the young lady in question was most persuasive. Didn't want me to leave."

The two men erupted into laughter, earning dark looks from their fellow travellers on the congested road.

"Do they ever shut up?" groaned Harley, several steps behind. "This has been going on for hours."

"Now you know how the rest of us feel, Harls," replied Meredith, nudging the younger girl playfully in the side.

"Hey, my stories aren't that boring."

"Would the two of you be quiet," seethed Kirkwood. "I'm trying to listen. Some of this stuff could come in useful down the line."

"Useful? Two meatheads bragging about how many drunken punch-ups they've been in? Hardly." Meredith grimaced as the mud once again threatened to pull the boot from her foot.

"You don't know when it might come in handy. We're meant to be soldiers. Will do no harm to pick up the odd war story or bit of slang."

"You're such an anorak, Kirkwood." Harley rolled her eyes as she trudged alongside him. "I've no idea what Emily sees in you."

"Harley!" hissed Meredith.

"Sorry," sulked the younger girl. "But it's true."

"We're just friends," stammered Kirkwood, wishing the drenched soil would open up and swallow him. "And anyway, I haven't time for that nonsense, none of us do. We have to stay focused." He silently counted to ten, praying Harley would take the hint and change the subject. Emily needed to be firmly dispatched to the back of his mind if he was to have any chance of surviving the impending bloodbath.

Ahead of them, Wesley let rip with a stream of expletives, which had them all gaping in his direction. He stood before them, hands on hips, as several soldiers toiled at the rear wheels of a wagon wedged on its side in the ditch. One of the men looked up to establish the cause of the outburst and redoubled his efforts when he caught sight of Rodriguez and Wesley.

"Sorry, Sergeant," he wheezed, thrusting his shoulder against the recalcitrant wheel and shoving until his face turned the colour of the tunic he'd unbuttoned to the waist. "Dog ran out in front of us and spooked the horses."

"You should have run over the damned dog then," scowled Rodriguez. "Come on, let's get this contraption back on four wheels. I can hear their bellies growling up the road. The boys can't be expected to fight the frogs on an empty stomach."

Wesley removed his pack and cap, before rolling up the sleeves of his tunic to reveal muscular forearms. "Come on, you scoundrels, put your backs into it," he shouted, putting a shoulder to one of the stricken wheels and shoving until the veins of his neck throbbed alarmingly.

"Well, don't just stand there, gawking," howled Rodriguez at his young companions. "Give the man a hand." Muttering all the while, Meredith and Harley descended into the ditch, followed by Kirkwood, and soon half a dozen of Wellington's finest were covered from head to toe in Belgian muck.

Taking command at the front, the big Portuguese Sergeant baited and bullied the overworked horses in harness. The combination of equine and human muscle finally started to overcome the gluey hold on the wheels as they began to turn, inch by inch, until with a sucking pop, the horses pulled the wagon clear of the ditch. Rodriguez let out a roar of triumph as the poor souls at the rear were carried forward by their own momentum face-first into several inches of boggy water.

"Good work, lads. Now, get that wagon up to the regiment, double-quick. If I hear about you getting stuck again, I'll kick you up and down this road till you're black and blue. You'll be praying for the French to come. Wesley, you're in charge. I'll be back in time for breakfast."

"Yes, Sergeant. I'll save a plate for you. Make the most of your night out in the city. Remember..."

"It could be my last." The two big men hollered with hearty laughter and exchanged a bear hug as a drenched Kirkwood, Meredith, and Harley emerged from the ditch.

"And look after those three drowned rats," shouted Wesley over his shoulder before turning and sauntering down the road after the loaded wagon.

"Drowned rats with hypothermia," spluttered Meredith, wringing out her beanie before placing it on her head, hair plastered to her face.

"Oh, stop crying like a little baby," growled Rodriguez. "Another hour or so will have us in Brussels. Put your best foot forward, and you'll be dried out by then. I'll find us a comfortable tavern for the night. The King's shilling goes a long way in this city, I'm told." He produced a small purse from the pocket of his long coat and jangled it before them. "Plenty of wine, woman, and song for us, young Kirkwood, eh?"

"All I care about is making sure Skelly doesn't put the Duke's nose out of joint at the ball. Plus, you're spoken for Rodriguez. The

Priestess wouldn't want to find out you've been playing away from home now, would she?"

"Nor your white witch," countered Rodriguez. He burst into laughter at seeing Kirkwood's flustered expression. "Oh relax, Senor Scott. Why must you be so serious all the time? Live and enjoy the moment, for it might be your last. I learnt that much in the army if nothing else."

The four unlikely companions trudged on through the crowds towards the city as the sound of distant cannon fire intensified in the distance. It was the early afternoon of 16 June 1815, and the Battle of Quatre Bras had begun.

CHAPTER 95 - GOING IN HEAVY-HANDED

The Drummer Boy clung to the pain, as for a long time, it was all he had. Without the pain, there was no reference point, nothing to cling to—to remind him he still existed. Without the pain, there was only darkness. A darkness from which they said there was no return. Yet, he had still believed, holding to the thin thread of pain, hauling himself inch by inch along its length towards redemption and repentance. A second chance, another opportunity to prove himself as worthy of repaying the debt he knew he still owed the old man. Now was that time, and he was ready.

Nobody knew the old man like him. A father figure, a mentor, a commander, a god. He'd marched with him to the very gates of hell and beyond, never wavering in his resolve, always maintaining a steady rhythm and cadence. Others had fallen by the wayside or proven themselves woefully lacking. Gunther at the bridge, and now Rodriguez betraying the hand that had fed him for so long. It had stung to learn he'd then turned to Maura Miller, a mere camp follower not fit to lace his boots. The Colonel was always partial to a pretty face, that's what had gotten them all into this damned mess in the first place. Couldn't keep his hands off Abervale's daughter, and condemned us all to that bloody ridge.

Not that he'd ever dare say as much to Skelly, he didn't have to, for the Colonel knew the truth better than anyone. All the rumours, all the idle gossip that soldiers thrived on to fill those long, dull hours of waiting, waiting, waiting. Waiting for the beat of the drum. The call to arms, the thrill of the advance. The maddening rush that drove men insane long before the first volley of musket fire tore into their ranks before the first cannonball danced its merry, bloody path through flesh and bone.

Skelly knew the truth. He knew what caused Wellington to bring the 49th up to fill the gap beneath the ridge. The gap that never featured in any of the memoirs or regimental histories. The 49th effectively ceased to exist that day, both literally and in the history books. Their magnificent legacy and tales of valour erased to satisfy the ego and pride of a man who should have known better. Skelly had his faults, many of them, but he didn't deserve that. None of them did.

"You do realise this will be your last chance?"

"Yes, sir."

"Your very last chance. I had to argue your case long and hard with the powers that be. They're not the most forgiving bunch; the higher you go up the food chain."

"I appreciate your faith in me, and I won't let you down again, I promise you that."

"Don't make promises you can't keep," spat Skelly. "Just bring me results. You used to be good at that."

"Just tell me what I have to do, sir."

"Maura, wherever her pretty head might be now, succeeded in re-opening the portal. Used her feminine charms to persuade that wittering fool, O'Sullivan, to facilitate our request. Much appreciated, although I've no idea where he is now. Probably moping around somewhere like a lovesick puppy. He's no longer a concern to us, he's given me what I need."

"He's a stray, though. Shouldn't we put him down just to be safe?"

"You'll do what I tell you to do, and no more, do you understand?"

"Yes, sir, absolutely." Careful does it. Maybe a bit soon to start poking the bear. Get back into his good books first, and don't take anything for granted. Small steps.

"With the portal opened onto that damned plane, the others will fall within days. Samuel knows that and is desperate. Hence this last throw of the dice, looking to strike beneath the armour at our underbelly. Get at me before I assumed my current job title."

"He's gone back, sir?"

"Glad to see the abyss didn't fry all your brain cells. Yes, he's gone back. Or rather sent those three damned brats who house the Presence. If I don't die in the prescribed manner at Waterloo, then I don't exist in my current format. None of the Company do, which causes a problem for our current employers."

"Without us, sir, the portal would not have been re-opened. They will be thwarted in their ambition to possess and destroy all the planes if the natural order at Waterloo is disturbed."

"Exactly. Which is why I need you to go back, William. Ensure I die. Maintain the status quo."

The Drummer Boy, William Fotheringham, felt his chest swell with pride. To be allotted such a mission by the Colonel was an honour beyond words. All he could do was nod eagerly. He would not let Skelly down—he could not. Ardgallon would be avenged, he would crush them just as he'd crushed Dobson before their disbelieving eyes. The Forsaken were no match for him, nor was Kirkwood Scott and his mongrel pack.

Skelly smiled, pleased with his decision to recall the angelic choirboy. For beneath the blonde curls and wide, blue eyes was a ruthless killer. An operative who would stop at nothing to run his enemies into the ground. He would triumph, and this time there would be no mistake. The Company would go in heavy-handed.

"Who do you wish to accompany you? I place the Company at your disposal. No expense spared."

"Bad Bill," replied William without hesitation.

Skelly nodded appreciatively. "A fine choice. Is that it?"

"I prefer a small team, it's less cumbersome. I'll take McPeake as well. And the Numbers Man."

"Numbers?" Skelly raises an eyebrow in mild surprise. "You'll have your hands full with that lot, but so be it. Just don't let me down. I want no mistakes, no repeat of what happened at Ardgallon."

"Don't worry, sir." William's expression was anything but cherubic. "I'll make sure they all die. Rodriguez, Scott, his wenches, and most of all, you. In the square. As it's meant to be."

Skelly sat back in his armchair. Once more, the pendulum had swung in his favour. For the final time, he hoped.

CHAPTER 96 - THE NUMBERS MAN

Wesley had been walking for less than an hour, the wagon rolling awkwardly in front of him when he caught a flash of red tunic amongst the monotone grey of the rural community descending upon Brussels.

"God save us, are any of the 49th still in camp? Where are you two ruffians going?"

"And a fine good morning to you as well," replied the fattest soldier in the regiment. "I see you've located the wagon. What tasty treats have you got under that canopy for me?"

"Hands off, McPeake. You need your belly trimmed, not another plate of grub. If the Frenchies come up this road, your waddling behind will be the first to be skewered."

"I've stayed ahead of them for six years so far, and I've no intention of stopping now. Many a skinny runt is dead and buried, but I've got *this*, the only muscle that matters." He tapped his head with a stubby finger, multiple chins wobbling beneath the chin strap of his cap.

"I see you've brought your boyfriend to keep you company. Numbers." He nodded at a second soldier, as thin as McPeake was portly and standing six inches above him. He glowered at Wesley and pushed back the peak of his cap to reveal a receding head of greying hair. Nobody knew his age, but the talk was he should have been retired out of the regiment years ago. Whenever he was asked, he would skilfully avoid the question, maintaining that "age was only a number." The nickname had stuck.

Numbers looked Wesley up and down before speaking, a broad Welsh lilt betraying his Swansea roots. "Move aside, we're on regimental business, or didn't they teach you to respect your betters in Africa or wherever the hell they found you?" He made to push past, but the big man placed a hand firmly on his chest.

"I'm from the Caribbean island of Jamaica, as well you know, Numbers. I suggest you commit that to your memory, for if you say that again the next time we meet, I might not take it so kindly." He released his grip on the other man's tunic, and he bustled past, studiously avoiding eye contact. "Come on, McPeake, we haven't time for this nonsense." The rotund soldier nodded a farewell to Wesley and followed suit, not speaking until they were well out of hearing range.

"What was all that about?" hissed McPeake at the taller man. "We're supposed to be keeping a low profile."

"I won't let that ingrate talk to me like that, alive or dead. I could have set his head on fire with a click of my fingers, watch him fry to a crisp."

"Yeah, smart move, old man. Blow our cover sky high. Do you want to end up in the abyss like Fotheringham did? Our orders are to find Rodriguez and then report back. Leave the dirty work to the Drummer Boy and Bad Bill."

"I'm no idiot, McPeake. I know what needs done. They can't be more than an hour up the road. We'll have no problem finding them. Brussels isn't that big a place, and there can't be that many giant Portuguese sergeants lumbering around it. Relax."

"I'll relax when the job's done, and we've reported back to Fotheringham. Not a second sooner."

The two soldiers continued to bicker as they weaved through the throng, occasionally shoving a hapless peasant to one side. They paid little heed to what was going on behind them and failed to notice that they were being stalked through the mass by a young man dressed as a simple farmer. Adam O'Sullivan never took his eyes off the back of the redcoats' necks, for they were going to lead him to his main target—one Sergeant Martim Rodriguez. The Priestess had left him in no uncertain terms as to what she expected—the bearded brute returned by whatever means necessary to New Jerusalem. She had no interest in the others, they were irrelevant to her, he could do as he wished with them.

O'Sullivan quickened his step, anxious not to lose them in the crowd. She had warned him to be wary of them, but this Company did not scare him. They were all the enemy to him, and he'd kill as many of them as he needed to in order to get at the three women in his life. For his harem of hate was growing. For years it had been solely Ariana Hennessy until her airhead friend, Tess, stuck her nose into his affairs. Now there was a third, the delectable, deceitful Maura Miller. He'd find them all, and he'd kill them all.

"So many women, so little time."

∞ ∞ ∞

"What do you mean he's gone?"

"I mean exactly that, Ariana. He's not there anymore." Tess pointed across the river towards New Jerusalem from their vantage point atop a landrover bonnet on their own side of the river. On either side of them, two Security Solutions soldiers crouched, their rifles raised as they scanned for signs of an impending attack.

"What about the Priestess?"

"Oh, she's there, alright. But O'Sullivan…he was there one minute, the next it was as if he…"

"Planed?" Ariana did not like where this conversation was headed.

"Yeah," replied Tess, struggling to piece together the mental jigsaw forming in her mind. "But how did she…"

"I'm beginning to think this Priestess character is a bit more than meets the eye. We know she has powers, has some sort of a protective forcefield that limits what we can do over there, but if you're telling me she can plane, it's almost as if she's…"

"One of them." Tess ended the sentence for her.

"But that can't be right. She hates Skelly as much as we do. If it wasn't for him, she'd still be playing happy families with Rodriguez over there. And Maura Miller was the only woman to die inside the square. She told us as much."

"Ariana?"

"Yeah?"

"Are you ready for the icing on the cake?"

"Knock yourself out."

"I've worked out the new coordinates for O'Sullivan. "You're not going to like this, not one little bit."

"I don't care," replied Ariana. "Where he goes, I follow."

"Well, hold onto your boots then," replied Tess, her eyes wide. "Because he's at Waterloo, Ariana. Water-Bloody-Loo."

CHAPTER 97 - DINNER IS SERVED

Emily sat on the bottom step of the cellar, knees pressed together, and hands folded primly on her lap. Opposite her, propped up against a beer keg, sprawled a comatose Gerry, snoring loudly, chin rested on his chest. In his hand was a near-empty bottle of whiskey.

"I'll give you this, Gerry. You're a man of your word."

She rose lightly to her feet and climbed the steps from the cellar, out into the bar. It really was the grottiest of places. How people spent their free time and money in such a dump, of their own volition, really was beyond her. She ran a finger along the surface of a table as she passed, accumulating a thick layer of dust on the outstretched digit in the process. *Gross.*

"Kirkwood Scott. If you and I are ever going to make a go of it, there are going to have to be some serious changes when all this is over." She laughed at the absurdity of her words. Here she was, a dead girl at the end of the world, worrying about relationship goals with a young man about to be plunged into one of the bloodiest conflicts of all time. Oprah would have had a field day with that one.

Outside, the sky was black even though the clock on the wall behind the bar told her it was mid-afternoon. Emily reached the door and clutched the handle, pausing to take in a deep lungful of air. Those weren't clouds out there. The atmosphere was clogged with an army of evil, the Scourge holding court and swooping as they saw fit to wreak further misery and pain on the few remaining survivors. It would soon be over if left to run its unnatural course. Which was where Emily came in.

Thanks to the heroic efforts of the drunken Gerry, Emily was free to operate on this plane within his inebriated dreamscape. Samuel had issued her with very clear instructions. The Earth was being choked, drained of all life, sucked dry. Her task was to delay the Scourge for as long as she possibly could in order to allow the others a time buffer to complete their respective missions. If she failed, they all failed, and the world burned.

Pulling the door open, Emily stepped out into the murky light onto the empty street. She stared up towards the black blanket above, waiting for them to detect her essence and begin the descent towards it.

"Well, what are you waiting for, you great big ugly donuts? Dinner is served. Come and get it."

It was as if they heard her and responded to the verbal gauntlet being thrown in their direction. One by one, small flecks of darkness wheeled away from the pulsating mass and began to drop towards Earth, taking clearer form the closer they plummeted towards her. Part of her wanted to run screaming back into the confines of the bar, join Gerry in the cellar, and drink to forget the horrors currently filling her vision. Their eyes blazed red, gorged with the blood of a million victims. Emily's mind was filled with images of them feasting on their hapless prey. Beaks slick with blood, jagged incisors tearing flesh from bone, a feeding frenzy that would not end until every last living soul was no more.

The silver-haired young woman closed her eyes and thought of her friends. When she walked this Earth, she'd been a vain, flighty girl. Everything was image, endless selfies, and acts intended to draw attention to the Emily O'Hara show. Until she met Meredith, a friend who taught her there was more to life than follower counts and designer trinkets. Meredith Starc—the best friend she'd chosen to turn her back on when she needed her most. Well, not now, and never again, Meredith. She was here for her. Here for Meredith, Harley, Ariana, even silly, vacuous Tess Cartwright.

"Here for you too, Kirkwood."

She arched her back, flinging both hands behind as she screamed at the beasts above. Her platinum mane fanned out around her as if her body had been possessed by an electric current. Her slight body glowed with an inner light before it erupted from her eyes, twin beams shooting upwards, obliterating the first wave of creatures as they neared her. Others twisted in the air, attempting to evade the light, but it tore through them, ever upwards, cutting a swathe until it connected with the main body of the Scourge. A small pocket of blue sky revealed itself, and tentative rays of sunlight peeked through. Bathing Emily in its comforting warmth as she continued her lone battle on a ravaged planet. For as long as there was light, there was life. And as long as there was life, there was hope.

CHAPTER 98 - GAME CHANGER

"If I can convince him..."

"You mean *we*," corrected Kirkwood.

Rodriguez glanced at him cynically as they trudged up an incline, which showed no sign of ending. "I mean, I. He's hardly going to listen to three new recruits he's never set eyes on before. You might be a big deal with Samuel, but remember, Senor Scott, you are nothing here. Nada."

"Alright then, Sergeant High and Mighty. How are you going to persuade Skelly to exchange the social event of the year for the blood, mud, and guts down the road?"

"Simple. I tell him the truth. That the French are coming. That tomorrow the greatest battle in the history of the world is going to take place. A chance for him to attain the glory he's been seeking all his career. Even the most beautiful woman in the world won't hold him back from that."

"Most beautiful woman in the world? Really?" Meredith sounded far from impressed as she trudged behind them. "What's her Instagram handle so I can check her out?" Harley and Meredith started to snigger, unfazed that they were pointedly ignored by Rodriguez.

"I know not what she looks like," he confided quietly to Kirkwood. "But I know men have fought over her, duelled to the death. Her beauty is the talk of Brussels society. As is the gold coin of her father. Secure the hand of Sienna Melrose, and a man has it all."

They cleared the top of the climb, and Kirkwood stopped dead in his tracks at the sight before him. Meredith and Harley clattered into the back of him, all three slipping and slithering down the other side before coming to rest in an undignified heap by the roadside. Men, women, and children shuffled past them without a glance, their dead, sunken eyes fixed on the rooftops of the capital city, a refuge from the coming storm.

"I give you the city of Brussels," enthused Rodriguez, his dark eyes sparkling. "We head there." He pointed towards a green area situated in the middle of the sprawling array of streets and houses. "The Abervale estate where half the Allied army is currently camped. And where the ball will take place tonight. That's where we will find Skelly, or my name isn't Martim Joacquin Frederico..."

"Rodriguez!" a voice roared from behind them. They turned in unison to be greeted by the sight of a British officer sat atop a giant black horse, steam rising from its flanks as it snorted and twisted, eager to be on its way again.

"What the devil are you doing up here? And who are these reprobates?" He twisted in his saddle to get a better view of Kirkwood, Meredith, and Harley.

"Regimental orders, sir," replied Rodriguez. "I can show them to you if you want. These three are fresh off the boat and under my charge. I brought them with me for fear they might desert."

"Desert?" snorted the officer. "Any wretch tries that on my watch, and I'll personally take the birch to their hides. Do you hear me?" He sat forward in his saddle and glowered down at them. Thin lips sat beneath a bushy black moustache, matched only in its darkness by a pair of black, unforgiving eyes above a long, tapered nose. He was a young man, not thirty yet, but his poise and manner spoke of an experienced and respected soldier.

"I'll take good care of them, Captain."

"See that you do, Sergeant. You know I've a mind like a steel trap when it comes to faces. If I see any of these three in front of me, I'll be holding you personally responsible, do you hear me?"

"Yes, Captain Mulligan."

Mulligan edged his mount forward, never taking his eyes off Kirkwood as he neared. He pulled up beside him and peered down, his eyes burrowing deep within the younger man. Kirkwood tried to hold his gaze but eventually cracked and looked away.

"Do I know you?"

"No, sir." stammered Kirkwood. Meredith and Harley followed his cue and bowed their heads. Now was not the time for sarcastic comebacks. Rodriguez sought to intervene and alleviate some of the pressure.

"Like I said, Captain, green as the grass, straight out of the garrison. They barely know one end of a musket from the other. They'll be lucky if they're still alive this time next week."

Mulligan continued to stare at Kirkwood, a snide smile creeping across his features. "Well, let's hope they learn quickly then. A lot can happen in a week, we both know that, don't we Rodriguez?"

"Yes, sir." Rodriguez had no more than uttered the words when Mulligan flicked the reins, giving his steed the little encouragement it needed to power down the other side of the hill. He turned in his saddle before disappearing round a bend in the road. "Get that hill cleared, Sergeant. Convoy coming through in two minutes, and they'll be stopping for no man, woman, or child in their path."

Rodriguez shrugged before staring at his three companions. "Well, you heard what the officer said. Clear the road," he roared, before hissing more quietly. "At least look like soldiers while we're here. Just push a few people back, shout a bit. Remember the glamour. They look at you, but they see infantrymen from the 49th. They're terrified of us, use it to your advantage." He started to climb the hill again, waving his arms to clear the ragtag procession streaming towards him.

"Come on, move to the side, or be run into the ground, you wretches. Make room for the King's business." Kirkwood joined him, half-heartedly doing likewise, while Meredith and Harley launched into their roles with rather more gusto. Their fellow travellers began to reluctantly filter to either side of the track, whispering amongst themselves as to who or what might be approaching. Necks craned to see what all the fuss was about. Kirkwood noticed they had been joined by a handful of other soldiers attempting to create order from the melee. Within minutes the road was cleared.

"Who was that guy?" asked Kirkwood, positioned with Rodriguez facing the docile crowd, their backs to the road. "He gives me the creeps."

"Captain William Mulligan of the 49th. Or Bad Bill as we like to call him. He's been with the regiment since day one, commissioned from the ranks and the meanest snake you could hope to meet. Because the other officers still regard him as rank and file, he goes out of his way to treat the lads like dirt. How do you say, he has the chop on his shoulder?"

"I think it's chip," replied Kirkwood. "He freaks me out. The way he stared at me there, it was like he recognised me."

"The last thing you want is Bad Bill recognising you. He will make your life hell. My friend, Callaghan—Bad Bill personally took the birch to him after catching the poor sod asleep on sentry duty. Flayed him to the bone. He never got over it. Wounds never healed, and he got an infection, was dead within a month. Nothing was said or done about it, Skelly turned a blind eye."

"Is he in the Company?" Kirkwood pressed ahead, given the big Portuguese sergeant appeared willing to talk.

"He died in the square, so yes. But I don't see much of him. Skelly uses him sparingly; don't ask me why. Which suits me fine. Nineteenth-century Bad Bill is bad enough without Skelly's version of him turning up here."

"How will we know the difference?"

"We won't," laughed Rodriguez harshly. "But worry not. Skelly doesn't know we are here. Not yet, anyway."

"What about Wesley, your friend? Is he one of them?"

Rodriguez looked genuinely sad as he answered. "Wesley never made it to the square. We lost him earlier in the day. There was a lot of hard fighting before then, and we lost a lot of good lads. A blessing in many ways. Better a quick, clean death and oblivion than this hell." He fell silent, and Kirkwood turned his attention back to the throng of people in front of him. Up until then, Rodriguez had been a bitter enemy who would have snapped his neck in a heartbeat. It was too soon to treat him with anything nearing friendship.

"Rodriguez...I mean Sergeant...sir...whatever," hollered Meredith. Kirkwood turned to see a tightly bunched group of riders approaching at speed. The crowd became agitated, jostling to get a better view of the approaching party, and Kirkwood strained to push back one particularly curious man. The sound of hooves to his right increased, and a cry went up from the crowd.

"C'est le Duc. C'est Wellington."

Kirkwood glanced to his right as history itself passed him by. He had read much of Sir Arthur Wellesley, the Duke of Wellington, in his efforts to unravel the mystery of Augustus Skelly. In all accounts, Wellington had been the hero. Portraits of him at the time were reasonably accurate, thought Kirkwood. The aloof manner, long, gaunt face, and distinctive angular nose. "Old Hooky," was an apt nickname. Kirkwood stared open mouth as the Duke cantered past, flanked by a phalanx of aides and his personal bodyguard.

"Scott." Kirkwood snapped out of his stupor to see Rodriguez glaring at him. "Stop gawking and concentrate." Despite his size and strength, the big man was struggling to hold the increasingly restless crowd back. More soldiers materialised, and a thin line of red was all that stood between a clear pathway and pandemonium.

"Pain, Pain," the cry went up.

"Pain? Is somebody hurt?" queried Harley, her slight frame losing ground against the weight of bodies pressing against her.

"It's French, you numpty, it means bread," replied a breathless Meredith. "You push me again, and you're getting a slap," she roared at a painfully thin man.

"Well, I didn't know. I dropped French for German in Year 10."

"Just shut up and help me out here, Harley."

"What's wrong with them?" Kirkwood was being inched backwards, his boots struggling to get a grip on the slippery surface.

"They're starving," grunted Rodriguez. "Most of them left their farms days ago. They haven't eaten since. They think it's food wagons coming through." To their left, a shot rang out as a soldier fired his musket in the air as a warning. Rather than placate the crowd, the shot only seemed to enflame the situation further. A young girl, no more than seven or eight years old, stumbled forward onto her knees between Kirkwood and Rodriguez. Kirkwood bent down to help the child to her feet again but was rewarded for his act of kindness with a kick from an unseen assailant in the crowd, which sent him sprawling into the middle of the road just as the next rider crested the hill. Their horse bucked and swerved to avoid Kirkwood, who froze, unable to get out of its way in time.

The rider, displaying incredible horsemanship, clung to the neck of their huge charge, its eyes wide, nostrils flaring at the unexpected obstacle before it. Somehow, they eked a response from the animal, and it hurdled Kirkwood, it's hooves clearing his prostrate form by mere inches. Meredith and Harley turned from their own marshalling duties, to watch in horror as their friend evaded death or serious injury by the slimmest of margins.

Kirkwood lowered his hands from his head to watch the departing rider. Twisting in the saddle, he turned to reveal an unmistakable scowl.

"Skelly." Kirkwood mouthed the word in horror as Meredith and Harley broke rank to run to his aid.

"Rodriguez, learn to control your men or next time they'll damn well hang," roared the voice that had haunted Kirkwood since childhood.

"He...he didn't recognise us," croaked Harley, on her knees, checking Kirkwood for injuries. Kirkwood waved her away but allowed them to help him to his feet. The near-miss had stunned the crowds on either side of the road. Anxious mothers clutched wide-eyed children to their skirts while the men hung back, fearful as to how the redcoats might respond to almost losing one of their own.

"Of course he didn't recognise you. That was the Skelly who walked this Earth, not the monster he became following his death. Although he wasn't a particularly pleasant man even then, as you saw." Rodriguez started to help Kirkwood to the side of the road when another two mounted officers trotted past. "Carriage coming through," snapped one. "Get off the bloody road." Kirkwood gingerly placed his weight on his right ankle and winced in pain, doubling over.

"What's wrong?" asked Meredith as the clatter of approaching wheels announced the arrival of the carriage. Two magnificent bay horses pulled it, the driver slowing down as he saw the mass of civilians and soldiers on the brow of the hill.

"I think I went over on my ankle. Just help me off the road so I can get these boots off. It's probably swollen. Don't suppose your medics carry ice packs and ibuprofen, Rodriguez?"

Rodriguez snorted. "The only painkiller you'll get here, if you're lucky, is a shot of rum. Here, sit down, and I'll have a look at it. Move, you lot, we've an injured man here." A space was cleared on the muddy verge, and Kirkwood sank onto it, uttering a yelp as he did so.

"Honestly, Kirky, you're such a drama queen," said Meredith, looking down on him, hands on hips. "You'd think it needed amputating the way you are carrying on."

"Shut up," hissed Rodriguez. "Don't mention amputation. The surgeons here are butchers. That's their answer to everything. Lop it off and send you on your way."

"I'm fine. Stop fussing." He loosened the laces on his left boot and tenderly eased his foot out of it, leaning forward to peel off his sock and inspect the damage.

"Ewww," gasped Harley, having dropped to a knee to get a better look. "When did you last cut your toenails, man? They're rank."

"Uber cheesy," added Meredith. "Don't ever show Emily those if you harbour any hopes of getting off with her."

Kirkwood opened his mouth to unleash a volley of expletives in their direction but halted as the ornate carriage crested the hill, the driver pulling hard on the reins to bring both horses to a halt. They stood, pawing the ground, none pleased at being asked to curtail their journey.

A head appeared out of the carriage window. That of an elegant, grey-haired woman in her fifties, her ears, and neck dripping with diamonds. She pulled a fur shawl over exposed shoulders and shivered as she peered down at the sorry spectacle of Kirkwood on the roadside.

"What's going on here?" she asked, curling her lip in distaste at the mass of mud crusted faces looking back at her. Kirkwood stared, lost for words, and was thankful when Rodriguez spoke.

"Nothing, ma'am. Just a twisted ankle. We'll get him strapped up and will be on our way soon. Thank you for your concern," he simpered, earning derisory looks from Meredith and Harley.

"Concerned? Don't be ridiculous, man. I just want the road cleared. I've the social event of the year later tonight and a million and one things to do. You lot just make sure Bonaparte doesn't arrive in the middle of it and ruin everything. We've been planning this for months. Damned French. Such an inconvenience." She turned to speak to someone else in the carriage. "It's just a silly soldier has fallen over, dear. Nothing to concern us. Carry on, driver."

The driver nodded and flicked the reins, the horses stepping forward smartly in tandem. A shout from inside the carriage caused him to pull up again, however, as raised voices continued for several seconds before the door opened and a flurry of skirts revealed a pair of shapely, stockinged legs.

"I'm just looking, mother," a soft voice pleaded from a young woman whose head was turned as she spoke back into the carriage.

Kirkwood squinted upwards as watery sunlight broke through the cloud cover. He blinked and readjusted his vision, not sure if he was hallucinating. Words failed him. The same could not be said for the others.

"Puta Merda."

"Oh, my God."

"What the..."

Despite the fine silk dress, dark braided hair over one shoulder, and modest make up it was unmistakably her. The same emerald, penetrating eyes and full, red lips. The Priestess stood before them, a quizzical look on her face.

"Good heavens," she cried. "You poor souls. You look like you've just seen a ghost."

"Sienna," the older woman called out of the window. "Get back in the carriage this instance. Those are common soldiers. Have you lost your mind?"

"But mama," she replied. "This poor man is injured. Fighting for King and Country. The least we can do is give him a lift to the city. The field hospital there will be able to help him."

"I'm not having a dirty redcoat in the carriage, and that is my final..."

"Hush, mama." Before he knew it, Sienna Melrose, the Priestess, or whatever her name was, had her head under the shoulder of Kirkwood and was helping him to his feet. "Come on you lads, give your friend a hand." Rodriguez nodded numbly and took

Kirkwood's other arm, for once lost for words. Meredith and Harley looked on in shock as, despite the vociferous protests of the Duchess, Kirkwood was bundled into the carriage.

Closing the carriage door behind her, Sienna turned and leaned out of the window again. "We will take him to the hospital. She removed a purse from her sleeve and dropped a handful of gold coins into the hand of the Portuguese Sergeant. "You and your men make sure you get a hot meal when you get to the city. We, the people of Brussels, will forever be in your debt, you brave boys." She nodded towards the driver, and the carriage took off, leaving three stunned soldiers in its wake.

"I've seen it all now," whispered Meredith.

"You're telling me," added Harley. "Rodriguez, can you please tell us what the hell is going on?"

"I have no idea," he replied. "I have no idea about anything, anymore."

Around them, the road was filling again as the tide of bodies began their shuffling, stuttering procession towards the city. The sound of far off cannons reminded all of the impending storm. It was Meredith who finally spoke.

"Come on," she said, starting down the hill towards the rooftops of Brussels. "We've got a war to win."

CHAPTER 99 - I'M KIRKWOOD SCOTT

The carriage rocked from side to side as it bounced over the uneven road surface, but the discomfort of the journey and pain in his ankle was forgotten as Kirkwood stared into the face of a young woman who, last time he saw her, would happily have wrung his neck. She stared back, a warm smile on her face, gloved hands demurely perched on her lap.

"How long have you been a soldier?" she asked.

"Oh, Sienna," the Duchess cried out in exasperation. "Bad enough you let this man ride with us, now you want his life story. Your father will be most displeased when he hears of this."

The young woman ignored the outburst, instead gesturing for Kirkwood to speak.

"Er...not long. This will be my first battle, in fact."

"Do you think the Duke will stand and fight? I sincerely hope so. I shall ask him tonight."

"You'll do no such thing," snorted the Duchess. "Sir Arthur is attending the ball tonight for the purposes of relaxation. The last thing he needs is being interrogated by a slip of a girl about his strategies and tactics."

Sienna rolled her eyes, and Kirkwood could not help but smile. It was such a Meredith Starc thing to do. He started to relax a little. This young woman was oblivious to the monster she would somehow turn into. His mind was assailed by a thousand theories as to how this polite, caring soul became the deranged killer he encountered in futuristic Belfast. Was she a doppelgänger, an evil twin? He sensed the tendrils of an obsessive thought beginning to curl its way around his cerebral cortex but resisted, aided by the strength of the Presence within him. Focus, Kirkwood, focus. This was an opportunity to get to Skelly, through the object of his lecherous desire.

"What regiment are you with?" persisted Sienna, oblivious to her mother's venomous glare.

"The Somersets, my lady. The 49th," croaked Kirkwood. The carriage went quiet as Sienna, and her mother exchanged a hurried, unspoken communication.

"Mother...no..."

"You're one of Colonel Skelly's men. Well, in that case, I insist you are treated by my personal physician. Our family is close friends with Sir Arthur, and Colonel Skelly is one of his most trusted officers. Indeed, I am hopeful one day of Sienna being wed to the Duke. Both the Duke and the Colonel will be at the ball tonight, no doubt vying for her attention. Isn't that right, Sienna?" She smiled at her daughter, but it lacked any maternal warmth. Sienna's eyes pleaded with her mother, but eventually, she dropped her gaze to the carriage floor, docile in defeat.

"Yes, mama."

"It's really no problem, your highness...majesty," spluttered Kirkwood, sensing the tension in the carriage.

"Your grace," corrected the Duchess, playing with an expensive earring as she stared out of the carriage window, countryside now being replaced by dwellings as they entered the outskirts of the city. She was a woman used to getting her own way, and as far as she was concerned, the conversation was at an end.

"Yes, your grace. Thank you, your grace." Kirkwood turned his attention to Sienna, who bit her lower lip and fidgeted awkwardly. Her body language screamed that she was no fan of either man. Kirkwood shoved the mystery of the Priestess to the back of his mind and saw a frightened young woman. Regardless of who she became, he vowed to do everything in his power to help her and somehow unravel the mystery of what happened to turn Skelly and Wellington into such mortal enemies. An enmity which ended with the annihilation of the 49th in the square. Sienna Melrose was at the root of the mystery, he was convinced of that. Rodriguez and the others would have to catch up. He sensed the Presence strongly, Meredith and Harley were still with him, moving towards Brussels. He would do it for them, he would do it for Emily, wherever she was, and hell, he would even do it for Rodriguez.

The carriage clattered over a stone in the road, and its three occupants bounced off their upholstered seats before resuming their original positions. Kirkwood chanced a smile at the troubled young woman opposite him. He knew her pain, and that pain connected them; it was a thread of humanity in a very inhumane world.

"Thank you, my lady," he mouthed.

"You're welcome," she whispered in response, beyond earshot of her mother. "And please, it's Sienna." She deliberated over her next words before asking. "And what is your name?"

Kirkwood smiled more openly this time. "I'm Kirkwood...Kirkwood Scott."

CHAPTER 100 - THE END OF EVERYTHING

"The agreement was, we did not become involved in one another's affairs, was it not?"

"That was before you went back on your word and decided to wipe out my plane."

Skelly flinched slightly, not used to his verbal serve being returned with such force. He decided attack was the best form of defence given the opposition before him.

"Which is why you pulled your petty prank of stealing Rodriguez from under my nose?"

The Priestess crossed her arms and laughed. "Rodriguez? Oh, he was easy—a pleasant distraction at the time. He was my insurance policy. I thought you wouldn't release the Scourge so long as I held onto your second in command. Seems I was wrong, though."

"Collateral damage, my dear," smirked Skelly, sensing he was gaining the upper hand again.

"I know that better than anyone, Augustus. You couldn't leave me alone, even in death."

"I'm afraid the matter was out of my hands, Sienna." Skelly crossed his legs and made a point of looking at the woman facing him from top to toe. "No exceptions could be made even for old acquaintances like yourself." Again, that knowing smirk, as a point was scored.

"You really are an evil bastard," she spat, her face a mask of revulsion.

"Now, now, don't be like that. Can't we let bygones be bygones and focus on the matters at hand? We're on a bit of a sticky wicket. You and I need to put our heads together."

"I'll never forgive you for what you did to me, Skelly. All I asked for was some peace, but you couldn't even allow me that small dignity."

Skelly started to pick at one of the yellow, gnarled claws which masqueraded as a fingernail on his right hand, yawning and studiously avoiding the murderous stare of the Priestess. Eventually, satisfied with the examination of the offending cuticle, he looked up at her with thinly veiled disinterest.

"Quite finished, are we? Ready to get down to business? For that's what this is, Sienna, a straight-down-the-line business proposition. I'll talk to my employers, see what I can do to save your rancid little kingdom. What do you call it, New Jerusalem? What a load of codswallop. Since when did you start believing in all this religious mumbo jumbo?"

"I give the people what they want," she replied, standing tall and proud. "And who are you to judge? None of us knows the full story. The Forsaken hold secrets yet to be revealed—Dobson hinted at their origin. Even the mighty Augustus Skelly doesn't know the whole truth."

"Pah. I know enough. I know that treacherous bearded villain and his bloody friends are out to hijack my destiny. They think if I don't die in the square, everything will be prancing ponies and sparkling rainbows. I will not allow centuries of work to be undone by a pathetic wretch like Kirkwood Scott." He slammed his fist onto the arm of his chair, and the icy flames flared up in the fireplace casting the Priestess in an ochre light.

"I have your word? As to New Jerusalem?"

"No promises, but I'll do what I can," he wheezed. "I can be most persuasive, as you know." His dead eyes twinkled with malicious glee at the unspoken slur. "But what can I expect from you, Sienna? Your lily-white, butter wouldn't melt in your mouth, 1815 incarnation is of little use to me. What can you bring to the table?"

She ignored the slight. "I still have influence on that plane. You know my powers. I may not be part of your damned Company, I may not have died in that square, but I too was tainted by its legacy. You know what I went through, what you put me through."

"Yes, yes," sighed Skelly. "Must we revisit..."

"Yes, we must. I curse the day you were spewed screaming onto the Earth, Skelly. I curse you every day." Her eyes screamed hatred, the veins on her elegantly pale neck rising to the fore. She regained her composure as quickly as it left, her breathing returning to something approaching normal. "You have your deal. I'll use my influence in Brussels to ensure everything is as it must be."

"Excellent. I knew you'd see sense in the end." Skelly surveyed the Study before delivering his parting words. "Off you trot then and do your thing. The Company is already in position. I'll be in touch."

He waved a hand in her direction, and the Priestess was gone, leaving the old man alone with his rancid thoughts.

A pretty little thing in her day and her father had owned half of Lincolnshire, but she meant nothing to him now. He would use her as he saw fit like he had before and then crush her like he would crush the rest of them. Samuel, Rodriguez, Scott, his risible harem—they would all perish, and he would be triumphant. The Scourge would consume them all.

Skelly raised his glass. "A toast," he raised. "To the end. Of everything."

∞ ∞ ∞

She sat in her chambers until the shivering ceased. Bringing herself back under control after the vitriolic bile of the Study was a slow and tiring process, yet a necessary one. Her people could not see her like this, nobody could. She was the Priestess, the Chosen One, a messenger sent to prepare a broken world for the return of their Lord and Saviour. Hell, she played the role so well she almost believed it herself. They needed that character, that strong, fierce woman not the naive, idealistic girl she once was. That girl was gone, Skelly made sure of that.

Skelly. The master manipulator. Well, two could play at that game. She did not fear him, and that infuriated the stinking bag of flabby flesh. She had passed over, tied to the horrors of the square by his wickedness, an embarrassing reminder of the brute he was.

He had tried to buy her silence, and for a while, New Jerusalem sufficed, giving her what she needed. Yet her hatred of him was always simmering. Quietly beneath the placid waters, waiting to erupt and shower her with the irreconcilable truth, the need for vengeance. Now was that time.

She cared not for this Kirkwood Scott and his pitiful friends. Deacon and his army across the river were trivial inconveniences, whom she could swat aside on a whim if she saw fit. All she saw now was Skelly. The beast who had stolen Rodriguez from her and so much more before that. The scab had been ripped away, and the raw wound within her soul exposed again. She craved healing, but the only way she could required the spilling of fresh blood. It was time to rewrite history, to delve back, and ensure Augustus Skelly remained dead and buried in a mass Belgian grave. Instead, a new power would rise from the square to avenge the memory of Sienna Melrose, the Lady Abervale.

A quiet knock on the door to her chambers caused her to swivel, instantly recognising the timid request to enter. "Come," she intoned, and the doors opened, two Maidens entering, their distinctive long white dresses rustling as they set a tray of food on the expansive dining table.

"Thank you, Tara, that will be all," breathed the Priestess. "I hope you are suitably chastised now after your momentary lapse of judgement with the outsider. The auburn-haired girl meekly nodded and backed out of the room, her gaunt features a patchwork of purple bruises. "Ruby, I have an errand for you. Close the door behind you, Tara."

The second girl nodded obediently and faced the Priestess, head bowed. "What do you require, Mistress?"

"You can drop that now, Ruby, it's just you and me." The Priestess studied her closely. They looked nothing like each other. Whereas she was dark, the girl was fair, strawberry blonde hair and blue eyes, the bridge of her nose adorned with a smattering of freckles. Barely in her teens, the rumours amongst the inhabitants of New Jerusalem were already reaching her door. The Maiden who did not age.

"Yes, Mother."

Sienna Melrose, the Priestess of New Jerusalem, rose from her chair and smiled. The gloves were well and truly off now, and as the old devil himself always said, every war had its casualties. Well, time for one more, Augustus.

"That's better." She stepped forward and ran a hand down the girl's cheek. "I think it's time I finally introduced you to your father."

ACKNOWLEDGEMENTS

Thank you to everyone who continues to support me on my writing journey. Special thanks to River Dixon and everyone at Potter's Grove Press for taking a chance on me. Many thanks to my eagle-eyed beta readers – Ruarí de Barra, Megan Dell, Una Hamill, and Lydia Russell. Finally, thank you to you, the reader, for picking up this book.

Printed in Great Britain
by Amazon